William Richard Wood Stephens

The Life and Letters of Edward A. Freeman

William Richard Wood Stephens

The Life and Letters of Edward A. Freeman

ISBN/EAN: 9783744689120

Printed in Europe, USA, Canada, Australia, Japan

Cover: Foto ©Raphael Reischuk / pixelio.de

More available books at **www.hansebooks.com**

THE

LIFE AND LETTERS

OF

EDWARD A. FREEMAN

D.C.L., LL.D.

BY

W. R. W. STEPHENS, B.D.

DEAN OF WINCHESTER

AUTHOR OF 'THE LIFE AND LETTERS OF DEAN HOOK,' ETC., ETC.

IN TWO VOLS.—VOL. I

London

MACMILLAN AND CO.

AND NEW YORK

1895

𝕺𝖝𝖋𝖔𝖗𝖉

HORACE HART, PRINTER TO THE UNIVERSITY

PREFACE

THE following memoir was undertaken at the request of Mr. Freeman's family. He numbered amongst his friends so many men highly distinguished as historians and scholars that I felt greatly honoured in having such a task entrusted to me. I entered upon it with some diffidence, but with a sincere desire to do justice to one to whom I owed much, and for whom, in the course of nearly twenty years' friendship, I had learned to entertain increasing regard and affection. The work therefore has been one of great interest to me, although it has involved a great deal of labour, owing to the method of treatment which it seemed to require. Mr. Freeman's life, although one of incessant activity, was not eventful in the sense of being marked by many striking incidents. Consequently the memoir had to take the form mainly of a record of his literary industry, and of the growth of his opinions. For this purpose it was necessary to extract the essence of his articles and essays on a great variety of subjects.

It is much to be regretted that his correspondence with some of his oldest friends has, from various causes, been lost, but a vast residuum of letters remained, which have been placed at my disposal, and I venture to hope that the careful selection which I have made from them will serve to bring out in their truest colours all the most striking features of his strong and original character.

In the collection of letters and other biographical materials I received invaluable assistance from Mr. Freeman's eldest daughter, the late Mrs. A. J. Evans. Never was a daughter fonder or prouder of a father than she was ; never did a daughter labour more assiduously than she did to help on the work which was to perpetuate her father's memory. It has been a sad thought to me in writing the following pages that they will not be read by one who took such a deep interest in the preparation for them.

While thanking collectively the large number of persons who have supplied me with letters and reminiscences, and who have most kindly answered all my inquiries for information, I must express my special obligations to the Right Honourable J. Bryce, M.P., Miss Edith Thompson, the Rev. North Pinder, and above all the Rev. W. Hunt, who has done me the very great service of reading nearly all the proof sheets of the work, and making many valuable criticisms and suggestions.

Mr. Freeman's letters abound, as the reader will notice, in historical allusions, references and quotations, as well as in peculiar words and names, and turns of expression. These I have endeavoured to explain in foot-notes: but in spite of much care bestowed on this part of my work, readers will probably discover some errors and omissions ; and I shall be thankful to have my attention called to them, that I may rectify them in a future edition of the book, should it be called for.

After much consideration it has been decided to reserve the correspondence between Mr. Freeman and Mr. John Richard Green for publication in a separate volume at some future date. The letters of two such remarkable men, who criticized each other's work with much candour, and exchanged their opinions on all manner of subjects with the utmost freedom, are of peculiar interest, and it has been felt that it would not be possible to bring out quite clearly and fairly the precise relation in which the two friends stood to each other without publishing both sides of the corre-spondence.

W. R. W. STEPHENS.

DEANERY, WINCHESTER.
March 20, 1895.

CONTENTS OF VOL. I

ILLUSTRATIONS

LIFE OF
EDWARD A. FREEMAN

CHAPTER I.

CHILDHOOD AND SCHOOL LIFE.

A.D. 1823–1841.

EDWARD AUGUSTUS FREEMAN, the youngest child of
John Freeman, Esq., and Mary Anne his wife, was born
at Mitchley Abbey, in the parish of Harborne, Stafford-
shire, on August 2, 1823.

He was named Augustus after the month in which he
was born. Owing to his delicacy, he was privately baptized on August 18, and was not received into the Church
till July 14 in the following year. His grandfather,
Mr. Joseph Freeman, of Pedmore Hall, near Birmingham,
had been a wealthy man, but his will being disputed,
a considerable part of the fortune which would have
come to the eldest son John, and his two brothers Keelinge
and Joseph, was swallowed up in a long law-suit. Referring in one of his letters to this event, E. A. Freeman
remarks, 'Brougham was counsel for my father, which
some say was the reason why his enemies gained their

† VOL. I.　　　　B

suit.' His mother was the second daughter of William Carless, Esq., of the Ravenhurst, Harborne. The family of Carless, or Carlos, as it was sometimes spelt, had resided in or near Birmingham from the middle of the seventeenth century, and Mrs. Freeman's branch of it claimed descent from Colonel William Carless, who was distinguished for his valour at the battle of Worcester, 1651, where he was said to have been the last to abandon the fight. He sought concealment and shelter in an oak which stood in an open field near Boscobel House, and persuaded King Charles to share his retreat, where the two remained for more than twelve hours, whilst their pursuers were searching a neighbouring wood [1]. Carless risked his life more than once by descending from the tree to get food. He afterwards escaped to France, where he remained with Charles till the Restoration. He was granted a coat-of-arms by Royal Patent, in which an oak tree was a conspicuous part of the device, with the motto 'Subditus fidelis regis et regni salus.' The descent of Mrs. Freeman's branch of the family from Colonel Carless cannot be traced very directly, but they use his coat-of-arms and possess a curious seal which, according to the family tradition, was given to him by King Charles. In a volume entitled *Original Ballads by Living Authors*, edited by the Rev. H. Thompson, and published in 1850, to which E. A. Freeman contributed several pieces, is one on William Carless or Carlos, with a short prefatory note, in which he says 'that the personal character of the ballad may perhaps be excused by the fact of the writer's being maternally descended from the Carlos family.'

Before he was eighteen months old, Edward Freeman

---

[1] See *History of the Commonwealth*, by S. R. Gardiner, vol. i. p. 452.

lost both his parents. His father, who had for many
years been subject to severe and painful attacks of rheu-
matic gout, died on Nov. 21, 1824. His mother, who fell
into a consumption when he was six months old, died
only four days after her husband, and by a strange coincidence their eldest child, Mary Anne, aged 14, died on
the same day. Out of a family of five children there
were now only three survivors, Sarah Elizabeth, aged 13,
Emma, aged 10, and the infant, Edward Augustus. The
orphans were taken charge of by their grandmother,
Mrs. Emmete Freeman, who, in a letter to a friend,
describes the boy as a 'lovely and engaging creature.'
His sister Emma died in April, 1826. Though he was
only three years old at the time of her death, he retained
a vivid and fond recollection of her, and whilst he was
yet quite a young child, wrote some verses upon her
which have been lost. She died at Weston-super-Mare,
where old Mrs. Freeman had settled in 1825. The town
of Weston is overhung by a steep promontory which
forms the end of the high limestone ridge called Worle
Hill, and Freeman used to say that his interest in geography was first excited by the view from this hill, to
the top of which he was often taken as a child. The
view is indeed one of great variety and extent: facing
northward, the tawny waters of the Bristol Channel can
be traced for a long distance on either hand, broadening
westwards till they are merged in the ocean, narrowing
eastwards until they are hidden by enclosing hills. Immediately below rise the dark islets known as the Steep
and Flat Holms, and on the opposite coast, behind busy,
smoky Cardiff, the eye rests upon the dark purple hills
and mountains of Wales and Monmouthshire, with their
many flitting lights and shadows. Following the line of

the Somerset coast, which is curiously broken into a succession of low green flats and bluff headlands, looking west-
ward the eye is first caught by the horn of the bay that is
opposite to Worle Hill, a high green promontory called
Brean Down, really an outlying spur of the Mendips,
beneath which the river Axe winds its way into the sea.
Further westwards, beyond the wide sweep of the flat
bay where the Parrett empties itself into the sea, rises
the soft outline of the Quantocks, and in the dim and
misty distance the sterner and heavier heights of Exmoor.
On the eastern side, immediately below Worle Hill, on
a low grassy tongue of land jutting out into the water, the
ruins of Woodspring Priory may be descried peeping out
from amongst a cluster of elms; while further eastwards,
beyond a long stretch of green level, rises the headland,
on the slopes of which is planted, tier above tier, the
town of Clevedon. Turning inland, the eye ranges to
the north and east over a tract of gently undulating
country, lying between the Mendips and the Kingswood
hills, rich in pasture and wood, from which emerges here
and there the grey spire or tower of some village church.
Southwards the view is bounded by the wall of the Mendips, behind which Wells and Glastonbury lie concealed.

One reason probably why his grandmother took up
her abode at Weston was that she might be near her old
friend, Mrs. Hannah More. She herself had been educated at the school kept by Hannah More's sisters at
Bristol, and her eldest granddaughter was sent about 1826
to the same school, which was then conducted by a Miss
Mills and Madame Amélie. An elder Miss Mills lived
with them, and on one occasion, when little Edward was
taken to see his sister, he startled and rather shocked
the old lady by asking her if she was the mother of the

young one. From time to time he was also taken by
his grandmother to see Hannah More, at her country
residence, Barley Wood, in the parish of Wrington. On
one of these occasions, when he was five years old, a certain
Dr. Randolph, a clerical friend of Hannah More's, came
to pay a call. Just as he rose to take his leave, the
child ran up to him and stopped the old gentleman with
the abrupt question, ' Do you think St. Paul wrote the
Epistle to the Hebrews? He is called the Apostle to
the Gentiles, so why should he have written to the
Hebrews ? '

The precocious young critic seems to have been
a great favourite with Hannah More, whose interest in
him is said to have been first excited by discovering
that when he was only two years and a half old he knew
the coats-of-arms of all the English episcopal sees. Her
first present to him was a small volume of hymns, with
a slip of paper enclosed, on which was written, ' For the
dear little rogue who is expected to tell the titles of
all the Bishops at his next visit to Barley Wood.' She
afterwards gave him a copy of the *Eton Miscellany*,
which is inscribed on the fly-leaf as ' The gift of Mrs.
Hannah More to Edward Augustus Freeman, with her
best love and good wishes.' ' From this book,' he used
to say, ' I first learned the name of William Ewart
Gladstone.'

Mrs. Freeman and her grandchildren left Weston in
1829. A book entitled *Bible Poetry* was probably
Hannah More's parting present to the boy, and is inscribed in her own hand as ' The gift of Hannah More to
E. A. Freeman, with the assurance of her fond affection as
long as he loves learning, fears God, and prays to be made
a good Christian. 4 Windsor Terrace, Clifton, March 27,

1829.' She died in 1832, and he did not see her after he left Weston, but the following letter which has been preserved in her own writing proves that the good old lady and her young friend did not forget one another.

MY VERY DEAR YOUNG FRIEND,

I am so delighted with your kind remembrance of me in your pretty letter, that I must write a line to tell you how much I continue to love you. I have sent you a few little tracts of my own writing, as I thought you would think them the better for that. I hope you continue fond of reading, and that you will make a wise choice in your books, on which your future character will much depend. You will therefore take the advice of the wise and the good, till you attain an age when you may be able to chuse for yourself. The Bible must have the pre-eminence of all other books. History opens a vast field to a youthful reader. But always inquire the character of the author. Poetry and polite literature must be deferred till the proper age. My best regards to Mrs. Freeman.

Ever yours with great affection,

HANNAH MORE.

He always looked back with interest to this early friend-ship with Hannah More, and was accustomed to say that she was a direct link between himself and Samuel Johnson, for he had been a pet of Hannah More, as she had been a favourite of the learned Doctor. He was also fond of referring to Lord Macaulay's acquaintance with her when he was a boy, only observing that he himself had not, like Macaulay, offered her a glass of old spirits [1].

After leaving Weston, his grandmother settled at Northampton, in order to be near her son, the Rev. Joseph Freeman, who was then Rector of Charwelton. At

[1] Hannah More called one day at old Mr. Macaulay's, and was met by his little son, aged four, who informed her that his parents were not at home, but that if she would be good enough to come in he would bring her a glass of old spirits. See *Life of Lord Macaulay*, vol. i. p. 27.

Northampton he was sent as a day boarder to a school in Sheep Street (facing the round church, St. Sepulchre's), which was kept by the Rev. T. C. Haddon, assisted by two brothers. His name appears in the school list of 1832, the earliest which has been preserved, but he probably entered the school before that year. I do not know whether he had learned any Latin before he went to this school; if not, he must have made remarkably rapid progress, for in December, 1833, he received as a prize for Latin Pitt's translation of Virgil's *Aeneid*. In some manuscript notes which he has left of his life, he says that he cannot remember a time when he was not interested in historical study. ' I remember reading both Roman and English history with intense pleasure before I began Latin ; that is, before I was seven years old.' In his second public lecture as Professor of History, after observing that ' our earliest notions of history are not so much drawn from any book, good or bad, as picked up at random from all manner of chance sources,' he continues :—

' I believe I was exceptionally lucky. I was told by my nurse that an emperor has a great many kings under him. That saying was not strictly true at the time when it was uttered, but it had been true only a few years before, and it was going to be true again not very many years after. It is not impossible that that childish piece of teaching may have helped my way to a notion of the Roman Empire clearer than that of some other people [1].'

Mr. Haddon died a few years ago, but the following letter, written in November, 1883, to his old pupil, shows what his opinion of him was :—

[1] *Methods of Historical Study*, p. 107.

DEAR EDWARD FREEMAN,

Perhaps I am the only man in Europe who would presume to address you so, nevertheless I claim the right. Whatever you are to all the world, to me you are still *the boy*, the most remarkable pupil of the hundreds I have had in a long life of pedagoguery.... Many a reminiscence of your schoolboy days is vividly with me. I often go to Northampton, and we often drive past the beautiful old Cross, never without my having vividly before me the scene of your schoolboy days. A mob of riffraff snobs had attacked our party, and had been repelled with ease. I see one of ours, with outstretched arm, and indignant gesture, declaiming 'Odi profanum vulgus et *arkeo*[1].' Who was that?

By his schoolfellows at Mr. Haddon's he seems to have been regarded with mingled curiosity and awe, as a prodigy of learning, who took no part in their games, but devoted all his time to the study of Greek, Latin, and Hebrew, together with the composition of verses, some of which he set up in type at a small printing-press which he kept at home. His schoolfellows say that he never walked, but always ran, or rather skipped, with an odd jerky kind of movement, which earned him the nickname of 'Hoppy-skippy.' He refers to this habit in a letter to his eldest daughter, written in 1888, and says, 'I dare say I skipped at Oxford, as I certainly did at Northampton. I am not sure that I don't now, when my legs give me a chance.' His figure at this age was slight, his face fair and freckled, with long curly flaxen locks, and a somewhat hard set look in his keen grey eyes. Owing to the peculiarity of his gait, and of his dress, a long blue frock-coat, shaped and buttoned much in the style of the Bluecoat boys, with rather short

---

[1] 'I hate the unhallowed crowd, and say, Avaunt.' Horace, *Odes*, Lib. iii. 1. 1.

nankeen trousers, displaying white cotton stockings and low shoes, he was subjected to some ridicule and rough handling from his schoolfellows. One of them[1] has still a vivid recollection of his first sight of him, when this singular little figure was being tossed and lugged about on the shoulders of other boys, half frightened yet laughing loudly, and shouting at the top of his voice (probably in the hope of being released), 'Do you know, my boys, there is a game at marbles called Pyramids?' He was still considered so delicate that some persons doubted whether he would ever grow up to manhood, and some of his schoolfellows remember how they used to be scolded by his grandmother if they had made him run home so fast as to be tired or hot. His grandmother and his sister, who was twelve years older than himself, were no doubt fond as well as proud of him, but their fondness often manifested itself in rather fidgetting and exacting ways, which were apt to irritate the object of their affection, and sometimes led to violent outbursts of resentment. The only successful pacificator at such times was a medical friend of the family, to whose son, the Rev. W. L. Smith, Rector of Dorsington, I am indebted for some of these schoolday reminiscences. He recalls two occasions on which young Freeman accompanied him to his father's house in the country, a few miles outside Northampton, to be cured of his rebellious fits. On one of these visits, he was taken out by his young companion to witness the performances of a terrier dog renowned in the family for its wonderful skill in rat-killing. Young Freeman would take no part in the sport, and surveyed the proceedings from a dis-

---

[1] The Rev. T. Field, Rector of Bigby, Lincolnshire, formerly Fellow of St. John's College, Cambridge.

tance with a somewhat scornful air; but he afterwards composed an account of the dog's exploits in Hudibrastic verse, intimating, however, that it was rather a condescension on his part to lower his muse to such a theme. Another schoolfellow remembers that one day when Sir Walter Scott's *Lady of the Lake* was being discussed, some one remarked that Roderick Dhu was a mere robber, whereupon young Freeman maintained that it was not fair to call him a robber, because 'the times had made him what he was.'

From time to time Mrs. Freeman took her grandchildren to Cromer, and some of his earliest verses, written in 1834, when he was eleven years old, were printed in the *Cromer Telegraph*. These were, for the most part, on public events, and show, for a child of that age, an astonishing knowledge of past as well as contemporary history, together with a very considerable command of language. It is amusing to read, in view of his future sentiments, a loyal rhapsody upon William IV of England, praying that—

'Long may he flourish, and in splendour shine,
Long may he lead on earth great George's line.'

Another piece, containing a fierce denunciation of Louis Philippe and an exhortation to the French to restore the Bourbon line, is headed 'À bas Louis Philippe,' and opens with the following lines:—

'May every tyrant fall,
And proud usurpers all,
But chiefly Louis Philippe and his train—
That sequel of Equality's fierce reign.
May the fifth Henry to his crown succeed,
And all the foes of glorious Bourbon bleed!

> May the arch-traitor never reign in peace,
> And may the line of Capet never cease !
>
> Is this the people of the "Grand Monarque,"
> Who to their throne have raised the tyrant clerk ?'

And more in the same indignant strain. On the other
hand, he sympathized with the attempt of Don Carlos
in 1833 to win the Spanish throne, because, as he said in
later years, it was 'the assertion of the local rights of
Navarre and the Basque provinces'; and one of these
early poems, dated September 10, 1834, celebrates
a victory gained over the army of Queen Isabella by the
commander of the Carlist forces, Zumalacarregui, whose
unmanageable name he contrives to work into his verse
by eliding the a before the l.

In an article entitled 'A Review of my Opinions,' which
appeared in *The Forum*, an American periodical, in
April, 1892 (the month after his death), he attributes his
early interest in public events and politics to living
mainly with people much older than himself.

' I was used,' he says, 'in childhood and youth, to the talk
of those with whom the French Revolution was an event
of their youth, and the American War of Independence án
event of their childhood. . . . I suspect that living mainly with
people a great deal older than oneself, as it helps to bring
the past somewhat nearer to one, helps also to make one take
an early interest in the present. I was, so to speak, introduced
to both the present and the past very early. I certainly have
not kept the impressions of my earliest days, which were for
the most part strongly Tory, but I am not sure that it is a bad
thing to have been a Tory in childhood. I have the dimmest
remembrance of Catholic Emancipation as something very
dreadful, but I can remember when George IV was king.
I remember the coming in of Lord Grey's Ministry in 1830;
I vividly remember the great Reform Bill; most vividly of all

do I remember the local parliamentary elections in the years
1830, 1831, and 1832. I was very eager then, at the age of
from seven to nine years, on behalf of the candidates whom
for the past forty years and more I should have looked on as
the wrong ones. All this I took in from my elders, but I took
it in with a warmth of my own. And I went off into regions
of my own choosing. I took a very early fancy to foreign
politics. The French Revolution of 1830 was the first foreign
event which deeply struck me. And from France I went on
to dabble in the affairs of Spain and Portugal. Of course I was
everywhere on the wrong side, though I am not sure that in
Spain it was wholly the wrong side. The cause of Don Carlos
came most clearly home to me, as the assertion of the local
rights of Navarre and the Basque Provinces. I must, without
knowing it, have been something of a Home Ruler already.
Of course I really knew nothing about foreign politics, but
I learned one piece of knowledge that I have kept : I learned
boundaries. I used an atlas, Wilkinson's, which showed the
map of Europe as it had been before the French Revolutionary
wars, and as it was at the actual time. I was never tired of
studying these maps, of comparing and copying them. And
from that process, I got first of all to feel a dislike for the
power of Austria. . . . Thus I was brought up a Tory on home
politics, but I began very early to make an eclectic creed for
myself in politics beyond the sea. I think that Wilkinson's
Atlas affected me for life, and other things kept me from the
beginning away from the received Tory creed in foreign
matters. The Tory creed was not then exactly what it is now.
It did not imply the same fierce hatred of Russia, or the same
romantic love of the Turk. . . . I was not taught to look on the
battle of Navarino as an untoward event. It always came to
my childish ears as something honourable. And I was most
likely further impressed by seeing a Panorama of the battle,
which was carried about the country. Since then Greece, her
rights and wrongs—to grow in after days into the rights and
wrongs of all South-Eastern Europe—have never been out
of my thoughts. I remember, while still very young, lighting
in some book or newspaper on a doctrine which has often been
repeated since—the doctrine that the power of the Turk was

something needful to be maintained in the interest of England or of all Europe. This saying came upon me as a strange paradox. How could it be for the interest of England and of Europe to prolong the oppression of European and Christian people, at the hand of barbarian and infidel masters? And I have not yet found the diplomatist or the writer of leading articles who has been able to answer the question.'

Although, as he says, he thought out many things for himself, yet his early views on foreign politics were partly influenced by a man of remarkable ability and great force of character. This man was Mr. Thomas Attwood, a banker in Birmingham, who was his uncle by marriage with his mother's elder sister, Miss Elizabeth Carless. Mr. Attwood, during the first thirty-five years of this century, was undoubtedly the most powerful and popular man in Birmingham, which was then a great and important town, but without parliamentary representation or municipal constitution. He was a true patriot, and in the highest sense of the word a demagogue, for he had the best interests of the people at heart, and was free from all selfish aims. He was an enthusiastic leader in the great struggle of the people to obtain parliamentary reform and the redress of public wrongs and abuses of every description. But although he made eloquent and fervid speeches in the open air to enormous multitudes, sometimes exceeding 100,000 persons, yet he never used any inflammatory language, or sanctioned any seditious act. In 1830 he founded the Birmingham Political Union, which became the most powerful organization in the country in the great contest for parliamentary reform. But one of the first rules of this Union was, that the members should be good, loyal, and faithful subjects of the King; that they should obey the laws of the land; and where these failed to protect the rights, liberties, and interests of the people, efforts should be made to get them changed by just, peaceful, and legal means. 'Remember, my friends,' he said in one of his speeches, 'our weapons are peace, law, order, loyalty, and union. Let us hold fast to these weapons, and I tell you the day is not far distant when the liberty and prosperity of our country will be restored.' In a letter written in 1838 he modestly sums up his principal achievements by saying, 'I have lived to see some changes. I began the war against the East India monopoly: I saw its downfall. I began the war against the American Orders in Council : I saw their abolition. I began the late war against the borough-mongering parliament : I saw its reform.' Speaking at a great banquet given in Mr. Attwood's honour at the Mansion House on May 23, 1832, after the passing of the Reform Bill, the historian, Mr. Grote, said, ' It is to him, more than to any other individual, that we owe the success of this great measure. He has taught the people to combine for a great public purpose, without breaking any of the salutary restraints of law, and without violating any of their obligations as private citizens. He has divested the physical force of the country of its terrors, and of its lawlessness, and has made it conducive to ends of the highest public benefit [1].'

'As a child,' says Mr. Freeman in his article in *The Forum*, ' I knew him very well. Of course I was taught to believe that his Radical goings on were not at all the right thing, but

---

[1] For information respecting Mr. Thomas Attwood I am mainly indebted to a very complete Life written by his grandson, Mr. C. M. Wakefield, of Belmont, Uxbridge. Mr. Wakefield's sister is the wife of Mr. Freeman's eldest son Harold.

I believe that he influenced me in one way. It was the time of the first revolt and re-conquest of the kingdom of Poland, sixty years back. Attwood was almost as zealous for Poland as he was for parliamentary reform, and that side of him was allowed to affect me. I took great interest in Poland, and when I had to choose a prize book I chose Dunham's *History of Poland* in Lardner's Cyclopaedia. Large parts of it I know by heart now. It seems strange to me now that I knew my Polish kings before I knew my emperors. The necessary references in Dunham's book to the affairs of the Empire used to puzzle me. I believe my Polish zeal grew cold, like my Greek zeal. It did not fit in with my Tory theories. It was then the Tories whom Whigs and Radicals used to charge with cringing to Russia, and my Polish history taught me that both Poles and Russians were very much like other people. Each nation, I learned, had done the other a shrewd turn whenever it had the chance. And I always had the advantage of knowing my boundaries, that is, of knowing that it was Prussia and Austria, not Russia, which swallowed up the true Poland in 1772-1795.'

In October, 1834, Mrs. Freeman, on returning from Cromer to Northampton with her grandchildren, spent a week with Mr. and Mrs. Robert Gutch, at Segrave Rectory, Leicestershire. Mr. Gutch, who was the second son of the Rev. John Gutch, the well-known antiquary, and Registrar of Oxford University, had been a Fellow of Queens' College, Cambridge, and an assistant master in a school kept by the Rev. Jonathan Boucher at Epsom, where E. A. Freeman's father, and also his uncle Mr. Joseph Freeman, had been educated. Mr. Gutch had married a stepdaughter of Mr. Boucher, Miss James, whose mother was a great friend of old Mrs. Freeman. On this visit to Segrave, her grandson saw for the first time his future wife, Miss Eleanor Gutch, who remembers how the boy astonished the family by arguing some question with her father concerning Nathanael and the fig-tree. Her sister, Miss Gutch, thus records the arrival of the Freemans in her diary:—

' *Oct.* 2, 1834.—Mrs., Miss, and Edward Freeman arrived to-day. . . . Edward one of the most extraordinary boys I ever heard of. Only eleven, yet well acquainted with Latin and Greek, and three years ago began to teach himself Hebrew as an amusement.'

In 1837 he was sent to a preparatory school for about forty boys at Cheam in Surrey, which was a kind of overflow from a larger and more famous school kept by Dr. Mayo. It was a rough place, after the fashion of those days. The only provision for washing was in a narrow corridor downstairs, where eight basons of cold water had to serve the turn of forty shivering boys in a quarter of an hour. Of the Head Master, the Rev. W. Browne, a Fellow of Worcester College, Oxford, Freeman used to say 'he did not know much, but what he did know he could teach.' Even this mild degree of praise, however, could not be bestowed on the ushers, who were, for the most part, a low, coarse set of men, paid exceedingly small salaries for teaching very little, and that little wrong. Some of them on leaving the school sank to lower depths; one of them was reduced to drawing pictures in coloured chalks upon the London pavement. Yet the school was an expensive one, to which sons of noblemen were often sent, and as a proof that rough living and bad teaching cannot permanently stunt the intellectual growth of boys who are both clever and industrious, not a few who began their education there were able, like Freeman himself, to rise to distinction afterwards. Such were James Riddell, who became a Fellow of Balliol and was one of the most finished Greek scholars that ever adorned the University of Oxford; Edward St. John Parry, the late Bishop of Dover; Mr. Clements Markham, C.B., F.R.G.S.; the Rev. R. E. Bartlett, afterwards a Scholar and Fellow of Trinity, Oxford; and others who might be named.

At Cheam, as at Northampton, the singularity of Freeman's gait and of his general appearance and demeanour subjected him at first to some ridicule and rough treatment at the hands of his schoolfellows. As a rule he took no part in games, though one of his schoolfellows thinks he remembers seeing him play hockey now and then, and once bowling a hoop[1]. He was somewhat lanky in figure and ungainly in his movements; nervous also, and fidgetty to an extraordinary degree. The nickname of 'Hoppy-skippy' or 'Hoppy-kicky' still clung to him. The long blue coat had now been exchanged for a green jacket, which was too short for him, and was made of some coarse cloth which the boys were pleased to call green baize, and which they delighted in scratching with their fingers, because the process was exceedingly annoying to the wearer, so that the tears were sometimes seen to roll down his cheeks when one of his tormentors succeeded in drawing his nail from the collar to the waist in one continuous application. Yet, much as he disliked it, the smallest urchins were permitted to scratch the green baize with impunity, so that either he did not know his strength, which was now considerable, or else he had scruples in using it. His kindness of heart, indeed, soon procured him many friends, while his absolute straightforwardness and fearless love of truth gained him general respect. On one

---

[1] The Rev. R. E. Bartlett.

occasion the head master had found fault with him for falling out of place when the boys were drawn up in line, before going into school. Freeman made a deprecatory face, and was then reproved for 'distorting his visage.' 'It is better to distort the visage than to distort truth,' was the reply. Mr. Clements Markham bears testimony to his kindness to the younger boys in the school. Mr. Markham was eight years old when he entered Cheam in 1838, Freeman being then fifteen.

' He was always very kind to me,' he says, ' and took a good deal of notice of me. He gave me the nickname " Pope " from my name Clements, and used to ask me, when I was going to the Vatican. I used to wonder what sort of place that could be and where it was, and at last I asked him. Then he told me a long story about Papal Rome, and left me filled with dreamy wonder. He struck me as unlike all other big fellows, because he was perfectly unconscious of his superiority, while we were more or less afraid of other big boys.'

After their schooldays Mr. Markham lost sight of him for many years.

'The occasion of our acquaintance being renewed was when he wrote a review in the *Saturday* of my *Life of Lord Fairfax*, and another of an account I wrote of the battle of Nieufort in *The Geographical Magazine* about 1871. He then wrote and asked me, if I was the " Pope " he remembered at Cheam. We cordially foregathered, and ever afterwards he took a friendly interest in all my affairs and undertakings.'

'When Freeman came to Cheam,' writes another of his schoolfellows[1], 'he knew as much at least as any of the masters there. He had moreover taught himself Hebrew, and he also brought with him a Septuagint, of the very existence of which I believe the whole school, masters and pupils alike, were

[1] The Rev. Warren Auber Brooke, Incumbent of Holy Trinity, Port Melbourne, Australia.

ignorant. I also had learnt a smattering of Hebrew, so here was a bond of union between Freeman and me, and many were the discussions we had about the Hebrew points, he insisting that they were modern, I as persistently affirming that Hebrew was created with points. A crucial test which I could never get over was afforded by a verse in the Psalms (vii. 12), 'God is angry with the wicked every day,' which the Septuagint renders μὴ ὀργὴν ἐπάγων. Now, said Freeman, the Hebrew copies which the LXX had before them could not have had points, otherwise they must have translated ὁ Θεός, such being the reading of the pointed versions. But if they had unpointed manuscripts they were quite right to render by the word μή, because the Hebrew word, so far as letters are concerned, means "not" as well as "God." Like many other people older than myself, as I could not answer Freeman, I contented myself with getting into a passion and—retaining my own opinion. I do not really think that Freeman learned anything during the two years he was at Cheam, except what he learned by himself, for he was an omnivorous reader of books, excepting novels, and works of modern science. I remember that on one occasion when he had fallen into disgrace with the head master, he was ordered as a punishment to translate a French treatise on geology, which advocated the then novel theory, that the earth was once in a state of incandescence. This theory Freeman abhorred, for he was severely orthodox, and any notion which seemed to contradict the Bible met with no mercy at his hands. It was therefore laughable to see and hear him as he plied his unwelcome task, fidgetting about, groaning, shouting, and calling the Frenchman by the names of all the atheists and heretics in existence.'

He insisted, indeed, so rigidly at this time on the truth of Holy Scripture in its most literal sense, as gravely to argue that the earth was motionless, from the verses in the Psalms, 'He hath made the round world so sure that it cannot be moved,' and 'He laid the foundations of the earth that it never should move at any time[1].'

[1] Ps. xciii. 2 and civ. 5 (P. B. vers.).

Before he went to Cheam he had written out the first thirty Psalms in Hebrew, together with a translation and notes made by himself. This occupation, however, seems to have been dropped at Cheam, and Hebrew gradually gave place more and more to the study of Latin and Greek, especially the latter, so that before he left Cheam he had transcribed the whole of the *Antigone* of Sophocles in Greek, adding his own translation and notes together with disquisitions on the metres of the choruses. The deeply religious tone of his mind appears in a letter written to his aunt, Mrs. Joseph Freeman, shortly after his confirmation in the first year of his residence at Cheam. It is the earliest letter from him that has been preserved, and is written in the firm, clear, upright hand which was always characteristic of him, but the signature is an elaborate and intricate device like some of the signatures of our mediaeval sovereigns.

Cheam, Oct. 28, 1837.

MY DEAR AUNT,

I had intended all the half-year to write to my uncle, but the receipt of five shillings has induced me to write to you instead. This present was exceedingly acceptable, as my finances were very low, but this and the same sum received from grandmama has quite set me up again. I suppose grandmama has informed you that I have been confirmed. This took place at the hands of the Archbishop of Canterbury[1], on Thursday, Sept. 28. I was, as may be supposed, deeply affected at the solemn ceremony, and at the awful responsibility I took upon myself, yet the awe was mingled with joy at the prospect of being admitted to the Table of my God, to partake of the sacred elements representing His Body and Blood, lacerated and shed for my transgressions. Nothing could exceed the solemnity of the Litany with which the ceremony opened. Though the words were trite and familiar

[1] Dr. Howley.

to me, yet I never listened so intensely, I never heard anything
read with such solemn emphasis as they were by Sir John
Harrington, the grandnephew of my grandfather's old friend.
It will be a fortnight to-morrow since I received the Communion from Mr. Wilding, the excellent although somewhat
eccentric Curate of Cheam, and Mr. Boucher, or, as he chooses
to spell his name, Bouchier. He also read very solemnly, and
it deeply affected me. Give my love to my uncle, cousin
Joseph, &c., and with all wishes for your and their welfare,
and thanks for your kindness,

Believe me,

Your affectionate Nephew.

Before the close of his school life at Cheam he had
become deeply interested in the religious revival commonly known as the Oxford Movement. He seems to
have read not only the famous *Tracts for the Times*, but
also a great deal of the ancient literature to which they
directed attention, and modern works written by distinguished members of the Tractarian School. When he
left Cheam in 1839 he gave as a parting present to one
of his schoolfellows two volumes of sermons by Dr. Irons
on the Holy Catholic Church and Apostolical Succession,
and he had already given him, a few months earlier,
a copy of the *Lyra Apostolica*. The same friend says :—

'The fearless expression of his sympathy with the principles
of the Oxford writers brought him into collision both with his
schoolfellows and the masters, who had not risen above the
ignorant Protestantism or Erastianism prevalent at the time,
but as he had the advantage derived from study of books which
they had not read, they were unable to cope with him in
argument, and contented themselves with sneers at his earnestness, and confident predictions that he would speedily develop
into a Romanist.'

In the course of his two years at Cheam he wrote
many short poems, of which a few have been preserved,

† VOL. I.

including 'The Jews at Babylon,' 'Palmyra,' and 'An
Epitaph on Bishop Heber,' all written in the spring of
1837, 'An Ode to Time,' composed in February 1839,
and some lines on ' Jephtha's Daughter,' dated December
of the same year. Some of these early pieces are marked
by a depth of thought and feeling and a command of
language and rhythm rarely to be found in compositions
of a boy of fourteen or fifteen. A few lines may be
presented as specimens from the 'Epitaph on Bishop
Heber.'

> ' Brighter his glory than of mighty kings,
> Whose conquering step the enraptured poet sings.
> Warriors have fought, and nations been enslaved ;
> Heroes the powers of death itself have braved.
> The widow's curse attends the victor's tread,
> But blessings rest upon the Christian's head.
> Loved and revered and blessed was he by all,
> And India streamed with tears at Heber's fall.'

The following stanza, from the poem on ' Jephtha's
Daughter,' describes her going to meet her father.

> ' First of a bright and tuneful choir,
> The damsel speeds to meet her sire,
> The tresses of her raven hair
> Circling her neck, divinely fair :
> Her dark eyes sparkle as she spies
> The distant vision of her father rise.'

It was in the autumn of 1839 that he began to enter
into correspondence with the Rev. Henry Thompson,
who for some years to come was of great service to him
in directing the course of his studies and the formation
of his opinions and tastes. Mr. Thompson was at this
time Curate-in-charge of Wrington, and afterwards Vicar

of Chard in Somerset. He was a Cambridge man, an excellent Greek and Latin scholar, with a good knowledge also of Hebrew and German, which was rare in those days. He was also well read in theology and general literature, and by very industrious and methodical habits seems to have successfully combined the duties of an active pastor with the charge and instruction of three pupils. He was the friend and biographer of Hannah More, and it is most probable that he first saw Freeman at her residence, Barley Wood. After the death of Mr. Thompson, Freeman's letters to him were unfortunately destroyed, with the exception of a few which had accidentally become mixed with a collection of autographs bought by a London publisher[1]. The purchaser has kindly lent them to me for the purposes of this biography. Mr. Thompson's own letters, of which many are written in Greek or Latin, also furnish a useful index to the mind of his correspondent, enabling us to see what were the subjects upon which it was at work; and some parts of them are well worth reading for their own sake, as coming from a man of extensive reading, clear views, sound judgement, and elegant scholarship. His first letter, dated September 2, 1839, is evidently a reply to one which Freeman had addressed to him concerning his *Life of Hannah More*, then recently published. After expressing delight at receiving a letter from Freeman, 'the first,' as he hopes, 'of a long and agreeable correspondence,' and saying that his remarks on 'the bit of biography are already deposited among the critical κειμήλια,' he proceeds:—

'You ask me my opinion of the Oxford Tracts. To say that I have not derived instruction and benefit from them would

[1] Mr. Elkin Mathews.

betoken a want of comprehension, or a want of humility, or both. I say not so: I am deeply grateful for the edification they have brought to me, as well as to the Church at large. But I can say with Dr. Hook that they have not taught me any new *principle*: their views, in the main, are the views that have been ever entertained by all well-read Churchmen. . . . I could not have believed, had not the outcry against the Tracts proved it, that there had been so many professed Churchmen wholly ignorant of Church principles as it seems there are. The Tract-writers have done wisely in the form they have adopted. Had they written a folio, they would have gone to Lethe with the great kindred spirits to whose writings they have called attention.'

The remainder of the letter deals with the 'quinquarticular controversy [1],' about which Freeman had asked for information. Considering what the subjects of his young correspondent's letter had been, the postscript is significant and not surprising. 'I hope you will not think me impertinent if I ask what is your present age. I assure you it is no idle curiosity.'

The next letter from Mr. Thompson, dated October 28 of the same year, is on foolscap paper, closely written and crossed on three sides, but, as always in his letters, the hand is so exquisitely neat and clear that it can be read without difficulty. Freeman had taken exception to some expressions in his former letter, which seemed to imply disapproval of Prayers for the Dead, and had asked him for 'scriptural, patristical, and liturgical arguments' in support of his opinion. After dealing with this question at considerable length, the writer goes on to discuss the meaning of 'Election,' which had been

---

[1] 'The five-article controversy,' so called from the five points on which the Arminians insisted in their Remonstrance against the doctrines of the Calvinists at the conference at the Hague in 1610.

another subject of inquiry. After referring to some of the attacks which had been made on the Oxford Tracts, and saying that Freeman was much better read in them than he was himself, he concludes by congratulating him that, 'although so young,' he had 'been enabled to take such clearsighted views of Divine Grace.' But he adds as a warning, ' I trust you will never forget *Who* has made you to differ so remarkably from the generality of boys in intellectual stature and information. It is a mighty gift, a gift which lays the recipient under deep responsibility. Beware how you permit it to minister to vanity, the instrument with which the Tempter will most probably beset you.' He also expresses a hope, that while he ' pursues his scriptural and ecclesiastical studies,' he will not neglect 'Greek and Latin literature, which expands, refines, and strengthens the mind, besides forming an admirable background for an ample and liberal study of divinity.' The letter is signed ' yours very affectionately,' and from this date a regular correspondence was maintained between the two friends for about ten years, and at rarer intervals for a yet longer period.

The next letter, dated December 14, 1839, is a reply at considerable length to one in which Freeman had inquired in what sense the Holy Eucharist might be considered a sacrifice, and also respecting the validity of lay baptism, the question being asked on behalf of a friend, who was doubtful whether he had been baptized by a cleric. Mr. Thompson was expecting a visit from him in the Christmas holidays, and ends his letter by quoting the thirteenth and fourteenth verses of the third Epistle of St. John in Greek, adding ' thus in the words of the Apostle of Christian love, take the present farewell of your affectionate friend.'

It had been the wish of Freeman's uncle that after two years' work at Cheam he should be sent to Shrewsbury School, then at the height of its reputation under Dr. Kennedy. But the boy was so averse to going there, or to any public school, and begged so hard to be allowed to become a pupil of Mr. Gutch, to whom he had taken a great fancy, that his request was complied with, and after the Christmas holidays in January, 1840, he became an inmate of Segrave Rectory. Here he had the advantage of the ordinary classical teaching, with more freedom and leisure to follow studies of his own choice in other directions than he could have enjoyed at a public school. On the other hand, his shyness, awkwardness, and impatience of views different from his own, were probably increased by the want of intercourse with lads of his own age. He himself was sensible of these drawbacks, but he thought that the balance was on the whole on the side of advantage. Writing near the close of his life, he says :—

'Am I to set it down as a gain or a loss, that I was never at a public school ? I feel that in some things it has been a loss, perhaps not now, but certainly when I was younger. But I suspect that it has been on the whole a gain. I think that I am thè more independent for it. There is a certain superstitious feeling about public schools, a certain wonderful bowing down to head masters, which I feel I am better without. And would Harrow or Eton in 1836 or 1837 have set me to read the book which I was set to read in my private school? That book was W. C. Taylor's *History of the Overthrow of the Roman Empire, and the Foundation of the principal European States.*

'The book is utterly superseded and forgotten : I have not looked at it for years, and I have no doubt that it is far below the standard of 1892, but from that book, coming to it with all the freshness of a boy's first real powers of understanding, I learned things better worth knowing than anything that

I could have picked up at Eton or Harrow. I had already some dim notion of a Western Empire; from Taylor's book I first learned that there was an Eastern Empire. I learned also what Saracens were. I learned that there were Sassanian Kings of Persia, Bulgarians also, and many things that have been good for me throughout life. I did not read Gibbon till many years later, and I believe that I took in many of these things in a better way, through coming on them first in the inferior writer.'

His mind continued to be much occupied after he went to Segrave Rectory with questions of theology and ecclesiastical history. From a letter of Mr. Thompson's dated February 25, 1840, it appears that Freeman had been consulting him on the distinction between Regeneration and Renovation, and on the position of the Non-Jurors.

'In your estimate of the Non-Jurors,' writes Mr. Thompson, 'I am happy to concur with you. The Non-Jurors were not, as such, schismatics. Holding themselves to be, as they were, Bishops and Presbyters by an authority which no act of the State could invalidate, they felt it their duty to exercise their ministry, though they could no longer do so within the pale of the Establishment, which you rightly consider to have been only a part at that time of the reformed Catholic Church in England. That their ministrations therefore were valid is, I should conceive, a point unquestionable by every Catholic.'

He then pleads for a milder and more equitable estimate than that which Freeman had formed of the character and conduct of William III, 'the Great Deliverer.'

'William had come to mediate between the King and his people, but James was cowardly as well as cruel (the common combination); he feared the popularity of the Prince and the temper of the people ; he dared not call a Parliament ; he absconded. What was to be done?

ἀναρχίας δὲ μεῖζον οὐκ ἔστιν κακόν·
αὕτη πόλεις ὅλλυσιν, ἥδ' ἀναστάτους
οἴκους τίθησιν¹.

The Convention did what they were *obliged* to do, and William did in my opinion only what he ought. He could not be expected to have a very exact knowledge of the peculiar constitution of our Church, as differing from the Protestant communion in which he had been educated, and his bias must have been towards his own form of Protestantism.

'For this we must make allowance. While we deeply venerate the memory of the pious men who sacrificed emolument to conscience, we can scarcely blame a sovereign *de facto* for vacating appointments where the holders refused allegiance, where indeed they would openly, before whole congregations, have prayed for our Most Gracious Sovereign Lord, King James. While therefore I honour the Non-Jurors, I must do justice to our " deliverer " from " Popish tyranny and arbitrary power²." '

A letter from Mr. Gutch to Freeman's grandmother in April, 1840, when he had been about two months at Segrave, testifies to his progress in classical studies, and also to his pertinacity in maintaining some of his peculiar opinions. He still held that the earth must be immoveable, on the strength of the verse in Psalm 104.

'But our arguments,' says Mr. Gutch, 'are always maintained in a very friendly spirit. We cannot but admire his intrepid avowal of what he conceives to be the truth, and his consistency in acting up to his professions. His ascetic habits are not at all excessive, and are more likely to be favourable than injurious to his health, nor are they particular, except as being more openly avowed than is usual in the present very relaxed state of society, in which each person's private judgement is commonly regarded as his standard of right and wrong, and deference to authority, especially ecclesiastical, is

¹ Soph. *Antig.* 672 sq.
² From the Service for Nov. 5 in the Prayer-Book: abolished in 1859.

thought a ridiculous weakness, rather than an obligation upon the conscience.'

The ascetic habits alluded to in this letter probably consisted of a certain degree of fasting, and perhaps abstinence from some ordinary amusements, on Wednesdays and Fridays, practices which he continued to observe for some years to come. About this time he consulted his friend Mr. Thompson respecting a systematic course of reading in divinity, who replies in a letter dated May 21, recommending in the first place a critical study of the Hebrew and Greek texts of Holy Scripture without any other commentary than what is purely philological. Collaterally with this, he says:—

'Study ecclesiastical history and geography; then the Scriptures again with the commentators, but not more than three or four of the best on each book; then some of the best ecclesiastical historians and the Apostolic Fathers, with selections from others, as the Apologies of Justin Martyr, some of the earlier treatises of Tertullian, the *Philocalia* of Origen, and the whole of Lactantius. The Commentaries of Chrysostom and Theophylact might also be read with the parts of Scripture on which they treat. Then evidences, then Anglican theology and sermons.'

That Freeman did his best to act upon this advice without delay is clear from another letter of Mr. Thompson's, dated October 22 of the same year. Like many others at this period, the letter is in Latin. He begins by saying that he thinks Freeman must be a Phoenix, for he certainly is a *rara avis*. The fertility of his brain is delightful, but so overwhelming in the quantity that it produces as sometimes to give his friend a headache. He makes verses almost faster than his correspondent can read them, and seems to be reading and translating

Greek, Latin, and English classics, and studying the Greek and Latin Fathers of the Church all at the same time.

THOMAIDES LIBERIO SUO S. P. D.

' Phoenicem, mi Liberi, omnino te esse suspicor, raram enim te avem esse quis dubitet? Sed et ex cerebri tui proventu idem conjicere licet qui mirâ quidem dulcedine est, me tamen capitis dolore aliquando excruciat. Eâ enim ubertate istum tuum cerebellum est, ut carmina paene citius condas quam ego legere valeam. Proh Sancte Phoebe! Aeschylum, Sappho-nem, Campbellum, Milmannum, Prudentium, Enchespalum [1] uno omnes tempore mihi et legere et convertere videris! Omnibus ecclesiae patribus Justino, Irenaeo, Cypriano, Chry-sostomo curam simul impendis. Sed quum mihi tam ingentem campum recluseris brevitati consulendum est : quocirca ne verbum quidem amplius addam, et ad respondendum tuis tam variis epistolis me confestim accingam.'

He then goes off into a careful criticism of Freeman's translations from the *Persae* of Aeschylus into English, and of some of Campbell's poems into Latin verse, and ends with a long dissertation upon the use of the Mixed Chalice, a subject which was constantly being discussed between the friends at this time. Freeman had been reading Dr. Brett's work, and was convinced that the mixture was the practice of the Primitive Church. Mr. Thompson was doubtful, and quotes some passages from Chrysostom which he thought rather implied the contrary, but ends one of his letters by saying, ' I have not read Dr. Brett, and as he appears to you and to the *Remembrancer* [2] to have proved his point, I dogmatize not.'

The earliest of the few letters from Freeman to Mr. Thompson which have been preserved is dated

[1] I. e. Shakespeare.
[2] The Review called the *Christian Remembrancer*.

August 12 of this year, and it appears from this letter
that he had only just begun to write Greek verses, and
that he was now paying special attention to translation,
and Greek and Latin composition, with a view to trying
for a scholarship at Balliol College, Oxford, in the following November, but from the end of the letter we see
that the liturgical question had still a large share of his
thoughts and interests.

My dear Friend,

    I send you hereby the translation from your friend
Enchespalus, which you bid me write and send to you. You
perceive, no doubt, many corrections in Mr. Gutch's writing,
several of which are nevertheless of my own devising. You
see that I have not scrupled to lay the dramatists under con-
tribution for anything I thought might be of service. I hope
that you will view this with the indulgence that is due to
a first attempt, but I trust that by November I may be able
to bring out something pretty tolerable. This Enchespalian
translation is the thing in my approaching examination at the
'Balliol.' Of the mathematical portion I have a kind of vague
dread.

Τρομερὰν φρίκᾳ τρομερὰν φρέν' ἔχω·
    διὰ σάρκα δ' ἐμὰν
    ἔλεος ἔλεος ἔμολε[1].

I must also try what I can do with regard to the translation
of English into Greek prose, which is I believe also required,
and in which perhaps I am less likely to succeed than in the
iambics, as my Greek studies have lain for the most part
among those poets.

'Unde nil majus generatur *ipsis*,
    Nec viget quidquam simile aut secundum:
    Proximos illis tamen occupavit
        Flaccus honores[2].'

---

[1] Eurip. *Phoen.* 1285-87.
[2] An adaptation of Horace, *Odes*, Lib. i. 12. 17.

Well, this can hardly be so far called an original note, for, as you see, it takes after its brethren, the Latin themes which I showed you at Wrington, my verses in that language being rather τῶν γενομένων μιμήσεις, as my friend Aristotle, upon whom I have just made a second attack, has it, or something to that effect. Some manuscripts however I believe read τοῦ διδομένου with the scholium σκίπωνος.

But to change the *metals*, the legality or illegality of which I leave to those more skilled in κηρυκεία. I will leave the σιδηρόγλωσσον στόμα χαλκοστόμου κώδωνος, as I have it in my translation[1], for the divine Χρυσόστομος[2], as I wish to make a little further inquiry into that passage which you cite as a condemnation of the mixture, a practice which I think that Bishop Brett has clearly demonstrated to be Catholic, and even scriptural, but which I cannot but imagine rather refers to the Encratite (query teetotal) heresy. I have many reasons to urge in favour of this supposition, but I must first examine whether Mr. Gutch's library contains a copy of the works of that holy father, and indeed the subject demands a more detailed inquiry. So I hope that you will write to me as soon as convenient, and among other things, enter upon this subject, upon which I will not at present dwell further. In the last *British Magazine* was a paper of mine ' On the Situation of the Inferior Clergy and Laity.' With best remembrances to Mrs. Thompson and the rest of your family, and many thanks for the pleasure and improvement afforded me during my stay at Wrington,

Believe me,

Your affectionate Friend.

The paper referred to in the latter part of this letter appeared under the signature of S. P. C. in the August number of the *British Magazine*, 1840, which was edited

---

[1] No doubt of the passage in *King John*, Act iii. Scene 2 :
' If the midnight bell
Did with his iron tongue and brazen mouth
Sound on,' &c.
[2] Chrysostom, i. e. ' He of the golden mouth.'

at that time by Dr. Maitland. Freeman seems to have
been moved to write it by the perusal of a pamphlet
which had recently appeared written by Dr. Hook, but
published anonymously, entitled 'Presbyterian Rights
Asserted.' The design of the pamphlet was to vindicate
the rights of Presbyters against the exercise of a too
arbitrary power on the part of Bishops[1]. The paper in
the *British Magazine* does not enlarge much upon this
topic, but rather calls attention to the neglect by the laity
of their rights and privileges as members of the Church,
and to the mischievous effects of the vulgar notion that
the clergy formed a body apart, with distinct interests
from the laity, the Bishops being merely like magistrates
to keep the clergy in order. He illustrates the prevalence
of this notion by a reference to the incorrect expression
more commonly heard then than it is now, that when
a man was ordained to Holy Orders he 'entered the
Church,' as if he had not already been admitted into it
when he was baptized, an expression, he observes, about
as correct as if any one should say that when a person
became a magistrate he entered the nation.

The translation from Shakespeare into Greek iambics
referred to in his letter was his first effort in that species
of verse-making. Mr. Thompson, in his reply, says that
he 'likes them exceedingly,' pronounces them 'wonderful
for a first attempt,' and sends him a version of the same
passage made by Dr. Kennedy, to which his own verses
presented some remarkable parallels.

In his next letter, a Latin one, dated September 20, he
highly praises some Latin hexameters in the style of
Juvenal and some lyric verses in imitation of Catullus.

---

[1] For a full account of this remarkable essay see the *Life and Letters of
Dean Hook*, by the present writer (6th edition), pp. 267-272.

The hexameters—which have been preserved in a book
into which Freeman copied at this time, in an exquisitely
neat hand, most of his Greek and Latin compositions—
consist of a lamentation on the religious indifference and
ignorance of the times, which he traces back to the
Revolution of 1688, winding up with an outburst of
indignation at the appointments of latitudinarian Bishops
made by Lord Melbourne. The great hope of falling
Church and country was to be found in such staunch
prelates as Henry of Exeter and Edward of Salisbury.
His friend, while expressing great general admiration of
the poem, and sympathy with his sentiments, is constrained to reprove him for his intemperate condemnation
of William III and commiseration of James.

'Verum (ut ad hexametros redeam) vix exprimere possum
quanta me voluptate affecerint! optimae sententiae! et quibus
me assentientem facile habebis, si modo excipias quae de
Liberatore paullo liberius, ne dicam ἀσεβεστοτέρως, proferre
ausus es, et lacrymas quibus indigne Caroli martyris sanctis-
simi indignissimum filium ornasti.'

With pathetic earnestness, the hardworked and not
overpaid curate of a non-resident rector exhorts his
young friend to use this golden season of leisure while
he may, and congratulates him upon the wisdom with
which, while devoting much time to the ancient classics,
he prefers the sacred writings to them all. Would that
he himself had made as good use of his opportunities!
As it is, he has no leisure for severe studies, and his friend
must pardon him if he seeks relaxation in the perusal of
the German poets.

'Utere, amice optime, aureo isto otio, dum licet perfrui.
Quam vellem ipse quondam usus essem! Nunc mihi liberi

docendi, oves pascendae, vixque suppetit unde legam. Quod si germanis poetis plus satis indulsisse videar id ne mihi vitio vertas, quum nova studia animum felicius reficiant, neque semper arcum tendere Apollo ipse sustineat.'

In November Freeman went up to be examined for a scholarship at Balliol. The successful candidates were his old schoolfellow James Riddell, and Matthew Arnold. Freeman, however, must have been 'proxime accessit,' for in later years, when he had conceived a great dislike for Balliol, he was accustomed to say that he owed Matthew Arnold a debt of gratitude for having saved him from becoming a Scholar of that College.

He is described as being at this period slight in figure, rather awkward in manner, and very shy and silent in the presence of strangers; but to persons with whom he felt at ease he talked very freely upon all subjects in which he took the keenest interest, more especially ecclesiastical architecture, Liturgical forms, and matters connected with the polity and ritual of the Church. He found an earnest inquirer into these subjects, and an attentive learner, in one of the daughters of his tutor, and to her in course of time he became deeply attached. No positive engagement took place then, or would have been permitted by her parents or by his uncle and guardian. They probably thought that the young people were too young to know their own hearts, and that with Freeman's removal to Oxford the strength of their attachment would gradually diminish. On the contrary, however, it steadily increased, and seven years later Miss Eleanor Gutch became his wife. His feelings at this time were confided to his old friend Mr. Thompson, who in one of his long Latin letters, dated April 10, 1841, gives him some wholesome advice on the situation. He

bids him remember that marriage means either the
greatest happiness or the greatest unhappiness, 'nuptiis
nihil felicius, nihil infelicius.' He entreats him to do
nothing precipitately, 'tantum id suadeo ut nihil agas festi-
nantius'; and warns him that lovemaking is fraught with
peril to the study of letters. Wherefore he exhorts him to
take care that his Eleanor does not hinder his devotion
to his Thucydides and Tacitus. 'Nihil est litterarum
studiis amore periculosius : neque facilè quis Minervam
simul ac Cupidinem coluerit. Caveas ergo ne Eleanora
tua Thucydidi et Tacito obsit.'

Certainly there is no evidence that this early attachment caused any relaxation of his studies at Segrave ;
for a great part of this same letter from Mr. Thompson
is filled with remarks upon his translation into English
verse of the *Agamemnon* of Aeschylus, some parts of
which his correspondent thinks worthy of Milman. It
also contains criticisms of some observations made by
Freeman in recent letters upon Aristophanes, Euripides,
and Ovid. He had been led astray by his great admiration of Aristophanes (with which Mr. Thompson heartily
concurs) into an unworthy estimate of Socrates, and he
had unduly depreciated Euripides and Ovid. Euripides,
Mr. Thompson observes, is a master of pathos, and Ovid,
in the judgement of Milton, would have surpassed Virgil
if the edge of his genius had not been blunted by exile
and sorrow.

As Freeman's Greek and Latin letters to Mr. Thompson
have been lost, with the exception of one which was
written some years later when he was at Oxford, I insert
here a letter to his friend the Rev. T. W. Barlow, dated
April 2, 1840, as a specimen of his Latinity when he was
barely more than sixteen and a half years of age.

AD VIRUM REVERENDUM T. W. BARLOW, M.A.

Per mihi gratum fecisti, Presbyter Reverende, quod versi-
culos istos quos plus toto abhinc anno animi causa scripseram,
ab amico tuo viro planè humanissimo, itemque eruditione summâ
instructo limatos ad me remiseris. Ex quâ censurâ et ex
versiculis eximiis, neque veterum quolibet indignis, quos
Salopiae Chartis tradidit, liquidó constat illum amicum tuum
eum esse cuius consuetudo maxime me delectaret. Haud
temere dixit Muretus, auctor gravissimus, nihil aetati meae
diligentius cavendum esse, quam quibus sodalitatibus utar ado-
lescentulus. Quare ne tanti viri sententiae immemor sim,
mihi semper maximae curae est ut proborum atque sapientium
amicitiis utar. Quod ad versos meos attinet eo nomine gavisus
sum quod eos D. Dukes castigatione dignatus sit: nam ut
verum fatear nisi quod illius annotationes servare vellem
emendationis ignibus ipse dederim. Quamobrem, ut scias
quantum in arte poeticâ profecerim neque me plane Maevium
aut Hyarbitam esse judices, versus quosdam, haud multis
abhinc diebus a me scriptos, ad te mittere decrevi. Quae in
his praeceptor emendavit obelo notavi. Vale, Reverende
sacerdos, atque omnibus meis salutem dic, tui semper ob-
servantissimum me habe.
                                        EDWARDUS A. FREEMAN.

Dabam Segraviae Quarto Nonas Apriles, CIƆIƆCCCXL.

But although he did not relax his diligence in classical
studies, he must have occupied a great part of his leisure
during the next two years in the composition of poetry,
most of which he dedicated to Miss Gutch, including
a tragedy (recast from a yet earlier and longer poem),
entitled *The Captives*; the plot of the drama being
that a German crusader returns home with a Grecian
bride, which causes his former love Leoline to bury
herself and her grief in a cloister. The piece is described on the title-page as being written 'chiefly in
imitation of Aeschylus,' and in accordance with the
Greek model it contains monostich passages, and is fur-

nished with a Chorus and a Messenger. He also wrote
another tragedy of 1240 lines on *St. Thomas of Canterbury*, in which some of the stirring scenes in the Primate's
life, and the murder in the Cathedral, are depicted with
considerable force and skill; and lastly, in the same
year he wrote a long poem entitled *Thoughts on the
most Holy Eucharist according to the use of the Catholic
Church of England*. It consists of a series of stanzas in
various metres upon every part of the service in order,
his aim being to bring out the spirit and significance of
each, and show its relation to the whole. It is dated
October 26, 1840; so it must have been finished just
before he went up to try for the Balliol scholarship in
the following month. Its style bespeaks a writer who
was familiar with the *Lyra Apostolica* and *The Cathedral*
of Mr. Isaac Williams. Some of the notes appended to
it show how entirely he was in sympathy at this time
with the spirit and teaching of the more advanced leaders
of the Oxford Movement. The Introits, he observes,
retained in the Prayer Book of 1549 'were expunged by
Act of Parliament in 1552, together with much that was
ancient and Catholic, to gratify the foreign innovators.'
To the wounds inflicted on the Church by the blind fury
of Bucer, Peter Martyr, and other fanatics of the same
school, reference is made throughout the rest of these
stanzas.

'The Commandments,' he says, 'were introduced into the
Communion Service in 1552. In the Church of God in Scotland, the officiating minister, if using the Scottish Liturgy, is
allowed to substitute our Saviour's Summary of the Law. The
legal formulary is more appropriate to a Church in bondage
like ours; the evangelical to one rejoicing in freedom from the
yoke of Erastianism.'

In a stanza on the Offertory, he expresses much indignation that this primitive and scriptural method of providing for the maintenance of the sanctuary and its services is comparatively neglected, in favour of such worldly devices as bazaars and musical performances, given in sacred buildings, professional singers, possibly Romanists, or infidels, being hired to take part in them. In a note on this passage he remarks :—

' I hope this will not be understood as expressing any unkind feeling against the Roman Church.   The true Churchman does not look upon the errors of any branch of the Catholic Church as subjects for hatred, but for pity ; least of all, those of a Church to whom we owe so much as to the Church of Rome.   If that Church claimed and exercised an undue authority, let us not forget that our own land was in a great degree evangelized by its missionaries.'

But he goes on to maintain that the Romanists in England were a schismatical sect, and that it was a false liberality which invited such persons to assist in desecrating the sanctuaries of the English Church—for a desecration he considered it to be, if musical festivals were held in Cathedral Churches at which money was paid for admission, and professional singers were engaged to perform.   And to this opinion he adhered to the end of his life.

In a note to the stanza on the Prayer of Consecration, he says:—

' The alterations made in this prayer to gratify the foreign sectaries are well known.   All that more particularly referred to the doctrines of the Real Presence and the Commemorative Sacrifice was mutilated.   These Catholic doctrines are indeed still contained in the service, but so expressed that only those who understand the spirit and language of the ancient Church will always be able to perceive them.'

A few lines extracted from the stanza on the Consecration Prayer clearly express his faith in regard to the Sacrament of the Holy Eucharist. After lamenting the corruptions introduced into the service by the influence, first of Rome, and afterwards of foreign reformers, he proceeds:—

'My spirit yearns for holier days than these,
When on our Church no foreign yoke had weighed,
And in such strains as these her prayers she made.

All glory be to Thee, O Lord,
For ever be Thy name adored.

.   .   .   .   .   .

With angels now our songs we raise,
Ever to celebrate Thy praise,
Whose mercy gave Thy Son, our God,
To shed for us His precious Blood,
And suffering death upon the Tree
To reconcile the world to Thee.
By one oblation duly made,
Even as Thy will, O Father, bade,
Who in that last and awful hour,
The season of infernal power,
When by His own betrayed, denied,
For us He suffered, bled, and died,
His Flesh and Blood vouchsafed to give
That Adam's guilty race might live,
And bade us for our Saviour's sake
This spotless Sacrifice to make [1].
Wherefore, O Father, heavenly Lord,
In meek obedience to His Word,
We on Thy Holy Altar lay
The tribute we are bound to pay.

.   .   .   .   .   .

[1] 1 Cor. xi. 24, τοῦτο ΠΟΙΕΙΤΕ εἰς τὴν ἐμὴν ἀνάμνησιν.

O gracious Lord, eternal Sire,
Incline Thine ear to our desire ;
In mercy to their voice attend,
Who at Thy dreadful Altar bend;
And with Thy Spirit from on high
Vouchsafe to bless and sanctify
Thy holy gifts of Bread and Wine,
Which now we offer at Thy shrine.
Make them, O Lord, the Flesh and Blood
Of Jesus, our incarnate God,
And all who shall hereof partake,
Thy true and faithful servants make.'

. . . . . .

Those who are familiar with the English Liturgy of
1549 will recognize in these lines a very faithful reflexion
of the language and spirit of the Consecration Prayer.
The following is the note appended in reference to the
words 'His Flesh and Blood vouchsafed to give':—

'That Christ did in a mystical manner offer Himself up to
the Father at the institution of the Eucharist has always been
the belief of the Church. It is also manifest from the words
of Scripture. St. Luke xxii. 19, 20, τὸ ὑπὲρ ὑμῶν διδόμενον, refers
much more naturally to a present than to a future action ; and
in the next verse we have τοῦτο τὸ ποτήριον ἡ καινὴ διαθήκη ἐν τῷ
αἵματί μου, τὸ ὑπὲρ ὑμῶν ἐκχυνόμενον, where the commonest rules
of grammar show that ἐκχυνόμενον must refer to ποτήριον and not
to αἵματι. "This Cup which is poured out for you, is the New
Testament in my Blood": no one, I imagine, will give this the
low sense of "this Cup poured out for you to drink," and indeed
τὸ ὑπὲρ ὑμῶν ἐκχυνόμενον is analogous to τὸ ὑπὲρ ὑμῶν διδόμενον in
the last verse, which I think refers to τοῦτο rather than to σῶμα.
We have here then, in Scripture, the ancient expression for
consecrating the Eucharist, "offering the gifts."'

In the first week of June, 1841, he gained a scholarship at Trinity College, Oxford, being the second out of

four who were elected Scholars at the same time [1], and in the following October he went into residence.

[1] The three others elected Scholars with him were : Arthur De Butts, first class in Classics 1843, afterwards Fellow of Oriel: died at an early age.   E. T. Turner, first class in Classics 1844, now Fellow of Brasenose and Registrar of the University.   Henry Musgrave Wilkins, first class in Classics 1845, afterwards Fellow of Merton; died 1887.

CHAPTER II.

THERE was probably no College in Oxford where
Freeman would have found himself in such thoroughly
congenial society as at Trinity. The Scholars of Trinity,
twelve in number, were at this period generally distinguished by singular purity and simplicity of life, by
a very high standard of religious thought and feeling,
by a remarkable combination of manliness and refine-
ment, and by a genuine love of learning for its own sake.
They were, for the most part, excellent Greek and Latin
scholars, and not a few of them gained the Ireland and
Hertford Scholarships, the highest prizes for Greek and
Latin learning which the University has to bestow.
They were not always so successful in obtaining the
highest honours in the Schools, as many of them dis-
dained to adhere strictly to the course of study most
necessary to that end, and diverged into paths of their
own choosing, some in the direction of theology, others
of modern history, or general literature, or of art and
archaeology. Most of the Scholars were drawn more or
less within the influence of the Tractarian Movement and
touched by the magic spell of Newman's genius; nor
indeed could the College ever forget that he had once
belonged to it. The old-fashioned type of College

Fellow, kindly, good-natured and convivial, but somewhat
secular in tone, was represented by Mr. Thomas Short.
On the other hand, the quiet but deep religious earnestness of Mr. Isaac Williams and of Mr. Copeland, who
were both of them in turn curates to Mr. Newman,
could not fail to make an impression upon all who were
brought into contact with them. They did, in fact, bring
the principles and spirit of the Tractarian Movement to
bear with remarkable effect upon the daily habits and
practice of the younger members of the College, Fellows
as well as Scholars. Much less wine was now drunk in
Common Room than had formerly been the fashion, and
some men, following the example set by Mr. Williams
from the time he became Fellow, absented themselves
from dinner in Hall on Fridays. Mr. Williams ceased
to reside in 1842, but the accession to the body of
Fellows of Mr. Arthur West Haddan, and later of Mr.
Samuel Wayte, helped to preserve the high tone of the
College. With Mr. Wayte (who in 1866 was elected
President of Trinity) Freeman became especially intimate, and was accustomed to consult him on all
matters in which the sympathy and help of a wise and
prudent counsellor and friend were needed.

The Scholars of Trinity had the reputation of being
exceedingly High Churchmen, and in politics they were
generally strong Tories. The liking of many for the Non-
Jurors may have been caught from Mr. Copeland, who had
much sympathy with them, and was familiar with their
writings. The Scholars lived on terms of free and friendly
intercourse with the younger Fellows of the College,
while amongst themselves they formed a close brotherhood united by the bonds of common interests, tastes, and
habits of life ; and although many of them in later years

drifted into opposite schools of opinion, both political
and religious, yet in most instances the tie of friendship
formed in the old happy Oxford days survived all
differences. Amongst the more distinguished Scholars
elected during Freeman's residence in Oxford, who
were all of them his friends, may be mentioned W. Basil
Jones, the present Bishop of St. David's; George Bowen,
now the Right Honourable Sir G. Bowen, G.C.M.G.;
H. J. Coleridge, who became a Jesuit priest, and was for
some time the editor of *The Month*, a Roman Catholic
journal; W. Gifford Palgrave, the great Oriental traveller;
W. G. Tupper, a man of singular gentleness and sweet-
ness of disposition, who became Warden of the House
of Charity in Soho, and died in the midst of his self-
denying labours; Wharton Booth Marriott, afterwards
Fellow of Exeter and assistant-master of Eton, who,
combining a healthy manliness of tone with almost
feminine tenderness, helped to correct a tendency in
some of his fellow Scholars to an excessive and morbid
asceticism; Frederick Meyrick, now Rector of Blick-
ling and Canon of Lincoln; W. Foxley Norris, the
present Vicar of Witney; I. Gregory Smith, an
Ireland and Hertford Scholar, now Vicar of Great
Malvern; and G. W. Cox, now Sir G. W. Cox, Vicar
of Scrayingham, whose writings are well known to
all students of history. Out of these a kind of inner
circle was formed, consisting originally of W. Basil
Jones, E. A. Freeman, H. J. Coleridge, W. G. Tupper,
W. B. Marriott, F. Meyrick, and Foxley Norris. To
this set, as time went on, Mr. Cox and Mr. Smith were
admitted, and also three Commoners of the College,
James Patterson, now the Roman Catholic Bishop of
Emmaus; J. W. Ogle, now an eminent London physician;

and Thomas B. Colenso, who died of consumption not long after his election to a Fellowship at Exeter— a disease of which he had probably laid the seeds by the rigorous frugality of his undergraduate life. His relations were poor, and to lessen his College expenses he was accustomed to go without dinner twice a week. In close touch with this society were two of the most distinguished Scholars, afterwards Fellows, of Balliol—James Riddell, who died in 1866, and Edwin Palmer, the present Archdeacon of Oxford.

Of the Scholars of Trinity, one who was a member of the body and afterwards a Fellow of the College, writes [1] :—

'Religion was recognized by all as having a right to the dominant control over our acts, words, and thoughts. Never once during my undergraduate career did I hear an oath from one of the Trinity set; never once did I hear a word uttered, or a subject discussed, which might not have been spoken or discussed in a lady's drawing-room. Never once did I see one of the set the worse for wine; never did I know one of them commit any of those transgressions of the rules of morality or of College discipline which are young men's temptations.'

As a rule, to which there were few exceptions, they all attended College Chapel twice daily, at 7.30 in the morning and at 5 in the evening. During the season of Lent some were in the habit of breakfasting before Chapel, and withdrew from dinner in Hall on Wednesdays as well as Fridays. Many also attended the weekly celebrations of Holy Communion which were instituted at St. Mary's by Newman, on Sunday mornings at 7 o'clock. Thus the atmosphere in which Freeman

[1] The Rev. F. Meyrick, in a chapter contributed to Dr. Hort's *Memoir of the Rev. Wharton Booth Marriott.*

found himself at Trinity tended to confirm and deepen
the religious temper of mind and habits of life which he
brought with him from the country Rectory at Segrave.
The entries in the Journal which he began to keep in
1843 show that he generally attended Chapel twice
daily, and that he almost always went to the University
sermon at St. Mary's on Sunday morning, and not
infrequently to the early celebration of Holy Communion
in that church.   Neither his Journal, however, nor his
letters supply any evidence that his mind was violently
disturbed or excited by events connected with the
Oxford Movement which agitated the whole Church
of England as well as the University—the publication of
Tract XC, the condemnation of Dr. Pusey's sermon on
the Eucharist and his consequent suspension from the
University pulpit, the retirement of Newman to Littlemore, followed by his secession to the Church of Rome.
The Tractarian Movement was many-sided and far-
reaching in its effects: it touched almost every subject
of human interest, for while it stirred the deepest
questions which can be raised in religion, philosophy,
and history, it also gave an impulse to music, painting,
and architecture in their connexion with religious worship, as well as to the study of all matters which had
to do with ritual and ecclesiastical discipline ; and it
was on the side of these more external matters that
Freeman was drawn within the current.   For purely
theological or philosophical speculations he never had
any strong taste or aptitude, and in time they became
positively repugnant to him.   Not improbably the vehemence and heat with which such questions were
debated in his time in the Common Rooms and social
gatherings of Oxford men, often without any profitable

or practical results, rendered them increasingly distasteful to him, and impelled him more and more in the direction of those historical, architectural and archaeological studies in which his thoughts and interests became ultimately centred.

At the outset of his Oxford career, pure scholarship naturally occupied a great deal of his attention, and the letters to Mr. Thompson, written shortly before he went into residence and immediately afterwards, must, judging from the contents of the replies, have been chiefly concerned with the Greek and Latin compositions which he had submitted to his friend for criticism. In a long letter in Greek, dated June 16, 1841, Mr. Thompson expresses surprise and admiration at his wonderful versatility, ὥς σε θαυμάζω, ὦ Ἐλευθέριε, φέριστε καὶ φίλτατε, τῆς πολυτροπίας, for after imitations of Lucretius, Anacreon, and Aristophanes, he has now turned himself into a Xenophon and a Sophocles. The latter impersonation, however, refers to his English poem of *St. Thomas of Canterbury*, which was cast in the mould of a Greek play. Mr. Thompson pointed out that he had not yet formed a correct estimate of Socrates. Xenophon was to Socrates as Boswell to Johnson : both were truthful chroniclers, but neither of them had any power of discrimination, and so recorded many things which were not worth recording, and sometimes only served to place their heroes in a ridiculous light.

Οὐ γὰρ Ξενοφῶν ὥσπερ Πλάτων ποιητικὸς τῇ φύσει, μᾶλλον δὲ ἱστορικὸς καὶ διηγηματικός. Ἀλλὰ καὶ λάλος δὴ καὶ λόγων γραώδων ἐράμενος ὑπῆρχε καὶ ἐν τῇ ἱστορίᾳ μόλις διακρίνων τὸ ἀξιόλογον ἀπὸ τοῦ ἁπλῶς ἀληθοῦς· ἔοικεν ὥς μοι δοκεῖ τὸ πλεῖστον τῷ ἡμετέρῳ Βοσβέλλῳ ὃς περὶ Ἰονσώνου ἀληθέστατα ἔγραψεν ἀλλ' ἀτοπώτατα.

He highly commends his correspondent's last Greek

letter, and his Iambics, and swears by his Eleanor that they are most exceedingly graceful—

νὴ τὴν Ἡλεανώραν χαριεστοτατιστότατα,

adopting a kind of exaggerated superlative, which was a favourite word with the two friends at that time.

From the next letter, dated July 24, it appears that Freeman had some thoughts of publishing his three English dramatic pieces, *Leoline*, *The Captives*, and *St. Thomas of Canterbury*. Mr. Thompson had only read the last, but he thinks, if the other two are equally good, the venture may be made, and he advises him to consult Mr. Isaac Williams on the subject. He has received a set of Latin odes, the joint productions of Freeman and his friend James Riddell, and he finds them so nearly equal in merit that he has great difficulty in deciding to which he will give the preference. From the latter part of this letter, it appears that Freeman was still so far swayed by the arguments of Non-Jurors as to question the validity of Archbishop Tillotson's appointment to the See of Canterbury.

The special service appointed to be used on November 5th had not yet been abolished. It was entitled, 'A form of prayer with thanksgiving for the happy deliverance of King James I and the three estates of England from the most traitorous and bloody-intended massacre by gunpowder, and for the happy arrival of His Majesty King William on this day, for the deliverance of our Church and nation.' His own dislike and that of others to the commemoration of this latter event is indicated in Freeman's diary, under the date November 5, where we commonly find the entry, 'Did not go to Chapel because of Dutch Bill,' or ' The Dean, after much straining, bolted Dutch Bill.'

In the spring of 1842 Freeman tried for the Ireland Scholarship, which was gained by his friend and fellow scholar, Mr. Basil Jones, the present Bishop of St. David's. The late Dean Church, in a letter written to Freeman in 1885, says that he has accidentally lighted on a memorandum, dated March 5, 1842 :—

'Ireland Scholarship. Basil Jones, Trinity; Temple[1], Balliol; De Teissier[2], Corpus; Poste, Oriel, with another man, Freeman, who is most likely to get it another year.'

The Dean adds, 'It looks like an extract from a note, but I do not know from whom. You must have been a little chap to fight with those big fellows[3].'

He stood for the Ireland again in 1844, when it was gained by John Conington, afterwards Professor of Latin, but I have no record of his place in the examination this year. He also tried more than once, unsuccessfully, for the Latin Verse Prize, and for the Newdigate prize for English Verse. Not improbably, as his mind became more absorbed in the study of architecture and history, his scholarship may have become somewhat less finished. In 1843 he began to keep a diary, a practice which he continued to the end of his life. It is a bare record, without any reflexions, of the persons he met, the places he visited, the number of hours he read and what he read, the letters which he wrote and received : yet it helps us to form a clear picture of the character of his daily life. He does not seem to have arranged his day at this period according to any fixed method. Sometimes he reads all the night to two o'clock in the morn-

---

[1] The present Bishop of London.
[2] Rev. G. F. De Teissier, afterwards Fellow and Tutor of Corpus.
[3] They were all senior to Freeman in academical standing.

ing, at other times he gets up early, occasionally even at
four o'clock, and this generally in the winter, but now
and then on account of cold, goes to bed again, and so
sleeps over the Chapel hour. If he misses Chapel, he
never fails to record the fact, and commonly adds
'Rebuked by Patterson.' At other times he falls asleep
in the evening, wakes about midnight, and then reads on
to three or four o'clock, goes to bed, and gets up again
in time for Chapel. He seems to have had a remarkable
faculty for dropping off to sleep at all sorts of odd times.
On one occasion he records in his diary, 'Fell asleep in
evening Chapel in the middle of the Nunc Dimittis.'
He and his fellow scholars, with a few of their intimate
friends outside their College, were constantly meeting in
each other's rooms, to discuss, often to a late hour in
the night, questions in philosophy, theology, history, and
art, to all of which the Oxford Movement had given
a fresh impulse. The evidence of the diary proves that
a very large proportion of his time was devoted to the
study of architecture. He was an active member, and
for a time secretary, of the Oxford Architectural Society,
and the restoration of the great Abbey Church of
Dorchester was, in its beginnings, largely due to his
efforts. He was most diligent in collecting funds for
the purpose, and in paying visits to the place, accompanied by friends whom he interested in the work.

Those parts of the vacations which he spent at Northampton with his grandmother must have been dull and
trying. She was now in feeble health, very deaf, and
rather querulous and exacting. He had to read aloud
to her by day, and to play backgammon with her every
evening, except on Sundays, when he was condemned to
read a homily or sermon aloud. From these uncongenial

E 2

occupations it must have been a great relief to escape for occasional rambles amongst the towns and villages of Northamptonshire and Leicestershire, sketching the churches, and making rubbings of the brasses, which he mounted after his return home. The country was not covered with a network of railways in those days, and these excursions were oftener made on foot and on horseback than by rail or coach. Journeying in this leisurely fashion, he became thoroughly familiar with the places that he visited, and had good opportunities for observing the characteristic features of the country through which he passed. He sometimes made his journeys between Oxford and Northampton on foot, spending two or three days on the road.

In July, 1844, he spent a fortnight at Cambridge with his friends Warren and Foxley Norris, occupying most of his time in sketching churches and college chapels. On July 30, they started at three o'clock in the morning to walk to Ely, where they spent two or three days. Some of the sketches which he made of Ely Cathedral have been preserved. They are bold, spirited, vigorous drawings in pen and ink, from eight to twelve inches in height, and from four to six in breadth. The most highly finished one of the interior of the great central octagon tower is not unworthy of the hand of Mr. Petit, whose style of drawing he imitated. In addition to five views on this scale, several pages of the same book are filled with drawings of details, such as sections of piers, mouldings of arches, and tracery of windows.

After his return to Northampton on August 2, the day on which he came of age, he wrote to Miss Eleanor Gutch making an offer of marriage. As long as he was under age, he said, he considered that

his guardians had absolute authority over him, and his
lips were sealed. Now the case was changed : he felt
a tenderness for his grandmother's old age, and a high
respect for his uncle's judgement, nor would he act
lightly or wantonly in opposition to either ; but he
considered that they had now no positive right to
command or forbid. He had expectations of a sufficient
income, but it was partly derived from coal mines, and
the shocking disclosures recently made respecting the
treatment of colliers made him doubt whether he could
conscientiously draw an income from that branch of
industry until the system was reformed. His offer was
accepted by Miss Gutch, subject to the approval of her
father and his uncle. Their consent was obtained without much difficulty, but his grandmother was furiously
angry with him, and remained obdurate for some time
to come, which occasionally led to stormy scenes between
them. His friends Patterson and Tupper were staying
with him, and gave him much sympathy, and probably
some good counsel respecting his behaviour to his grandmother under these trying circumstances, as in his diary
for August 7 occurs the entry, ' Rebuked by T. and P.
after dinner.'

On the following day, the three friends set off for an
excursion to Winchester, Romsey, and the Isle of Wight.
A week was spent in Winchester and the neighbourhood,
and much sketching was done there and at St. Cross,
also at Romsey, and at Netley Abbey. In the Isle of
Wight, a quiet retreat in those days, not the hunting
ground of hordes of tourists from all parts of the kingdom,
they were joined by his fellow scholar, Mr. Meyrick,
and a week was spent in quiet rambles and bathing, and
drives in curiously constructed cars, one of which is

described in the diary as 'like a bedstead,' another like a 'pew and tea-tray combined.' Sunday, August 18, was spent at Freshwater: it was the eleventh Sunday after Trinity, and the four friends repeated in turns to one another parts of Keble's verses in the *Christian Year* for that Sunday. The day was marked in the calendar of their memory as one of peculiar enjoyment, and they were accustomed to refer to it thenceforth as 'our Sunday.'

The news that his uncle and Mr. Gutch consented to his engagement was received during this tour. He had dreamed the night before that his proposal had been fiercely repulsed, and that he was rolling in agony on a brick kitchen floor. He had been holding forth to his friends on the advantages of a monastic life; he now recommended them to found a house for themselves, reserving for him a visitatorial jurisdiction only.

After a short but happy visit to Segrave, he returned to Northampton, and the dull routine of reading aloud to his grandmother and playing backgammon with her began again, occasionally varied by passionate reproaches from the old lady on the subject of his matrimonial engagement. The frequent entries in the diary, 'Great storm with my grandmother,' or 'More revilings from my grandmother,' show what he had to bear. A letter to Mr. Thompson, dated September 10, refers to these scenes, and as it is the only Latin letter to him which has escaped destruction, it may be read with interest partly on that account.

LIBERIUS THOMAIDOE SUO S. P. D.

Ignoscas velim silentio tam longo, tamque insolito, crebriores enim epistolas posthac jure expectes : lingua enim cui nil hodie

silentii erga dilectissimam sponsam nostram Eleanoram ser-
vandum est, vel ad alios plus habet libertatis. Olim enim
pupillus tacebam, nunc autem fraenum excussi. Primae nobis
curae fuit ex quo nostri juris facti sumus ut foedus matrimonii
inter nos compingeretur, idque neque patruo, neque patre illius
improbante, re autem compertâ truculentum in modum debac-
chata est avia. Nos autem amore mutuo securos hujusmodi
tempestates minus vexant.

Magna nostra itinera conspexit haec Vacatio. Cantabrigiam,
Eliam, Wintoniam, Insulam Vectim, Westmonasterium, duobus
e necessariis comitantibus, inspeximus, quanta voluptate vix
opus est dicere. Singulari etiam quodam gaudio nos affecit
Coenobium Romsiense, quod abest ab Hamtoniâ Meridionali
circa septem millia passuum. Pulcherrimae sane ecclesiae
pepercit Henricus iste, nummis scilicet meliorem in partem
inductus ; incolae enim templum emerunt C libris : ita ut hodie
totum exstet aedificium praeter Capellam B.V. M. Architectus
fuit Henricus de Blois, Ep. Wintoniensis, Regis Stephani frater,
qui magnam ecclesiae partem more Romano condidit, idque
egregium in modum : pars autem occidentalis Gothicam exhibet
artem, ita tamen ut mirificè congruat. Coenobium etiam
Netleiense vidimus, minus felici praeditum fortunâ : est autem
vel ruinis pulcrum : multa exstant aedificia praeter Ecclesiam,
atrium, culina, etc., quae apud Romseiam nulla sunt, ne claustra
quidem exstant.

Apud Cantabrigiam diutius commorati sumus, ab amico
quodam in hospitium excepti : ita ut permulta mirari liceret.
At neque urbem neque ecclesias, neque Collegia Oxoniensibus
aequanda putavimus, praeter capellam Coll. Regalis ; cui nil
habemus conferendum, sive ad magnitudinem spectes, cujus
vix dimidium vel Cathedrali nostrae ecclesiae jactare licet, sive
ad pulcritudinem quâ omnia nostra aedificia vincit. Tuum
quoque Collegium inspeximus, e quo haud pauca nos incredi-
bilem in modum delectant, praecipue tui memoria. Certiores
etiam facti sumus te praemia duo in Academiâ olim meritum
esse : de qua re nihil unquam ex te audivimus.

Quid censes de rebus Oxoniensibus ? Timeo enim ne a
Philippo tuo Hiemali redemti, in fauces Ingentis, quem dicimus,

Benjaminis incidamus, maximae sanè pestis et verae disciplinae inter acerrimos hostes[1].

Vale, mi Thomaide, neque aliquid memoriae tuae nostra ex mente intercidisse putes. Id tibi non ingratum fore putavi, quod et Eleanora nostra tuâ de salute ex nobis percunctata est. Mi Thomaide iterum atque iterum vale. Dat. Northamptoniae A.D. iv. Id. Sept. Año Dñi CIƆIƆCCCXLIIII.

There can be little doubt that the flutter of hopes and fears respecting the issue of his attachment had agitated and distracted his mind a good deal, and to this cause his repeated failure to obtain the honours for which he competed, may partly be attributed. Writing to his future wife on August 31 of this year, he says that he had read hard for the Trinity Scholarship because he knew that he could not pass through Oxford without the aid of one, and when he feared that he should be cut off for ever from the object of his attachment, he had thrown himself into study, as the only relief to his feelings. He had made up his mind to speak when he came of age, but he had considered rejection as only too probable, and he had brought himself to look upon a Fellowship, if he could get one, and Greys Rectory[2] in his old age, as a possible and endurable destiny; but he had not read steadily or regularly enough to warrant the hope of obtaining a First Class, and now that his offer of marriage was accepted, Oxford studies and modes

---

[1] The passage refers to the appointment of a new Vice-Chancellor which was about to be made. Dr. Wynter ('Philippus Hiemalis'), President of St. John's, who had just vacated the office, was succeeded, as the writer feared, by Dr. Benjamin Parsons Symons, Warden of Wadham, commonly called 'Big Ben' ('Ingens Benjamin') on account of his size and stature. Both were much opposed to Dr. Pusey and his party.

[2] Rotherfield Greys, near Henley-on-Thames, a Living in the gift of Trinity College.

of life had not the same charm for him, he would rather
go in for an ordinary degree, but he should in any case
stand for a Fellowship, though with a very faint prospect
of getting one.

In the Michaelmas Term of this year he began to
read rather more steadily for the Schools, but much of
his time was still occupied with the business of the
Architectural Society, and of a Debating Society to
which he had recently been elected.   Mr. Wall, of
Balliol, was his coach in logic, but he disliked the
subject so intensely, that in the spring of 1845 he
speaks in one of his letters of having given it up.   He
read his Aristotle with some degree of interest, but from
the evidence of his diary, it appears he often fell asleep
over his Butler.   Nevertheless, in after life, he acknowledged that he owed much to the compulsory study of
these authors.

'Left to myself,' he says, 'I should, perhaps, never have
read the Ethics; I should certainly not have read them as
I did read them.   I should most likely have looked to see what
historical facts I could get out of the book, and not much more.
But, having to read the book thoroughly, I felt that I drew from
it a new power, a power of discerning likenesses and unlike-
nesses, of distinguishing real and false analogies, which I had
not before, and which has helped me ever since.   I have written
the History of the Norman Conquest, I am writing the History
of Sicily, all the better for having been made to read about
μεγαλοψυχία and ἐπιχαιρεκακία.

'To Aristotle I must add Butler.   Him I believe the march of
reform has swept away, hardly to the clearing of men's minds.
I do not so much mean the *Analogy* as the wonderful sermons.
From the *Sermons on Human Nature* one learns, and one does
not straightway forget, what manner of man one is[1].'

[1] 'Review of my Opinions,' *Forum*, pp. 151, 152.

On December 18, 1844, a Society was founded in Freeman's rooms called the Brotherhood of St. Mary, of which the avowed design was, 'to study ecclesiastical art upon true and Catholic principles.' The original members, in addition to Freeman himself, were Patterson, of Trinity, Parkins, of Merton (some time Secretary of the Oxford Architectural Society), and Millard, of Magdalen (afterwards Master of Magdalen College School). To these, about a dozen more were afterwards added, including H. J. Coleridge, F. Meyrick, N. G. Tupper, G. W. Cox, all of Trinity, and a few from other Colleges. The discussions seem to have ranged from large questions of principle, such as the place of architecture amongst the arts, to small details of practical construction, as the comparative advantages of high and low pitched roofs. After a time, different branches of inquiry were assigned to the different members, symbolism to Coleridge, coloured decoration to Patterson, ritual to Millard, monasticism to Meyrick, construction and internal arrangement of churches to Freeman. Gradually, however, the Society changed in character, and when it became rather a Guild for the regulation of religious life than an association for the study of religious art, Freeman withdrew from it.

The purpose of reading for Honours was not abandoned. He went into the Schools in Easter Term, 1845. As he had anticipated, however, he failed to obtain a First Class, but he was afterwards informed by the Examiners that he only very narrowly missed it. The names of his friends James Riddell and Goldwin Smith appear in the First Class the same year. Whatever vexation he may have felt at the result of the examination was forgotten in the joy of being elected a probationary Fellow of his College on Trinity Monday, May 19. His gratification was all the greater, inasmuch as during the examination for the Fellowship, he had been so unwell from a severe cold, and nose bleedings, that he had been compelled to leave one of the papers untouched. Writing in 1892, he says, 'it has seldom come into my head to think whether I was first, second, third, or fourth in the Class List, but I have never at any moment of my life forgotten that I was once a Scholar and Fellow of Trinity.' He thus describes the circumstances of his election in a letter to Miss Gutch.

DEAREST ELEANOR, Trinity College, May 22, 1845.

I have been lionizing Isabella and Emily about all the morning, and having safely deposited them at Long Wall and seen your father and James to a lecture of Dr. Buckland, I have sat down at two of the clock to write you some account of myself in my new capacity. All Monday morning I was in the greatest state of mind I ever remember to have experienced ; it was much worse than the Schools or anything else, and, knowing that probably there would be a close division, it was the greatest possible state of suspense—not knowing whether to expect success or defeat, a probability either way would have been a comfort. And to sit helplessly in this state, knowing that the Dons were all in the Chapel judging one's fate. Happily I had some men in my rooms most of the time, Turner, Coleridge, Marriott, and Meyrick, otherwise I know not what would have become of me. At last herds of men, I cannot tell who was the first, came rushing up with the news, which I could scarcely believe at first, but, rushing down into quad, I had the agreeable tidings confirmed by Hickley the Dean, who presently ushered me into the Chapel, where the great Bursar[1], was the first to hold out his hand in congratulation, and every one seemed pleased, except Short, whose countenance

---

[1] Bursar Smith.

betrayed ineffable disgust. After the requisite cursing and swearing—the former, as usual, directed against his Holiness—I knelt down before the President, and was admitted a Probationary Fellow of this noble society. The payments amounted to one guinea to Dr. Bliss, and £1 2s. 6d. in gratuities, chiefly for ringing of bells. Of course we had a fine spread at High Table and Common Room ; in the latter I had to make a brief speech on the health of the newly-elected Fellow being proposed. Old Scholefield, who was a tutor here many years back, made a speech about seeing a son of an old pupil of his added to our body.

Since this I have been chiefly engaged in investigating a great problem as to wherein the duties of a Probationary Fellow consist, for, as far as I have yet gone, my chief business is reading newspapers in the Common Room, and drinking ale out of a silver tankard instead of a crockeryware mug. I shall make my first appearance at High Table since Monday to-day, as my out-college friends have provided for me several days this week. It entails the necessity of getting up more sprucely than is required of a Scholar.

A constant correspondence with Miss Gutch during the three years which had still to pass before their marriage, supplies the most exact record of his occupations, and the most faithful reflexion of his feelings and opinions on subjects of all kinds. In one of his letters written soon after he has taken his degree, he says that he intends to read most of the subjects which he had studied for the Schools, only more leisurely and with more real benefit to himself, ' for the way in which many men read, not for learning, but merely for a Class, is odious.' And his opinion on this subject remained unchanged in 1892.

' Happy in most things,' he writes, 'as was my Scholar's life, there was still the drawback of having to read for an examination. I suppose examinations cannot be got rid of ; I suppose

they are necessary evils, but they certainly are evils. Reading
for an examination, even if it be real reading, and not taking in
tips from a crammer, is not what reading should be. A lower
motive comes in; it is not simply reading for the sake of
knowledge.

'To me the examination was a mere bugbear, a something
that hindered real work. I shall never forget my joy when the
examination was over. One of my first thoughts was, 'Now
I can really begin to read, and in October, 1845, I did begin.
I began by reading my Herodotus over again. That was the
beginning of a course which, in February, 1892, is not ended.
Truly, the more one learns the more one finds one has to
learn [1].'

The question of a profession was much revolved in his
mind during the years 1845 and 1846, and discussed
with his College friends, as well as with his future wife.
For some time, the two alternatives debated were Holy
Orders and Architecture. Writing to Miss Gutch in
1845, he says that if he determines upon Ordination, he
shall probably resume his study of Hebrew, and shall
certainly attend Professor Hussey's Lectures on Ecclesiastical History. His own feelings were in favour of
Ordination. He feared, however, that he was not well
fitted for the duties of a Parish Priest, but if he could be
certain of securing any office, however humble, in a Cathedral Church, he would not hesitate to take the step.
Sometimes he had thought of taking up the study of
Canon Law. Ecclesiastical architecture was the study
most after his own heart, only he doubted whether the
profession ranked high enough to be worth following,
owing to the miserable pretenders who crowded into it.
But after all, why should he adopt any profession, he
hoped to have a private income of more than £600

[1] 'Review of my Opinions,' *Forum*, p. 151.

a year, and if a change was made in the law for the regulation of mine labour, which would enable him conscientiously to sell the coal-pit for a good price, the amount of his income might be trebled. His final decision against Ordination turned on the conviction that celibacy was the most proper and desirable condition for the clergy on all grounds. In this conviction he had been encouraged by his friend, Mr. Samuel Wayte. Writing on January 25, 1846, he says,

'I have almost entirely given up the idea of Ordination, as I am getting every day more fully convinced of the necessity for the clergy to observe celibacy for every reason, both as in itself the holier estate, and therefore especially incumbent upon *them*, and also for the avoidance of secularity and sacrilege. We were a nice little party in the Common Room yesterday, Haddan, Wayte, and myself, and, there being no Short or Bursar to awe your poor timorous lover into silence, we had a very pleasant discourse on the affairs of this Church and Realm. I told Sam that I had come over to one of his dogmas which he had been endeavouring to instil into my mind last term, that of clerical celibacy. Haddan then asked if I meant to take Holy Orders, to which I replied " Most likely not," and Wayte said I was quite right, adding that it was "not my vocation."'

And writing again on March 22 he says that his convictions on the question of clerical celibacy are now so strong that he has finally determined to remain a layman. In the same letter he says that he has often thought of learning the practical part of architecture while he was in Oxford, but he adds

'I doubt whether I could rightly so employ myself while Fellow, as I seem to have a plain vocation : viz. to carry on the line of study which one has begun as an Undergraduate, and to do all I can for our own Scholars . . . If I take up any

profession it would be architecture, but I would much rather
if I find myself sufficiently well off have none. I have begun
a course of reading which if I carry it on would go a good
way through a tolerably long life. Besides philosophy, I work
chiefly at history, of which I should much like to be master.
My great ambition would be to get one of the History Professorships here.'

The idea of practising architecture, however, was not
yet finally abandoned. Writing in May, he says that he
is thinking of engaging a coach in the practical details
of that art, and he actually designed a chapel for the
workhouse at Wantage.

The summer vacation of 1845 was spent in paying
visits to Segrave and Charwelton, his uncle's parish, and
in making archaeological rambles by himself in the
midland counties. He still travels partly by coach, and
a great deal on foot, but sometimes has recourse to the
railway, and finds it very odd to be whirled so rapidly
past places between which he had been accustomed to
make long and toilsome journeys. The following is
a specimen of a well-filled day as described in a letter
to his future wife. On August 13 he went by rail from
Northampton to Higham Ferrers Station, midway
between that town and Irthlingborough ; walked to
Rushden and sketched the church there, 'a very fine
cross church, with a glorious tower and spire at the west
end'; then went to the village inn, where he was invited
by the landlord and his wife to join them at their dinner,
which consisted of 'good stout stiff Yorkshire pudding,
such as you can cut with a knife, not stuff that falls to
pieces like sago and other such sick food, which was
followed by a shoulder of mutton, and French beans, all
very much to my liking.' Thence he walked on to

Wymington, examined the 'very pretty, though in some respects rather odd little late decorated church,' then returned to Rushden to contemplate the interior of the church there, and thence to Higham Ferrers where he had tea, and had yet time before the train started for Northampton to walk up to Irthlingborough, and to examine the church there. Everywhere he made rough and rapid pencil sketches, which he worked up in the evening with pen and ink, and where he had not time to sketch he made notes. In excursions of this kind he laid the foundation of those vast stores of architectural learning derived from personal observation to which he was continually adding down to the last days of his life. He was in constant correspondence also at this time with Mr. Petit, Mr. J. H. Parker, and Mr., afterwards Sir Gilbert, Scott. A letter dated from the Swan Inn, Wells, August 31, describes his first visit to places with which for so many years in after life he was to be intimately associated. He travelled by coach from Northampton to Oxford, where he found his friend Mr. Wayte reading hard, 'I suppose for Ordination, as all human learning he has acquired already.' Thence he had a starlight drive in a gig to Steventon to catch a train for Bath, where he was joined by his friend Patterson. They proceeded to Wells by coach 'through a most glorious country,' and spent three days of intense enjoyment in seeing for the first time the ruins of Glastonbury, and the matchless group of buildings at Wells. Their visit included a Sunday, when they attended service twice in the Cathedral, and heard Dr. Jenkins, who was Dean of Wells as well as Master of Balliol, preach in the morning. 'In his Bidding Prayer,' says Freeman, 'he returned thanks for the comforts and conveniences as well as the necessaries of life, the latter I suppose being the Mastership of Balliol, and the former the Deanery of Wells.'

From Wells the two friends travelled on by coach through Salisbury to Winchester, where on September 9 Freeman read a paper on St. Cross before the members of the Royal Archaeological Institute, the first which he had contributed to that Society. He did not begin to write it till four days before the meeting, but he could write rapidly because he was full of his subject, having made careful drawings and notes on his former visit. It was an honour for so young a man to read a paper before the distinguished men who used to attend the meetings of the Institute in those days, and who were present on this occasion, Professor Willis, Mr. Petit, Mr. Albert Way, Mr. Beresford Hope, and Mr. Parker. The paper was illustrated by Freeman's own pen and ink sketches and by some drawings of P. H. de la Motte. It is remarkable not only for the fulness of knowledge and power of criticism which it displays, but also for the religious and reverent spirit by which it is pervaded.

'The Hospital,' he said, 'has that peculiar attraction which belongs to whatever is first of its own class. The Cathedral, the College, the Royal and Episcopal Palace, may be found elsewhere, individually at least in equal beauty, but nowhere, to the best of my knowledge, does there exist any foundation of a similar nature, which can for a moment compare with the architectural beauty, the historical associations, or the calm and holy air pervading the whole of this truly venerable establishment. Whether among the numerous similar Societies which fell beneath that spirit of sacrilegious rapacity which could not spare the very resting-places of aged poverty, any existed which at all approached St. Cross in wealth and splendour, I know not; it stands, I should suppose, incomparable among its own class, the roof and crown of such foundations. No one can pass its threshold without feeling himself landed as it were in another age. The noble gateway, the quadrangle, the common refectory, the cloister, and, rising above all, the lofty and massive pile of the venerable church ; the uniform garb and reverent mien of the aged brethren, the common provision for their declining years, the dole at the gate house, all lead back our thoughts to days when men gave their best for God's honour and looked on what was done to His poor as done to Himself, and were as lavish of architectural beauty on what modern habits might deem a receptacle of beggars as on the noblest of royal palaces. It seems a place where no worldly thought, no pride or passion or irreverence could enter, a spot where, as a modern writer has beautifully expressed it, " a good man, might he make his choice, would wish to die." '

He had the privilege of hearing Dr. Arnold deliver his lectures in 1841 and 1842 as Professor of Modern History, and he speaks of him in his own inaugural lecture in 1884 as ' that great teacher of historic truth, that greater teacher of moral right,' from whom he ' first learned what history is and how it should be studied—first learned the truth which ought to be the centre and life of all our historic studies ; the truth of the unity of history.' Yet while he listened to Arnold's teaching of history with delight and admiration, he held his opinions on church matters at this time in utter abhorrence.

In truth, throughout his life at Oxford he continued to be both in opinion and practice a rigid High Churchman. His principles, as we have seen, had been formed before he came up, and were derived partly from his own early reading of the Fathers and of standard theology, partly from his intercourse with men of the old High Church School, like his tutor Mr. Gutch and his friend Mr. Thompson. The Oxford Tracts, and all the literature to which ' the movement ' gave birth, seem not so much

to have directed his mind to certain conclusions as to
have strengthened opinions which he had already formed
for himself. The only effect indeed of 'the movement'
that is traceable in his letters, was an occasional doubt
whether the Church of England, in which there was so
much laxity of practice, latitudinarianism in doctrine,
and bondage to the State, could be a true branch of the
Church Catholic. Yet it is significant of the independence of his mind that, in his remarks upon this question,
he never refers to the writings of Newman, Hurrell
Froude, Ward, or any other leaders of the Oxford movement. It could not be said with truth that he was ever
a disciple of Newman or Pusey, or, speaking generally,
of the Oxford school. In one of his letters to his future
wife he says, that he is sometimes surprised to find how
entirely he had thought things out for himself, and that
he could not attribute his opinions to the direct influence
of any one man, however eminent.

In 1846, Dr. Hook, then Vicar of Leeds, published his
famous pamphlet on National Education, in the form of
a Letter addressed to the Bishop of St. David's, Dr.
Thirlwall, and entitled *The best means of rendering
more efficient the education of the people*. In this
Letter he advocated compulsory elementary education
by the State, in rate-paid schools to be open to the
children of all denominations, the ministers of each
denomination being impartially admitted at certain
hours and on different days to the children of their own
communities [1]. The Vicar's proposal subjected him to

---

[1] A fuller account of this pamphlet, in which Dr. Hook anticipated with
remarkable foresight some of the principal educational needs and difficulties of the present day, and suggested a solution of them, will be
found in the *Life of Dean Hook*, pp. 403–407, sixth edition.

a storm of obloquy and abuse from nearly all parties in the Church, and all kinds of unworthy motives were imputed to him. Freeman was too stiff a Churchman at this time to look favourably upon this scheme, nevertheless he took a calm and dispassionate view of it, recognizing in it an honest attempt to deal with a real difficulty.

'Certainly,' he says in a letter to Miss Gutch, 'some of his statements appear very startling, but I should not think of entertaining the apparently uncharitable views you mention, till I know more about the scheme. He seems to me rather from the letter I have seen, like a person despairing of any recognition on the part of the State of the divine character of the Church, and the consequent duties of the State, and therefore putting matters on the merely legal and political view of an infidel government. Not of course that I agree with this, as I think we should maintain the Church's rights, but I can quite understand the view, if this really be the ground in question.'

The first indication that he had been revolving in his mind the possible validity of the claims of the Roman Church, is to be found in a reply from Mr. Thompson, dated St. Stephen's Day (Dec. 26), 1845, to a letter which has unfortunately, like so many others to him, been lost. Probably the sound and sensible judgement of his old friend helped to allay his doubts.

'I quite agree,' says Mr. Thompson, 'with your views respecting catholic doctrine. We or the Romanists are schismatics : if we have decided in our minds that they are right no doubt we ought to join them at once : to defer the deed is, even on the ground of mere human consistency, absolutely ridiculous. But consistency seems to have fled to the stars. It is my great comfort that Newman and his followers, have not "developed" Church principles into Romanisms, but have been obliged to abandon Church principles in order to become Romanists. The development theory places Romanism in bold and avowed opposition to Catholicism, and "quod semper, quod ubique, quod ab omnibus," is to yield to "quod nunc, quod Romae, quod a nobis." Rome *cannot* stand upon antiquity. She professed to take her stand upon Scripture till Scripture became read, and then she shifted to the Fathers : now that the Fathers have been studied she takes refuge in a principle which would justify the wildest fanaticism. But no person without the most manifest unfairness, can say that the principles of the Tracts for the Times have led to Popery, for it is only through rejecting those principles and adopting their opposites that the apostasy is sought to be justified.'

From time to time, however, Freeman was so much dissatisfied with the condition of the Church of England that he owns, if matters became much worse, the position would be intolerable. Sometimes he was shaken by the intemperate denunciations of Rome from the University pulpit. Thus on January 25, 1846, he writes : 'this morning I went to St. Mary's, where Dr. Jeune, the Master of Pembroke, treated us to a most violent sermon about the worship of St. Mary. If I had to sit under many more such, I should certainly go clean over.' And again, on Whit Sunday of the same year, he writes :—

'It is just midnight, rather more than twelve hours since I came out of St. Mary's after listening to a very long and pestilential discourse of Garbett's, a furious invective against Rome, which went off finally from the declamatory into the blasphemous. This kind of thing, had I to hear it often, would infallibly make me Roman, as it always makes me find out arguments against what is said. This sermon and the heat together made me feel very queer.'

Sometimes he is disgusted and unsettled by the deplorable and neglected condition of some country church, and the miserable way in which the services were conducted in it.   Writing from a village in one of the midland counties, he says :—

'I cannot conceive anything more distressing, than the circumstances of the Communion here : a damp squalid chancel, everything as bare and meagre as possible, thanks to the shameless selfishness of the non-resident pluralist who consumes the revenues of the Church on his dogs and guns, a solitary priest to officiate with no vestment but a surplice, while the worshipper is fastened up in a large pew utterly cut off from Priest, Altar, or Congregation.'

He mourns over the mutilation and inadequacy of our present Communion service, yet he owns that Rome has no great advantage over us here, her own service, though clearly adequate, being meagre and confused by the side of the Oriental and Scottish liturgies.   On the whole he gravitated more towards Rome when he was in the country than when he was at Oxford, where the occasional outbursts of Protestant partisans in the University pulpit were corrected by the sounder teaching of men like Pusey, and counterbalanced by excesses in the other direction of the extreme Tractarians.   Writing from Wrington, where he was staying with his friend, Mr. Thompson, he says :—

'You may suppose I have a great deal to talk about to Thompson, as we deal in nearly the same topics, save that he superadds gardening, for which I have no taste, and German, for which I have a great though at present distant respect ; and we take much the same views of most things, save Dutch William and the Pope, for whose jurisdiction he has much less reverence than I have.   Being out of Oxford, I am immediately getting Popish, according to my wonted flux and reflux.'

But it was characteristic of his straightforward nature

that he considered it an act of disloyalty in any one who
was still a member of the English Church to attend
a Roman Catholic service for the sake of mere curiosity
or of drawing comparisons between the two Churches
one way or the other.

'What business had A,' he writes, 'at a Roman service at all,
my view is simply that I am not called upon to decide whether
their service is better or worse than our's. For us to attend their
worship is manifest schism. But to go as A says he and his
pupil did, to stare and scoff and come back and make a flourish
of trumpets about "pure and apostolical," is much worse than
schism, being to my mind simply profane.'

Referring in another letter to an article by Mr. Mozley
(afterwards Regius Professor of Divinity) in the *Christian
Remembrancer* for January, 1846, written after the secession of Newman, Ward, and Oakley, and entitled 'The
Recent Schism,' he says, 'Wayte compares me with the
description of Froude there, and I think he is right.' The
Froude here alluded to was Richard Hurrell Froude,
and Mr. Mozley, in his essay, had drawn a contrast
between the attitude of Froude's mind towards the Church
of England and that of Newman's mind as it had been for
some time previous to his secession. He maintained that
Mr. Newman, with a lurking suspicion, gradually increasing
to conviction, that the Church of England was not the
true Church, did nevertheless for a long time sincerely
do his best to throw himself into the position of the
Church to which he belonged, and defended it with all
the skill of a subtle and powerful advocate. His position,
therefore, although sincere, was yet in a sense artificial.
Mr. Froude's position, on the other hand, was thoroughly
natural, genuine and artless. 'He had the real intrinsic
feeling of belonging to his Church as a branch belongs

to a tree; he regarded her straight and not through a medium. In this way he had very strong, sharp feelings about different portions of her history. He felt against the Reformers; he felt *with* the Caroline divines.' What he felt he freely, sharply, vehemently expressed, but all this declamation against what he called 'the Reformation spirit,' 'Church . of England-ism,' ' Establishmentism,' and 'Smug parsons,' co-existed with a deep and genuine loyalty to the Church of his baptism. Against abuses in the Church he used strong language, to the Church itself his attachment did not waver. This union of devotion to the Church of England with an honest, vehement and fearless denunciation of its abuses, was no doubt the point in which Mr. Wayte rightly discerned a likeness between him and Freeman. Referring to this same article, Freeman concurs with the description which it contains of Mr. Newman's position.

'I do not see,' he says, 'that the article need produce any unfavourable opinion of Newman, though it lays open a very extraordinary state of mind nearly approaching to self-deception. It seems that, like yourself on another occasion, inclination led one way, and duty another, and that he tried to throw himself into a particular line from a sense of duty. I can thus quite enter into his strong language against Rome, while himself inclining to Rome, his language expressing not so much what he really felt, as what he supposed he ought to feel.'

Although he was not a devoted disciple of any of the Tractarian leaders, yet the slight allusions which occur in his letters and diary to the conflicts in which they were engaged with their opponents, both in the University and outside it, show that his sympathies were on their side. 'Ward degraded; bad luck to them,' is the entry in his journal for February 13, 1845, the memorable day when the Convocation of Oxford, amidst vast excitement, passed a resolution by 568 votes to 511 for the degradation of Mr. Ward, Fellow of Balliol, from the degrees of B.A. and M.A. on account of the opinions advocated in his book *The Ideal of a Christian Church*.

The following letter to Miss Gutch refers to the first sermon which Dr. Pusey preached before the University after he had been suspended from preaching for three years on account of his sermon on the Eucharist.

DEAREST NELLY,   Trinity College, February 1, 1846.

I am now again, as you requested, seated down to write to you in my own rooms; it being Sunday morning and the hour for *the* sermon not yet having arrived. How everybody is to get into the Cathedral I know not, thanks to Cardinal Wolsey for pulling down three arches of the Nave to make room for his wretched College. James Riddell told us yesterday that he should go down and eat his breakfast on the step. Mrs. Parker has affirmed long ago that she would book a place over night—by the way, I wish women and lay persons would keep away. The sermon is to be on Absolution and Confession. I could rather have wished he would preach on swearing and covetousness, or something to which no one could object; but perhaps in his peculiar circumstances just now, it might seem rather as if he shrank from maintaining his principles.

. . . Well, I have been to the sermon, which was upon the subject I mentioned, and preached to a huge congregation, every inch of available space being crowded—very many of course standing. I do not exactly see what there was in it that any one could lay hold of, though to be sure the wickedness of Golightly and the Hebdomadal Board will compass anything, yet, as Turner just now told me—' They cannot well suspend him, unless they suspend the Prayer Book, which however is suspended in most places six days in the week.' He showed the nature and necessity of sacerdotal absolution, and obviated Protestant objections. I hope it may be printed, though I fear not, as he has rather a dislike to doing so. . . .

Thanks for Bishop Ken's lines, which I will employ, dearest Eleanor, as you suggest. I have seen them before, though I did not remember that you had ever sent them to me. If they are not part of the Evening Hymn, which you may know is much longer than the part sung in churches (an use for which it was never intended and yet is never unfit, though the folly is not so great as when men call on their souls—precious sleepy souls they must be—to 'awake and early rise,' at eleven o'clock a.m.), it is part of the Midnight Hymn which is comparatively little known.

During the autumn of 1845 and the beginning of 1846 he was busily engaged in collecting materials and writing for the Chancellor's English Prize Essay, the subject set being ' The effects of the Conquest of England by the Normans.' Up to this time there is no evidence that he had read many original authorities on mediaeval history. In his diary for October, 1845, he notes that he had begun to read William of Malmesbury, and about the same time he began to study the works of Thierry, Lingard, and Palgrave, with a special view to the subject of the Essay, upon which he set to work in January, 1846. He worked hard at it for three months, became profoundly interested in the subject, and set his heart upon getting the prize. His essay was the longest and fullest of fourteen which were submitted to the judges, consisting of forty-six large quarto pages, very closely written in a beautifully neat clear hand, with a marginal summary and a few short footnotes and references to authorities. But the prize was won by Mr. Chichester Fortescue, of Christ Church, the present Lord Carlingford. His failure to gain this prize was undoubtedly the most severe of the many disappointments which Freeman suffered in his Oxford career. As in former instances, however, so in this, disappointment only stimulated him

to deeper and more diligent study, and thus in after
life he came to look upon this failure as a piece of good
fortune. Writing in 1892, he says :—

'The Norman Conquest was a subject that I had been thinking
about, ever since I could think at all. I wrote for the Prize;
I had the good luck not to get it. Had I got it, I might have
been tempted to think that I knew all about the matter. As it
was, I went on and learned something about it[1].'

Thus in some sense we are indebted to his rejected
essay for his great *History of the Norman Conquest.* But
it is instructive to notice, that most of the main positions
laid down in the essay are the same which were afterwards maintained in the History. That the Conquest was
not so much a starting-point as a turning-point in the
history of England, that a plausible appearance was given
to William's claims upon the throne by a skilful combination of fallacious arguments, more especially Edward the
Confessor's alleged bequest and his own nearness of kin,
together with the sanction of the Pope ; that so far from
feudalism having been introduced by William, he checked
it in one direction, and only strengthened existing tendencies in another; that the chief political changes effected
by the Conquest were the increased communication of
England with the Continent and the establishment of
a feudal aristocracy in the midst of a conquered people ;
that neither English law, nor the English language, nor
English forms of architecture were violently displaced or
extirpated, but only gradually changed by the infusion
of new elements—all these points, which are worked out
exhaustively in the History, find their place in the essay.
The only subject touched upon in the essay which is not

[1] 'Review of my Opinions,' p. 154.

directly dealt with at all in the History is the effect of
the Conquest upon the morals of the people. On this
point he accepted the statements of William of Malmesbury as to the gross intemperance and profligacy of the
English before the coming of the Normans. The original
authorities to which he refers are William of Malmesbury,
Matthew Paris, Roger of Hoveden, and the *Chronicle*;
the last is quoted only once. The secondary authorities
on which he relies are Thierry, Palgrave's *History of the
English Commonwealth*, Lingard, Turner's *History of
the Anglo-Saxons*, Keightley, and Schlegel on Literature,
and in drawing historical contrasts and parallels he frequently refers to Niebuhr's *Rome*, Arnold's *Thucydides*,
and Taylor's *Overthrow of the Roman Empire*, with
which, as we have seen, he had been familiar from boyhood. His style at this time, and for some years to
come, lacked the freedom and vigour by which it was
afterwards distinguished, but it was not marked by so
many peculiarities. In that part of the essay which
deals with the effect of the Conquest upon language,
after showing that our modern English, 'like the men
who speak it, is neither French nor Saxon, but a fusion
of the two,' he remarks, 'yet in our forms and con-
structions the Teutonic element decidedly prevails,
and it affords expressions mostly of greater force than
their romance synonyms for all purposes of general
literature.' He did not, however, as yet rigorously
prune his sentences of romance words, and in some of
the more rhetorical passages there is a tendency to be
florid and redundant. From the following letter to Miss
Gutch, written immediately after his failure to get the
prize, we learn that he was aiming at a purer and simpler
style of writing, which he found very difficult to acquire.

Trinity College, June 12, 1846.

DEAREST NELLY,

I am at last able to give some information as to the prizes, but I am sorry to say not favourable either to Trinity in general, or to its junior Fellow in particular. All the prizes, which appeared this morning, though they were not expected till Monday, have been disposed of elsewhere, the English Essay to a certain Fortescue of Christ Church, whom I do not know, but had heard mentioned as a formidable antagonist. I must confess I am a good deal disappointed. I had, as you know, given great pains to it, and it was as it were my last chance of University distinctions, as so favourable a subject will hardly be given again, if I have the heart to make a second attempt. I not only thought I had a far greater probability of success in this instance than in any other attempt I have made, but success I had hoped would have been in a manner shared with you, at least crowned with your presence; and this, as it of course made me very much more desirous to win, so it has increased my disappointment tenfold. I am only afraid that you may feel it even more than I do: but I must beg of you, dearest Eleanor, not to trouble yourself more than you can help, much as I am sure it will disappoint you to be deprived of the pleasures we had fancied we might enjoy. I was very much cut down at first, but I do not think it is my nature to make the worst of anything, and I am now pretty well myself. I have been thinking over my career here, my peculiarly fortunate and agreeable elections as Scholar and Fellow, with my invariable failure in any attempt to win mere honours. It seems as though I met with everything relating to my real welfare—my admission at the first moment of my Academical life to a comfortable maintenance and the greatest advantages in other respects that Oxford or the world could furnish: then my peculiarly comfortable election as Fellow directly after my degree without any time of suspense or searching about for a place, or even having to go out of College—while anything that might feed formal vanity—certainly a foible of mine—in the way of honours and reputation is denied me. On the other hand, I have known men of far more brilliancy in honours and reputation who have repeatedly tried and failed to obtain a Fellowship. If all this be not actually meant as a lesson to me, I think I may fairly draw one from it.

I am now very busy with my article for the *Ecclesiastick* on Spelman, or rather on Sacrilege generally, which, as I trust you will peruse next month, I will not make any remarks upon it now. I did not quite understand whether you meant to ask if I were requested to write the article, or requested to write it as I expressed it 'in pure English.' The former I was—the latter was my own device, which I found so hard that after a few pages I gave it up.

Besides the article for the *Ecclesiastick*, referred to in this letter, he had even, when he was writing the essay, contributed several papers to the *Ecclesiologist*, and to the journals of various Archaeological Societies. An article in the *Ecclesiologist* on the development of Roman and Gothic architecture, in which he maintained Perpendicular to be the most perfect style, was criticized in the March number of that periodical by Mr. Beresford Hope. To this article Freeman wrote a long reply in May. In the summer of 1846 he wrote another paper for the *Ecclesiologist* on 'The True Principles of Church Restoration,' which elicited expressions of warm admiration from Mr. Gilbert Scott and Mr. Petit. In the spring of 1846 he had also written, at the request of Mr. J. H. Parker, an architectural chapter for a new edition of *The Memorials of Oxford*, receiving in remuneration £5 a sheet. In the autumn of the same year, he thought of writing a new *Guide to Oxford*, which was to be free from the silly and pretentious trash with which guide-books are commonly filled.

'Such books,' he says, writing to Miss Gutch, 'generally praise everything and everybody, "the picturesque seat of Mr. Tomkins," "the enlightened taste of the churchwardens, who have lately pulled down an old screen, erected a commodious gallery, and inserted a neat plaster ceiling," or again, "the liberality of the Dean and Chapter has provided the verger with a very convenient residence in the south transept of the Cathedral, they have also shown great judgement in blocking off half the Chapter House so as to form a very appropriate and commodious dining-room." '

In 1846 he began to study Anglo-Saxon, in company with his friend J. Riddell, under the direction of Professor Buckley, and though he was not one of the college tutors, he acted as coach to some of the Scholars. Writing on March 14, 1846, he mentions with great satisfaction and pride, that one whom he calls 'my Scholar,' I. G. Smith[1], had won the Hertford Scholarship. ' It is a marvel,' he adds, 'that we have no Scholar standing for the Ireland this year, but I intend my boy to get it next year'—which he did.

There are but rare references in his letters and diary at this time to any books of a light kind, save the novels of Walter Scott and Fouqué's Sintram and Undine. For the writings of this author he seems to have had a special liking. Probably Fouqué's intense truthfulness, and his deep sense of the mysteries of religion, as well as his high-minded patriotism, rendered him peculiarly attractive to Freeman. For the study of pure theology he had little inclination or indeed capacity. He began reading Hooker's *Ecclesiastical Polity* in 1846, but found it 'dreadfully hard.' ' I understand little or nothing,' he says, 'as far as I have gone ; Butler is child's play to it, though there does not seem to me to be really so much in the learned and judicious divine.'

During Commemoration week this year, some members of the Cambridge Camden Society paid a visit to

[1] See above, p. 45.

Oxford, and were entertained by the Oxford Architectural Society. On June 25 they were Freeman's guests at dinner in the Bursary at Trinity College. The party included Archdeacon Thorp, Sir Stephen Glynn, Dr. Mill, Mr. Benjamin Webb[1], Mr. John Mason Neale[2], and Mr. Philip Freeman[3]. 'With Archdeacon Thorp,' he says, ' I am delighted, and also with Webb. Neale is the gravest and most reserved man I ever saw, quite different from what I should have expected from his books.'

There was much correspondence and discussion during the following autumn and winter about his marriage, which he was anxious should not be delayed much longer. Month after month the matter seemed on the point of being settled, and then fresh difficulties and obstacles were interposed by his grandmother and uncle till his patience was nearly exhausted.

At length these vexatious hindrances were overcome, and on April 13, 1847, the long-engaged lovers were married in Segrave Church. The first part of the honeymoon was spent at Lincoln, where, of course, many sketches were made of the Minster and of other churches, both in the city and in the neighbouring towns and villages.

After paying visits to the uncle at Charwelton and to the grandmother at Northampton, and sojourning for a time in lodgings at Oxford, the young pair took up their abode at Littlemore in a small red-brick house, or rather large cottage, by the road side, a short distance

[1] Then Editor of the *Ecclesiologist*, afterwards Rector of St. Andrews, Wells Street, and Prebendary of St. Paul's.

[2] Afterwards Warden of Sackville College, in Sussex, author of a *History of the Holy Eastern Church*, and many other works.

[3] Afterwards Archdeacon of Exeter—no relation of E. A. Freeman.

beyond the churchyard gate. It had once been occupied by Newman himself, and was afterwards inhabited in turn by Mr. Isaac Williams, Mr. Bloxam, and Mr. Copeland when they were his curates.

Freeman's personal appearance at this period is fairly represented by the portrait prefixed to this volume. His figure was still slight, and his old habit of skipping in his walk was not yet quite outgrown. He had also an odd way of flapping the sleeves of his Scholar's gown like wings, which earned him the nickname among his fellow Scholars of 'the bantam cock.' He was as we have seen an active walker, though even at this age he was now and then crippled by the hereditary enemy, gout, from which he suffered grievously in later life. The first notice of this malady occurs in his diary under the date of September 12, 1845, where he writes 'did not go out for toe woe.' His ordinary recreations besides walking were riding and bathing, though he occasionally played at bowls in the College garden, and once he records in his diary, as if it was a remarkable event, that he had played a game of hockey with his friend Millard.

In his Fellowship, which he vacated by his marriage, he was succeeded by the only man who has in our time equalled him in historical learning in England — Dr. Stubbs, the present Bishop of Oxford.

The following reminiscences of him in his college days have been kindly contributed by his old friend Sir G. W. Cox :—

'I saw Edward Freeman for the first time in May, 1845. He was elected Fellow of his College on the day when, along with Gregory Smith, now Vicar of Great Malvern, I was elected Scholar. I remember the kindly words of greeting, which led me to look forward with no small eagerness to further acquaint-

ance with him, when my time for residence should come.. Nor
was I disappointed. I found in him not a particle of that
assumption of superiority which is supposed to characterize the
young Oxford don ; and in spite of some peculiarities he seemed
to me to treat those undergraduates who became for him anything more than mere acquaintances as in every way his equals.
For myself there were circumstances which soon led to closer
intimacy. We found that we had the great aims and objects
of our life in common. He was already a historian who was
drawing out the lines of work which he followed with splendid
method and perseverance throughout his life.

'His work, so far as I could share it, seemed to me to satisfy
all my wants. I had the good fortune, after the first term
of my residence in College, to be placed in rooms on the same
staircase and on the same floor with his ; and from that time our
breakfasts were commonly taken together, and when there were
no other engagements, we spent together as much time in the
evening as we could spare. I look back to this time with the
happiest of memories. We had the freshness and vigour of
youth ; and although we had ample enjoyment, we were never
idle. We shared the fashion of the time in the matter of days
of abstinence. On Fridays we dined, not in the College hall,
but in our rooms ; and, during Lent, our absence from the hall
dinners was extended to two or three days in the week. Our
frugal meals of eggs and bread were happy ones, at which
I always learnt much from him. He was, in fact, constantly
helping me on by the knowledge which his wider historical
reading had given him. We could speak with the utmost confidence, and I felt that with him I had not a single secret.

'We had also not a few tastes in common. The ballads of
our own country we enjoyed as songs telling of great deeds
in English history: and I found that he had no small powers in
throwing into the form of ballad and song the stories of great
deeds recorded in the wonderful history or epic of Herodotus. In
short, we were passing through our phase of song-making ; and
the result was that, a few years later, in 1850, we published
a volume of *Poems Legendary and Historical,* of which each of us
contributed one-half. This phase was, I am sure, distinctly of
benefit for us, and I confess that, looking lately into the volume,

I find nothing of which either he or I need to be ashamed.   In a not very temperate article, entitled 'The Prevailing Epidemic,' Mr. Charles Kingsley, in the pages of *Fraser's Magazine*, charged us with substituting false sentiment in place of common sense and sober thought. Freeman said at the time, and never changed his opinion, that our songs of the Norman Conquest were as much part of our political education as the reading of the *English Chronicle* itself could be.

' Nor was this the only subject for which we had a common enthusiasm. We were not less earnest in our architectural studies. In this field I found that I could work on in complete agreement with him, although he looked on the Perpendicular or Continuous period as the one in which the national architecture of this country reached its highest perfection, while I gave the first place to the Geometrical styles, and looked on the development of the Flowing and Continuous styles as belonging to the period of decay.

'In the evening the finishing of his pen and ink drawings of buildings, which he sketched with amazing rapidity, as well as accuracy and fulness of detail, never interfered with his enjoying and taking part in the conversation which might be going on round him. Of these drawings he amassed an immense store, and to the end of his life he never grew weary of adding to their number. It should, however, be remembered that these drawings were, and were meant to be, strictly careful records of actual facts. They made no pretence to thorough exactness of perspective or to serve in any sense as pictures, such as those with which Mackenzie delighted the eyes of all who care for colour as well as form. Of grandeur Freeman had a deep sense ; of beauty apart from real grandeur or historical association he had little or none. A picture, even of Prout, had for him no charm and no value, except in so far as it might furnish him with certain lines or forms on which he could rely as truthfully drawn from the building. In spite of this, his drawings were very impressive, and the vast wealth of illustration thus brought together added a deep interest to his conversation. In every way they might be placed in comparison with the sketches, also in pen and ink, of his friend, Mr. J. L. Petit.

' In this way a year and a half of my undergraduate life passed away, during which our friendship became more and more intimate. I was aware that this close association was not to last. He was engaged to be married ; and his marriage led, of course, to the resignation of his Fellowship, and to our losing his help as, so the phrase went, Rhetorical Lecturer[1]. To me his departure caused a great blank. The friendship in after years might not be less : and assuredly in our case it was not less. But the old days could not come again, and when he brought his young wife in the Easter term to bid us farewell, I felt much as though the sunshine was taken out of my life.'

CORRESPONDENCE, 1844-1847.

To Miss Eleanor Gutch.

Oxford, October 24, 1844.

. . . As to the matter of Advowsons, I cannot see any valid objection to the sale thereof. An Advowson certainly involves a very high responsibility, but it is still a right and a property, and therefore an object of sale ; and as no patron can present a person who is not already in Priest's orders, the Bishops have only to blame themselves if improper persons are presented to them, as they should either not have ordained them in the first instance, or, in case their offences have been since their ordination, have exercised ecclesiastical discipline against them. Remember that what is sold is not (as some foolishly or wickedly talk) either the spiritual office or the temporal profits annexed to it, neither of which of course are capable of sale, but simply the *perpetual* right of presenting a Clerk to the Ordinary for institution ; remember also, I say, the *perpetual* right, for as to the purchase of a single presentation ' to set up a son in the Church,' to ' buy him a living,' I cannot see that it differs in one

[1] The ' Rhetorical Lecturer ' at Trinity delivered a lecture four times a week immediately after morning Chapel. It was nominally on Rhetoric or Philosophy, but considerable latitude was allowed in the choice of subjects.

jot or tittle from the damnable and accursed sin of simony, and I believe that it is only by some legal juggle that it is not punishable as such.

. . . Speaking of the sacramental character of other rites than the two great Sacraments, a difference struck me the other day between them and any others, viz. that in Baptism and the Sacrament of the Altar, grace is conveyed not merely by a *ceremony*, but by a *material substance* representing something spiritual; by bread and wine, and water, the *substances* being in some mysterious and awful way made the *vehicles* of grace to our souls; while in Confirmation and Orders the grace is conveyed by a *ceremony*, the laying on of hands, but not through the intervention of any *material substance* like the elements at Baptism and the Communion. The other three approach far less to the idea of a Sacrament than Confirmation and Orders. Penance and Matrimony have no outward sign at all that I can make out, and Extreme Unction seems a sheer corruption, at least as it is looked upon in the Roman Catholic Church; but unction of the sick, as described by St. James, is surely a scriptural and Catholic practice, the omission of which in our own services strikes me as a great deficiency. We may thank the hereticks of the Continent for this, as for so much mutilation; the free and deliberate judgement of the Church of England retained it in the First Book of King Edward, the best exposition of her own mind uncorrupted by the fantasies and irreverent cavillings of Protestantism.

I have given you a bit of a sermon, but you asked for it yourself . . . I think the only thing of much consequence we are likely to split about is the observance of Sunday, but just look if you can find a word in the New Testament at all favouring the Jewish theory, and remember that your way was never heard of for 1600 years, and is now peculiar to Britain, as both Catholics and Protestants abroad agree in allowing amusements, though I fear it is too often violated by traffic among foreign Catholics, as by school-teaching among English. I sometimes wonder at myself, how utterly I have thought out everything for myself gradually, and how little is to be attributed to 'that man,' or anybody else. I know others that have done the same, but, except in such absolute saints as Tupper, I should think the imbibing of truth from childhood is likely to have a better effect on the moral system. I think all inquiry, all exercise of mere intellect on the subject of faith, though continually necessary, is to be avoided if possible. The Athanasian Creed is, of course, an invaluable treasure, but I should suppose reverence would have been better fostered had heresy never rendered definitions on such awful subjects necessary.

To turn from the spiritual temple to the material, I think Adderbury would have delighted you. Bloxam gives a print of the nave roof, soaring at a great height with all its intricate framing: the effect is admirable. The chancel, I told you before, is Perpendicular—every church I see convinces me more and more that this is our peculiarly English style; it is the perfection of Gothick architecture—the roof is also of wood, of lower pitch than that of the nave, but more richly ornamented, much in the style of the roofs about you, but with smaller corbels.

To J. L. PATTERSON, ESQ.

Ely, January 18, 1846.

. . . They are going on with the restoration of the Cathedral here, but much has not as yet been done beyond a little scraping. We went to both services to-day, which were beautifully done, the minor canons either having learnt to chant since July, 1844, or else only practising that art on Sundays. There are some peculiarities here; after the Nicene Creed, all men went out into the nave or quasi-nave (being, as you may remember, part of the constructive quire), where a sermon was preached, the clergy sitting in their surplices among the others. The preacher told us what seemed to me a very odd doctrine, viz. that each man had some sins which he had done so long ago that there was no good his troubling himself to repent of them, a position which might be a comfort or convenience, if one could but believe it, ἀλλ' ἀδύνατον. After sermon we went back into the chancel, where there was Communion, with the very smallest congregation I ever saw. As this is no particular day, nor the first Sunday in the month, I infer that it is weekly. In the afternoon was no sermon at all.

To Miss Eleanor Gutch.

Trinity College, Oxford, February 1, 1846.

. . . So you think all my friends have a leaning towards Rome, and you think that to avoid their pernicious influence I had better be removed from Oxford as soon as possible to the Protestant atmosphere of a wife and a drawing-room. What will you say when I tell you that I have been thinking whether I could not manage to combine both? I really do not know how I could leave Oxford altogether, and there are so many married tutors and such people that I should think there must be some sort of ladies' society, which is the thing which they say is wanting. Well, dearest Nelly, we can settle this some time, and I am sure I should be happy anywhere with you, though I should most certainly object to a place where 'the Prayer Book is suspended six days in the week.' However, I feel myself very much bound to Oxford for many reasons; most of my friends are here and likely to stay here; then there is such advantage in the way of libraries; and I must confess that I do not wish entirely to leave the Architectural Society; but, above all, it is the place itself, the whole idea of Oxford, from which I hardly should like to be severed. Still it is a weighty matter, and I should like to hear what you say about it, and I should consult one or two people here.

. . . I have a world of things to do. I am going to give myself a regular course of history and moral philosophy, which I have already begun. Then I have to write or rather to finish writing a certain essay on the Conquest of England by Duke William Fitz-Robert; also to transcribe a certain document in our Archives about our stained glass ; also to finish a certain history of the Church of Purton and others thereabouts; also a certain history of the Collegiate Church of St. Peter at Irthlingborough ; also a certain essay on windows, with illustrations; also to write a certain article, I know not yet what about, for the *Ecclesiastick,* and to touch up one on chancels for the *Ecclesiologist*; finally, to abridge the life of Ambrose Bonwicke [1] for *Sharpe's*

---

[1] A non-juror, Head-Master of Merchant Taylors' School from 1686 to 1691, when he was deposed because he would not take the oath of allegiance to King William.

Magazine. This, you will think, is enough. I have no pupils, and go to no lectures; for the former I am not very sorry, as it gives me more time for my own studies, although on the other hand the tutor often learns as much as the pupil.

I should recommend you to get the *Ecclesiologist* for this month, which, as I believe I told you, is to contain a review of my Developement Paper[1] by Hope. I am most anxious to see it: I suppose it will be out to-morrow. I have seen the advertisement on the cover of the *Ecclesiastick*—in the middle of the contents comes, ' Mr. E. A. Freeman on Roman and Gothick Architecture.' I give the capitals as I find them. ' Such is Fame.'

To THE SAME.

Oxford, March 24, 1846.

. . . As to royalty, I hold the peculiar sanctity of a king, as distinguished from a governor of any other sort, to consist exclusively in his consecration and unction. This of course renders rebellion against him not only a breach of order, but something sacrilegious and impious. But hereditary right, though of course it has its advantages, is surely merely a rule of convenience, and I hold a man to be rightfully king who obtains that place by the established order of that country. My *ideal* of succession, though it would hardly do now, is election from among the Royal Family by the great prelates and nobles of the kingdom, as was done in the Saxon times. As the family—at least up to the times of Henry VIII, since which it has been evidently withering away in body and mind under the curse of sacrilege—would be likely to contain at least one qualified for the office, we have all the prestige about the line, the being descended from elder monarchs, &c., without the absurdity of entrusting the destinies of a whole kingdom to a weak or wicked person merely because he is the next in succession.

To THE SAME.

Trinity College, March 29, 1846.

. . . I need not say, dearest Eleanor, how much I have been affected by the contents of your letter of this morning, both for

[1] *Developement of Roman and Gothick Architecture.*

your sake and that of the rest of your family; and I may add
for my own, as you know I always was very fond of poor
Emily[1]. Poor I should not say, as we may trust she is now
better off—good and gentle and patient as she always was—
awaiting that perfect consummation and bliss to which it will be
my fervent prayer that she may attain. It is a great comfort to
hear that her last moments were so tranquil and without pain—
though it must be an awful thing to die without the Sacraments.
As for you and all, I know that you will all look for consolation
in the only place where it can be found, and when I remember
the Christian fortitude and resignation with which your parents
and all of you endured what I should suppose must have been
a far heavier trial, I cannot doubt but that God's Holy Spirit
will bear you all safely through this present affliction, and that
you will find your sorrow to be not a consuming but a refining
fire.

The news quite cut me down, as I expected nothing less than
anything of the sort, and I did not observe the black seal on
your letter. To me it bids us look forward to the time when
a still sterner blow must in all probability separate for a while
even our united hearts, and to hold ourselves ready for the
rending of the dearest earthly ties. And you will now feel the
practical comfort of the Church's doctrine of the unseen world;
that the death of the righteous is at most a mere removal from
sight; that they still share with us in the invisible, though far
more real bond of fellowship, the Communion of Saints; that
not only we may look forward with sure and certain hope to
a reunion in another world, but that even now we may believe
that their prayers may avail much for us, and that they may
share in the benefits of our prayers, and in the holy Sacrifice of
Christ's Body and Blood.

. . . I will not fail, dear Eleanor, to commend in my prayers
both the living and the dead to the mercy of our Heavenly Father;
for you, that you may be enabled to bear up under the temporary
withdrawal from sight of one who we believe is not dead but
sleepeth, and for herself and all of us, that 'we may find mercy
and favour together with all His saints who from the beginning
of the world have pleased Him in their several generations;

---

[1] Sister to Miss Gutch.

that He may give them and us rest in the region of the living, and vouchsafe to bring them and us to the full enjoyment of His heavenly kingdom[1].' This, dearest Eleanor, has been the language of Christ's Church from the beginning with regard to her departed members, and in which I trust you will feel yourself able to join with a good heart and conscience.

To the Same.

Trinity College, Thursday before Easter, 1846.

. . . I have finished my account of Christ Church, except a little touching up, which will also, I fear, involve a little abridging to get into the required space[2]. I got admission to-day to the Chapter House, which requires a special order from a Canon, with Parker and Jones; it is a most glorious Early English room, but mutilated and desecrated like every other part of that unhappy church. After that ceremony I walked with Jones to Forest Hill; I have had very little exercise this week; I set out indeed for a walk with Riddell on Monday, but we had not got farther than Somerstown, when a heavy storm of hail and rain compelled us to seek for shelter in a hovel, where we abode I should think as much as an hour, discoursing divers matters; and Tuesday and Wednesday, what with rain, and what with work in the Cathedral, I had scarcely any time for walking, so that a good long expedition was very acceptable. We went in the evening to St. Peter-le-Bailey; they seem to have stopped the chanting this week, for which I see no occasion, for, as Jones says, there is no reason why music should not be made edifying in a penitential as well as a joyful manner. You know that the chanting there has no organ with it. There was a sermon, preached by Heathcote, on the occurrences of the day in the Gospels : it seemed to be part of a series for the week. It seems to me so strange your not

---

[1] This passage is not a direct quotation, but rather a kind of patch-work, the elements of which are derived from the Liturgies of St. Basil and of St. James, from the Scottish Communion office and possibly other ancient sources.

[2] Probably for the notices of churches which he was writing for a new edition of *Memorials of Oxford*, published by Parker.

having prayers even this week; if said in the house how would it be harder to say them in church? But it is of course the deadening spirit of, thank God, a past age, from which even men as much superior to their generation as your Father have not been able wholly to escape. Not only in Oxford, but in such an out-of-the-way place as Littlemore, there is always a very good, often quite a large congregation at any of the daily services when I have happened to be present. To-night the church was very full. I do wish the President would let us have chapel in the afternoon, as no one compels him to come, if he does not choose; I suppose it will be to-morrow. I should think there must be a great deal in this week's services to comfort any one under affliction; the feeling must occur so repeatedly that the bitterest suffering we endure is as nothing compared with what our Saviour bore for us, and that even the best of us 'receive' in our afflictions only 'the just reward of our deeds, while this Man hath done nothing amiss.' Heathcote said in his sermon that of old this night was passed without sleep, and told us, if that was too much, at least to 'watch one hour.' I could wish our Church had retained the nocturnal services, at all events in cathedrals and colleges; though we ought rather to be thankful that we have anything left; and I always tell men who are longing for something more, to wait first till all that we have is made use of, till every church in the kingdom has daily prayers, and at least weekly Communion, and then we may be in a position to consider whether anything further is needed.

. To the Same.

Trinity College, April 1, 1846.

I write by return of post, as I thought you might perhaps be better pleased to have nothing to disturb you on the day fixed for the melancholy, yet I doubt not consoling ceremony which is to separate your dear sister for a little while from your earthly sight. I shall not forget to think of you at the time; and the better to join with you in spirit, I will go over to Littlemore that day, where there is service at three o'clock. We have now no afternoon chapel, so we have to look out for service how we can, and I think all the services in Oxford are later. It will no doubt be a severe trial to all of you to feel completely separated from her bodily presence in this world, yet, when all is over, and you will gradually return to your usual occupations, you will I trust, under God's grace, become reconciled to your great loss—though I suppose there will always be things occurring, circumstances connected with her who is gone, which will be always calling up remembrances painful indeed, but I should hope still comforting and edifying. I shall hope soon to be with you, and I trust my coming may not only be a comfort to you but profitable to myself.

Many thanks for your father's prayer, and the extract from his letter, both of which are conceived in that spirit of true Christian resignation which has always distinguished him. I hope you will say everything kind for me to him and to everybody else.

I feel quite relieved at having got rid of my essay, whatever may prove its destination, it is almost the same as coming out of the Schools, so great has been the labour and weariness the last few days.

To the Same.

Trinity College, April 5, 1846.

. . . Now that the last sad rite is over, you will be the more reconciled to your late deprivation. I hope you were all enabled to endure the trial as well as we could have hoped for. I went over to Littlemore Chapel, as I mentioned I thought of doing; and did not forget to offer up my prayers equally for the repose of the departed and the edification of the living, myself included. You ask me about a monument. You must tell me whether you want a coped stone, or only a small cross at the head; these two being of course the only two sorts I can recommend. You can find very good examples in Paget's tract upon tombstones, and Armstrong's paper on monuments; neither of which, being mere pamphlets, costs much. If you decide upon any form I can get a working-drawing; I think there are some in the *Instrumenta Ecclesiastica*, or at all events I can get Millard to make one. The inscription, I think, is better without the age; I never saw it in an ancient one, and for a good reason, namely, that in the other world days and years do not reckon. A text, I think, is also as well away ; and I should simply put, after the old model :—

'Here lieth Emily Gutch, who deceased the twenty-eighth day of March in the year of our Lord God MDCCCXLVI, on whose soul Jesus have mercy.'

If it is to be read by the villagers, the old characters, which are otherwise of course infinitely preferable, are out of the question ; as the common ones are so ugly, I should recommend a letter like this :

HERE LIETH,

and above all things you must have 'who *deceased*,' not 'who *died*,' the latter word being, I believe, *never* found in ancient tombs of those who are not dead but sleep in Christ. And, if you stumble at the conclusion of the epitaph in the only form in which a Christian epitaph can conclude, remember it was in use after the so-called Reformation, so long as anything like religion remained in these matters.

To the Same.

May 16, 1846.

. . . Have you seen the review of Carlyle in the last *Christian Remembrancer*? I never read any of his books, for though divers people profess to understand and admire them, the few passages I have looked at seem always such absurd and unintelligible rant that I feel no desire to go on further. They say that his style is formed on German writers, and that an acquaintance with the language would make me appreciate them, but I do not see what is gained by that so long as the affected ass professes to talk English. If I write this sentence, 'True valour is the man who going against his enemies they do not turn him back but fights to the death,' I conjecture it would not avail much to tell you that it is an exact imitation of the style of Thucydides. I intend to go on to German and the other Teutonick languages when I have got up Anglo-Saxon, though a bar is put to our progress just now by the illness of Mr. Professor Buckley.

. . . Hope has sent me part of the proof of his answer to

me [1]; we seem to write in geometrical progression, his answer being infinitely longer than my letter, as mine was than the original review. I am also composing an article ' On the Position and Duties of Architectural Societies ' for the —*ologist*, and am to review a book which I think you are rather looking out for, the new edition of Spelman's *History of Sacrilege*, for the —*astick*, where you must also look out in the next number for the second part of my discourse on Chapters.

To the Same.

Trinity College, June 9, 1846.

. . . It seems now tolerably certain that the prizes will not be given out before Monday next, or Saturday at the earliest. Rumour assigns the Latin verse to Marshall of Trinity, and the English to Tupper, but of that in which we are more immediately concerned I hear nothing. Our festivities yesterday [2] went off very well ; we sat down twenty-one to dinner, including the President, and we had wine, &c., afterwards in the Hall, which I like much better than removing to the Common Room. It seems as if we at last had some cool weather, to my no little delight, as I am so utterly good-for-nothing during those great heats. I can hardly talk, read, write, or even think. One thing or another has hindered me from bathing since last Saturday.

. . . It is certainly a very grand protest of the Bishop of Exeter against the whole schismatical affair at Jerusalem [3]. The second

---

[1] Mr. Beresford Hope wrote a review in the *Ecclesiologist*, for March, 1846, of a paper by Freeman on the *Developement of Roman and Gothick Architecture*. Freeman, in the May number, answered his criticisms in a long letter, to which Mr. Hope wrote a yet longer reply in the number for June.

[2] Trinity Monday, the Gaudy Day at Trinity College.

[3] The scheme, sanctioned by Act of Parliament in 1841, whereby the King of Prussia and the Sovereign of Great Britain were alternately to nominate to a Bishopric of Jerusalem. The project was regarded with abhorrence by the majority of High Churchmen in England, and its adoption was one of the causes which impelled Mr. Newman to secession. See on the whole subject *Life of Dr. Pusey*, ii. 248 ; *Life of Dean Hook*, pp. 336–340, sixth edition.

reason seems merely to mean that if they were determined to send any such person, it might have been done without implicating the Church of England in any way by his title or otherwise Happily our Church is really not at all implicated, as Convocation has never sanctioned the matter, so that Dr. Alexander's [1] consecration was merely a private act of schism on the part of the officiating bishops. I hear that Gobat [2] was to be ordained priest by the Bishop of London yesterday, and that Dr. Mill, the Archbishop's Chaplain, intended to appear and object to the ordination on the ground of his heresy. This is also a capital move, though bearing only indirectly on the bishoprick question.

To the Same:

Trinity College, Whitsunday, 1846.

. . . I am afraid you will think that both I and my guide Wayte are somewhat changeable, when I tell you that a discourse with him on Friday evening has made me give up the idea of Architecture as a profession. I think there are strong objections to it : its study now would require more time and expense and a greater absence from College than I am inclined for, and I should not be likely, if ever, to get any return till it would probably not be an object to me. I hope to have enough to marry on from private sources earlier than I should be likely to have from this. Then, you see, it would shackle me very much and altogether break up the line of study upon which I have entered, and into which the theory of architecture enters ; and it is for this only that I have ever felt any turn : the practice would involve a good deal for which I have no ability whatever. I have, therefore, concluded to give up the idea, as also the chapel at Wantage. I hope you will not be disappointed at this—I really do not see why you should be, except that you seemed pleased with the other. I then asked Wayte about a residence—he recommended a cathedral town, and among them Exeter. I do not know, however, whether

[1] The first Bishop appointed under the scheme.
[2] Nominated as successor to Dr. Alexander by the King of Prussia.

I should not prefer the country if ecclesiastically qualified, as more places are continually becoming. I do not want to be anywhere where there would be much common visiting, which I do not think you would desire either.

To J. L. PATTERSON, Esq.

Northampton, September 7, 1846.

. . . About your difficulty as to the Institute—I, you know, have withdrawn already, so I am perhaps a prejudiced witness. It strikes me that the Socinian committee-man is not actually a further objection, the wrong point being the moral possibility of the election. I say *moral*, because in our Society it is equally possible by the letter of the rules, though there we have a moral certainty against it. At the same time I should wish our rules to speak more plainly on this point. The grand objection to the Institute seems to me to be what its name expresses, that it is merely archaeological on points where mere archaeology is worse than useless. I do not object at all to a numismatic society, or a society for digging up old pots, or tracing out pedigrees. I should not belong to it for exactly the same reason that I should not belong to a chemical or botanical society, because I have no interest in those particular pursuits. A society for any of these matters I should consider innocent and laudable (so far as its particular science is so), if it simply be not irreligious. But the Institute is wrong in applying to higher matters the merely antiquarian tone which belongs to inferior ones. It examines examples of the highest arts, painting, sculpture, architecture, and of those arts devoted to the highest of ends, without recognizing either their aesthetical or their religious character. Their avowed principle is to consider them, not as consecrated things to be treated with reverence, nor even as helping in what is surely a very high branch of philosophy, but merely as facts, curiosities, antiquities. Their manner of treating heathen remains would be absurd, unphilosophical, unartistick; when applied to sacred things, it is all this, and irreverent into the bargain. Nor is it merely an abuse which the presence and example of Hope or Markland may rectify, but an inherent evil; so far as they can introduce anything higher, it is merely adventitious, belying the name and constitution of the Society. An *archaeological* institute necessarily excludes both philosophical and religious views, an *architectural* society ought to involve the former and give scope for the latter, an *ecclesiological* society involves the latter as its essence, and requires the former as an auxiliary. You see then I am quite in favour of you and the rest of our friends withdrawing; the Socinian only strengthening, but not adding to my objections. You cannot make it what you wish without its ceasing to be an archaeological institute; and what you wish you have already to your hands in the Camden—excuse the old name.

To Miss Eleanor Gutch.

Oxford, October 30, 1846.

. . . Now for a sermon, as you have asked me again about the Bishop of London's happily defunct Church Discipline Bill. Setting aside minor objections and absurdities, of which there are not a few, and also one's general objection to matters of this kind being done by Parliament, while Convocation is impiously suppressed, the chief atrocities are :—First, that the whole goes on the theory of the clergy, priests and deacons, being the whole ecclesiastical body, with bishops as magistrates or constables to look after them and correct them when naughty. Of the laity, the mass of the Church, we hear not one word as amenable to Church discipline ; it is only the correction of clerks that is thought of; and of clerks only of the two lower orders. Not one word is said of correcting bishops ; yet the archbishop has, and must have, as full a jurisdiction over any bishop in his province as the bishop has over any priest or deacon in his diocese, otherwise he is not an archbishop but a mere primus, as in Scotland, who is merely president of the college of bishops, not archbishop with jurisdiction, which I cannot but think a defect in the constitution of that Church. And do either reason or experience teach that a bishop may not be immoral or heretical, as well as a priest ? Bishops of *Rome* have been deposed before now on both grounds, and I do

VOL. I. H

not see that the sees of Chester or Cashel have any prescriptive right to propagate heresy uncensured. Secondly, the archiepiscopal authority is intruded on in another way by his courts being deprived of their appellate jurisdiction. The bishop is, *quâ* the Church, to be constituted absolute tyrant ; the rights of metropolitans and presbyters are equally trampled on, for the jury of the bishop's nominees is, of course, a mere mockery; the power which Canterbury and York have had for 1200 years is to go to the Judicial Committee of the Privy Council. In fact it seems as if all authority in the Church is to be gradually merged in 'her most gracious Majesty,' &c., practically in whatever Jews, Turks, infidels or hereticks, may have attained the high places of the common law. The Papal protection is gone, the Metropolitan is to follow. The question of the rights of the presbytery involved in my phrase of 'Co-rulers' would be a very long one, but like the other it turns on the question, is the Church a body of priests and deacons, with bishops to keep them in order, or a body of laymen with bishops and priests to feed and govern them in their several degrees of authority ? The former is the opinion of the Bishop of London and Sir Robert Peel, the latter, which I expressed in the phrase 'Co-rulers,' that of the Catholic Church in all ages and countries. I would refer to a pamphlet published some years ago[1] under the title of *Presbyterian Rights Asserted*—I know not the author[2]—but the whole matter is most lucidly and cogently expressed. There can be no doubt that a priest has to his own flock, for his own functions, an authority perfectly independent of, though inferior to, and committed through, that of the bishop. So is the bishop's in his diocese to that of the archbishop. And in his purely episcopal acts nothing of consequence would, in a well-ordered diocese, be done without the assent of the chapter, as more largely is expressed in the *Ecclesiastick*. But I cannot go on about this for ever, or I should fill a ream of paper, and be too late for the post. I shall have a penny to pay as it is.

[1] 1839.   [2] Dr. Hook, then Vicar of Leeds. See above, p. 33.

To J. L. Patterson, Esq.

Northampton, April 10, 1847[1].

. . . Woe is me ! in the excitement τοῦ exire in saecula saeculorum I forgot a most important part of my goods, viz. my desk, which was ready packed up, and when I tell you that it contains, among other comforts and conveniences of life, that holy symbol of wedlock abhorred by the Puritans, and also Father Jacobs' certificate of the threefold publication of banns, you will be able to estimate the perplexity in which the loss, were it, like the decease of Short's godmother, irreparable, would involve a pair whom it might hinder from being 'respectably' joined together in holy matrimony.   But it is in you to repair it, ἐν σοὶ γὰρ ἐσμέν, as the Greek hath it ; could you then burthen yourself with it on your journey ?   Once in my rooms, you cannot fail to know it, a portable desk in a leather case. And as this would involve opening my room, could you extend your favours so far as to take order for the sending of Murphy's *Mahometan Empire in Spain* to the Union, about which I am not quite certain that George understood ; and, farther still, could you allow me so far to trespass on your liberality as to ask you to bring the latest edition of Bloxam of which I am possessed.   All this will, I trust, be a relief to you in the intervals of Common Prayer and human compo, as it will be a never-to-be-forgotten obligation conferred upon

Your sincere well-wisher and, especially under these circumstances, most anxious expecter.

To the Same.

Northampton, November 22, 1847.

. . . I have got two curiosities ; one philological, the other ecclesiological, both of which may well be communicated to Jones or others interested therein.   The first is from the surrender of St. Andrew's Priory here, in which the monks confess that they had spent their revenues on 'continual ingurgitations and farcing[2] of their carayne[3] bodies.'   The other is from *Perran-*

---

[1] Written three days before his wedding.
[2] l. c. stuffing.
[3] I. e. fleshly : derived, like carnal, carrion, &c., from the Latin ' caro.'

zabuloe, or the Lost Church Found, where the author states of the *ruins* thereof : ' On entering the interior, it was found to contain none of the modern accompaniments of a Roman Catholic place of worship. Here was no *rood-loft for the hanging-up of the host,* nor the vain display of fabricated relics —no latticed confessional, no sacring bell, no daubed and decorated images. . . . The most diligent search was made for beads and rosaries, pyxes, and Agnus Deis, censers and crucifixes—not one, not the remnant of one, could be discovered.' The Church was forsaken in the twelfth century (as he says), and would they not have taken the furniture to the new one ? Besides, the new use for the rood-loft is only to be paralleled by the use of a chapter as conceived by the M.P. for Manchester, namely, as ' a machinery which, if properly worked, would render a bishop unnecessary.'

CHAPTER III.

THE sojourn at Littlemore was a time of gentle
transition from academical life to country life. Scarcely
a day passed in which Freeman did not see some of
his Oxford friends and associates, more especially
Mr. Wayte, Mr. Patterson, Mr. Haddan, and Mr. Cox.
He and his wife usually attended the two daily services
at Littlemore Church, and often walked together into
Oxford, where they would have tea with one of his
college friends, or at the 'Auntage,' as they called the
residence of two Misses Gutch, aunts of Mrs. Freeman[1]. And of course he regularly attended the
meetings of the Architectural Society.

---

[1] Mr. Newman was curate of St. Clement's, Oxford, from 1824 to 1826,
when Mr. John Gutch, then an octogenarian, was the rector. During
these two years he did a great deal of hard parish work, in some of
which, especially the establishment of a school for the poor, he was
much assisted by the daughters of the Rector, Mrs. Freeman's aunts.
One of them was still living when he visited Oxford after he had become
Cardinal, and he did not forget to call upon her.

In January, 1848, his grandmother died. This event brought him an increase of income, and during the spring he was busily engaged in seeking a new home. His diary for April records visits for this purpose to Winchester, Christchurch, Wimborne, and Exeter. He clearly wished to settle, if possible, under the shadow of some great minster, but finding nothing suitable in these towns, he travelled on through Somerset into Gloucestershire, where he succeeded in finding a house to his liking called Oaklands[1], beautifully situated in the valley of the Cam, and facing the wood-clad heights of Stinchcombe hill near the small town of Dursley. One attraction in this place, no doubt, was its proximity to Stinchcombe, of which Sir George Prevost, a friend of the leaders in the Oxford Movement, and himself one of the writers in the Tracts for the Times, was vicar, Isaac Williams, who had married his sister, being the assistant curate. In May the young couple had to give up their small house at Littlemore, and went into lodgings in Oxford until Oaklands was ready for them. On June 29 they bade farewell to their Oxford friends, and after a week spent at the inn in Dursley, whilst their goods were being removed and unpacked, they entered their new home. The event is thus recorded in the diary, ' July 7, ST. THO. CANT., Matins. Took possession of Oaklands. Bought dog. Examined boy. Chose pony, and rode it to the turnpike.'

And now began that quiet life in the country, which for a married man with a competence, is perhaps the most favourable of all conditions for steady literary work and study. What may be lost by living at a distance from

---

[1] The name is now changed to Rednock.

the intellectual atmosphere of a University or some great
centre of literary activity, is more than compensated
by independence, and freedom from interruptions and
distractions of various kinds, while the visits of friends,
and correspondence with them, refresh and invigorate the
mind, and send the scholar back to his work with
renewed ardour and zest.   He tried to persuade his
friend Patterson to apply for a curacy in the neighbouring
parish of Cam.   Writing to him on September 20, he
says :—

'If you do think of leaving Oxford at all, you will hardly turn up
so pleasant a thing in a hurry, as you would be among congenial
people, having (not to mention Mr. Madan himself and ourselves) Isaac Williams and Sir George Prevost very near.   The
parish is large and somewhat scattered, but all rural, the vicar
resident and very active.   There is a daily service in the
morning in the parish church, newly restored, in the evening in
a chapel of ease newly built.   We are just out of the parish, to
my sorrow, but we attend the church three days in the week,
when our own service is at 10.30.'

Mr. Patterson, however, was not inclined to act on the
suggestion of his friend, and from Freeman's next letter
to him, dated September 27, it seems he was beginning
to show symptoms of the dissatisfaction with the Church
of England which ended in his secession to the Church
of Rome.

'What is the matter with you about the Romans?   Don't do
anything rash.   I have not thought much about them lately,
but as far as I have, my present studies have given me a push
the other way, and my faith in B. Gregory VII is somewhat
shaken, as the sender over of those abominable Norman thieves.
I shall not be satisfied till the Queen passes Bills in English,
and till every man may hunt on his own ground according to
the laws of King Cnut of blessed memory.'

We have now reached the point at which Freeman's real work begins. From the time that he left Oxford and settled in the country as a married man, he continued to the end of his life with untiring patience and zeal to be a student and writer of history. He formed a larger conception of history than was common at that time, and he improved upon the earlier methods of studying it, so that he became, if not the founder, certainly one of the most conspicuous leaders, of a new school of historical learning. In his early youth there were, with the splendid exceptions of Gibbon and Hallam, no English historians of first-class merit. For children indeed, Mrs. Trimmer and Goldsmith had given way to Keightley and Mrs. Markham, but for older readers the chief authorities for Greek and Roman history were Mitford and Hooke. When he went to Oxford they were just beginning to be displaced by Arnold and Thirlwall, and when he left it in 1847, the first four volumes of Grote's *History of Greece* had appeared. English history was still presented through the medium of the cold dry intellect and narrow prejudices of Hume, who was beginning (but slowly) to be supplanted by Lingard, while the chief authority on the general history of Modern Europe was the superficial Robertson.

Freeman early grasped the idea that the history of the Aryan nations in Europe should be studied as one great continuous whole. The revival of classical learning in the fifteenth and sixteenth centuries had, in his judgement, wrought one evil together with much good. The range of human interests and tastes had been narrowed by the prevailing notion that the only forms of language and of art, and the only portions of history which deserved the attention of cultivated men, were those that belonged to certain periods, called 'classical periods,' in the history of Greece and of Rome. One consequence of this limitation of the field of vision was, that a sense of the true distinctions even between subjects which fell within the sacred pale of these chosen periods was lost. Under the common name of 'the Ancients,' or 'the Classics,' poets and historians were lumped together, as widely separated in time and character as Homer and Virgil, Herodotus and Tacitus. It was truly remarked by Macaulay, that as some simple folk, imagining that all the people in India live together, charge a friend setting out for Calcutta with kind messages to Bombay, so in like manner to Rollin and Barthelemi all the classics were contemporaries [1].

The comparative method of study in philology, mythology, politics, and history, which took its rise in France after the peace of 1815, under the direction of such men as Sismondi, Guizot, and Michelet, had been taken up in Germany, and was finding its way into England about the time when Freeman had taken his degree at Oxford. Following this method, and starting from the study of Herodotus, which, as we have seen, he began to read again as soon as he was set free from the Examination Schools, he gradually formed the conviction that the history of the Aryan nations in Europe was one great drama ; that their language, their institutions, their dealings with one another, all formed one long chain of causes and effects, which could not be rightly understood except when viewed in their connexion. The centre of this great drama he found in Rome. Rome was the vast lake in which all the

---

[1] Lord Macaulay's *Miscellaneous Writings*, vol. i. p. 272.

streams of earlier history lost themselves, and from which all the streams of later history flowed forth. The world of independent Greece stood on one side of it, the world of modern Europe on the other. In this great drama, the two most marked and important divisions were the second century B.C., when the final overthrow of Carthage by Rome fixed the position of Rome as the mistress of the civilized world, and the fifth century A.D., when the Teutonic races were breaking up the empire and forming the modern nations of Europe; the age which saw the settlement of the Goths in Spain, of the Burgundians and Franks in Gaul, of the Angles and Saxons in Britain. The latter of these two epochs formed the nearest approach which he would ever recognize to a boundary line between ancient and modern history. The special interest and value of the work of Gibbon was that his history connected, like a stately arch, the events which lay on either side of this line ; and in like manner, the reason why Ravenna had a peculiar and almost unique charm for the student of history was that it represented, as Freeman expressed it, an isthmus joining two worlds. Standing on that isthmus amid Roman, Gothic, and Byzantine monuments, the student might realize more vividly than in any other place what the history of the Roman Empire really was : how abiding its power and influence were even in the days of its decline and decay, how thoroughly Rome had led captive her Teutonic conqueror, even as she herself had been led captive by the conquered Greek.

His conception of the unity of the history of the Aryan nations in Europe was based partly on a consideration of the common characteristics traceable in their language, habits, and institutions, partly on the fact that they were

all drawn more or less within the influence, and most
of them within the boundaries, of the Roman Empire,
and that they were all, sooner or later, converted to
Christianity. These three conditions divided their history by a strongly marked line from that of other
nations which differed from them in origin or in religion.
Civilization and progress were co-extensive with those
portions of the world in which the Romans had securely
established their empire, and in which the Christian
Church had been firmly planted. The fate of the civilized
world had always hung upon the strength of the Aryan
nations to repel the attempts of Asiatics to force their
way into Europe, and to flood the western world with
oriental ideas and habits, modes of government and
forms of religion. The struggles of Greece with Persia,
and of Rome with Carthage ; the struggles of Greeks,
Romans, and Teutons with the Saracens ; the conflicts
extending to our own times with the Turks, were but so
many acts in one long drama of which the earliest scenes
were to be found in the pages of Herodotus, and the
latest might be studied in the telegrams of the daily
newspaper. And one great attraction to him in the
history of Sicily was that the island had twice been the
battle-field in which this great strife between East and
West had centred. And as Greece was the original
parent of the arts, the literature, and the political
ideas which were afterwards diffused throughout the
western world through the medium of the Roman
Empire, and handed down to the modern nations which
grew out of it, so the enslavement of Greece by the
alien and infidel Turk was to him the most melancholy
and distressing event in all history. The recovery of
St. Sophia at Constantinople for the Christians was

the dream of his life. Bondage to the Turk was a fatal obstacle to the prosperity and happiness of south-eastern Europe; an obstacle which, in his opinion, for the sake of civilization and of Christianity, the European powers ought to combine to remove.

His conception of the continuity of European history was originally derived, as he himself said, from the lectures delivered at Oxford by Dr. Arnold as Professor of Modern History. And it was from Arnold also that he learned to regard the essence of history as consisting in the record of man's political being. Arnold defined history as the biography of a political society or commonwealth, and he divided this biography into the record of the external life of a state—its dealings with other commonwealths, which consisted very largely of wars ; and the record of its internal life, which was primarily concerned with forms of government, institutions, and laws. All other elements of national life, as literature, science, and art, though they had their influence in moulding national character and shaping the course of events, were only of subsidiary importance for the historian [1]. Freeman heartily adopted this view, and expressed it in his well-known and favourite maxim, ' history is past politics, and politics are present history.' He admitted, indeed, that every branch of knowledge which had to do in any way with the affairs of mankind was at least potentially useful for the purpose of the historian. Theoretically, he acknowledged all forms of art to be deserving of the historian's consideration, as being elements of the national life, though in practice he confined his attention to architecture. The reason,

[1] See Arnold's *Lectures on Modern History*, more especially his inaugural lecture.

however, of this limitation was that he had a strong
natural taste for this particular art, and a very thorough
knowledge of it, while for the others he had no aptitude
or liking, and he would never presume to write about
subjects which he did not understand. The study of
geography and chronology, which have been called 'the
two eyes of history,' he considered to be of primary
importance, but he did not neglect or despise any
branches of learning which might help to throw side
lights upon his main subject, such as a knowledge of
coins, inscriptions, and antiquities of every description.
And only secondary in importance to geography and
chronology he placed the sciences of geology and language. The physical formation of a country combined
with climate had no small share in determining the
character and condition of the inhabitants, and consequently of their history, while language was the most
trustworthy evidence of nationality. More especially
in cases where the population was mixed, as in England
after the Norman Conquest, and in Gaul after the
settlement of the Franks, the character of the language
spoken at any given time indicated which nationality
was in the ascendant.

Travelling was involved in the study of architecture,
but it was no less necessary for identifying the sites of
battles and the scenes of great events, for forming
a more vivid and accurate idea of them, and for observing
the characteristic features of the country as a whole.
Travelling, as a direct branch of the historian's business,
is quite a modern practice, owing to the expense, difficulty, and even danger, which attended it in earlier
times ; but few modern historians, if any, have made it
such an essential part of their work as Freeman did.

As his conception of the unity of history, and his belief that the essence of history lay in the political element, were derived from Arnold, so also did he heartily embrace Arnold's doctrine that history is a great moral lesson—that the inner life and character of a nation are determined by the nature of its ultimate aim, and that if the end at which it aims, either as a people or through its responsible rulers is an unrighteous one, its highest welfare and truest happiness cannot be attained. The blackness and ugliness of a national crime could never be gilded in his eyes by apparent success, and he utterly refused to believe that the best interests of England or of any country had been, or ever could be, promoted by injustice or cruelty towards other nations.

In his youth there was probably no country in Europe of which the history was worse represented than our own. The conscientious labours of Thomas Fuller and Jeremy Collier in the seventeenth and eighteenth centuries had not been followed up by later writers comparable to them in learning or industry. Remarkable ignorance prevailed respecting the earliest periods of English history, not only because vast stores of material were inaccessible or very difficult of access; but also because in their scorn and contempt of what men were pleased to call 'the dark ages,' historians did not take any serious pains to master the materials which were within their reach. The way indeed in which the histories of Greece and Rome were studied, presented a direct contrast to the way in which the history of England was studied. All that was most generally and thoroughly known concerning Greek and Roman history was derived from the earliest authorities, Herodotus and Thucydides, Livy and Tacitus. Of later historians, such as Polybius and Diodorus, Ammianus Marcellinus, and the Byzantine writers, knowledge was rare, and for the most part slight. Of English history, on the other hand, the later portions dating from the sixteenth century were by far the best known and understood. Hume had written his history backwards. The first two volumes covered the period from the accession of James I to the Revolution of 1688. Two more volumes dealt with the times of the Tudor sovereigns, and two more were afterwards added to these, into which he crowded all the events of the preceding ages from the landing of Julius Caesar to the accession of Henry VII. Hallam's *Constitutional History* also starts from the latter date.

But it was not merely in their neglect of the early history of their country that our writers in this century were deficient. They were so steeped in the political and religious prejudices of their time, and so entirely convinced of the superiority of their own age to all preceding ages, that they were incapable of forming true conceptions and fair judgements of the characters and actions of men in remote times. They looked down upon them with a kind of cynical disdain. More especially did they fail to do justice to the influence of the Church, to point out how much it had done for learning and the arts of civilization in rude and barbarous times, and how much help it had given to the people in some of their struggles with tyrannical sovereigns for civil and political rights. They could not give ecclesiastics credit for any purity of motive, and were perpetually sneering at the hypocrisy, superstition, and priestcraft which they imputed to them. In the conflict between the authority of the State and of the Church in mediaeval times, in the contests of Anselm with William Rufus and Henry I, it was always assumed that right rested with the secular side, which was wronged, oppressed, or outwitted by its crafty adversary. Even Hallam is not free from these faults, vastly superior as he is to Hume in range of knowledge and research, in breadth of sympathy and fairness of judgement. And, of course, smaller histories written for the young followed the lead of the larger ones. These wretched little compilations, dry lifeless epitomes, excluding everything which could excite enthusiasm for what was grand, or noble, or poetical, in their references to the struggles between the secular and spiritual powers, invariably assumed that the State was right and the Church was wrong. It was one part of the work of the Oxford Movement to exhibit the Church, both of primitive times, and of the Middle Ages in truer colours; to enable men to see it as it really was, not through the mists of eighteenth-century prejudice. No doubt in this reaction the sympathies of some swung back too far, and, the 'dear, delightful, Middle Ages' were credited by imaginative and romantic spirits with greater charms and virtues than really pertained to them. But such exaggerated admiration was checked in a historian who took a careful and critical survey of all the circumstances of the time. And this was precisely the position of Freeman. He had studied the history of the Christian Church from boyhood: he knew what Christianity had done for the heathen world ; how it had inspired the old corrupt Roman Empire with fresh life, how it had trained and educated the young and rugged races which broke up the Empire and formed the modern nations of Europe. He estimated at its full value the influence of the Church in moulding national character, he could appreciate the virtues of the mediaeval saint or hero, as well as the beauties of mediaeval buildings ; but his strong historic sense, and his habit of looking all round his subject and viewing it in all its bearings saved him from blind admiration. His eyes were open to defects as well as to merits, to vices as well as to virtues, but he could often perceive that these defects and vices were but the natural offspring of the times in which they were manifested. His historic instinct in this direction had shown itself, as we have seen[1], in early boyhood when he maintained that Roderick Dhu ought not to be called a mere robber, for the times had made him what he was. And in his essay for the Chancellor's prize at Oxford, in speaking of the Benefit of Clergy, as the exemption of clerks from trial in secular courts was called, he observes that this privilege had often been assailed as a monument of superstition and priestly dominance. ' But,' he says,

' without positively deciding on the good or evil character of the measure, it may be remarked that its. acknowledged inexpediency at the present day does not prove that it may not have been a wholesome and necessary provision in another state of society.'

and he concludes by remarking that

' . . . We are not called upon to condemn the Middle Ages because they resemble not our own days, nor yet to under-value our own position because we live not among the chivalrous devotion of earlier times.'

Although it is true that the early history of our country had of late been much neglected, some laudable efforts had been made to rescue it from oblivion and con-

---

[1] Above, p. 10.

tempt[1]. At the beginning of the century Sharon Turner had published his *History of the Anglo-Saxons*. In the preface to his first volume he observes that the subject of Anglo-Saxon antiquities had been nearly forgotten by the British public.

'The Anglo-Saxon MSS.,' he says, 'lay still unexamined, and neither their contents nor the important facts which the ancient writers, and the records of other nations had preserved of the transactions and fortunes of our ancestors, had ever been made a part of our general history.'

To Sharon Turner belongs the credit of having awakened some interest in these neglected materials which led to an inquiry being made about the matter in Parliament in 1800, and the appointment of a Commission ' to methodize, regulate, and digest the records.' The slow and imperfect labours of this Commission were followed in course of time by the grand series, which is still going on, of records published under the official sanction of the Master of the Rolls. Meanwhile in 1839, two years before Freeman went to Oxford, John Mitchell Kemble had begun to bring out his collection of early English Charters under the title of *Codex Diplomaticus*. He had studied at Göttingen, and had become convinced that the true beginnings of English national life dated from the Teutonic settlements in Britain in the fifth and sixth centuries. His fellow-worker in the same field, Sir Francis Palgrave, had already published in 1832 his *Rise and Progress of the English Commonwealth*, a work to which Hallam

---

[1] A few of the statements which follow were suggested by an admirable article on Mr. Freeman contributed to the *Yale Review* for August, 1893, by Mr. Hannis Taylor, the United States Minister at Madrid, though the chapter as a whole was written before I had seen his article.

acknowledged his obligations. In 1840, Benjamin
Thorpe brought out his collection of *Ancient Laws
and Institutes of England*, and in 1849 appeared another
work of Kemble entitled *The Saxons in England*, the
most systematic attempt which had yet been made to
arrange and apply the materials which his industry had
brought to light. Lastly, the interval between 1851 and
1854 was marked by the production of Sir Francis
Palgrave's *History of Normandy and England*.

The issue of this work, and of Kemble's *Saxons in
England*, nearly coincided with the time when Freeman
was settling down to the methodical study of history as
the main business of his life. He immediately recognized their value, and to the end of his life he always
spoke of these two authors in terms of the greatest
admiration and gratitude. But he detected from the
first certain errors of judgement and method in both
writers which made him long for the appearance of an
historian who might combine their merits while avoiding their defects. In a review of Kemble's book which
he wrote for the *Guardian* of February 15, 1849, he
pronounces him to be not so much an historian
as an antiquary, though an antiquary of a very high
class. He heartily concurs in the opinion expressed in a
rhetorical passage in Mr. Kemble's preface, that to the
institutions and principles of government inherited from
our Teutonic forefathers, England owed in a great measure
her pre-eminence amongst European nations, her real
dignity as the seat of justice and order, her stability and
security at a time when 'on every side of us thrones totter
and the deep foundations of society are convulsed[1].' But

[1] The reference is to the shock produced by the French Revolution of
1848.

he points out that Mr. Kemble had not succeeded in tracing the gradual growth of these principles, or in showing how far Saxon institutions survived in those which existed at the present day. His work was in truth not so much a history as a collection of detached essays. Most of these, however, were of very high value, and more especially those which dealt with the question of feudalism. On the other hand, he considered Kemble's treatment of ecclesiastical matters, especially the relations between the Church and the State, extremely unsatisfactory and misleading. Kemble failed to distinguish between a just resistance by the State to ecclesiastical encroachments on secular authority, and an unjust intrusion of the secular power into matters which were purely spiritual; nor did he make a sufficient allowance for differences in character, and in the circumstances of the times, not perceiving that the interference of an Alfred or an Æthelstan in the affairs of the Church might be allowable and beneficial, while in the case of a William Rufus or Lord John Russell it was pernicious and unwarrantable.

Of Sir Francis Palgrave it is needless to say that Freeman formed a much higher estimate. He wrote a review of the first volume of his *History of Normandy and England* for the *Guardian* in July, 1851, in which he pronounces him to be the first English writer of great original powers who had devoted himself to the early history of his own country. Whatever faults he had were not on the side of defect, but sprang from the exuberance of a mind of strong natural power, only not always sufficiently restrained by sober judgement and discretion. Freeman had such a high respect for his ability that, as he said, he could almost be content to go wrong in his company; yet he was convinced that some of his theories were overpressed. He rated, for example, far too high the influence of imperial and Roman ideas both in northern Gaul and in England. Clovis and Offa were regarded as representatives or survivals of the imperial idea ; as successors of Tetricus and Carausius, rather than as national kings of Franks and Angles. He himself, on the contrary, could not discover any continuous traditions of Roman imperial power in England : no idea of the consulate, or of a Caesar or Augustus had survived. If any imperial notions or titles had been retained, they were not fragments of the fallen and shattered Empire of the West, but only imitations of that living corpse of Rome which was still lingering on the shores of the Bosporus. The historian who should be able to form a true estimate of the influence of laws and institutions on the one hand, and of race and conquest on the other, in shaping the growth and progress of the English nation, would supply the want of the age— a history of early English times which might rank with the great histories that our countrymen had already produced of Greece and Rome.

His own views at this time on the relation of history to other branches of learning and on the proper methods of studying it, are very clearly expressed in three pamphlets which he published with reference to the establishment at Oxford of a new School of Modern History [1]. The first of these pamphlets, entitled *Thoughts on the Study of History*, was written in 1849, when the project was still under consideration. He begins by observing that an

[1] (i) *Thoughts on the Study of History.* (ii) Second edition with a Postscript to the same, 1849. (iii) *Thoughts on the Third Form of the New Examination Statute.* All published by J. H. Parker, Oxford.

increased attention to the study of history as well as to
the study of physical science was a distinctive feature
of the age.   Philosophy, poetry, and art, though none of
them were despised, had perhaps seen better days; but
the age of Niebuhr, Arnold, Thirlwall, Grote, Guizot,
Thierry, Palgrave, and Lappenberg, must be reckoned as
one which had outstripped its predecessors in historical
learning, however much it might hereafter be itself outstripped.   One reason, perhaps, of this development of
the study of history simultaneously with that of physical
studies, was that it had more points of contact with them
than was the case in any other branch of mental or
moral science.   History, it is true, was concerned with
mind, but with mind, so to say, under its most material
aspects, mind surrounded with the conditions and accompaniments of physical existence :—

'History does not deal with abstractions, nor does it ever
teach first principles.   It has primarily to deal, like the physical
sciences, with outward facts or phenomena; and though it
assigns those facts to the working of certain laws or principles, it does not pretend to invest these laws with the character
of eternal and immutable truth.   They are, like the laws of
physical science, only generalizations from instances, a high
class of probabilities, hardly amounting to moral certainty.'

There were, moreover, some branches of inquiry
which were common to the student of history and the
student of physical science: such were physical geography,
which often supplied the key to many otherwise dark
passages of history, and the kindred science of geology.
Closely connected with these was the study of the effects
of race and of climate upon the bodily and mental condition.   And yet from another point of view the study
of history was 'the protest of mind against matter in

a material age': it was an acknowledgement that there
were other and nobler objects of pursuit than the
discoveries of physical science: that the rise and fall
of empires was a grander subject for contemplation than
the ebb and flow of tides: that the mind of man
contained deeper and richer treasures to be explored
than the bowels of the earth could supply, and was
a more glorious and awful subject for investigation than
'system beyond system of suns and constellations.' And
let it not be said that in physical science we contemplated
directly the works of the Creator, but in history only
the actions of His creatures. 'The deeds of Pericles,
and Decius, of Charlemagne and Alfred, are as much
creations of Almighty power as the earth we tread or
the sky we gaze upon'; but while the study of natural
science led chiefly to the contemplation of creative
power, the study of history led more directly to the
contemplation of a moral governor of the world.

The study of history then was the point from which
it was possible to start with the most reasonable hope
of influencing the present age for good. Not only had
the study become generally diffused, but every depart-
ment of it had its own workmen. There were diligent
pioneers in the shape of 'antiquarian collectors of
charters and letters, the editors of chronicles, and
elucidators of individual facts : there were constitutional
antiquaries who traced out the growth and decay of
different forms of government : there were the sober
judgement and sound criticism of Thirlwall and Lappenberg, the life-like grouping and glowing colouring of
Thierry, the intuitive divination of Niebuhr, and above
all, the wide grasp, the majestic eloquence, the moral
dignity of Arnold.' But, for the early history of our

own country, no adequate historian had yet appeared. 'Our truest and most national antiquities have as yet been so enveloped in clouds of vague theory on the one hand, and of dead archaeology on the other, as to have found no historian in the highest sense, none at least whose works are not open to grave charges either of excess or defect.' Men's minds, however, had at last waked to the fact that Greece and Rome did not exhaust the world's stock of wisdom and greatness. 'We have learned that such a monopoly of dignity was never granted to any age or nation: that the soil of Teutonic Christendom has brought forth as glorious works of art and genius, as mighty deeds of national and individual greatness, as aught that southern heathendom can boast. We have at last learned where to look for our own fathers: we have at last discovered that we owe not more to Athenian forms of beauty, to Roman laws and government, than to those seeds of liberty and glory which the despised " barbarian " planted in his German forest or on his Scandinavian rock.' To the principles of government and to the institutions inherited from their forefathers, the northern nations owed the security and stability which they alone enjoyed amidst the political convulsions of Europe. Such a contrast must of itself force upon Englishmen the peculiar claims which the history of their own country had to their careful and attentive study. Unfortunately, however, there was no study in which 'shallow, half-knowledge, baseless theories, without facts, or dull facts not expanded into principles,' were more to be apprehended. Modern history was a study which stood open to all, men, women, and children, who plunged into it without that sound training, at once sobering and enlarging the mind, which the University enforced upon all who pursued the line of study which her wisdom had marked out. All, 'indocti doctique,' could rush at it without treading that hard and toilsome path by which the study of the ancient world had to be approached, without puzzling through the involved sentences of Thucydides, or wearying the brain over the refinements of Greek philosophy and mediaeval logic. But, in truth, there was no royal road to modern, any more than there was to ancient, history : no one could rightly understand the former without having thoroughly grasped the latter. If any one thought it possible, let him correct his error by reading Arnold's preface in the third volume of his *Thucydides*, or the 'six goodly and learned volumes[1]' of Mr. Grote's *History of Greece*.

Meanwhile, members of the University of Oxford were informed that the Oxford system of learning was narrow and antiquated, and they were invited to enlarge it by the introduction of Modern History, as 'a direct subject for University studies and examinations.' The proposal raised two questions : first, as to the expediency of the change in itself: secondly, as to the method recommended for effecting it. He met the question of expediency with a direct negative. The study of history formed part of the academical course, but that course was not designed to make the scholar who went through it a finished historian, though it put him in the way of becoming so if his inclination led him to follow that line of study in after life. It was not intended to teach all history, which was impossible, but the principles of historical philosophy, principles which must be studied in their practical workings. And the only way in which

---

[1] Six more volumes were published in course of time.

this could be done was by giving a sample, as it were, of this working. And where was such a sample to be found? Primarily in the history of Greece, and in an inferior degree. in the history of Rome. The history of Greece might be defined as 'the history of the world compressed into dimensions practicable for this purpose.' The astonishing rapidity with which Greek, and especially Athenian, institutions developed and decayed, as compared with those of more modern states, rendered the history of Greece of incomparable value to the student. Three centuries, from Draco to Phocion, measured the duration of historic Athens, and its most important and brilliant period was contained almost within the life-time of one man. Thus the history of a few generations became an epitome of the history of political society, and was a sufficient school for instruction in all the principles of an historical philosophy. And in the most critical period the student enjoyed the inestimable advantage of having the events recorded by a contemporary historian of first-rate excellence. Thus, partly from its own nature, partly from the character of its principal writer, the early history of Greece supplied the very sample which was specially marked out for the requirements of academical study. The history of Rome, though in some respects more impressive and important, did not present either of these advantages in so eminent a degree. It was, indeed, a history of law and government : it was the history of a state whose influence on subsequent ages could scarcely ever be effaced. But the march of events in the history of Rome was not so fiercely rapid as in the history of Greece, and the subject was far too vast to be embraced in an academical course. Moreover, 'except in the

small portions handed down to us by the stern historian
of tyranny,' there was no writer like 'the almost infallible
guide on whom we rely in our Grecian studies.' The
attention, therefore, of the student was generally confined to that portion which exhibited the growth to
perfection of a constitution surpassed only by our
own, and in which the deficiences of ancient authorities
were wonderfully supplied by the almost unerring
divination of a modern genius. What Aristotle and
Butler were to moral philosophy, Thucydides and
Niebuhr were to history.

But 'any attempt to introduce the almost infinite field
of modern history as a subject of ordinary study and
examination on the same level as Grecian and Roman
history must be utterly fruitless.' Moreover, he strongly
deprecated setting up a distinct school of modern history
as false in principle. It was to build up and fortify that
wall of separation which it had been the great aim of
Arnold's historical labours to level with the ground : an
aim which he had avowed when he expressed the hope
that his edition of *Thucydides* might 'contribute to the
conviction that history is to be studied as a whole, and
according to its philosophical divisions, not such as are
merely geographical and chronological : that the history
of Greece and Rome is not an idle inquiry about remote
ages and forgotten institutions, but a living picture of
things present, fitted not so much for the curiosity of
the scholar, as for the instruction of the statesman and the
citizen.' But if the new scheme was rejected, as Freeman hoped it would be, should things be left precisely
as they were? 'Not exactly,' he replied. ' If we look at
things dispassionately, without any wish either to uphold
abuses simply because they are old, or to adopt inno-

vations simply because they are new, we shall perhaps
see that while our historical course stands in no need of
being revolutionized, it might with advantage be con-
siderably expanded.' This expansion he proposed to
effect by encouraging the practice of illustrating ancient
history by comparisons with the events of later times,
and by giving weight to it in examination.

' If a question be set concerning the Lacedaemonian constitution and the relations between the conquering Dorians and the
conquered Achaeans, let it be understood that no information
really illustrating the relations of conqueror and conquered in
all ages will be considered out of place in the answer. Let it
be allowable to carry out the analogy suggested by Dr. Arnold
between the Spartans in Laconia and the Normans in England :
to show the almost perfect identity between the first stages of
both, the total dissimilarity of the result in each, and to point
out the causes to which the different course of events may be
most probably traced. In considering the wars and revolutions
of the various Grecian cities, let it not be considered amiss to
illustrate them by references to similar scenes in the republics
of mediaeval Italy.'

More life and spirit would, he thought, thus be given
to the existing system without forsaking the sound
principles on which it was founded, or wildly grasping
at what was unattainable.

Soon after the publication of this pamphlet the proposed examination statute appeared in a revised form,
but the features which he considered most objectionable still remained. The portion of history required
to be taken up for the new school was defined as
being 'at least a knowledge of the history of England,
or France, or Germany during the sixteenth and
seventeenth centuries.' He did not hesitate to say that
a worse choice of a period could not possibly have been

made. Not that he would depreciate the great importance of a full and accurate knowledge of those stirring and eventful centuries. No periods better deserved the careful attention of the finished historical scholar when the course of his studies had brought him to them, and he was qualified thoroughly to appreciate the great principles they involved and the disputed facts and characters in which they abounded. But a premature study of those days of controversy, though it might fill the Union with fluent declaimers, would not help to adorn the University with sound historical scholars. The events of those times were viewed through the mists of passion and prejudice almost as much as the events of our own day. People felt as strongly and bitterly for or against the proceedings of the Council of Trent or of the Long Parliament, as for or against the Reform Bill or the Corn Laws. But, in truth, to pick out any late epoch for separate study could only tend to superficial and inaccurate knowledge. To understand for example the cause and origin of the seventeenth century conflict between the prerogative of the Crown and the privilege of Parliament, we must retrace our steps a thousand years : we must look back, on the one hand, to the 'All-thing' and the Mycel-gemot, and, on the other, to the combined elements of imperial and feudal tyranny : 'we must recognize the spirit which dictated the Petition of Right as the same which gathered all England around the banners of returning Godwin, and remember that the "good old cause" was truly that for which Harold died on the field and Waltheof on the scaffold.'

The new examination statute underwent yet another revision, and in its third form an option was given to

the student of two periods, from 1066–1509, or 1509–
1789. The first period was in Freeman's judgement
a bad selection, because the year 1066 was not, properly
speaking, a starting-point in English history[1]. Our
most truly national history, the history of the germs of
all our institutions, lay in the ages before the Norman
Conquest. Macaulay had truly remarked, that the
history of England for a considerable period after the
Conquest is not English history at all, but French[2].
It was not till the reign of Edward I, at the earliest,
that our kings and nobles could be regarded as really
our fellow-countrymen. On the other hand, some of
the greatest and noblest of our English heroes had
lived in the ages which preceded the Norman
Conquest. Alfred was only the most brilliant star in
a bright galaxy: no later periods could furnish a series
of such great names as Edward the Elder, Æthelstan
and Edmund I, the great rivals Canute the Dane and
Edmund Ironside, the patriot Godwin, and last and
greatest of all, his glorious son. 'I cannot conceive'
he adds, 'that the external history of the days of Crecy
and Agincourt, with all their tinsel frippery of chivalry,
can ever be brought into real comparison with those of
true and unmixed Teutonic greatness.' Should it be
determined, however, to ignore early English history, it
would be better to start from a later date than 1066.
And a fair starting-point might be found in the first
appearance of our present House of Commons in the
days of Simon de Montfort and Edward the First. That
was the beginning of a gradual development in the

---

[1] *Thoughts on the Third Form of the New Examination Statute.* Oxford :
J. H. Parker, 1850.
[2] *History*, i. p. 13.

constitutional history of England, and required less knowledge of what went before it than the reign of William the Conqueror, which, being a period of strife between two races, could not be properly understood without a previous knowledge of the position and character of the contending parties.

In his study of the history of England, Freeman himself faithfully adhered to the principles laid down in these pamphlets. It has been seen what value he attached to the labours of scholars like Kemble, Lappenberg, and Palgrave, and it was a happy coincidence that just when new sources for the early history of England were being discovered, and more enlightened methods of historical study and research were being established, a scholar appeared who was eminently fitted to make the most of his opportunities : gifted with broad sympathies, strong critical judgement, an astonishing capacity for work, an ardent love of truth and justice, and a power of imagination sufficient to call up vivid pictures of the past before his mental eye, yet not so exuberant as to escape from the control of reason and judgement.

This imaginative faculty, which is a most essential part of an historian's equipment, was strengthened in Freeman by his practice in early life of writing ballads illustrative of memorable events and the deeds of great men. He was a contributor to two volumes of Ballads which were published in the year 1850. Of these, the earlier, entitled *Original Ballads by Living Authors*, was edited by his old friend Mr. Thompson. Nine ballads in this volume were written by Freeman, the other principal contributors, besides the editor, being Archdeacon Churton, and the Rev. John Mason Neale.

Freeman's ballads are nearly all concerned with countries, places, events, and characters which throughout his life were most dear to his heart and stirred his deepest emotions. The subjects of the principal pieces are 'The triumph of Aristomenes,' the hero who led the Messenians to victory over their Spartan conquerors; 'The Meed of Heroes,' a song supposed to be sung over the graves of the slain at Marathon; 'The funeral of Harold'; 'The last Eucharist in St. Sophia'; 'The last address of the Emperor Constantine Palaiologos to his people on the eve of the capture of Constantinople by the Turks'; 'The martyrdom of Abbot Whiting' (the last Abbot of Glastonbury); 'The death of Lord Brooke in the siege of Lichfield'; 'William Carlos or Carless,' his maternal ancestor, the hero of the Battle of Worcester; and 'The farewell of Don Carlos to Spain,' a subject upon which he had composed some lines when he was eleven years old [1].

The second volume, entitled *Poems, Legendary and Historical*, was a joint production by himself and his friend, Mr. G. W. Cox. Of the twenty-three pieces which it contained, Freeman contributed nine, which, like those in the former volume, were mostly concerned with the early histories of Greece and England. 'The Meed of Heroes,' and 'The Funeral of Harold' were repeated in this volume, and to them were added 'Poseidon and Athene'; 'The Persians at Delphi [2]'; 'Othryades'; 'Harold and Edith'; 'The Battle-field of Hastings'; 'Waltheof at York'; and 'Alaric at Rome.'

[1] See above, p. 11.
[2] Some parts of this poem have recently been set to music as a ballad for men's voices by the Rev. J. H. Mee, Mus. Doc., late Fellow of Merton College, Oxford.

With the exception of a few rough or weak lines here
and there, which indeed are common defects in all ballad
poetry, these pieces are on the whole full of vigour and
spirit.   They breathe that love of freedom, and that
admiration of courage and self-sacrifice in the defence
of national liberty, justice, and righteous laws, which
were always characteristic of him.   A few stanzas from
the 'Meed of Heroes' are here quoted as samples of his
style.

'Awake, ye sons of Marathon,
    Day yokes her golden car ;
Her milk-white steeds are chasing
    The gloom of night afar.

The rosy-fingered morning
    Hath lit the dark-blue wave,
And pours her gentle brightness
    Upon the heroes' grave :

The grave which is our altar,
    Where we this morn must pray,
And to the fallen heroes
    Our richest offerings pay.

.   .   .   .   .

Soft sweeps the blue Aegaean
    Around the heroes' grave,
Soft sweeps the breeze of morning-land
    Where rest the fallen brave.

The mountains bend in homage,
    The trees wave soft in awe,
Over their graves who perished
    For freedom and for law.

But in the gloom of midnight,
    When all beside is still,
Then doth the cry of battle
    Float back from every hill :

Then rise the shadowy warriors,
  And meet again in fight;
But none may see their faces,
  Nor harness glittering bright.

Yet ever on the breezes
  The shouts of war are borne;
The clashing of their weapons,
  The blast of flute and horn,

The clang of shivering harness,
  The neigh of gallant steeds:
As meet the Grecian spearmen
  And quiver-bearing Medes.

  .   .   .   .

But while ye bend in homage,
  To greet the fallen brave,
Think not their dauntless spirits sleep
  Within the voiceless grave.

Their bones below are mouldering,
  Their shadows flit around,
But a happier home than we may tell,
  Their holy souls have found.

Far, far beyond the western hills,
  Where sinks the Sun-god's car:
Beyond Hesperia's laughing plains,
  And Atlas frowning far:

Beyond the stream of Ocean,
  Fast by his farther shore,
Their spirits dwell for ever,
  And sorrow taste no more.

For ever and for ever,
  In bliss that passeth song,
The spirits of the blessed
  Lead the fair hours along.

Theirs is no gloomy midnight,
    Theirs is no noon-tide blaze;
But the Sun-god ever shining
    Glads them with gentle rays.

No winter binds their rivers,
    No summer blasts their fields,
But one fair spring for ever,
    Each choicest floweret yields.

They labour not for ever
    Nor stem the tide of fight:
They pass not o'er the wine-dark seas
    Nor mountain's weary height.

For ever and for ever
    In bliss we may not tell,
By father Chronos' hoary tower
    The happy spirits dwell.

    .   .   .   .   .

Who dies for truth and freedom,
    Who keeps his hands from wrong,
Who gives his people holy laws,
    Who twines the wreath of song;

There in the happy island
    By Ocean's western shore,
Reck not of earth's wild passions,
    And fight and toil no more.

Of this ballad, Mr. John Mason Neale, in a letter to
the author soon after it appeared, remarks, 'I cannot
help writing to say how very much I admire it. I think
I never read one which more fully came up to my idea
of what such a thing should be.' And the poems of
both authors received a hearty tribute of praise from
Sir E. Bulwer Lytton.

'I have just read them,' he writes on February 10, 1851, 'with
very great pleasure, and very great admiration. It is delightful

K 2

to me to see the true and great school of poetry—poetry which, free from verbal affectation and puerile subtleties of thought, warms the blood and stirs the heart—upheld with singular ability. I earnestly wish your work all popular favour for the sake of the good it should do in elevating the public taste.'

Shortly before the appearance of the ballads Freeman's *History of Architecture* was published, a closely printed demy octavo volume of 450 pages. It was a work for which he had been preparing for many years, and represents a great deal of reading [1] as well as of personal observation. The latter, however, had been confined to the buildings of this country, as he had not yet visited the continent.

He claims at the outset the highest place for architecture in the category of art, because, while the other arts, painting, sculpture, and music, owed their origin to a love of beauty and a taste for refinements which belong to an advanced state of civilization, architecture started from the primary physical need of shelter, and gradually took all the other arts into its service.

'The art whose name bespeaks it the chief and queen of all, which presses the noblest of other arts into its service and bends them to its will, is thus at once their beginning and their end: the most lowly in its origin, the most glorious in its perfection: slowly and gradually has it risen, enriched by the contributions of every age, and creed, and nation, from the log-hut of the savage, we might say from the lair of the wild beast, to the fairest works of mere human and heathen beauty; and by a more soaring flight has attained to the unearthly majesty of the Christian minster.'

The design of the work, as stated by the author, was ·to trace the history of the art in its developments

[1] More especially the works of Mr Thomas Hope, Mr. Petit, Professor Willis, Dr. Whewell, Mr. Petrie, and Mr. Gally Knight.

among all nations.'   Hitherto, in his opinion, the study
of architecture had been pursued too much in the spirit
either of the mere antiquary or of the ecclesiologist.
The methods of both were too narrow : but the antiquarian method was not only narrow, it sometimes
became positively irreverent.   It was not merely
that for the pure archaeologist the most sumptuous
specimen of Grecian or Gothic art had scarcely any
higher interest than a barrow or a kistvaen, a rusty
dagger or an antique potsherd, but that he had no
more regard for a building consecrated to Christian
worship than he had for an old barn or an old kitchen.
On the other hand, the interest of the ecclesiastical
antiquary in architecture was directly and essentially
religious, and only incidentally artistic.   His study of
architecture was for a distinctly practical purpose ; his
field was both too narrow and too wide for the purpose
of an historical inquiry : on the one hand it was restricted
to ecclesiastical architecture, on the other it included
a variety of subjects which were concerned with the
furnishing and adornment of churches, and not directly
with their construction, such as painting, sculpture,
wood-carving, glass-staining, embroidery and metalwork.
His own sympathies were entirely with those whom he
calls 'the authors of the great ecclesiological movement ;
the men who have fought the battle of the Church in
her material sanctuaries, and have stood forth so manfully amid suspicion and slander, to convert the modern
preaching-house into the Catholic temple of prayers
and sacraments.'   At the same time many of the disciples of this school were so exclusively devoted to
Gothic forms of architecture, that the historical study
of Grecian and Roman buildings was viewed by them

with suspicion, and even northern Romanesque barely escaped reprobation by being reckoned as a species of Gothic.

In contrast to the narrow methods of these two classes of specialists, his endeavour was to take a comprehensive survey of the growth of architecture in the several styles throughout the known world ;—Pelasgian, Indian, Chinese. Egyptian, the ruined cities of central America, Grecian, Roman, Romanesque, Saracenic, Gothic, and the Renaissance ; Revived Italian, and Revived Grecian. It is interesting to notice that in this early work he had arrived at certain principles and convictions from which he never afterwards deviated. That all architectural styles fall into two main groups, distinguished respectively by the use of the entablature and the arch, of which the Grecian and Gothic are the most perfect developments ; that Egyptian architecture, though bearing some resemblance to Grecian, was not the parent of it ; that the earliest development of Romanesque may be traced in Diocletian's buildings at Spalato, where the entablature is discarded and the arch rises clear from its own supports ; that the perfection of Romanesque is to be found in the Norman form of it rather than in the Lombard or German varieties ; that our Anglo-Saxon forefathers built in a style of their own, differing essentially from the Norman, yet having an equal claim to be regarded as a distinct branch of Romanesque ; that the main idea pervading all Gothic forms is vertical extension, and that the most perfect development of Gothic is the Perpendicular style; that Saracenic architecture was of Roman origin, but resembled Gothic in some of its features, especially the pointed arch, although destitute of the spirit which gives to Gothic its beauty and charm : all these are positions upon which he insists in the treatise, and all his later studies and observations served to strengthen his conviction of their truth. But what is specially remarkable in this early work is the way in which he tries to penetrate to underlying causes, and to trace the influence of race, climate, national character and geographical position in determining structural forms. From this point of view the book may be regarded as a kind of philosophy of architecture, and exhibits a method of inquiry which he never afterwards pursued to the same extent in connexion with architecture or any other subject.

Thus after observing that extreme simplicity is the grand characteristic of Grecian architecture, since the horizontal principle of construction which pervades it is not susceptible of infinite variations like the vertical principle of Gothic, he points out that this simplicity was thoroughly in harmony with the character of the Greeks and of their religion.

'In all the best Greek writers we observe the same simplicity, the almost childlike outpouring of nature, which distinguishes their architecture . . . The Greek tongue is indeed capable of expressing the very subtlest distinctions of thought, it is in truth the very language of metaphysics, but the Greek mind was not in the same degree as the Oriental speculative or abstract. It could not rest upon the dim imaginations of informal powers : it was utterly incapable of all conception of the spiritual and the infinite. The world of the Greek was man : it was among the scenes of common humanity that he found his truest element . . . He looked indeed beyond the grave, but not to an existence of shadowy contemplation, his paradise was local and human, peopled with the valiant and the just of whom his poets had sung. In his lively imagination all nature was full of life : sky, sea, and earth, woods, mountains, and rivers teemed with beings higher than man, but still beings of human form and swayed by human passions. He bowed indeed in adoration to one mightier and more enduring than himself, but still to one like himself personal and human. The deity to whom he prayed was the ancestor from whose blood he was descended, he was one who dwelt in his temple and animated his statue : he could feel love and hatred, gratitude and resentment . . . For such a worship no shrines could be so fitting as those which Grecian art reared . . . A structure whose extent was measured and could be grasped at a single glance well suited a deity who was subject to the accidents of humanity and dwelt in his temple as a mortal prince in his palace. There was no need of aspiring forms to raise the soul of the worshipper above the earth on which he trod . . . He needed no spire to point out a heavenward path, while his very heaven was on earth, far away indeed, and in lovelier regions, but still within the bounds of this lower world, and where the existence that he hoped for was but a brighter form of that which he led in his own city . . . Contrast this merely human beauty, this local, definite, circumscribed temple, with the embodying of the infinite—that ἄπειρον which the Greek deemed a form of evil— in the interior of a Christian minster, especially in its noblest form, the soaring and heaven-pointing Gothic. Place yourself where you will, the view is boundless, nothing occurs to force a limit on the eye in any direction . . . every feature suggests something beyond itself. Stand a little west of the rood-screen : you see into the transepts but you see not their full length : the eye is caught by their eastern arcades, suggestive of the aisles and chapels beyond. If the rood-screen is pierced you see the choir stretching before you, the slim arches beyond the high altar giving a faint glimpse of chapels yet far away, or the mighty reredos proclaiming while concealing their existence : if all this is hidden, you at least see the roof line stretching on till it is lost in the distant perspective. . . . Even the apertures of the triforium, and the narrow passages of the highest range give a hint of something yet further, of interminable mazes leading you know not whither.'

Was not such a pile, which no human eye could comprehend in its full extent at a single glance, and which was vast and boundless in its conception, even when not actually very large, the most fitting 'shrine of the God of the Christian, who dwelleth not in temples made with hands, the Incomprehensible, the Infinite?'

Again, Roman architecture was typical of the Roman character. It was pre-eminently the architecture of strength, the material expression of the stern resolution, the dauntless, inflexible will of a people which subdued the world.

The ideas pervading Romanesque buildings were ' rest and immobility,' while a free, upward, soaring tendency traceable in all parts of the structure was the characteristic of Gothic. The two styles represented two conditions of the world and the Church. During the Romanesque period the influence of Rome still remained paramount, her northern conquerors submitted to her sway in religion and law and the arts of civilization: much of Europe was still Pagan; among many of the Teutonic nations the work of the Church was still of a missionary character, and even in Christian countries she had not arrived at her full influence.

The Romanesque style was the type of the Church thus imperfectly recognized and developed, it was the language of an age of martyrs and confessors. Gothic, on the other hand, ' the pure, the glorious, the peculiar heritage of our own northern race,' was ' the language of the Church when she throws off her mourning, and going forth in triumph over her persecutors, arrays herself with a victor's wreath of the fairest foliage.'

The peculiar charm in his eyes of Gothic was its soaring character, owing to the use of the vertical principle. A Gothic minster was one harmonious whole, the eye throughout was guided upwards, no part seemed an afterthought, but each seemed to grow out of that which was beneath. The Mahometans indeed made a systematic use of the pointed arch, but not being accompanied by vertical details it was merely a solitary feature, and not a development of the vertical principle ; a kind of dead Gothic, the form without the soul.

The publication of the *History of Architecture* was followed within two years by an *Essay on the Origin and Developement of Window Tracery in England*[1]. It was an expansion of three papers which he had read before the Oxford Architectural Society in the course of the years 1846 and 1848, and was now brought out in four parts in 1850 and 1851, making up together an octavo volume of nearly 300 pages. It contained many hundred diagrams of window-heads, executed from his own drawings, illustrating the growth of tracery in three principal styles, the Geometrical, the Decorated or, as he called it, the Flowing, and the Perpendicular ; the examples being grouped in various divisions and subdivisions, as unfoliated, trefoiled, quatrefoiled and subarcuated. Some drawing-books have been preserved which are filled with the original sketches for this work all carefully numbered and indexed.

In 1850 a Royal Commission was appointed to 'inquire into the state, discipline, studies and revenues of the University of Oxford.' The Commissioners were seven in number ; the Rev. A. P. Stanley was secretary, and Mr. Goldwin Smith assistant-secretary. Their meetings were held month by month from October 1850

---

[1] Published by J. H. Parker, Oxford.

to April 1852. Information and suggestions upon the subjects of inquiry were invited from the Heads of Colleges and Halls, the Professors and public officers of the University, and other 'eminent persons who by their station and experience merited public confidence.' Freeman was included in the latter list.

In the circular letter addressed to the persons thus consulted, sixteen points were indicated upon which their opinions were specially invited. Of these Freeman dealt chiefly with eight [1], and first of all with the power of the University to make, repeal, or alter statutes. The power of legislation vested in the University seemed to him to be merely an instance of the right enjoyed by all Corporations to make bye-laws binding on their own members, provided that these regulations did not contradict the known laws of the land; but the actual constitution of the legislative body at that time was, in his opinion, open to many objections. Convocation, in which all who had taken the degree of Master of Arts were entitled to vote, could entertain such questions only as were submitted to it by a Board called the Hebdomadal Board, consisting of the Vice-Chancellor, the Heads of Houses, and the Proctors, and it could merely affirm or reject the propositions which were laid before it by the Board, having no power of amendment. He was of opinion that the sole right of making original substantive proposals to Convocation should be lodged in some board of πρόβουλοι, but the existing constitution of the Board was open to grave objections. It was adapted for executive rather than legislative purposes: it was in the strictest sense an oligarchy: its members

---

[1] *Report of the Oxford University Commission*, pp. 134-143.

were appointed for life, and were irresponsible: they formed practically a distinct rank, socially and politically, having but little interchange of sentiment with the University at large. The normal condition of the Board was one of simple conservatism. On the other hand, the individual members of the Board were open to influence in the way of ministerial favour, or of a popular outcry for sweeping alterations which more moderate reforms at an earlier date might have averted. The natural tendency of such a body was to postpone changes till they were forced upon it; in short, to 'diversify a normal state of quiescence by an occasional state of revolution.'

For this permanent irresponsible body he recommended the substitution of an elective responsible Board. Such a Board, consisting of members elected for some definite period out of the mass of Convocation, would contain an element of life favourable to constant but moderate reform. But while he thought that the initiative should be confined to this Board of preliminary councillors, he was strongly of opinion that a right of amendment should be granted to Convocation. Under the existing system Convocation was in the awkward position of being compelled to accept entire, or to reject entire, any measure which was submitted to it. It often happened that some modified form of the measure would be far more satisfactory than either of these alternatives. As it was, a measure approved in principle might be rejected on account of faulty details, or it might be accepted with objectionable details, because the general principle was approved. The necessity of sending back all rejected measures to the Hebdomadal Board, introduced a clumsy and tedious mode of proceeding: a measure once rejected might be proposed again and again, and perhaps at last carried by reason of sheer weariness. The new Examination Statute was a case in point: it had been produced in four shapes and carried piecemeal: probably no one was exactly satisfied with it at any stage, but voted for or against some portion as the lesser of two evils.

He strongly advocated a University examination for Matriculation. As things were, the standard of admission was left to the discretion of each College. In some Colleges the examination was a reality, in others little more than nominal. A uniform standard he considered to be most desirable, and one pitched much higher than the average at that time; he should suggest almost as high as the standard for the ordinary degree: for if boys had not attained at school the small amount of classical learning required for the latter, it was hard to imagine to what their studies during so many years had been directed. As to rendering the higher degrees real tests of merit, he doubted the possibility of imparting any very practical character to the three higher faculties of Divinity, Law, and Medicine, but he strongly recommended that the degree of Master of Arts should not be conferred simply as a matter of course, after a certain lapse of time, upon all who might with whatever difficulty have obtained an inferior degree, but that it should be made a really honourable distinction conferred upon those who had passed a real searching examination. By such a system, while the numbers of Convocation would be diminished, the quality of the body would be improved, for the members would be of the *élite* of the University. The degree would remain optional as at present, only those who sought it would have to enter upon a further course of study. And if there were real examinations for Matriculation, and for the M.A. degree, it followed almost as a matter of course, that the length of time required for the first degree might be diminished.

As to the effect of existing limitations in elections to Fellowships and in their tenure, he deprecated any sweeping change on any general theory. If Fellowships and Scholarships were simply rewards of merit, of course all limitations should be abolished, but that was not the view taken by the founders, and he did not see how, even under all changes of circumstances, it could fairly be put forward at the present day. Regarding a Fellowship or Scholarship as a provision for a student in the University, there seemed to be no wrong or absurdity in a founder giving a preference to persons in some way connected with himself. Where the bounty of the founder did not habitually go to undeserving persons he could see no reason for interfering with the existing mode of election, merely to bring things into accordance with some pre-conceived system. With regard to the tenure of Fellowships, he said :—

'It can hardly be necessary to refute the wild notion of their being made tenable by married men : if the proposers of such a scheme think the Collegiate system bad in itself it would be much better directly to propose its suppression than to attempt thus covertly to destroy its most essential feature.'

But he thought it might be advisable to limit the tenure of Fellowships to a certain number of years. A Fellowship was an admirable position for a young man, but was hardly suited for one advanced in life. Elderly Fellows, and especially if they were non-resident, were too often a dead weight on the College.

With regard to the means of rendering Bodley's Library more generally useful, he maintained now, as he did ever afterwards, that the use of the Library would be very greatly increased, if books were, under proper restrictions and securities, allowed to be removed and consulted at home.

' For want of this power,' he says, ' I have individually made very little use of the Library, always preferring any other mode of obtaining access to a book . . . The necessity of consulting a book in the Library renders it almost impossible to make references at the moment when they are actually wanted —especially in cases when they are wanted for any literary composition. Notes taken in the Library and made use of at home, are a very poor substitute for the presence of the volume itself.'

Even allowing for occasional inconvenience arising from the book wanted by one reader being in the possession of another, he thought the Library would be far more profitable to students generally if some such plan as he recommended was adopted.

He concluded his paper by some remarks in justification of the appointment of the Royal Commission, which some persons resented as an unwarrantable attack upon the privileges and independence of the University and Colleges; refusing on this ground to give the evidence and information which they were requested to supply. Such a refusal he considered to be very ill-advised, because if the Commission was to present any report upon the state of the University, it was most desirable that it should be made as full and fair as possible by collecting statements of facts and opinions from all quarters and persons of all ways of thinking. Then, as to proposed alterations of statutes, he pointed out that in the Caroline or Laudian statutes by which the University had been governed since 1636, there were certain portions which it was generally understood could not be altered without the sanction of the Crown. One of these related to the constitution of the Hebdomadal Board, one of the evils which most needed reform, but it was not likely that the royal sanction would be given to any proposal for reform without a full and sufficient inquiry.

The case of the Colleges raised a more difficult question. They were for the most part governed by statutes given by persons long since deceased, in many cases without any power of alteration being reserved either to the Society or to any other authority, and the consciences of the members were bound by a solemn oath to observe these statutes and not to receive any others. Upon this point he observes :—

'With every respect for the possible scruples of others, I strongly incline to the belief that as the rights of the founder originally to impose such obligations must, by the very nature of civil society, have proceeded from the express or tacit licence of the State, every such obligation is incurred with an implicit reservation of the right of the Supreme power to revoke the licence originally given, and consequently that to admit new statutes sanctioned by the Legislature would not involve the guilt of perjury. I believe all rights and possessions both of individuals and corporations to proceed from the State, and to be at any time liable to *privilegia* affecting them. But the enacting of such privilegia has ever been esteemed the most delicate and difficult office of any legislative body: and the delicacy and difficulty in the case of corporations, though second, is only second to that which exists in the case of individuals . . . I believe then that the Legislature may lawfully alter statutes and that no corporation would be justified in offering resistance. Whether the existing members would be bound to resign their endowments is a question for their individual consciences. But on the other hand no power of the Legislature ought to be exercised with greater discretion and hesitation : the greatest possible presumption should be allowed in favour of the existing statutes, and no change entertained without some demonstrably weighty cause. Hasty meddling with such matters would be little less than a breach of faith on the part of the State, which is clearly pledged to strict observance of its charters under all ordinary circumstances.'

The principal reforms recommended in the Report of the Commissioners were embodied in an Act of Parliament entitled the Oxford University Act, passed in 1854. By the old conservative party in the University it was regarded with bitter animosity, and when the bill was first introduced in the House of Commons in 1853, a strong petition against it was prepared by the Hebdomadal Board, and submitted to Convocation. On the other hand, a protest against the petition was drawn up by members of the Tutors' Association, which was in favour of reform. Convocation met in large numbers, and amidst great excitement, on March 31, in the Sheldonian Theatre. The 'non placets' seemed to exceed the 'placets,' but a scrutiny was demanded. Freeman spoke earnestly against the petition, in Latin, in which all speeches in Convocation had to be made at that time except by special permission.

Insignissime Vice Cancellarie, vosque egregii procuratores ; nunquam ni fallor rem majorem nobis tractandam obtulit rerum status. Id enim decernendum est utrum Rogatio nuper de Universitate reformandâ ad Senatum lata consentientem sibi sit an repugnantem habitura Universitatem . . . Sunt scilicet qui dicunt inimicos nescio quos in Academiam conjurasse, quibus persuasum sit aliquid libertati nostrae Rogationis minitari auctores. Immo quidem si libertati illi academicae, rei mihi

quidem ante omnes carissimae, periculi aliquid impendere
censerem nunquam me sibi consentientem haberet Rogatio.
At longè aliter res sese habet. Quales enim homines hodie
res nostras tractant? Quales hodie rempublicam administrant?
Num homines ab Academia prorsus alieni, artium liberalium
ignari, Boeotiae camporum agricolae? Quinam verus Rogationis
auctor habendus est, cujusmodi viros consentientes habet?
Auctor est vir ille longè omnium clarissimus, Academiae
senator, Academiae simul ac patriae decus. Adstipulantur
tanto viro collegae minimè indigni. Qualis denique est ipsa
Rogatio? qualia aufert? qualia imponit? Oligarchiam nimirum
tollit, quam nemo praeter ejus participes unquam defendere
conatus est; libertatem ipsam cujus scilicet causâ Rogationi
inclamatur, libertatem quâ hodie vix, aut ne vix quidem,
fruimur, libertatem illam veram atque antiquam Academiae
reddere decrevit[1]. Hinc ni fallor illae lacrimae: instat enim
oligarchiae dies ultima: conventum illum Hebdomadalem cujus
cygneam hanc cantilenam hodie audivimus omnino delendum
esse statuit: Academiae autem veris Magistris, veris doctoribus
Academiae regimen more majorum tradit[2]. Quodsi (quod absit)
hujusmodi petitionem senatui obtrudamus, Academiam omnibus

[1] Originally, in all probability, the House of Congregation, in which all
the Masters had a seat, was the sole legislative body for the University.
Under the Laudian Statutes many of its functions were transferred to
the Hebdomadal Board, and those which it retained were purely formal.
By the Act of 1854 a new 'Congregation' was created, consisting of all
resident members of Convocation, and was invested with the power of
amending measures submitted to it by the Hebdomadal Council.

[2] The Act of 1854 substituted for the old Hebdomadal Board a new
body called the Hebdomadal Council, composed partly of official, and
partly of elected members. Thus constituted it corresponded very nearly
to the form which Freeman had suggested in his evidence to the Commissioners. The Commissioners themselves, in the conclusion of their
Report, had recommended a far more oligarchical body, of which Freeman
expressed strong disapproval in a pamphlet which he published soon
after the appearance of the Report. The Hebdomadal Council retains
the initiative in legislation formerly exercised by the Board, but every
measure has to be promulgated in Congregation, and may be amended
by that body, before it is submitted to Convocation for final adoption or
rejection. See preceding note.

civibus ludibrio, viris de patriâ optime meritis etiam impedi-
mento dabimus; neque aliquem, nisi forte factionis omnium
in Republicâ indoctissimae coryphaeos talis causae assertorem
habebimus . . . Quare huic petitioni minimè consentire
possum : vosque omnes Academici, si vobis Academiae, immo
si patriae, commodum ac libertas cordi sunt omnes hujusmodi
petitiones mecum obsecror antiquandas decernatis.'

The petition, however, was carried by the narrow
majority of two—193 to 191.

It is clear from the remarks which Freeman addressed
to the Commissioners as well as from his pamphlets on
the new Examination Statute, that his views in regard to
the University were those of a conservative reformer.
He wished to see abuses removed and improvements
effected by amending and remodelling ancient forms
rather than by creating new ones. And he strongly
deprecated alterations in the statutes or customs of
a College, unless they could be proved to work badly.
Varieties and peculiarities, when not positively evil, were
better than a dull dead level of uniformity.

His opinions on Parliamentary reform were conceived
in the same cautious spirit. In a letter to the *Spectator*
of November 8, 1851, referring to a motion in Parliament
by Mr. Locke King for leave to bring in a bill to place
householders in counties and in towns on the same footing
in respect to the franchise, he remarks, that the admission of the rural labourer to the franchise would be the
greatest political change which had ever been advocated.
In nearly all countries the landowners and the citizens
were the two classes which enjoyed political rights. In
England the peasant class had long been held back in
villainage. They had now obtained civil liberty : whether
they were yet fitted for the exercise of political rights

admitted of a doubt. He wished to see the suffrage limited to a certain standard : only let that standard be fixed at a point attainable by every steady, sober, and prudent man. Let the franchise, in short, be to the working classes a reward of industry and forethought. But what point would exactly meet this requirement he must leave to be settled by statists more skilled than himself. In a subsequent letter in the *Spectator* of December 20, he advocated some system by which the electors of members of Parliament should be themselves elected by the people. Many men who were not capable of weighing the comparative merits of two political candidates might very well be able to determine which of their neighbours were best qualified by natural ability, good sense, and honesty, to decide for them. He did not approve of the principle of 'one man, one vote.' It seemed to him unreasonable and unjust to compel a man to vote in one place only who might have an equal interest in other places, and he thought that wherever a man had property he was most likely to do his duty by it, if it carried with it a right to vote.

Between the years 1853 and 1855, he wrote several letters to the *Spectator* on the subject of the Crimean War. In the first of these letters, dated October 29, 1853, he declared himself to be in favour of the war. After quoting the old rhymes, expressing detestation alike

'Of the Russians and the Turks
With their Babylonish works.'

he said that he looked upon Russia as the embodiment of modern centralized despotism, the foe of political and civil liberty, the despoiler of Poland and Sweden, the abettor of Austria. He was willing to say 'Amen' to the old prayer which begged for deliverance from ' Pope and Turk,' and if the metre permitted, he would contentedly add the Czar to the same worshipful company. But he had come to the conclusion that in the present condition of affairs, if the choice had to be made between the Sultan and Czar, the former was the less evil of the two. There was, indeed, an irreconcilable antagonism between East and West, which had manifested itself through twenty-four centuries in a succession of contests between Greek and Persian, Roman and Parthian, Frank and Saracen, Goth and Moor, Venetian and Ottoman. The Western world was progressive, the Eastern was stationary. In the West, there had been a continuous development of political life from Theseus to Gladstone : in the East, there had been no advance from Nebuchadnezzar to Abdul Medjid. The day must come, and was steadily approaching, when a Christian state or Christian states must be formed south of the Danube : but if the Muscovite was admitted into those regions it might be indefinitely postponed. Russia was to south-eastern Europe what Macedonia was to Greece in the days of Demosthenes—a strong, semi-barbarous power threatening to overwhelm its weaker neighbours. And as Demosthenes courted alliance with Persia in order to save Greece from Macedonia, so might the support of the Turk be justified in order to save those parts of Europe which he held in subjection from falling under the yoke of a yet stronger despotism. Certainly it was a disagreeable and odious necessity, and there was an inconsistency in resisting the encroachments of the Russians in southern Europe when no opposition had been offered to them in crossing the Eider, and carrying their brigandage into the heart of Jutland. To have checked Russian aggression years before on behalf of gallant Poland, or of our own Swedish brethren, would have been a noble undertaking, and for his own part he abhorred the tyrant, Louis Napoleon, and Francis Joseph the so-called Emperor of Austria, just as much as he did the Czar. But on the principles on which European nations had acted for some centuries, he thought the war was just, and, once undertaken, it must be pressed with vigour.

But as the war went on, his opinions underwent a change which ended in the conviction that it had been unjust from the beginning. The causes of this change are clearly explained in a letter to the *Spectator*, April 16, 1855. There were five reasons, he said, which had formerly induced him to justify the war.

i. A belief that there was some treaty which bound England to support the integrity and independence of the Ottoman Empire.

ii. A belief that it was desirable on European ground to check the advance of Russia.

iii. A belief that for the sake of the Christians in southeastern Europe it was better to maintain things as they were for a time, because the weak despotism of the Turk could be more easily destroyed some day, than the strong despotism of the Russian.

iv. That on the principles of international law as defined by technical writers like Vattel, the war seemed to be just.

v. That it was acquiesced in by those men, like Mr. Gladstone, for whose judgement he had the highest respect.

Now of these five reasons, the first had turned out to be a delusion. There was no treaty, such as he had supposed, in existence.

As to the fourth, it must be borne in mind that international law was not obligatory like statute law.

International laws were not, strictly speaking, laws at all, but merely collections of maxims deriving their weight from the authority of the men who delivered them. On Vattel's principles the support of Turkey might be justifiable, but it was not obligatory.

As to the second and third reasons, he still held that it was not for the advantage of Wallachians, Slavonians, Bulgarians, and Greeks, to exchange the Ottoman for the Russian despot. Could he hinder such a result by merely giving a vote he would give it. But the difference was not so great as to justify us in sacrificing the lives of thousands of Englishmen in order to keep things as they were. He had formerly thought more lightly of war than he did now, since the events of the past year had brought him face to face with its horrors. He had now come to regard war as the most prodigious of all evils, except the loss of national liberty. Unless that was threatened there could be no excuse for war. Already the war had stopped all domestic legislation, and instead of a Reform Bill we had a Siege of Sebastopol. If he was asked whether he would surrender the position of England as a great European power, he answered, undoubtedly, if it could only be maintained at the price of misery and crime. As long as she retained free institutions England was a great power, and he supposed every one with a soul above that of a gentleman usher or a lady-in-waiting would rather be a free citizen of Norway, or Switzerland, than a French or Austrian slave. He was far from being indifferent to the greatness and glory of his country; only he regarded greatness and glory as consisting not in mere *bigness*, but in a free government at home, and a righteous policy abroad. He protested also against carrying on a war merely to guard against vague contingent possibilities, suggested for the most part by distrust of an opponent's sincerity. On such pretexts nations might go on fighting for ever. And the experience of history proved that wars to maintain what was supposed to be the balance of power were generally futile. England and Austria, for example, had once combined to force a king of their own choice upon the Spaniards, because it was feared that the balance of power would be disturbed if France and Spain were ruled by kinsmen. After a great deal of glory and misery the allies had to leave Spain in the hands of the French sovereign. But instead of combining to upset the balance of power, the royal kinsmen soon went to war about their own quarrels.

In another letter, written in August of the same year, he pointed out that after the Conference at Vienna, when some pacific overtures from Russia were rejected, the war had entirely changed its character. From being a war in defence of Turkey it had become a war of aggression against Russia, because Russia would not guarantee the integrity and independence of the Ottoman Empire. But to insist on a guarantee for the integrity of Turkey was an act of deliberate wickedness; for it meant a guarantee to perpetuate the Turk's oppression of his European subjects. It was the simple duty of the Slavonian and Hellenic subjects of the Turk to cast off the yoke if they could, and to guarantee the Turkish rule over them would be to force France and England to undo the glories of Navarino. When we were attacked, let us defend ourselves, and in monstrous cases of oppression let us arm to maintain the independence of nations: but let the balance of power, and the integrity of the Ottoman Empire be left to take care of themselves.

He believed in a God who judged the earth, and when men attempted to usurp the functions of Providence, Providence often took the wise in their own craftiness, and taught them in the end the folly of that long-sighted policy which inflicted immediate wrongs and evils in order to avert distant ones which might or might not happen. If, for instance, Russia should succeed in getting Constantinople, it was highly probable that the Czar's dominions would be split into two divisions— a Russian and a Byzantine Empire.

He felt perhaps all the more keenly on the subject of the Crimean War because he was giving particular attention at this time to the later history of Greece, and of the Byzantine Empire. The results of his studies in this direction found expression in two long and very able articles which he contributed to the *North British Quarterly Review* in August, 1854, and February, 1855. They are interesting also as being the earliest of many endeavours to prove the importance of neglected periods of history, and so to strengthen that idea of the unity of history which it was one great aim of his life to enforce. The first of the two articles is a review of Niebuhr's *Lectures on Ancient History*, and of the sixth, seventh, and eighth volumes of Thirlwall's *History of Greece*, but the greater part of it is devoted to pointing out the interest and importance of the Macedonian period of Grecian history, which had received, in this country at least, far less attention than it deserved. This comparative neglect was due partly, as he observed, to the want of a text book, after the student had lost the guidance of Thucydides, and Xenophon, and Demosthenes, and had to 'pick his way amidst the careless blunders of Plutarch, the impenetrable stupidity of Diodorus, the scandalous gossip of

Athenaeus, and the antiquarian twaddle of Pausanias ; '
and partly it was owing to the character of the history
itself, concerned as it was with the dregs of a nation the
vigour of whose political and literary life had passed
away for ever. Yet he maintained that the rise of the
Macedonian state under its two great princes, the spread
of Hellenism in Asia through the conquests of Alexander,
the great political phenomenon of the Achaean league,
and even the momentary glory of young Sparta under
the last Cleomenes, were events at once highly important
and instructive.

Niebuhr's lectures and Thirlwall's history had done
much to rescue this period from oblivion, but he considered that two works were still needed to complete that
cycle of ancient history, of which the writings of Arnold,
Thirlwall, Grote, and Merivale formed such noble portions.
One want was a history of Macedonia, tracing out all
that could be discovered of the ethnology and early history of that country, and narrating in detail the later
history of Greece after Macedonia became the dominant
power: and this should be written as far as possible
from a Macedonian point of view. The other want
was more difficult to supply—a history of Graeco-
Macedonian power in the East, tracing the fortunes of
the oriental kingdoms which rose out of Alexander's
conquests, and investigating the influence of Greek
literature, philosophy, and art on those countries which
became more or less Hellenized, as well as the reciprocal
influence of eastern modes of thought upon the later
Grecian mind. The interest of such an inquiry consisted
in contemplating on the one hand the decline of Greece,
yet accompanied by an increased spread of Grecian
influence over the world : and on the other, the slow and

sure advance of Rome leading the former masters of the
world 'down the gradual descent of alliance, dependence,
subjugation, and amalgamation.'   And if the gradual
advance of Roman power and its still more gradual
decline contained, as in fact they did, the history of the
civilized world, it was surely no uninstructive task to trace
the steps by which Rome gradually wound the toils of her
tortuous diplomacy around the fairest of her conquests.
Bishop Thirlwall had truly remarked that in such arts
the Roman Senate surpassed every cabinet, ancient and
modern : and it was to them, more than to its pilum and
broadsword, that Rome owed the reduction of Macedonia
into a province of a city of which Demosthenes and Philip
may have barely heard the name.   Again, if it was remembered how the Hellenized nations took up the name and
position of Romans, and preserved the political continuity
of the Roman Empire in a Megarian and Milesian colony
for hundreds of years after the old Rome had forgotten her
ancient mission, it would be no unprofitable speculation
to trace the steps by which the first impulse was given
to so strange and permanent a union between the intellectual supremacy of Greece and the political eternity of
Rome.

His second article, entitled 'Finlay on the Byzantine
Empire,' was a review of Mr. Finlay's *History of Greece*,
and more especially that part of it which dealt with the
events between A.D. 716 and A.D. 1453.   He welcomed
in this great work the first serious attempt to do justice
to a period which had been treated not merely with
neglect, but with the utmost scorn and contempt as the
barren record of an age of moral and political emptiness.
He observes that under the phrases of 'Greek Empire'
and 'the Lower Empire,' readers and writers were content

to veil their ignorance of a thousand years of eventful history. The popular belief seemed to be that from the fifth to the fifteenth century an empire of some kind maintained itself in Constantinople, but that during the whole of that time it was in a dying state, that the princes were mere tyrants, its people mere slaves and cowards with whose actions it was unnecessary to burden the memory; and that it was a good riddance when the last Byzantine historian was blown into the air by our brave allies the Turks. Yet this despised empire exhibited for ages the only regular systematic government in the world, and the legislation of Justinian, Leo, and Basil, gave to a large portion of the human race the then unique blessing of a regular, though despotic, administration of justice and of civil order. Nor need the military student disdain to study the exploits of Belisarius and Heraclius, of Nicephorus and Zimisces, and Basil the slayer of the Bulgarians. The legions of this power, despised as decrepit, had in one century restored the imperial sway from the Euphrates to the Ocean, and in the next planted the Roman eagle upon the palaces of the great king. This empire had endured the first onslaught of the victorious Saracen, had defended her frontier for three glorious centuries, had won back province after province and made the successor of the prophet tremble before the arm of the triumphant Caesar.

He points out that one cause of this portion of history being treated with contempt, was the unattractive character of the Byzantine historians. Few but professed scholars had the patience to read their bulky and tedious volumes. The consequence was that by English readers Byzantine history had been known, so far as it was known at all, almost exclusively through the

medium of Gibbon, who found in its events and characters only too many opportunities for indulging in
his faculty of sarcasm, and his love of anecdotes that
exhibited the weak or ludicrous side of things and persons. Moreover, the Byzantine Empire was essentially
a conservative, rather than a progressive or creative
power. And therefore it did not excite enthusiasm. ' It
was an aged state living in the memory of the past and
inheriting a power and a glory which it had to maintain or
to recover : unlike the youthful nations of the West, with
their future before them, and their power and glory yet
to be won.' It produced a never-failing succession of able
men, but few very great men, and only one or two of the
heroic type. Sagacious legislators, able administrators.
valiant generals, profound scholars, acute theologians,
were the natural products of the soil for century after
century. They rose one after another, each in his time
and place, to carry on the work of a scientifically ordered
machine of government. Strong men were they in their
day, but their strength lay in preserving and restoring,
not in creating. The Macedonian and the Roman must
yield the palm to the higher genius and purer virtue of
the Slavonian conqueror of Italy and Africa ; but while
Alexander and Caesar founded empires, Belisarius could
but win back the dismembered provinces of a decaying
one which was falling to pieces.

' At last, when all was over, when the political succession of
1500 years was doomed to extinction, when the day of restoration, reform, and preservation had all passed by, when the
Empire had shrunk to a single city, and that city contained but
one man worthy of the name of king or citizen, the last Emperor
of the Romans could but die in the breach before the onslaught
of the barbarian, while Italy was wasting her strength in the
warfare of selfish condottieri, and England shedding her best

blood to decide the genealogical quarrels of the White and the Red Rose.

'Again, the history of Constantinople is mainly a record of despotic power. It is the story of a government, not of a nation : of a government, indeed, which, with all its crimes, discharged for many centuries its functions better than any contemporary government in the world, but which never excited that warmth of patriotic affection which attaches to the stormiest republic in which the citizen feels that he himself is a partner, and often to the vilest despotism exercised by a tyrant who is still felt to be the chief of his own people. The Emperor of the Romans never became a national sovereign to the Egyptian or the Syrian, or even to the Sicilian or Peloponnesian Greek.'

Nevertheless, Constantinople continued to be for 9co years the greatest city in Europe, while the western nations were still wrapped in the gloom and confusion of the really dark ages.

' The history of the Eastern Empire is at once an encouragement and a warning to all highly civilized communities : it shows the vitality which may be imparted to a scientifically constructed machine of government, how great a superiority is conferred by the mere possession of civil and social order upon an aged and feeble power, supported by little or no national feeling, and surrounded by fresh and vigorous enemies. But at the same time it shows that this vitality may become something little better than "life in death," and suggests the idea that there may be circumstances in which civilization and civil government actually become impediments to human progress.'

Freeman describes with great clearness and succinctness the steps by which the Empire, whose seat of government was at Constantinople, gradually became less Roman and more Greek in character, mainly through the influence of the Church, which was the bond of union between those portions of the Empire which spoke the Greek tongue and adhered to the orthodox faith. The Church created a kind of artificial Greek nation: a philological, ecclesiastical and political, but not an ethnological unity, which has survived to the present day. The true Greek was distinguished by the combination of language and religion.

'The Russian and the Servian has not become Greek because he has the tie of religion only without that of language: the Mahometan or Latin renegade of Hellenic blood and speech is no longer recognized as Greek because he has the tie of language only without that of religion. This process of change was accelerated during the seventh and eighth centuries by the Arabian conquests which cut off first Syria and Egypt, always the least amenable to civil control and ecclesiastical discipline, and afterwards the Latin province of Africa. Spain had been already lost.'

The latter part of the review contains some interesting remarks upon the prolonged struggle of the Eastern Empire with Bulgarian and Russian invaders, and the question is raised, whether the cause of Christianity and of civilization might not have been promoted if Constantinople had fallen into their hands, or if it had become the capital of the great Servian Empire in the fourteenth century.

'The abiding majesty of the Roman name, and the personal greatness of the emperors who were engaged in these wars, make us sympathize almost mechanically with the Byzantine cause.'

But it had to be remembered that—

'the Bulgarians, Russians, and Servians were not mere savages like the wandering Huns, nor yet, like the Saracens and Ottomans, the representatives of a rival system of religion, polity, and social life. They were to the Eastern Empire what the Teutonic nations were to the Western, half conquerors, half pupils. They looked up with reverence to the city from which they had derived their religion, and whose civilization they had begun to appreciate and adopt. The rulers of Russia in those days were princes of our own blood—the Scandinavian conquerors of a Slavonian people. Established on the throne of the Caesars, a Varangian Emperor might have proved the Theodoric or the Charlemagne of the East, and a Russian conquest in the ninth century might have prevented the necessity of contending against one in the nineteenth.'

It is a remarkable evidence of the extent and variety of Freeman's studies at this period, and of the readiness and ease with which he could write upon widely different subjects, that within the compass of twelve months, besides the two articles already referred to in the *North British Review*, he contributed another to the *Quarterly Review* for June, 1854, upon 'Queen Elizabeth and her Favourites.' In this article the character of the great Queen, and the characters of her several favourites are drawn with much spirit and vigour. A strong resemblance to Macaulay, which begins to be traceable in his writing about this time, is especially striking in this article, in which all that can be said first on one side of the subject, and then on the other, is piled up after Macaulay's manner in a series of short incisive sentences, so as to make the contrast between the two views as sharply defined as possible. Such are the passages in which the good and bad qualities of Elizabeth are alternately summed up.

'Elizabeth as drawn by her admirers, and Elizabeth as drawn by her enemies, appear like the portraits of two wholly distinct women. And yet neither portrait is to be set aside as an entirely fictitious one. We need not dispute whether the shield is gold or silver, whether the chamaeleon is green or

blue . . . . The knight approaching the shield from one side
alone might well pronounce it to be all golden . . . . Most of our
kings have been men of more than average ability ; several of
them have been men of pre-eminent genius. But since the
mighty Norman first set foot upon our shores, one prince alone
has worn his crown who can dispute the first rank with the
daughter of Henry VIII and of Anne Boleyn. The first
Edward, great alike in war and peace, the founder of our
commerce, the refounder of our law, may indeed claim a place
by the side of one who in so many respects trod in the same
line of policy. During the forty-five years which beheld
England under the sway of Elizabeth, it rose from a secondary position among the powers of Europe to a level with the
mightiest of empires . . . . Under Elizabeth arose that naval
greatness which has since formed our chief glory : under her
auspices Drake, Frobisher, and Raleigh extended alike the
dominions of their sovereign and the limits of the habitable
world. She first raised her own England to the rank of
mistress of the ocean, and laid the first foundation of another
England on its further shore. She could not only boast of
hurling defiance at Parma and at Spain, but her diplomatic and
commercial intercourse embraced the Czar of Muscovy and the
Sophi of Persia.

'She was looked to by all Europe as the bulwark of Protestantism and of liberty, and was recompensed by the offer
of foreign crowns which she had the wisdom to refuse. At
home she established and maintained a government which
for those times was both firm and gentle, a despotism which
drew its power from the national affection. Nearly her whole
reign was one triumphal procession. Everywhere her people
gathered round her as round a parent : gracious and accessible
to all, no petitioner was repulsed from her presence. Stern
and unbending when necessity required it, she knew how to
give way with grace or, by anticipating remonstrance, to avoid
the necessity of yielding. She reared up the fabric of a Church
free alike from the superstition of the Papist and the licentious-
ness of the Puritan. . . . Versed in all the learning and accom-
plishments of her age, delighting in the gaiety and splendour
of a court, she never forgot the duties of a real ruler in the

idleness and dissipation of the vulgar mob of princes. She maintained the credit of her kingdom abroad without plunging into unnecessary or expensive wars: she encouraged the arts of peace without suffering the decay of a martial spirit: she maintained a magnificent court without its being purchased by the misery of the nation. The true parent of her people, she won the love in which she delighted : she ascended the throne amid their acclamations ; and if from the satiety which comes with long familiarity she did not descend to her grave amid their tears, her memory soon became dearer to them than ever from the contrast she presented to her inglorious suc-cessor, and remained thenceforward embalmed among the most precious recollections of their past history.'

He then invites the contemplation of her character from the opposite point of view.

'The mighty queen is transformed into a weak, if not a vicious woman . . . . From youth to old age she was the slave of the most egregious personal vanity. Queen and heroine. sacred Majesty and Defender of the Faith, were titles less acceptable to the royal ear than the flattery which extolled the royal person as surpassing the beauty of all women, past, present, or to come. The sovereign of seventy was never more delighted than when her courtiers exchanged the respectful demeanour of subjects for a strain of amorous adula-tion which might have disgusted a sensible girl of seventeen.... Her personal habits were those of one, who had thrown off alike the dignity of the monarch and the gentleness of the woman. Her diversions seem to have surpassed the ordinary brutality of the times. The "most godly queen" interlarded her discourse with oaths worthy of a Rufus or a John : she boxed the ear of one courtier, and spat upon the fringed mantle of another. The hand of the sovereign was open to receive, and shut when she should repay : her military schemes were ruined by an unworthy parsimony. . . . Her government was that of a despot : the rights of Parliament were openly jeered at : patents and monopolies enriched her favourites with wealth wrung from the scanty fare of the peasant and the artisan. Although her personal religion was doubtful, she enforced a conformity with her external standard by a rigorous persecution in all directions. While the fires of Smithfield still received an occasional Protestant, the lay votary of Rome had to struggle through life with confiscation or imprisonment, and his spiritual adviser lived in a perpetual apprehension that the last sight afforded him in this world would be that of his own bowels committed to the flames before his eyes. . . . Yet this woman takes her place by common consent among the very ablest of our rulers. Forty-five years of glory did England owe to her between the contemptible administrations of her immediate forerunner and her immediate successor : and the longer we contemplate her chequered nature the more we are impressed with the truth of the dictum, that in Elizabeth there were two wholly distinct characters, in one of which she was greater than man, and in the other less than woman.'

Oaklands was Freeman's home for seven years, during which his literary industry was incessant. In addition to the labours already described, he was now a regular writer of reviews for the *Guardian*, and he still frequently contributed papers to the *Ecclesiologist* and *Ecclesiastick* on historical and architectural subjects. In the course of the summer months he attended the annual meetings of the Archaeological Institute, and of various Archaeo-logical societies, more especially the Cambrian. The most important papers which he wrote during this period for the journal of the Archaeological Institute were—'On the Anglo-Saxon remains at Iver Church, Bucks,' read at the meeting in London in January 1850; 'On the preservation and restoration of ancient monuments,' read at Bristol, July 29, 1851. Of three papers written on Dorchester Abbey Church in 1852, the first two were read at a meeting of the Institute at Oxford, the third contains the substance of an address delivered at Dorchester itself. A paper 'On Harold

and Earl Godwine' was read at the meeting in Chichester
in July, 1853. Two papers on the life and death of Earl
Godwine appear in the journal of the Institute for 1854,
and a third in the journal for 1855. In 1850 he brought
out a small volume, published by Pickering, on the
Architecture of Llandaff Cathedral, including 'an Essay
towards a History of the Fabric,' and throughout the
time of his sojourn at Oaklands he was preparing, in conjunction with his friend Mr. Basil Jones, an elaborate history of the See and Cathedral Church of St. David's, which
involved many visits to that beautiful and remote spot,
besides a vast deal of research and correspondence.

It seems to have been his habit to anticipate the
summer meetings of the Archaeological Institute by
going into the neighbourhood a few days beforehand, and
rapidly visiting as many places as he could, sketchbook
and notebook in hand, so that he had observed the most
characteristic features of the buildings, and worked up
a good deal of local history before other members of the
Society came upon the scene. Thus before the meeting
at Chichester in 1853, he made a ramble by himself
through Sussex from east to west, visiting Bayham
Abbey, on the borders of Kent, Wadhurst, Rye, Win-
chelsea, Hastings, Pevensey, Hurstmonceux, and Battle.
And after the meeting was over he worked back again
eastwards through the western division of the county,
visiting Arundel, Tarring, Broadwater, Sompting, Old
and New Shoreham, Steyning, Bramber, Brighton. and
Lewes.

The quantity and the variety of the literary work
which he had on hand involved of course a great deal
of miscellaneous reading, but, the records of his diary
prove that he was also steadily working through the

The Historian of the Norman Conquest
Usk Castle : Monmouthshire
W.G. Smith del Aug. 18. 1876.

course of historical study which he had prescribed for
himself, stretching from the days of the greatness of
Greece and Rome down to modern times. Ten days after
he had settled at Oaklands he began Diodorus Siculus.
Between October, 1848, and the end of February, 1849,
he read volumes four, five, and six of Grote's *History
of Greece*, Thierry's *History of the Norman Conquest*,
Guizot's *History of Civilization*, and Kemble's *Saxons in
England*. Macaulay's volumes he rapidly devoured as
soon as they appeared. On September 26, 1849, he
began (though surely not for the first time) to read
Gibbon, and finished him on March 9, 1850. On
August 5, 1850, he began Sismondi, and finished him
on August 12, 1851. In February, 1851, he began to
read some of Amari's works (but which of them is not
mentioned), and in January, 1852, he set to work upon
Polybius. About the same time he was studying Niebuhr's
books, and the first mention of reading German occurs.

At no period of his life had he a very keen appetite
for works of fiction, but most of the greater novels of the
day were read, and one of them, at any rate, proved so
absorbing that other reading was put aside for it. He
began *Jane Eyre* on July 12, 1849, and finished it the
next day. Kingsley's *Alton Locke, Yeast*, and *Hypatia;*
Disraeli's *Coningsby*, and *Sybil;* and Thackeray's *Esmond;*
besides some of his old favourites by Sir Walter Scott,
were all read through in the course of one year. Other
books of which frequent mention is made in the diary
are Boswell's *Life of Johnson*, Sir Thomas Browne's
works, and the *Koran*, the latter of course being read in
a translation.

His favourite exercise at this time was riding. He
had two horses which he named Bruno and Otto, and on

one or other of these he rode almost every day. He
would gallop about the hills at a great pace, often
shouting out scraps of ballad poetry. This practice
may perhaps explain the somewhat startling entry,
'taken for a madman,' which occurs in his diary when
he was on a journey to Oxford on horseback. He
frequently records the falls of his horse, or his own falls
off his horse, but neither he nor his beast seem to have
ever been seriously damaged by these misadventures.
He was very tender-hearted towards all the lower animals,
and very gentle in his treatment of them; and when
a conflict of will arose between him and his horse, the
latter seems generally to have got the best of it. 'Set
out on Bruno, but turned back because of pranks,' or,
'Otto obstinate,' are not uncommon entries : on one occasion he notes that he dismounted to draw a church, but
'Bruno ramped in the churchyard,' and the sketch had to
be cut short. At one time the stock of animals kept at
Oaklands was a large one, including, besides cats and
dogs, and the two horses, a pony for the children, sheep,
pigs, and goats, a squirrel, and a raccoon. The births
or deaths which occurred in this numerous family
are always duly chronicled in the diary. When the
children were very small he was fond of training the
young goats to draw them in a carriage, and 'proved
kids' is one of the commonest entries in his diary
in reference to this practice. When some of them were
old enough to ride the pony he enjoyed walking by
their side to places where he could help them to gather
spring-flowers, chestnuts, or acorns, according to the
season. The following letters to his eldest daughter
are specimens of many which he was accustomed to
write to his children.

March 7. 1852.

From Papa to his dear little
MARGARET.

I dare say you were very glad
to see MAMMA at home again,
and that you had a great deal
to tell her. I hope to come home,
and see you all again in about
a week, when I hope MAMMA
will be able to tell me that
our little MARGARET has been

a good little girl. I hope
HAROLD and little Baby
are very well. You must
give the other letter in the
cover to MAMMA and ask
her to read this to you if
you cannot make it all out
yourself. How are the goats

and the guinea pigs and
Thora and everything. Pa:
:pa saw such big dogs

the other day, much bigger
than Thora, and a little girl
on such a little pony. riding

so fast. Kiss MAn:

MA and Bonny Boy and little
wee Baby and so good bye.
GOD bless you my own little
MARGARET.

33 Maddox Street,
London, March 3rd,
1853.

My dear little GRETCHEN,

We have come up to
this great town London
to-day, so you must tell
William to send the let-
ters as I have written

above. I am glad to hear that HAROLD is a good boy, but you should wait for him to say that you are a good girl, and not praise yourself. How are EDGAR and little HELEN ? Are the pups grown, and is there a kid born yet ? We have had a great deal of snow and rain at Waltham, but

it was finer to-day as we
came along in the train.
We will not forget to bring
you something, and I will
Write to the Bonny Boy
another day. We hope one day
to go to the Zoölogical

Gardens to see the

Giraffes or Cameloparde,
the Great Sagacious Ele-
-phant, and the other beasts.
So good bye, my little Tochterlein, and kiss Brothers
and little Sister for us,
and believe me
            Your own Father

            EDWARD FREEMAN

- ἐν Λονδίνῳ, τὴν 28 Μαΐου,
1857 -

φίλη θύγατερ Μαργαρίτη,
    ἅπασαν τὴν ἐπιστολὴν Ἑλ-
-ληνιστὶ γράφειν χαλεπώτερον ἂν
εἴη ἢ -ὥστε ἢ σοὶ ἢ ἐμοὶ ἡδομέ-
-νῳ εἶναι. διὰ οὖν ταῦτα τὰ
λοιπὰ Ἀγγλιστὶ γράψω.

We have heard something to-day
which I think will be a great plea-
-sure to you. How should you like
to come up and meet us in Oxford?

Mr Parker, whom we saw yesterday,
says he will be very glad to take you
in.. So I hope you will come on Tri:
:nity Monday. You will have to go
by yourself in the train as far as
Didcot, but there Mamma or I will
meet you and take you to Oxford. I
think you will like your visit very
much. We have been very busy,
running up and down, to one place.
and another, ever since we came
here, and have not much time for
writing long letters or doing any:

:thing else. I hope we shall get a sight of the Zoological Gardens and the Crystal Palace before we go, but we have not been able to, yet.

Mamma will write to you in a day or two, and tell you more about your journey, which will be quite a great event for you.

χαῖρε, φίλον κοράσιον· κύσον ὑπὲρ ἐμοῦ τώ τε ἀδελφὼ καὶ τὰς ἀδελφάς.

ὁ σὸς πατὴρ
Ἐδούαρδος Ἀ. Φημμανος.

Some of his old Oxford friends paid him visits from
time to time, and he enjoyed meeting his neighbours,
Sir George Prevost, Mr. Isaac Williams, and Dr. White,
formerly Professor of Anglo-Saxon at Oxford, but he
never had any inclination to join in what is called
general society. And in truth he had little leisure
for it. With the exception of the two or three hours'
walk or ride in the afternoon, the whole of the day
and much of the night were devoted to reading and
writing. The earlier part of the evening he occupied
in working up his sketches with pen and ink, while his
wife read aloud or sang, after which he returned to his
study and read or wrote to a late hour of the night,
or into the early morning. On Sundays he put his
regular work aside, but wrote a great many of his letters
between the hours of Church services, and in the evenings he worked at his sketches again, as on other days,
while his wife read aloud, generally from some of the
writings of Newman or Isaac Williams, or from the
Christian Remembrancer, a quarterly journal to which
Mr. R. W. Church (afterwards Dean of St. Paul's), and
Mr. J. B. Mozley (afterwards Regius Professor of Divinity
at Oxford), and other writers of first rate ability and
learning frequently contributed at that time.

Certainly Oaklands well fulfilled the idea of 'a home
of industrious peace.'

To the Rev. B. Webb[1].

Oaklands, Dursley, April 22, 1854.

You see you read my heart well. I don't think I can promise
to come and talk at your Annual Meeting, first, because I much

---

[1] Editor of the *Ecclesiologist*, afterwards Rector of St. Andrews,
Wells Street, London, and Prebendary of St. Paul's.

doubt whether I shall find myself able and willing to be in London at the time you mention ; as I shall have to be there for another matter betwixt this and then, and may not wish to come again. Second, I have written and engaged to write so many discourses this year ('for I am torn in pieces by such blessed calls') that I really cannot undertake another. Third, I really fear whether a profane person like me, a carnal west-country alderman, in a white hat and brown holland trowsers, would not be somewhat out of character among the cloud of M. B. coats which I conceive a meeting of the E. C. C. C. S. (as Hope writes it) to present. I should be afraid of being scratched to pieces like Hypatia, or torn with pincers like Fra Dolcino. Then I suppose I should have to deliver my oration in the 'cantus collectarum'[1] under penalty of a censure from the secretary for Musical Matters, while I, poor musicless brute, don't know the Hypo-Lydian from Cambridge New, or the Tonus Peregrinus from the tune that the old cow died of. So I must pray you to excuse me as a weaker brother.

To THE REV. R. E. BARTLETT[2].

Oaklands, Dursley, August 2, 1854.

If the numerous dreams in which I find myself figuring as one of the legislators of this commonwealth could ever be fulfilled by daylight, I might be able to tell you something more about the practical working of representative government. But as things stand at present, I must refer you on that head to your host, W. Jackson, Esq., M.D., and only lay before you what I have theorized upon the subject.

First, I would recommend to your notice, albeit not written, as you seem to prefer, in the High Dutch language, a certain article in the current number of the *North British Review*, headed 'Greece during the Macedonian Period,' wherein you may possibly pick up a wrinkle or two. To prove the catholicity of the author, I may add that there is one from the

---

[1] The mode of chanting the prayers then becoming fashionable amongst high churchmen.

[2] Fellow and Tutor of Trinity College, Oxford, 1853-1860. Bampton Lecturer, 1888.

same hand in the current *Quarterly*, headed, 'Queen Elizabeth and her Favourites,' which however contains more fun than work.

But about representation, I conceive that the delegation of certain citizens to act on behalf of others in the sovereign assembly of any commonwealth, is the natural and necessary result of establishing a free constitution in an extensive country; and, as such, I do not imagine it to be older than mediaeval times, and, like all other practical institutions, to have been gradually developed. In the small republics of Greece it is clear that nothing of the sort was wanted or could exist; their animating principle was that every qualified citizen should personally discharge his political functions as a member of the sovereign body. This is equally the case whether that membership be confined to a few or extended to the mass. Oligarch or democrat, he must vote himself, and not send a representative to vote for him. The 'house' might, and generally did, appoint some smaller body out of itself as a βουλή or γερουσία for various functions, but the sovereign assembly itself, where the majesty of the people resided, invariably consisted of the whole of the qualified citizens (many or few), and not of a select portion of them.

Now it is clear that this kind of constitution could be practically worked only in the old city-commonwealths, where the whole territory of the state was so small that all the citizens could habitually assemble in one place. The history of Rome here comes in as a warning. She attempted to govern an empire with the constitution of a municipality. Whole nations were admitted to citizenship, and citizenship gave a personal vote in the comitia. The comitia therefore became an unruly mob, practically swayed by its least respectable portion, the city populace. The result was the establishment of despotism.

This case of Rome was remarkable, because a step was taken towards the representative system from the earliest period. Each citizen gave a personal vote, but his vote only counted indirectly, the votes being taken by tribes. It never seems to have occurred to Servius, Licinius, or any of them, to make each tribe elect certain of their own number who should give its vote for it. Yet this would clearly have been infinitely more convenient in the later days of the republic, when citizens were spread all over the world.

In the confederacies and federations, of course, you find something more like a representative system. Aeschines among the Amphictyons clearly acted as 'the honourable member for Athens,' or, considering the functions of that body, one should rather say, 'the Reverend Proctor for the Diocese of St. Athene.' Still, we do not know how the votes of the Ionian or Dorian tribe,—two, mind for each *tribe*, not each *city*— were got at; and we also hear of a more numerous body, the Amphictyonic ἐκκλησία, besides the formally commissioned Hieromnemons and Pylagoroi. But you see this is not a government; it is not a Parliament for internal government, but a congress of diplomatists to arrange matters affecting various sovereign states. Here you cannot avoid some sort of representation; but this is quite another matter from applying the same principle to internal government.

In fact the Greeks did not even apply the representative principle to the central government of a federal *Bund*. The Achaean League was constituted in very much the same way as the Roman Republic. Each city, great and small, had one vote in the Assembly at Aegium; but every qualified citizen of every city might attend and give his voice towards determining that vote. But it should be observed that in the League (vid. *North British Review*) it was impossible that all the qualified persons should have habitually attended the Assembly in the way they did at Athens. Business must have been done by a few leading men from each city, who would practically be the members for those cities. A formal election to that function alone was wanted.

The Lycian League went a step beyond the Achaean. The latter gave as much weight to Tritaea as to Corinth, just as Harwich with us counts for as much as Manchester, and as, till Tudor times, all constituencies, except, I believe, London did. The Lycians gave each city a greater or less number of votes according to its size. See Strabo, xv. 3. But he does not mention how those votes were determined; if each city sent as many citizens only as it had votes, they would, it is clear, be really representatives for the cities. But very possibly the number, as in Achaia, was indefinite, and the aggregate vote of all the Xanthians present reckoned for three, of a smaller town, two, and so on. Observe that the Roman and Achaean mode of voting admitted no *representation of minorities* in the several tribes or cities, and also that, just as in an election by nations in Glasgow University, a majority of tribes or cities was not necessarily a majority of citizens. Any three little towns of the old Aegialus could out-vote Corinth and Argos.

Under the Roman despotism one would hardly look for anything like representative government, but a remarkable instance of something very closely approaching it is mentioned by M. Guizot, in the second lecture of the *History of Civilization in Europe*.

Another point to which I think you should look, though I really know next to nothing about it myself, is the constitution of ecclesiastical councils. I need hardly say that the development of temporal institutions in Europe was very much influenced by ecclesiastical ones, and I cannot help fancying that you will find something like a real representative system in ecclesiastical assemblies earlier than in civil ones. And I suspect again that you would be likely to find it first among the monastic orders, which, for all their vow of obedience, always had a strong democratic element in them. Till the system got influenced by kings and popes, the monk might serve a despot, but it was always a despot of his own choosing.

I am not sufficiently versed in the details of mediaeval constitutional history to give you more than a few hints. You know I am no German scholar, and I need hardly refer you to Hallam, Guizot, Palgrave, Kemble, and the like. But I conceive the general course of events to be something like this. In all the Teutonic nations, the national assembly originally comprises every freeman of the dominant race ; as the nation spreads itself over a wider space, attendance becomes impossible, and the assembly either dies out, as in France, or is reconstructed, as in England, on a principle more suited to the wants of the age. I wrote a review some time back in the *Morning Chronicle* on Bonnechose's *History of France*, in which I remarked, what I think you will find worth working out more in detail, that England has always had a legislative assembly of some kind or other from the very beginning of things, while France has attempted it thrice in three different forms, barbaric, mediaeval and modern, and it has failed in all. Our Witenagemot went on flourishing, while Charlemagne and his successors could not get a house at the Champ de Mai. Our mediaeval Parliament was developed out of the Witenagemot, and was itself developed very gradually into its modern form. Meanwhile mediaeval France tried States General, which gradually came to nothing, and in more recent times half a dozen different sorts of conventions, chambers, and assemblies.

There is a book very well worth your reading, Lieber on *Civil Liberty and Self-Government*, which I also reviewed in the *Chronicle* since Bonnechose; as also Creasy on the *English Constitution*. The mediaeval system of representation is closely connected with the growth of the communes, and with the notion of estates. Our present notion is that of a representation of the whole people, local election being rather looked on as a convenient mode than anything else. Experience—including that of every American State—shows the necessity of revision by a second chamber of a less popular character; we find this ready made in our House of Lords, which one would not invent theoretically, but which, being ready made, does its work practically very well, and, being close, insures the presence of some of the best men in both houses, while in America, both houses being elective, the best men try to get into the upper one. But this system arose out of the accidents of a system whose theory was widely different. The full development of the mediaeval notion may be seen in Sweden, with the four houses, nobles, clergy, citizens, peasants. Each estate, each order, that is, of society, was supposed to have different interests and met separately. The consequence is that in Sweden now large classes of persons not strictly coming under any of those heads are altogether disfranchised. Citizens means only persons actually belonging to some civic or mercantile corporation—the professional class, and landed proprietors, whether noble or peasant, have no political existence.

In England, as feudalism came in, the Great Council consisted of all the king's tenants *in capite*. Gradually only the greater ones were summoned personally—House of Lords; while the lesser chose representatives—Knights of the Shire. As the towns grew, they got admission also. The details of this development are not at all clear, but the main outline is certain enough.

But observe several happy accidents. According to the Swedish system, the freeholders, the burghers, and the clergy would have elected separate houses; in France, too, nobility, clergy, and commons were distinct. In England—I know not from what good luck—we never had a nobility. The peer sat as a great tenant-in-chief, not as a person of noble blood; his sons had no privilege whatever. Again, thanks to Simon de Montfort, the representatives of the boroughs were allowed to sit with the knights, instead of forming a separate house. Again, all the attempts to make a distinct parliamentary order of the clergy failed; hence the strange anomalous position of Convocation. The result of all this is that, instead of nobility, clergy, citizens and peasants forming separate estates, one House of Commons represents all, while the House of Lords does not represent a distinct estate, but is merely a hereditary senate instead of an elective one.

You should also try to work out the difference between a representative of the whole body of citizens, only chosen for convenience sake by the citizens of a certain locality, and a delegate, the mere mouthpiece of local wishes. The former is our present idea, but I conceive the latter was the original one. In Poland, you know, it always lasted, and the deputy who betrayed his trust was commonly sabred for his pains. Connected with this is the apportionment of numbers to each electoral body. I do not know whether London always had four members, but certainly, for some centuries, every other place that sent members at all sent two. Now this, I believe, was to ensure local interests really getting a mouth-piece; *each member was a check upon the other telling lies.* The *Edinburgh Review*, in one of those capital articles, made a strange slip, saying this lasted to the Reform Bill. The Welsh constituencies, founded by Henry VIII, sent always only one member, and so did several English ones dating from the same century. By that time it must have been recognized that each member was to vote independently. But Yorkshire and Rutland sent two alike till George IV's time, when some Cornish borough was disfranchised, and its members given to Yorkshire. The Reform Bill, of course, did much more in the same way, but it did not begin it.

You should also look to the Scotch Parliament, where Lords and Commons sat together, and compare this with the fact that in the Convocation of York the Bishop and Proctors sit together instead of forming two Houses, as in Canterbury.

Well, here is a mass of paper. Instead of references, I have pretty well written the essay for you[1]. I hope I may get the prize. I didn't when I tried before.

About Dissenters ; I don't specially love them, but I hate them so much less than I do the Hebdomadal Board, that I am quite willing to take the Dissenters in exchange for the Board. I suppose we shall have a few from the orthodox Eastern Church ; at least as Nicholas sends our midshipmen[2] to the University of Moscow, under the special care of the rector, Cotton[3] ought surely by ἀντιπεπονθός to get a young Muscovite or two as parlour-boarders.

Why don't you come and see me, instead of going to Munich? Prythee tell the Bavarians the next new dynasty they set up, that I and Laing and Lieber and De Tocqueville will legislate a vast deal better for it than they did in Greece.

I am hard at work on Finlay for next *North British*, also Mahomet for *Quarterly*.

Do you ever see the *Ecclesiologist ?* I trow not, but if you can catch the August number, you will find my account of our doings at Cambridge, which may make you laugh.

---

[1] The subject set for the Chancellor's Prize Essay at Oxford in 1855 was 'The different principles on which the chief systems of popular representation have been based in ancient and modern times.' The prize was gained by the Hon. G. C. Brodrick, now Warden of Merton College.

[2] Taken prisoners in the Russian war.

[3] Then Provost of Worcester College, Oxford, and Vice-Chancellor of the University, A.D. 1852–1856.

CHAPTER IV.

Settles at Lanrumney Hall. Articles on Greek and Roman History. Beginning of Correspondence and Friendship with Mr. Finlay and Spyridon Trikoupes. The Ionian Islands. Offers Himself as a Candidate for Parliament. Letter on Church Property and Disendowment. First Tour Abroad. Examiner in History School at Oxford. Candidate for Professorship of Modern History. Domestic Habits. Correspondence.

A.D. 1855–1859

As Freeman's family increased, and his books multiplied, the house at Dursley became too small for his requirements. After some searching in various parts of southern England he found a home to his mind in Lanrumney, or Lanrhymney, Hall, near Cardiff—an old-fashioned house, situated in an undulating and well-timbered park in the beautiful valley of the Rumney, down which here and there glimpses may be caught of the Bristol Channel. The house is within the parish of St. Mellon's, but about a mile distant from the church, which stands above the village on the top of a steep hill whence there is a noble view of the Channel, and of the coasts of Somerset and Devon. It is, indeed, almost exactly opposite Worle Hill, with which, as the reader will remember[1], Freeman had been familiar in his childhood.

The following letters convey some notion of the new home and the surrounding scenery.

[1] See above, page 3.

To the Rev. B. Webb.

Lanrumney Hall, Cardiff, August 7, 1855.

You will indeed say that I have deserted my earlier Saxon love for a Llan- this or that, when I tell you that I have altogether changed my quarters, moved westwards, and taken up my abode here on the extreme confines of Gwent, within a stone's throw of Morganwg, but with communication therewith sadly impeded by lack of a decent bridge. However, this is not a *Llan-* but a *Glan-*, *Lanrumney* being a corruption of *Glanrhymney*, which you are perfectly welcome to direct if you please, only don't put *Llanrumney.* But *Lan* or *Glan*, I must confess to dwelling among the Cymry, among church-towers without buttresses, and with corbel-tables under their battlements. Also I dwell within a few miles of Llandaff; *therefore*, what you will hardly believe, at a great many miles distance from St. David's.

This reminds me, you may as well look up and notice the few last numbers of *Archaeologia Cambrensis*, wherein you will find papers of mine in your line on Brecon, St. Asaph, Ruthin, and Llanthony, as also some by Basil Jones and by Longueville Jones. Can't you get some of your rich men, Hope, Dickinson, and the like, to become members. . . . I don't go either to Shrewsbury or Llandeilo. My great move here is enough till I go to Edinburgh in the winter to preach about the Saracens. In the meanwhile, may Allah and the Prophet confound Louis Napoleon and Palmerston and exalt Gladstone and John Bright to the empire of the world.

To the Rev. Henry Thompson.

Glanrhymney, Cardiff, September 19, 1855.

Since I wrote to you last I may consider myself as having got quite settled in my new abode; for though we have still got both masons and gardeners about, I have been happy in my library—half a huge old gallery, with a grand cinque-cento chimneypiece—for many weeks; and we have even had guests tarrying with us. I need not say that we shall be happy to receive you in that capacity whenever you please to run across and explore Llandaff and Caerphilly.

I have been still labouring for peace since I was with you ; but the *Times* and all of them still seem frantic for bloodshed. Have you seen certain *Tracts for the Present Crisis*, published at Bristol ? *A priori* I conceive them to be written by Sir Arthur Elton. . . .

This is certainly a jolly place. From our churchyard and other elevated points we see all Zummerzet coast, and it is said that, from some of the mountains more inland one can see right across to the English Channel. Anyhow the Holms, Worlebury, Breandown, Uphill, Clevedon, Crooks Peak, are all conspicuous; yet more so is BRENTKNOLL, whereon one can dimly conceive a venerable figure, with bell, book, and candle, launching forth anathemas against the world in general, and the Lords of the Council in particular[1]. Glastonbury Tor I have not yet discerned.

Without deserting my books, I have turned farmer, and own

2 Horses,	1 Coon,
1 Pony,	1 Dog,
4 Pigs,	2 Goats,
29 Sheep,	4 Cows,
1 Calf,	Rabbits,
Ducks,	Cocks and hens.
2 Cats,	

Of these, two pigs and all the sheep and kine and ducks have been bought since I came here. We slay and eat patriarchally of our own, yet we do not eat so soon after death as Abraham did.

Welsh is much more the language here than I had expected, but the people are thoroughly δίγλωσσοι. My children and servants seem to be picking up a little ; Margaret saluting me with unintelligible greetings, and synonyms for βεκός[2], which sound like the second word in the Hebrew Pentateuch[3].

The five years spent at Lanrumney were largely devoted to the study of Greek and Roman history, more

---

[1] The well-known George Anthony Denison, Vicar of East Brent, and Archdeacon of Taunton.

[2] See Herodotus, ii. 2.   [3] בָּרָא = bara.

especially the former, as a mere enumeration of the articles which he contributed to various reviews will prove. 'The Greek people and the Greek kingdom' appeared in the *Edinburgh* for April, 1856[1]. 'The Athenian democracy,' which was a review of Grote's history, in the *North British Review* for May, 1856[1]. 'Alexander the Great' in the *Edinburgh* for April, 1857[2]. 'Ancient Greece and mediaeval Italy' in the volume of *Oxford Essays* published in 1857[2]. 'Colonel Mure and the Attic historians' in the *National Review* for January, 1858[2]. 'The Eastern Church' in the *Edinburgh* for April, 1858. 'Mr. Gladstone's Homer and the Homeric Age' in the *National Review* for July, 1858[2]. 'Mommsen's History of Rome' in the *National Review* for April, 1859[2]. The whole series of essays exhibits a knowledge of Greek and Roman history, marvellous in its extent, clearness, and firmness of grasp, ranging as it does from the earliest ages down to his own day. And his interest in the events related by Herodotus and Thucydides, was as vivid and keen as in those which were recorded in the history of the last Greek revolution by Spyridon Trikoupes, or in the daily newspaper. The essays abound also with interesting criticisms of the historians of Greece from Herodotus to Finlay and Trikoupes. In a few pithy sentences he sums up and contrasts the principal characteristics of Herodotus, Thucydides and Xenophon. He points out that Herodotus and Thucydides, though contemporary writers, were so diverse in temperament and style that they seemed to be centuries apart. The archaic taste

---

[1] Reprinted, with additions and alterations, in *Historical Essays*, third series.

[2] Reprinted in *Historical Essays*, second series.

of Herodotus imparted to his writings the flavour of
an age much earlier than that in which he lived. Thucydides belonged to no age or country: he was the historian of our common humanity, the teacher of abstract
political wisdom: Herodotus was hardly a political
writer at all: the few political comments which he made
were indeed always true and generous: but they were
put forth with an amiable simplicity which brought them
near to the nature of truisms. . . . Xenophon wrote
from the worst inspiration of local and temporary party
spirit. Herodotus lived in the past. Thucydides lived for
the future. Xenophon reflected only the petty passions
of the moment. Thucydides without Xenophon might
make us place the ideal Greek historian at a super-
human height above us. Xenophon without Thucydides
might lead us to drag him down to the level of a
very inferior modern pamphleteer . . . . No one could
thoroughly appreciate the merits of Thucydides, if he
did not make use of Xenophon as a foil. Without
comparing the two, we might be led to think that
Thucydidean dignity and impartiality was an easy commonplace quality, which did not entitle its possessor
to any special honour. When we turned to the Hel-
lenica, we could at once see how great were the
temptations to a contrary course which surrounded
a Greek who wrote the history of his own time. ' How
many opportunities must Thucydides have had, how
many must he have cast aside, for colouring, omitting,
exaggerating . . . . How hard a task (it must have been) to
keep the bitter revengeful spirit of the exile from
showing itself in every page.' Yet a certain unfairness
towards Cleon and Hyperbolos was the only accusation
which could be brought against him. And even here,

there was no reason to doubt the honesty of his narrative :
only the story, as he tells it, did not bear out the epithet
which he applies to the actors in it.   There were in
Freeman's judgement only three defects in Thucydides :
First, a certain coldness and unattractiveness of character.

'He does not, like many other writers, draw us near to
himself personally. What reader of Herodotus does not long
for a talk face to face with the genial and delightful old traveller
who had been everywhere and seen everything—who could tell
you the founder of every city and the architect of every temple,
who could recite oracles and legends from the beginning of
things to his own day, and who could season all with a simple
moral and political commentary, not the less acceptable for
being a little commonplace ? . . . Xenophon, again, would evidently not have been the less agreeable as a companion on
account of his unpatriotic heresies and his historical unfairness. . . . Genial simplicity, hearty and unconscious humour, are,
after all, more attractive than the stern perfection of wisdom :
a little superstition and a little party-spirit, if they render
a man less admirable, do not always make him less agreeable.
Impartiality is a rare and divine quality ; but a little human
weakness sometimes commends itself more to frail mortals.'

Another defect in Thucydides, was his occasional
obscurity.

'We admire, but we cannot bring ourselves to love, the man
who has clothed the words of wisdom with a veil so hard to
uplift. We are sometimes tempted to prefer a teaching less
profound in substance, but more conformable to the ordinary
laws of human and Hellenic grammar.'

The third defect, partly due to the very intellectual
greatness which placed him above the men of his own
time, and made his history an eternal treasure-house of
political wisdom, was that he confines himself entirely
to external politics, and affords the reader no insight

into the social, literary, artistic and philosophic life of
Athens in her greatest splendour.

'We should never have learned from him that Aeschylus,
Euripides, Pheidias or Anaxagoras ever lived. From Thucydides
alone we should never have found out that the Sophokles who
figures as an admiral in the Samian war was at least not less
illustrious as the author of the *Oedipus* and the *Electra*.'

And he ends by pointing out how the gossip and petty
personal anecdotes of Xenophon, spiced with party
spirit, present a more vivid picture of the age than the
dignified but colourless narrative of Thucydides. In
his criticisms of the modern historians of Greece, Mitford,
Thirlwall, Grote and Ernst Curtius, he endeavours to
assess the merits of each with the same careful discrimination. A conventional way of looking at Greek
history had grown up as early as the time of Plutarch,
when writers were in sympathy further removed than
the modern scholar from the age of Thucydides ; when
they had not the same habit of drawing historical
analogies, or the same wide field of historical experience
in which to seek their analogies. Greek history thus
gradually became—

'a collection of formulae, of misunderstood models, and of
sentiments fit only for a child's copy-book. Mitford, with all his
blunders and all his unfairness, did good service in showing
that Plutarch's men were real human beings like ourselves.
The calm judgement and consummate scholarship of Bishop
Thirlwall came in to correct, sometimes a little too unmercifully,
the mistakes and perversions of Mitford. But it was Mr. Grote
who first thoroughly tested our materials, who first looked
straight at everything without regard to conventional beliefs,
by the light of his own historical and political knowledge.
Mr. Grote indeed is throughout his history a partisan, the
champion of a side. The Athenian democracy is to him as

a party or a country, and he says all that is to be said for it. We read what he says, not as the sentence of a judge, but as the pleading of an advocate : but it is a great thing to have the pleading of such an advocate. We may not be prepared to go all Mr. Grote's lengths on every matter, but we should have thought that no reader of Mr. Grote ever shut up his book in exactly the same frame of mind in which he opened it. He will at least have seen that there is another side to a great many things of which he had hitherto only looked at one side.'

Now and always Freeman maintained that the publication of Grote's history in no way diminished the sterling value of Bishop Thirlwall's great work. ' Each,' he said, ' has its own use. The professed historical student cannot do without either.' And again, for those persons who, without being specially devoted to Greek history, wished to study it in something higher than a mere school-book, he recommended Thirlwall's history rather than Grote's, by reason of the comparative shortness, the greater clearness and terseness of the narrative, and its freedom from discussions and digressions. In his history of the Macedonian period also, Mr. Grote sank in his judgement far below the level of Bishop Thirlwall. Grote could not be fair to the Macedonians because they degraded, corrupted, almost extinguished the Athenian Demos, which was the darling of his affections. Yet, in Freeman's opinion, the supremacy of Macedonia was not at all more oppressive than the supremacy of Sparta. It did not interfere so much as Sparta had done with local governments, and the main difference between the supremacy of Macedonia on the one hand, and of Athens, Thebes, or Sparta on the other, was that the latter states were republics, while Macedonia was a monarchy. Grote was not, like Niebuhr, a reckless calumniator of Philip and Alexander, but he could not do justice to them. He regarded them as mere barbarian invaders of Greece, whereas Alexander undoubtedly stood forth as the champion of Hellas against the barbarian, and it was not until he attacked Persia that he appeared in the character of an aggressive invader. After criticizing the early authorities for the life of Alexander the Great, more especially Arrian, Quintus Curtius, and Diodorus, he observes that from such a mass of conflicting evidence, it was no wonder that different minds should draw different conclusions, but that

'high above them all the serene intellect of Bishop Thirlwall holds the judicial balance . . . . The oftener we read his narrative of this period the more disposed are we to see in it the nearest approach to the perfection of critical history . . . . In his treatment of the internal affairs of Athens in earlier times Mr. Grote far outshines Bishop Thirlwall : but nowhere does he equal or even approach the Bishop's admirable narrative of the period from the accession of Philip to the death of Demetrios Poliorketes. It is therefore the Alexander of Thirlwall rather than the Alexander either of Grote or of Droysen, who deserves to live in the memory of mankind, and to challenge the admiration of the world.'

No one, in Freeman's opinion, had done fuller justice to the effects of Alexander's conquests than Mr. Finlay in the first chapter of his *History of Greece.* These two great historians, the one of Greece independent, the other of Greece enslaved, were thus brought into strong contrast. By the historian of the Athenian democracy the Macedonian was cursed as a destroyer ; by the historian of the Byzantine Empire he was admitted to the honours of a founder. For in truth,

'if he overthrew the liberties of Hellas in their native seat he gave to the Hellenic mind a wider scope, and, in the end, a yet

nobler mission. He was the forerunner of Heraclius bringing
home the True Cross from its Persian bondage, and of Leo
beating back the triumphant Saracen from the walls of the city
which Philip himself had besieged in vain. The victories of
Christian Emperors, the teaching of Christian Fathers, the
abiding life of the tongue and the arts of Greece far beyond the
limits of old Hellas, perhaps the endurance of Greek nationality
down to our own times, all sprang from the triumphs of this, it
may be, "non Hellenic conqueror," but, in the work which he
wrought, most truly Hellenic missionary.'

Freeman's criticisms of Ernst Curtius appeared for
the most part in the *Saturday Review*, and date from
1868, when an English translation of his history was
first published, but it may be convenient to take notice
of them in this chapter. The strong point of Curtius,
in his opinion, lay in his geographical knowledge and
his power of vivid description. ' He brings out as clearly
as words can bring out, the physical conformation, the
climate, and the products of the different countries round
the Aegaean Sea, and the way in which the course of
their history has been influenced by these geographical
features.' In this part of his work Freeman thought
that he far surpassed Grote. On the other hand, on
the political parts of Greek history Curtius shed no
fresh light, and here it was to the English writer that the
student must look for originality, vigour and clearness.
In ethnological and philological knowledge again, Curtius
was in advance both of Thirlwall and Grote. He did
justice also to the literary, artistic, and philosophical
sides of Athenian history, but he did not make too much
of them.

'Some writers and talkers,' Freeman remarks, 'both on
ancient Greece and mediaeval Italy, have utterly wearied us
with poets, artists, and philosophers, till we have been some-

times tempted to wish that neither Greece nor Italy had ever produced any poets, artists, or philosophers at all. Curtius never errs in this way. He never forgets that if Athens did great things in the way of literature and art it was only by virtue of her position as a great and free city that she was enabled to do so.'

On the whole, though he recommended every student of Greek history to read Curtius without fail, he held that he was equally bound to read Thirlwall and Grote also. There were points in which each of the three writers was distinctly superior to the other two. The article which Freeman wrote for the *Edinburgh Review* of April, 1856, entitled 'The Greek people and the Greek kingdom,' was the occasion of much correspondence, which led to a lasting friendship, with the historian Mr. Finlay[1], although they never met, and with the

---

[1] Mr. George Finlay first went to Greece in 1823, when he was twenty-four years of age, and took an active part in the war of independence. He became acquainted with Lord Byron, and was the intimate friend of George Abney Hastings. After the conclusion of the war he bought an estate in Attica, and entertained hopes of being able to do something to improve the political and social condition of the country. In these hopes he was disappointed. In a letter to Freeman, written in April, 1856, he says, 'Literature was not my vocation. I came to Greece to work in active life, and it was only when I found that political corruption excluded me from the administrative service, and brigands prevented me from doing the duty I wished to perform as a landlord by residing myself in the country, that I took to writing. History was a medium for reaching the period of political discussion, and now, having reached it, I am enamoured of history and have some distaste for politics.' Many of his letters to Freeman, of which fifty-four have been preserved, are full of interest, as containing descriptions, by a very acute observer, of the country in which he had long resided, and of the people with whom he was intimately acquainted, though the disappointments which he had experienced led him to take rather an over-gloomy view of things, and to be rather harsh in his criticisms. His *History of Greece* was brought out in sections. *Greece under the Romans* appeared in 1844, *Greece to the Conquest of the Turks* appeared in

statesman, Spyridon Trikoupes, the Greek minister in
London, and his son Charilaos. The first letters
addressed to these two correspondents were written on
the same day and with the same purpose.

To SPYRIDON TRIKOUPES.

Trinity College, Oxford, June 13, 1855.

SIR,

I trust you will excuse the intrusion of a personal
stranger on a subject which I doubt not will attract your
sympathy. I am reading with extreme interest your *History of
the Greek Revolution*[1], on which I shortly contemplate an article
in one of the leading Reviews. I am one of those, who still,
now that English sympathies seem all but exclusively given to
infidels and barbarians, do not shrink from the once popular
title of Philhellenes; who can still admire the heroic struggle
which you have so vigorously depicted in your own language,
and who still do not wholly despair of its ultimate results. If
you should chance to have seen two letters in the *Spectator*,
signed E. A. F. and headed, 'What are the Greeks?' you may
know my general line of argument, but some portions of it
I wish to be able to strengthen by more minute facts, figures,
and documents. My two great positions are, first, that though
liberated Greece has not answered all the expectations of thirty
years back, it has nevertheless made great advances upon its
condition under the Turks. Secondly, that where it has failed,
the failure has been owing to the injudicious introduction or
imitation of Western habits and institutions, instead of developing the native energies of the people. For instance, the
boundary between 'Greece' and 'Turkey,' i. e. between independent and enslaved Greece, is something altogether absurd,

1851, *Greece under Ottoman and Venetian Domination* in 1856, and *The
Greek Revolution* in 1861. The whole work, as revised by the author,
was re-published in 1877 by the Delegates of the Clarendon Press,
Oxford, in seven volumes, very ably edited by the Rev. H. F. Tozer,
late Fellow of Exeter College. The references given in the present
biography are to this edition.

[1] Σπυρίδωνος Τρικούπη 'Ιστορία τῆς 'Ελληνικῆς 'Επαναστάσεως. Τόμοι Α'
καὶ Β'. 'Εν Λονδίνῳ : 1853-4.

a pure diplomatic figment which the national sentiment cannot be expected to respect. Again, I hold that the old municipal institutions, faulty as they were, should have been retained in an improved and developed form. Yet in spite of all this, I see your country and your countrymen making great strides in commerce, literature, and everything else. But to work this out thoroughly, I want details and figures to look well in the pages of a Review. If you can kindly do this, it will be at once a great favour to an unknown admirer of your own writings, and also, I would hope, not altogether useless for the interest of your country.

I am, Sir,
Your obedient servant.

To G. Finlay, Esq.

Trinity College, Oxford, June 13, 1855.

Sir,

I trust you will pardon the intrusion of an admirer of your writings, although personally unknown to yourself, on a subject which I am sure cannot fail to be as interesting to you as it is to myself. In the first place, however, allow me most sincerely to thank you, as a student of history, for the great benefit which I have derived from your works on the history of mediaeval Greece and the Byzantine empire. I am afraid your labours in rescuing from ignorance and misrepresentation that most important and neglected period of history are not yet appreciated as they should be; I feel sure, however, that they cannot fail in the end to lead the way to a more full and general acquaintance with a subject about which most people think it creditable to be ignorant. I have done my best in a review of your books in the *North British Review* for last February[1], in which I have gone into the whole subject, and I hope you will find that I have thoroughly appreciated your eminent services to historical knowledge, even though I may have expressed an occasional point of dissent.

The subject, however, on which I have ventured to trouble you on the present occasion is somewhat different, though

---

[1] 'Finlay on the Byzantine Empire,' see above, ch. iii. p. 155.

certainly not without a close connexion with the subject of your great work. I am contemplating an article in one of the leading Reviews, the object of which, I am sure, will command your sympathies, namely, the vindication of the Greek nation, as distinguished from the Greek government, from the misrepresentations with which our present unhappy war on behalf of their old oppressors has rendered it fashionable to overwhelm them. My two main theses will be, that Greece, even as it is, has greatly benefited by its emancipation from the Turkish yoke, but that it would have benefited still more had it been left to the development of its natural energies and not crippled by the interference of European powers. It will be a great favour to me, and I trust of some advantage to a cause which we both have at heart, if you would take the trouble to communicate to me any special facts, or to refer me to any documents, which may assist me in making out my case. There was a pamphlet of your own which I have seen referred to, and which I have ordered but have not yet obtained. But that was twenty years back, when the Greek kingdom was very young, and since that there has been a revolution, &c., &c. One special point I wish to enlarge on is the introduction of a centralized system, instead of developing and improving the rude elements of municipal government which had lived through both Roman and Turkish despotism. Can you help me to any special facts and figures on this head? But you will readily understand what will conduce to strengthen my argument, one in which I doubt not that you will agree. And for any information with which you may be good enough to supply me, I shall feel most deeply grateful.

I have the honour to be, Sir,

Your obedient servant.

To CHARILAOS TRIKOUPES.

Field Place, Stroud, June 20, 1855.

DEAR SIR,

I am most obliged for your letter which has been forwarded to me from Oxford this morning. I shall most thankfully receive and carefully return the *Spectateur de l'Orient*, and any other documents with which you may favour me, and should I require any further information, I will not scruple to avail myself of your permission to apply for it, as I am anxious to make my article as complete a refutation as possible to the fashionable calumnies against the Greek nation.

. . . I wish I could have written to you and your father in your own language ; I felt greatly inclined to attempt it, but my heart failed me, for during the last ten years, though I have read abundance of Greek, I have not had occasion to compose any.

Believe me,
Your obliged servant.

The attempt was soon made.

To Charilaos Trikoupes.

Ἐν Χάρδῳ (ἐν τῇ ἐπαρχίᾳ τῶν Σομερσήτων), τὴν 5 Ἰουλίου, 1855.

Φίλε Κύριε Τρικούπη,

Τὴν μὲν σὴν ἐπιστολήν, ἐξ Ἐξεκάστρου πρὸς ταύτην κωμόπολιν ὁδοιπορῶν, ἐξεδεξάμην, τὰ δὲ βιβλία παρὰ τῆς γυναικὸς μανθάνω πρὸς τὸν ἐμὸν οἶκον ἀφίκεσθαι. μεγάλην τῷ σῷ πατέρι χάριν ὀφείλω τῶν τῆς ἑαυτοῦ ἱστορίας τόμων. ταῦτα τὰ ἀντίτυπα ὡς κειμήλια ἐν τῇ ἐμῇ βιβλιοθήκῃ φυλάξω, ἃ δὲ νῦν ἔχω (ὧνπερ τὸν μὲν πρότερον τόμον ἔδωκέ μοι ὁ ἐν Κερκύρᾳ γραμματεὺς Γεώργιος Μπώην) τῇ τῆς ἁγίας Τριάδος ἐν Ὀξονίᾳ βιβλιοθήκῃ δώσω, ἵνα οἱ ἐκεῖ περὶ τῆς ἐν Ἑλλάδι καλῆς τε καὶ δικαίας ἐπαναστάσεως πλέον τι μανθάνωσι.

Εἴπερ ποτε ἢ σεαυτῷ ἢ τῷ σῷ πατέρι σχολήν τινα παρέχουσιν αἱ περὶ τῆς πατρίδος σπουδαί, εἰ δὲ ὑμῖν ἡδομένοις εἴη τὰ ἐν τῇ δυτικῇ Ἀγγλίᾳ καὶ τῇ Καμπρίᾳ ὄρη τε ὁρᾶν καὶ ἀνθρώπους, χαρᾷ ὅτι μεγίστῃ τοιούτους ἐν Λανρυμνίᾳ δέξομαι ξένους.

Εὔχομαί σοι πᾶν ἔφετον,
ὁ σός,
Ἐδούαρδος Φρήμαν.

[Translation of the above.]

To Charilaos Trikoupes.

At Chard (in the province of the Somersetans), July 5, 1855.

Dear Mr. Trikoupes,

    I received your letter on my journey from Exeter to this country town, and I learn from my wife that the books have arrived at my house. I owe your father many thanks for the volumes of his history. I shall keep these copies as treasures in my own library, and those which I now possess (of which the former volume was given me by the secretary in Corfu, George Bowen[1]) I shall present to the library of (the College of) the Holy Trinity in Oxford, in order that the students there may learn something more concerning the noble and righteous insurrection in Greece.

If your zealous labours on behalf of your country ever permit you or your father to have any leisure, and if it would afford you any pleasure to see hills and people in western England and in Wales, I shall be delighted to receive such guests at Lanrumney.

With every good wish, I remain, yours,

EDWARD FREEMAN.

Mr. Finlay replied on June 27 to Freeman's first letter, and wrote twice to him again at considerable length in the course of the summer and autumn. For the information which Freeman was seeking he referred him to some of his own pamphlets and articles in *Blackwood's Magazine*, published during the last twenty years, some of which had been translated in the *Revue Britannique*, and had therefore excited some interest in Greece, and elsewhere on the Continent. He expressed entire agreement with the general principles laid down in Freeman's letter, but he took a very gloomy view of the present condition and immediate prospects of Greece. He admitted that independence was a great gain, and worth a hundred years of revolution, but the condition of the country was still lamentable. 'We have had,' he says, 'a European monarchy for more than twenty-two years, and a representative government for twelve, yet not a single elementary measure has been proposed to

[1] Sir George Bowen, his old college friend, at that time Secretary to the 'Lord High Commissioner' of the Ionian Islands.

secure the increase and improvement of the agricultural population.' He was doing his best to persuade the people to improve their own condition, for he had lost all hope of help from protecting powers, kings, diplomatists, and representative chambers. Meanwhile, brigandage prevailed in all parts of the country, and was accompanied with acts of the most revolting cruelty, which the government took no vigorous measures to suppress.

Freeman's article in the *Edinburgh Review* for April, 1856, contains a clear and concise sketch of the history of the modern Greek nation as distinguished from the purely Hellenic race of classical antiquity, of the war of independence, and the subsequent condition of the country down to the time at which he was writing. But he first of all deals with the pretext for withholding sympathy from the modern Greeks, which alleged that they were mere impostors and not Greeks at all. Such an objection, absurd though it was, might be regarded as a natural retribution for resting the cause of Greek independence, as some persons did, upon grounds which were too narrow. There had been a vast deal too much talk about the descendants of Leonidas and Themistocles, about the glories of Marathon and Thermopylae. The Greeks and their friends were too apt to leap back two thousand years and ignore all history between the fight of Chaeronea [1] and the fight of Dragatshan [2]. They were too apt also to isolate the cause of the Greek from the general cause of subject nations. The real grounds for sympathy with the Greeks

[1] The decisive victory of Philip of Macedon over the Athenians and their allies, B.C. 338.

[2] The first great decisive victory of the Greeks over the Turks in the Revolution of A.D. 1821.

were, that they were an oppressed people rising against
their oppressors, and a Christian people, oppressed as
Christians, rising against infidel oppressors. The immortal associations of old Greece, the identity of language
and, in many respects of character, between its ancient and
its modern inhabitants, added, of course, a peculiar charm
which could not attach to any other land or any other
struggle: but the real merit of the Greek cause—the
cause of religion, liberty, and civilization—must not be
overshadowed by past associations, however glorious.
As to purity of race, if no one but a genuine Hellene
could claim our sympathy, and if no one was to be
admitted as a genuine Hellene who could not produce
a pure Dorian or Ionian pedigree, the cause might as
well be given up at once. The modern Greeks were
a very mixed race: but not more mixed than the
modern English. If Macedonian, Slavonian, Albanian,
Wallachian, Frankish, and even Turkish blood were
mingled with the pure stock of the old Hellene, so was
that of the old Anglo-Saxon mixed up with the blood
of every race which he conquered and of every race
which conquered him, as well as with that of every people
whom commerce or persecution had led to settle in our
island. Gael, Cymry, Dane, Norman, Fleming, Frank,
almost every nation of modern Europe had contributed
to the result. We generally rather boasted ourselves of
our mingled ancestry, but the mingled ancestry of the
Greek was supposed to make him a debased mongrel,
incapable of comprehending what national sentiments
were. If the Greek was a mongrel so was the Englishman: but the Englishman, after all foreign intermixture,
remained essentially and practically an Englishman,
and the Greek, after all foreign intermixture, remained

essentially and practically a Greek. By Greeks he understood, without regard to political allegiance or geographical position, all those who both spoke the Greek language and professed the faith of the Greek Church. As for their character, which was sometimes said to be so depraved as to be quite unworthy of sympathy, he maintained, that both in its good and bad points, it was very much the same as that of the old Greeks, allowing for the debasement inseparable from the loss of political liberty for two thousand years, of which the last four centuries had added the burden of the most grinding Mahometan oppression. After sketching the history of this modern Greek people, he traced the course of the war of independence which he divided into four periods. The first covered the year 1821, when the Turks were expelled from the whole of Peloponnesus and the adjoining provinces, and a national government was established. The second extended from 1822 to 1824, when the Porte attempted single-handed to recover the revolted provinces, and the Greeks were unhappily torn by internal dissensions. The third began in 1825, when Ibrahim Pasha came from Egypt to the assistance of the Porte and reconquered nearly the whole of the lost territory. The fourth and last period, extending from 1826 to 1832, was marked by the intervention of the great European Powers which took the settlement of the affairs of Greece into their own hands.

In establishing the Greek State two radical errors had, in Freeman's judgement, been committed. In the first place, it was far too small either to satisfy the national instincts of the Greek people, or to secure the political objects of their western protectors. A Greek kingdom ought, in all reason, to have included Crete, at least, at

one end, and Chalcidice at the other. Such a Greek
State need neither have been a tool of Russia nor an
enemy of Turkey. The existing State was so petty that
it could hardly fail to be both. The second error was
the character of the government which had been set up.
In a letter which Freeman wrote to the *Spectator* in
December, 1854, he pointed out that the history of the
Achaean League, of the Swiss and Dutch Republics,
and of the United States of America, proved that
a people who had won their own independence most
naturally adopted some form of federal government.
But the idea of a Republic or Federation of any kind
was odious to the Great Powers which settled the affairs
of Greece, and therefore it was decreed that Greece
must have a king. In an article in the *Edinburgh Review*
in 1856, Freeman admits that the strong hand of a single
ruler might be needed to control and direct a people only
just set free from a barbarian master, many of them in
consequence only half barbarians, and all utterly unused
to political self-government. But granting the necessity
of a monarchy, it need not have been bureaucratic or
Bavarian. A native king was ideally the best, but no
such king appeared. The crown was offered to Prince
Leopold of Saxe-Coburg, undoubtedly the best choice
which could have been made among princely foreigners,
but Leopold declined the offer[1]. And then the wisdom
of collective Europe selected a foreign boy[2] for the
throne, his power to be exercised by foreign regents

---

[1] He did in fact accept it on February 11, 1830, but resigned on
May 21 of the same year. See Finlay's *Hist.*, vii. 54-56. The narrow
limits prescribed for the kingdom of Greece by the Great Powers was
certainly one cause, if not the chief cause, of his retractation.

[2] Prince Otho, the second son of the king of Bavaria.

until he came of age. The king that was wanted was a practical, working king : a king who did not require a grand palace, a ceremonious court, or a vast army of officials. But the Bavarian notion of civilization was to thrust all these things ready made upon a semi-barbarous and impoverished country. Civilization and liberty took the form of debt, taxation, foreign governors, foreign legislation, and foreign habits. A palace was built at a ridiculous expenditure, but roads were left unmade, and agriculture was neglected.

A bloodless revolution in 1843 gave Greece a constitution which looked well at first sight, but was radically unsound. It instituted universal suffrage for the national assembly, but withheld it from the municipalities in which the chief magistrates were selected by the king from three persons nominated by a local oligarchy. The old municipalities of Greece had survived ages of Roman despotism and of Frankish and Ottoman bondage. Next to her national Church they had been mainly instrumental in preserving her national existence. They had been suppressed by the revolutionary dictator Capodistria. They were now nominally restored, but in such a form as to make them mere tools of the monarchy. It was a farce to institute universal suffrage for the great council of the nation, while there was not universal suffrage for the petty council of the village. The true education for the greater politics was to be found in the practice of the less. The parliament was paid : it met for an annual talk of ten months in the year. Yet it could not find time to make roads, suppress brigandage, or encourage agriculture, while it fettered commerce by absurd restrictions.

The very mean opinion which Freeman entertained of diplomatists may be traced in a great measure to this mismanaged settlement, so called, of the kingdom of Greece by the Great Powers. Two radical evils commonly pervaded the modern system of diplomacy and international intercourse. In the first place, when the limits of a new kingdom were defined, or those of an old kingdom were readjusted, the principle of nationality was neglected or ignored. Diplomatists set to work to map out a frontier, and to arrange a dynasty, according to their own technical ideas, with little reference either to the wishes or the necessities of the people who were principally concerned in the matter. They seemed to think that the signature of a note or of a protocol by parties who were distant and comparatively unconcerned, at once altered the circumstances and duties of those who were most deeply interested in the question, but who were not consulted about it. And the second evil was that the people of a new or resuscitated state were not left to the free and natural development of their own resources and national character, but an attempt was made to thrust upon them the political and social institutions of other nations. In older times nations had not generally been subjected to this kind of treatment. When the earliest of all struggles between Austria and freedom had crowned the Alpine shepherds with immortal honour, it did not occur to the Emperor at Constantinople, the King of Castile, and the Republic of Novgorod to arrange that Uri and Schweiz should form a monarchy under a prince of the blood royal of Poland, but that Unterwalden must retain its allegiance to its lawful sovereign. The Great Powers, however, which undertook the settlement of Greece, decreed that Peloponnesus, Attica, Boeotia, and Phthiotis might exchange an Ottoman for a Bavarian master, but that Crete, Chios, Epirus, and Chalcidice, must remain in their old bondage [1].

In the April number of the *Edinburgh* for 1858 an article appeared by Freeman on the Eastern Church, written by way of a review of Muravieff's *History of the Church of Russia*, John Mason Neale's *History of the Holy Eastern Church*, and W. Palmer's *Dissertations on subjects relating to the 'Orthodox' or 'Eastern Catholic' Communion.* Some of the criticisms of these authors and their works are in his most trenchant style, and are very amusing reading. But the greater part of the article consists of a vigorous sketch of the history of the Orthodox Church, viewed in its political and national, rather than in its strictly theological aspect. The great interest in his eyes of the Churches of the East lay in their being witnesses to the fact that a Church may be strictly national, admitting no foreign jurisdiction, and yet retain the fullest intercommunion with the equally

---

[1] The frontier between Greece and Turkey was drawn from the mouth of the Achelous to the mouth of the Sperchius.   In reference to it Mr. Finlay remarks, 'Diplomatic ignorance could hardly have traced a more unsuitable line of demarcation.   All Acarnania and a considerable part of Aetolia were surrendered to the Sultan.   That part of the Continent in which Greek is the language of the people was annexed to Turkey, and that part in which the agricultural population speaks the Albanian language was attached to Greece.   With such a frontier it was certain that peace could only be established by force : yet the protocol declared that no power should send troops into Greece without the unanimous consent of the allies.   This injudicious protocol concluded with a foolish paragraph. congratulating the allied Courts on having reached the close of a long and difficult negotiation.'   He adds in a note that Colonel Leake, who was known to be better acquainted with the proposed frontier than any man in Europe, was then residing in London, but he was not consulted. *Hist.*, vii. 54.

independent Churches of other nations. The Orthodox Church contained peoples, nations, and languages of various origins, under various governments, and in various stages of civilization. Greeks, Roumans, Slaves, Georgians, were bound together by the tie of a common faith and worship, not as in the Western Churches, by common subjection to one central power. This co-existence of national independence and religious intercommunion seemed to him to be the highest ecclesiastical ideal on earth, and to afford a good hope that there might some day be a more extended application of the principle among the divided branches of the Universal Church. The connexion which he was fond of tracing between the growth of the Byzantine Empire and the Orthodox Church has surely never been more clearly and tersely set forth than in the following passage :—

'For some time the Roman Empire and the Catholic Church were co-extensive; and to this day Christendom is nearly co-extensive with those countries which either formed part of the Roman Empire, or were once civilized and evangelized by the inhabitants. But within the Roman Empire and within the Catholic Church there gradually arose the great division into East and West. The Greek and Latin provinces split off into rival empires and rival churches. In the farther East the Syrian and Egyptian provinces which had never been really incorporated with the Roman Empire fell off from all allegiance, temporal or spiritual, either to the old or the new Rome. Meanwhile, both in the East and West, new races of men were coming within the sphere both of the Church and the Empire in a character strangely compounded of conquerors and disciples. Thus there arose a Western Empire with its Western, Latin, or Catholic Church, with its half oppressor, half pupil, the Teuton. Thus too there arose an Eastern Empire with its Eastern, Greek, or Orthodox Church, with its half oppressor, half pupil, the Slave. The Byzantine Empire and

the Orthodox Church, as we find them fully developed between
the seventh and eleventh centuries, were thus the result of
a triple series of events. The Oriental provinces were
violently dismembered ; the Latin provinces gradually fell off.
The residuum left by their loss was nearly co-extensive with
that artificial Greek nation, Church, and Empire which in the
two former characters is still living and vigorous. But the
Orthodox Church, thus closely united in its origin with the
Byzantine Empire, did not remain confined within the limits of
Byzantine political authority. It did however remain, and it
still remains, confined within the limits of Byzantine moral
influence. Numerically viewed it has been, for ages past,
a Slavonic Church. Morally and intellectually it has always
been, and probably always will be, a Greek Church. To the
Eastern Slaves the new Rome was the centre of civilization,
just as old Rome was to the Teutons. Bulgaria, Servia, Russia,
have often been the political enemies, but they have always
been the intellectual disciples, of the Empire and Church of
Constantinople.

The remainder of the essay is devoted to the consideration of the three processes which led to the formation of the Orthodox Church as a distinct form of
Christianity : (i) the loss of the heretical Churches in
the East : (ii) the separation from Latin Christendom ;
(iii) the conversion of the eastern Slaves, and the rise of
the Russian Church.

Freeman's review of Mommsen's *History of Rome*,
which appeared in the *National Review* for April, 1859,
is the earliest published expression of his views on Roman
history, and of his judgement on the principal writers
upon that subject. The same masterly power of taking
a comprehensive survey of long periods of time, indicating the character and comparative importance of each,
the same clear perception of the bearing of the past
upon the present which marked his articles upon Grecian

history, are conspicuous in this essay also. And having at this early age seized with a true instinct all the main points of Greek and Roman history, he had not, in later life, to recede from any of his positions, but was continually illustrating the truth of them by fresh instances as he added to the stock of his knowledge. The vastness of the history of Rome had for him a special fascination. It was the greatest of all historical subjects, because it was in truth the history of the world. He who would understand Roman history aright must know the history of the Semitic and Hellenic races which Rome swallowed up, and the history of those races of the further East which Rome herself could never overcome. He must go yet further back, and by the aid of philological research grope warily beyond the domain of history or legend. He must go back to unrecorded days when Greek and Italian were one people; and to days more ancient still, when Greek, Italian, Celt, Teuton, Slave, Hindoo, and Persian were as yet members of one undivided brotherhood. But if the historian of Rome was bound to look back, still more was he bound to look forward. He had but to cast his eye upon the world around him to see that Rome was still a living and abiding power. The tongue of Rome was the groundwork of the living speech of south-western Europe; it was still the ecclesiastical language of half Christendom. The law of Rome was still quoted in our courts, and taught in our universities; it formed the source and groundwork of the jurisprudence of other countries. Little more than half a century had passed since an Emperor of the Romans still held his place among European sovereigns, and, as Emperor of the Romans, claimed precedence over every meaner potentate. The title of a Roman office, the surname of a Roman family, was still the highest object of human ambition, clutched at alike by worn-out dynasties and by successful usurpers. Above all, 'in deep and vast significance towered the living phenomenon of the Roman Church and the Roman pontiff.' 'Look back to the first dim traditions of the European continent, and we look not too far back for the beginnings of Roman history. Ask for the last despatch and the last telegram, and it will tell us that the history of Rome has not yet reached its end.'

When Freeman wrote this essay, he had not quite made up his mind what was the point at which a special Roman history should most properly end, but he finally decided that Arnold was right in fixing it at the coronation of Charles the Great in 800. Down to the coronation of Charles, the Byzantine Emperor was at least nominal lord of the old as well as of the new Rome. With Charles began the various dynasties of German Caesars, which kept up more of local connexion with old Rome, but much less of the true Roman tradition, than their rivals at Byzantium. The date commonly selected for the close of strictly Roman history, A.D. 476, was too early, for it shut out Theodoric the patrician, and Belisarius the consul. But when the Roman Empire had practically become an appendage to a German kingdom, the old life of Rome was gone. The old memories still went on influencing history in a thousand ways ; but the government of Charles was not Roman in the same sense as the government of Theodoric had been Roman. There were henceforward two Roman Empires, and two Roman Emperors. Of these, the one fast tended to become definitely German, the other to become definitely Greek.

The views and the methods which had been success-
ively adopted in dealing with early Roman history, have
never been more clearly set forth than in the following passage, which forms an introduction to Freeman's
criticism of Dr. Mommsen and his work :—

'That Rome was taken by the Gauls seems to be the one
event in the annals of several centuries which we can be
absolutely sure was recorded by a writer who lived at the time.
Yet of these ages Dionysios and Livy give us a history as
detailed as Thucydides can give of the Peloponnesian war, or
Eginhard of the campaigns of Charles the Great. Till the
time of Niebuhr, all, save a solitary sceptic here and there, were
ready to give to the first decade of Livy as full a belief as they
could have given to Thucydides or Eginhard. And the few
sceptics that there were, commonly carried their unbelief to so
unreasonable a length as rather to favour the cause of a still
more unreasonable credulity. Till Arnold wrote, Hooke's was
the standard English history of Rome : and Hooke no more
thought of doubting the existence of Romulus than he thought
of doubting the existence of Caesar. Then came the wonderful
work of Niebuhr which overthrew one creed and set up
another. The tale which our fathers had believed on the
authority of Livy sank to the level of a myth, the invention of
a poet, the exaggeration of a family panegyrist : but in its stead
we were in our youth called upon to accept another tale, told
with almost equal minuteness, on the personal authority of
a German doctor who had only just passed away from among
men. Niebuhr's theory, in fact, acted like a spell : it was not to
argument or evidence that it appealed : his followers avowedly
claimed for him a kind of power of 'divination.' Since that
time there has been, both in Germany and in England, a reaction against Niebuhr's authority. The insurrection has
taken different forms. One party seems to have quietly fallen
back into the unreasoning faith of our fathers. Others are
content to adopt Niebuhr's general mode of inquiry, and
merely to reverse his judgement on particular points. This is
the case with the able but as yet fragmentary work of

Dr. Ihne[1]. Lastly, there comes the party of absolute unbelief, whose champion is no less a person than the late Chancellor of the Exchequer. Beneath the Thor's hammer of Sir George Cornewall Lewis the edifice of Titus Livius and the edifice of Barthold Niebuhr fall to the ground side by side. Myths may be very pretty, divination may be very ingenious, but the Right Honourable member for the Radnor Boroughs will stand nothing but evidence which would be enough to hang a man. Almost every child has wept over the tale of Virginia, if not in Livy, at least in Goldsmith. Niebuhr and Arnold connect the tragic story with deep historical and political lessons : but Sir George Lewis coldly asks : " Who saw her die ? " and as nobody is ready to make the same answer as the fly in the nursery legend—as Virginius and Icilius did not write the story down on a parchment roll, or carve it on a table of brass – he will have nothing to say to any of them.'

Freeman himself thought at this time, and continued to think, that the faith with which he and his contemporaries had in their youth been taught to look up to Niebuhr was, although exaggerated, not altogether misplaced. Niebuhr's doctrine that the current statements about early Roman history, although probably far removed from the literal truth, did yet contain a basis of truth, he held to be a sound doctrine. It required great caution and discrimination in its application, and Niebuhr had damaged his own cause by his arrogant and self-sufficient dogmatism : but his method, at once destructive and constructive, was in Freeman's judgement essentially sound. The estimate which he formed of Mommsen, after reading the first three volumes of his History, remained substantially unaltered in later years. He respected him as a consummate scholar, who had mastered more thoroughly than any former writer the antiquities and the

---

[1] His Roman History has since been published in five volumes both in German and English.

philology, as well as the history, of the people of whom he treated.   In addition to this primary merit, Freeman recognized another, equally sterling, that he always told his story clearly, and often with extraordinary force. On the other hand, Mommsen was daringly dogmatic ; as dogmatic as Niebuhr, while he did not, like Niebuhr, condescend to favour his readers with the reasons upon which his theories were based.   He sometimes indulged in a vein of low sarcasm unworthy of himself and of his subject, and seemed to worship mere force with a total indifference to the moral character of the actors or the nature of their acts ; while in purity of style he was vastly inferior to Curtius, owing to the needless intro-duction of a large number of French and Latin words. In mere knowledge Mommsen, of course, surpassed Arnold as he surpassed every other scholar, but Freeman maintained that Arnold, by his finer moral instincts and his warm sympathy with all that was great and noble and righteous, often drew a truer picture of persons and events than was possible to the colder nature of the German historian.

The series of articles on Greek and Roman history to which reference has been made, were far from exhausting Freeman's literary energies during this period.   In No-vember and December, 1855, he delivered six lectures before the Philosophical Institution at Edinburgh on the ' History and Conquests of the Saracens.'   He did not begin to write them till August, and had a great deal of other work on hand at the same time, but, being full of his subject, he composed with rapidity and ease.   They were published in the succeeding year, with the following dedication [1]:

[1] A second edition, with a new preface, was brought out in 1876.

'To George Finlay, LL.D., K.R.G., the historian of Constantinople and Mediaeval Greece, this record of the rival Empire is inscribed with feelings of gratitude and admiration.'

In the following year appeared the *History and Antiquities of St. David's*, a quarto volume of 400 pages, with illustrations by Jewitt engraved by Le Keux. This work, the joint production of Freeman and his friend Mr. Basil Jones, the present Bishop of that See, was the fruit of many years of industrious inquiry, research, and observation. The entries in Freeman's diary during the two years preceding the publication of this book, show how much of his time was occupied in correcting the proof-sheets and in making the index.

In the *Edinburgh Review* for April, 1859, he had an article on the second volume of Sir Francis Palgrave's *History of Normandy and England*, in which he again expresses his great admiration and respect for the ability and learning of the author.

' Few living men,' he says, ' have equalled him in the extent of his reading. Still fewer have surpassed him in sincere and independent inquiry. He has won the deep gratitude of every historical student by the new light which he has thrown upon the ancient institutions of our own land. He has at least deserved, if he has not always won, a gratitude deeper still for being the first to find the key to the great riddle of general mediaeval history. The man who discovered that the Roman Empire did not terminate in A. D. 476, but that the still living and acting imperial power formed an historical centre for centuries later, merits a place in the very highest rank of historical inquirers.'

But he criticizes Sir Francis unsparingly for grave faults of style in this volume of his history, and for want of discrimination in the use of his authorities. He accordingly discusses with carefulness and acuteness the

characteristics and comparative value of the three writers
who were the chief original authorities for French history of the tenth century: Frodoard, Canon of Rheims;
Richer, monk of the same city; and Dudo, Dean of St.
Quintin. Such an examination was characteristic of the
thorough and conscientious way in which he always
discharged his duty as a reviewer. However great
might be the quantity of work of this kind on his hands,
he never suffered himself to lapse into a habit of hasty and
superficial treatment. Before reviewing any important
historical work, he always studied some, at least, of the
original authorities upon which it was based. Thus, in
a letter written to Mr. Stubbs in November, 1857, he
says: 'I am hard at work on Thucydides and Xenophon
for one review, Dudo and Frodoard for another.' The
result of this method was, that most of his reviews have
a threefold interest. They contain critical examinations
of the author and his authorities, and a sketch, always
spirited and often masterly, of the whole subject from
his own point of view.

As an illustration of the range of his studies and
interests, it may be mentioned that, in addition to the
long articles on Greek, Roman, and early English, or
rather Norman, history produced during this period of
five years, he contributed another on a totally different
subject, 'The Court of Louis the XVth,' to *Bentley's
Quarterly* for October, 1859, besides writing nearly fifty
shorter reviews for the *Saturday Review*, which was
started in 1855, and nearly forty for the *Guardian*.
He also wrote, from time to time, for a series of tracts
edited by Sir Arthur Elton, entitled '*Tracts for the
Present Crisis.*' the object of which was to propagate
accurate knowledge respecting the past history and

present condition of south-eastern Europe, and to prove the iniquity of carrying on the war with Russia in support of the Turks. He frequently wrote letters upon the same subject but occasionally also on home politics, in the *Evening Star*, a strong Liberal paper, and he became for a time a paid writer of leading articles for that journal.

In the months of January and February, 1859, he wrote four leading articles in the *Guardian* upon the Ionian Islands, in reference to the appointment of Mr. Gladstone as High Commissioner Extraordinary to inquire into the grievances of the inhabitants, who asked to be incorporated with the kingdom of Greece. All proposals for a settlement of the difficulty short of acceding to this demand proved to be impracticable, and in 1864 the Ionian Islands were formally ceded to Greece. By a large part of the English press the discontented islanders had been denounced as rebellious and ungrateful subjects, and a plentiful stream of sarcasm and ridicule had been poured forth upon Mr. Gladstone and his mission, which it was thought witty to describe as an adventure of 'classical enthusiasm,' or 'an ethnological and literary amour.' Freeman, on the contrary, maintained in these articles that the demand of the Ionian islanders was natural and reasonable. They were not, properly speaking, British subjects at all. The islands had been made an independent Republic in 1815, under the protection of Great Britain; but the protecting power had military possession and exercised a virtual sovereignty. The inhabitants had assisted Greece in the war of independence: Greece was now delivered from the Turk, but the people who had helped them to shake off the yoke were still dependent upon a foreign power.

The English administration, although not cruel like that
of the Turk, had not been altogether wise or liberal.
No wonder, therefore, that the Ionian islanders desired
to be politically united with their brethren on the adja-
cent continent, with whom they were already one in
language, religion, and sympathy. It was vain to tell
them that they were better off under British rule than
they would be as subjects of King Otho. National
instincts and sentiment would be proof against such
arguments. It was impossible to dragoon men into
happiness.

It was natural that one who took such a profound
interest as Freeman did in politics, both foreign and
domestic, should have been ambitious of entering Parliament. He was a philanthropist and a sincere patriot,
and he often longed to be able to raise his voice in the
great council of the nation on behalf of the principles of
civil and religious freedom, humanity, and justice. He
was fully persuaded that the true honour and the highest
interests of the country depended upon strict adherence
to these principles; but he thought that in the strife of
party government, and in the complications of diplomacy,
they were perpetually in danger of being violated or
neglected. They were the avowed principles of the
advanced Liberal party, and in the ranks of that party he
might be generally reckoned, but he would never surrender
the independence of his conscience or of his reason to any
party or to any leader, however eminent. As a candidate
for Parliament, therefore, he might have been most fairly
described as an independent Radical. He came forward
for Cardiff in 1857, and for Wallingford in 1859, but on
both occasions he was too late in the field, and had too
little interest with the constituencies to have any chance

of success, and he retired from the contest without going to the poll. The following address was issued to the electors of Wallingford :—

Lanrumney, Cardiff, April 25, 1859.

GENTLEMEN,

Information which I have received from your Borough, has induced me to come forward at the last moment, as a candidate for the high honour of representing you in Parliament.

I have the misfortune to be personally unknown to you, but I am not unknown to many in other parts of the kingdom, as an advanced and earnest reformer, and I trust in a very short time to appear personally before you, and to explain my views more at length.

I do not come before you as the pledged follower of any minister or of any possible minister. I believe that powers far too irresponsible are at present confided to 'Governments,' or 'Administrations.' The result is a constant struggle for power, and the time of the nation, which ought to be devoted to sound legislation, is wasted on putting down and setting up successive ministries. I should go to Parliament prepared to support any measures which I approved, from whatever source they might proceed. I hold also that no Member of Parliament should pledge himself to vote this way or that on matters of detail. If I ever sit in the House of Commons, I will sit there as a representative, not as a delegate. It is, however, the duty of every candidate, to lay before the constituency he addresses, a full and frank exposition of his general principles. This I will now proceed to do.

I have given many years to the study of parliamentary reform. The creed which has been the result substantially agrees with that of the more advanced section of the existing Liberal party. With regard to the extension of the franchise, I do not bind myself to any particular scheme, simply because it may often be good policy to support measures which do not go the full length that one can desire.

I am, by settled conviction, a supporter of the ballot. I think that open voting is the better way, whenever open voting can

† VOL. I.   P

be combined with free voting. But, for the corruption and coercion now too often practised at elections, the ballot seems to me the only possible remedy.

I wish to see Parliaments elected for a shorter time than they now are, and to make them indissoluble during the time fixed for their duration.

The question of re-distribution of seats is one which I have very attentively considered, and on which I trust to explain my views to you more at length when we meet. I will now only say that, while I am for giving an increase of members to many of our great towns and counties, I could not support those sweeping measures of disfranchisement which are urged by many with whom I otherwise agree. I should prefer the grouping together of the smaller boroughs, rather than their total suppression.

I am for the total repeal of Church-rates, as an impost at once unjust to the Dissenter, and tending to bring the Church, to which I myself belong, into odium.

In the Continental war which seems unhappily impending, I should advocate strict neutrality on the part of England. In the quarrels of two despots, between whom it is hard to say whose cause is the worse, a free nation cannot be called upon to interfere. We can only hope that the cause of Italian and European freedom may gain in the end, by the dissensions of its enemies.

In a word, I raise as my motto the time-honoured cry of 'Peace, Retrenchment, and Reform.' If that cry is one which strikes any chord in the hearts of the electors of Wallingford, I call upon them to rally, even now at the last moment, round a thoroughly independent Candidate, and to make one strong effort to contribute their share to the popular element in the Parliament about to be assembled.

I have the honour to be, Gentlemen,
Your obedient Servant,
EDWARD AUGUSTUS FREEMAN.

On the subject of Church-rates, to which reference is made in this address, and which continued to be a cause of great contention between the Church and Dissenters until the abolition of compulsory Church-rates in 1868, he had expressed his mind fully and clearly in a letter to the *Spectator* of September 4, 1858. The plain principle of religious equality required that every religious body should have full power to preach its own doctrines, exercise its own discipline, regulate its own affairs, enjoy its own property. This principle was violated by Church-rates. The Dissenter was compelled to pay for the maintenance of the Church, and in return had a voice in the management of its internal affairs. Thus the liberty of the Dissenter was infringed by the compulsion to pay for the maintenance of a building in which he did not worship, and the right of the Church to self-government was violated by the Dissenter's power of voting upon its affairs.

On the other hand, he strenuously opposed at this time, and to the end of his life, the erroneous notions which have commonly prevailed, more especially amongst Nonconformists, respecting the nature of Church property, and of the connexion of the Church with the State in this country; and he pointed out that many of the arguments by which some advocated, and others opposed, the disestablishment of the Church of England were alike untenable.

The following letter, which appeared in the *Evening Star* of October 25, 1858, represents the substance of his opinions upon the subject, from which he never afterwards deviated.

CHURCH PROPERTY.

Lanrumney, Cardiff, October 19, 1858.
SIR,

There has been lately a good deal of controversy in your columns on the nature and rights of Church property.

P 2

As the question is one which is much misunderstood on all sides, I wish to put forth a few plain considerations on the subject, but I do not intend to enter into any controversy with any one about it.

The Legislature may do what it likes with Church property, because it may do what it likes with anybody and anything. There are no limits to its power; it is responsible to no one on earth. An Act of Parliament may at any moment override the ordinary law. It may cut off a man's head without trial, as in the case of Lord Strafford or Sir John Fenwick. It may set aside his will, as in the case of Thelluson. Till the passing of the late Divorce Act, it was in the constant habit of dissolving an engagement which both canon and common law held to be indissoluble. Every time it passes a railway bill, it takes away people's property, and gives them what they may think an imperfect compensation. It clearly might, if it chose, take it away without giving them any compensation. In all these cases the proceeding may be just and expedient, or it may be the opposite, but anyhow it is legally valid. It is therefore evident that an alienation or redistribution of Church property is at any time within the power of King, Lords, and Commons, and that King, Lords, and Commons must themselves be the judges of the justice and expediency of such a measure.

But this is very often not all that is meant. Many people, when they say that the State has a right to dispose of Church property, mean much more than that the Legislature is supreme over Church property, because it is supreme over all persons and things. They talk as if Church property were in some special way the property of the nation, different from all other property. Now, this notion is legally and historically false, and grows out of three distinct misconceptions.

1. Parliament is seen to be in the habit of dealing with ecclesiastical property much more frequently, and with much less respect than with private property. Hence it is inferred that it has some special rights over the former, which it has not over the latter. Now, if we take in railway bills, in every one of which private rights are always set aside, I very much doubt whether ecclesiastical property is just now dealt with

more frequently, or with less respect than private property. And, if it is, it arises from the very nature of corporate property. The cases in which it is just and expedient for the Legislature to touch corporate property will naturally occur more frequently than those in which it is just or expedient to touch private property. But the principle is the same in both ; it is the exercise of the extraordinary, not the ordinary, powers of the State.

2. It is supposed that the Church was some time or other endowed by the State. Now, if such were the case, it would clearly show, not that Church property is national property, but that it is not so. What a man gives away is no longer his. Therefore, if the State had endowed the Church, the recall of the endowment would still only come under the head of the State's extraordinary power. It may be quite just and expedient to do so, but not on the principle that a man may do what he will with his own. But, in truth, this notion of a State endowment is simply a mistake. The thing never happened. People take it for granted ; but they cannot tell one the date, or the circumstances of the event. The truth is, that, except some comparatively small and comparatively recent pecuniary grants, the Church of England owes all her vested revenues to the voluntary system. They are derived from property freely given at various times by various bene-factors. They differ in nothing but their greater extent and greater antiquity from the endowments common among some dissenting bodies. The law simply maintains the Church in rights, some of which are older than the Parliament or the monarchy. Of course, much Church property came from Royal gifts ; but in days when no man doubted that the Crown lands were the king's private property, a Royal gift and a State gift were two different things. One king gave to bishops and monks, another gave to minions or mistresses. Both gifts might be foolish, but both were legal. Neither constituted a State endowment.

3. It is said that in the sixteenth century Church property changed hands, that it was taken from one Church and given to another. In the mouth of a Roman Catholic this may mean that Roman Catholics ought to possess it ; in the mouth of

a Protestant, it is commonly an *argumentum ad hominem* to illustrate the power of the State. But here again, the event never happened. I am not speaking theologically, but historically. The Roman Catholic may be theologically right in holding that the changes of the sixteenth century deprived the Church of England of all right to be called a Church. I only say that, legally and historically, the Church before the Reformation and the Church after the Reformation are one and the same body. The Church presided over by Augustine, by Becket, by Cranmer, by Laud, and by Sumner, is one and the same society. There was no transfer from one society to another, but an existing society made certain changes in its own constitution. 'A Town Priest' says that gifts made to a Church which held the Papal supremacy cannot be fairly held by a Church which rejects it. Unless he can show that this or that possession was given specially to support the Papal supremacy, his argument is good for nothing. That is, it may be very good theologically, but it can prove nothing against the legal and historical identity of the society. 'A. B.' again, argues in the same way about masses for the dead. Does he not know that all foundations specially and directly for that purpose were abolished under Edward VI, that their revenues were seized by the Crown, and that (unless by subsequent gift in any particular case) they are not possessed by the existing Church? This sort of argument plunges us at once into the theological abyss. There have always been changes in the Church from Augustine onwards; the sixteenth century simply witnessed more extensive and more rapid changes than any other. If a Roman Catholic denies the right of the existing Church to donations made from 1066 to 1531 on the ground of theological difference, the existing Church may fairly challenge him to show his right on the same ground to donations made from 597 to 1066.

In conclusion, the gist of the whole matter is this. Let those who wish for a confiscation of Church property rest their case on the undoubted right of King, Lords, and Commons to do anything. Let them prove the justice and expediency of the proposed measure by showing that all endowments, or that such and such particular endowments, are mischievous to the

nation. That raises a fair question. I happen to think otherwise. I believe that there are a vast mass of particular abuses
about Church endowments which call for thorough reform ;
but I believe Church endowments, as a whole, to be the
opposite of mischievous to the nation. Here is a plain issue,
on which both sides may join on fair terms. I only ask that the
question may not be confused on either side, whether by.
statements which historically and legally are simply false, or
by purely theological positions of which no politician can take
any account.

I am, Sir, your obedient servant,

EDWARD A. FREEMAN.

He touched upon the same question in his letter to
the *Spectator* on Church-rates. He points out that the
clergy were not Government officials, like Post Office
clerks or Captains of Dragoons: they were not in any
sense stipendiaries of the State—their revenues consisted
for the most part of their own freehold endowments :
neither were the churches national property, but the
freehold of this or that local corporation, whether sole or
aggregate. The Church was just as much entitled to
her endowments as the Dissenters were to their endowments. The Protestant Church in Ireland was in
a totally different position to the Church in England,
and he already admitted that some measure of disestablishment and disendowment was no more than
justice demanded. In Ireland he saw pastors without
flocks, revenues without duties, parish churches and
cathedral churches without congregations, and sometimes
in ruins. Those who possessed them could not use
them, and those who would use them were not allowed
to possess them. The National Church and the people
of England had accepted the changes of the sixteenth
century. The National Church and the people of Ireland
had rejected them : and then the endowments which

belonged to the Church of the Irish people had been transferred to the Church of the English Colony. Here then was a case for the State to step in and redress the wrong. In England, on the contrary, there was no such call for any interference on the part of the State. The Church of England had a full, legal, and historical right to her emoluments: only by the abolition of compulsory Church-rates he wished to see her deprived of the unjust power of taxing the members of another communion.

His remarks upon the condition of the Irish Church were partly suggested by the observations which he had made when he was on a tour in the autumn of 1858, in the course of which he visited Drogheda, Kildare, Athlone, Galway, Kilconnel, Killaloe, Cashel, Limerick, and Waterford. His first tour on the continent was made in 1856, in company with his friend, the Rev. North Pinder, formerly Fellow and Tutor of Trinity College, Oxford. They spent the greater part of September in Aquitaine and the neighbourhood of the Pyrenees. It can easily be imagined with what intense interest Freeman now saw for the first time, and sketched with his own hand, the buildings with some of which he was already familiar through descriptions or illustrations in the various books on architecture which he had studied for many years. On the other hand he discovered that he had no relish for mountain climbing. He ascended the Pic du Midi, but he declared that there was neither interest nor beauty in the view to compensate for the toil of the ascent, and except for some distinctly historical purpose he would never in future be persuaded to ascend a mountain.

In 1857 and 1858 he was one of the examiners in the School of Law and Modern History at Oxford. The examiners issued a notice indicating the special subjects which candidates might take up, and recommending the principal books in which they were to be studied. After it had been in circulation about four months, the Vice-Chancellor and Proctors put forth a statement that the 'said paper' was 'without statutable authority.' This announcement, having been made in the *Times* newspaper without any previous communication with the examiners, excited Freeman's wrath, and he addressed an indignant letter to the Vice-Chancellor. Neither the act of issuing the paper nor its contents were in his judgement unstatutable. The examination statute was perfectly vague as regarded Classmen, neither defining the periods of history which were to be taken up, nor prescribing the books to be studied. For Passmen, certain periods were prescribed, but no particular books were recommended. It was obvious, he thought, that the examination could not be carried on unless there was some understanding between the examiner and the student as to the subjects of the examination. 'Modern History' was far too vast a subject for any student, or even any examiner, to be equally well versed in every branch of it. Unless some scheme therefore was drawn up beforehand an examiner might claim to examine, or a student to be examined, in some subject of which the other party was wholly ignorant. The examiners, he said, had most certainly required nothing but what the terms of the statute justified. He could hardly suppose that the Vice-Chancellor and Proctors looked upon it as an unjustifiable stretch of authority for the examiners in a School where English History was a *sine qua non*, to require of the candidates a knowledge of the chief towns and rivers in England and France. 'We found the most

deplorable ignorance,' he says, 'existing in this respect
among the students, and we thought that it was our
duty to remedy it. History without Geography is
simply meaningless.' One of his fellow-examiners, the
Rev. C. W. Boase, Fellow of Exeter, in a letter dated
November 13, 1857, remarks : 'I was told to-day in
a class that the Rhone was the chief tributary of the
Rhine, so the geography clause was not inserted before
it was wanted.' The Vice-Chancellor and Proctors
having issued their protest, took no further steps to
suppress the notice of the examiners ; but early in the
following year it was laid hold of by some members of
an association calling itself the Protestant Alliance, who
excited the alarm of that sensitive body by pointing
out a paragraph in which Lingard was recommended in
preference to Hume for the study of English History.
The committee of the Alliance thereupon addressed
a solemn letter to the Vice-Chancellor, directing his
attention to the obnoxious paragraph, and informing
him that 'the fact that a Romish writer was there
publicly preferred and recommended by the authorities
of a Protestant University' was regarded by the committee as 'one of painful importance.' The alarmists
were referred to the circular which had been put forth
by the Vice-Chancellor and Proctors in the preceding
October, declaring that the examiners had exceeded the
limits of their authority in issuing any list of recommended books, and with this comforting piece of information the Protestant Alliance professed to be
satisfied, although the list remained unwithdrawn. Freeman and Mr. Boase, who were the two senior examiners,
also addressed on their part a letter to Lord Shaftesbury,
who had presided at the meeting of the Alliance when

the subject was first brought forward. In this letter they stated that Lingard's History had been in use ever since the School of Law and Modern History had existed, and that Lingard and Hume had always been alternative books ; and they added :—

'In our recommendation of Lingard as preferable to Hume for the times before the Reformation (which alone are practically affected), we feel quite sure that we should meet with your Lordship's approval. Your Lordship could hardly fail to think us right in preferring the work of a really learned man and very moderate writer, though belonging to another Christian communion, to one not only full of historical errors, but written with an evident animus against the Christian religion in general.'

Early in the same year—1858—the Chair of Modern History in Oxford became vacant by the resignation of Professor Vaughan, and the names and qualifications of various candidates for the office, including R. W. Church, afterwards Dean of St. Paul's, were submitted to the Prime Minister, Lord Derby. Freeman himself was strongly recommended by Thirlwall, Bishop of St. David's, and others; but the choice of the Premier fell upon Mr. Goldwin Smith. No one could question the excellence of the appointment, and no one had a higher admiration for Mr. Smith's character as a man, and for his learning and ability as an historian, than Freeman himself. But it is remarkable that as it was the height of his ambition to obtain a Professorship of History, and as he was certainly well qualified for some office of the kind, he was destined to be disappointed time after time when he came forward as a candidate for various chairs, both in Oxford and elsewhere, until at last, when he did become Regius Professor, he was comparatively indifferent to the honour, and was too old to adapt himself readily to the change in residence and in habits of life which the office involved.

The life at Lanrumney was in all essential features the same as that which Freeman had led at Oaklands. The daily ride, in which he was now often accompanied by one of the children on their pony, was the most regular form of recreation, but he sometimes lent a helping hand in making hay, or pulling potatoes, or constructing a path. His intense dislike, on principle, to field sports, of which more will have to be said hereafter, brought him now and then into collision with the fox-hunters of the neighbourhood. If they had the temerity to invade his fields, within view of the house, he would rush forth from his study and peremptorily eject them, after delivering his mind upon the subject in plain and forcible language. 'Drove out hunters' is the brief but emphatic record in his diary of these scenes. On one occasion a gentleman of the hunt, deceived by his somewhat rough exterior, the shaggy beard, the shabby reading coat, and the other large, loose, ill-fitting garments which for the sake of comfort he always insisted on wearing, took him for an over-zealous bailiff or gardener, and endeavoured to soften his heart by an offering of five shillings, saying, 'Come, my man, don't be so angry; take this, and I'll make it all right with your master.' The reply of the supposed bailiff has not been recorded, which is to be regretted, as it was probably worth hearing. But the fields which were sternly closed against fox-hunters were readily thrown open for the innocent sports of the village school-children at their annual festival. He was, indeed, exceedingly fond of children. Their freshness and simplicity had a great charm for him, and were thoroughly congenial to his own honest and artless

nature. Nothing gave him more pleasure than to watch
their ways and listen to their remarks, and he was
delighted if a baby was bold enough to pull his great
bushy beard as his own children did. His friend James
Riddell, writing to Mrs. Freeman in 1856, says: 'I am
interested to know whether the children still climb their
father's knees by the help of his beard, or whether that
handle has ceased to be afforded them.'

In the relief of poverty and distress he was always
generous, often out of proportion to his means, and in
various ways he did as much as he had leisure to do for
the benefit, both temporal and spiritual, of his poorer
neighbours. He examined the children now and then
in the parish school, and took the chair at meetings of
the Young Men's Christian Association. He held for
a time the office of churchwarden, and finding that the
fine barrel-vaulted roof of the nave in St. Mellon's Church
was in a condition of decay, he got his friend Gilbert Scott
to advise upon the best mode of repairing it, and spent
£100 of his own money upon the work. The church
was a mile distant from Lanrumney Hall, and sometimes
from stress of weather on Sundays, he read the morning
or evening service, as the case might be, with his family
at home, occasionally giving his own exposition of one of
the lessons in place of a sermon.

When he was at Lanrumney he began the practice of
dining early, only varying the hour according to the
season, so as to secure about two hours of daylight after
dinner for a ride or a walk. Dinner thus became a move-
able feast ranging between the limits of one o'clock and
five. His guests did not always find this arrangement
conducive to good digestion, and perhaps, unknown to
himself, it was one cause of his headaches, and of the

sensations of lethargy and dullness, of which there are frequent complaints in his diary during this period ; for the long stretches of work from breakfast to afternoon dinner must have been a severe strain upon the physical powers. Nevertheless he liked this division of the day for the convenience of his work, and adhered to the custom for many years. Great as was the quantity of his literary undertakings and the extent of his correspondence, he found time to give his elder children some instruction in Greek, Latin, History, and Geography. The following patchwork letter to his eldest daughter, intended to practise her in the several tongues which she was then learning, is a quaint illustration of the theory which he always maintained, that the comparative method in teaching languages was the easiest and the most interesting.

To HIS DAUGHTER MARGARET.

Bristol, June 10, 1859.

MEIN LIEBES TOCHTERLEIN,

Hier sind wir χαίροντές τε καὶ ὑγιαίνοντες valde autem defessi. Pourquoi non? Nous avons visité πολλῶν ἀνθρώπων ἄστεα in provinciis Herefordensi, Salopiensi, Wigorniensi, et Glocestrensi. Die Mercurii (qui Anglicè dicitur Wodenesdæg) den Schloss von Ludlow εἴδομεν, où on peut voir *capellam* quandam rotundam. Τί δ', ὦ πρὸς Διός, πάτερ, λέξεις ἴσως, ἐστὶ τὸ Capella? Ne credas, precor, *capras* Salopienses tam crassas esse ; est autem Capella id quod Gallicè dicimus *Chapelle*, Teutonicè autem *Capelle*, Anglicè *Chapel*, Cambricè, ni fallor, *Capel*. Jetzt habe ich Babylonisch genug geschreibt, ἔχω γάρ τινα εἰπεῖν, ἄτινα, ὡς οἶμαι nisi Anglicè scripta sint, vous ne comprendrez pas.

There, little Gretchen, I hope you will be able to make all that out. And now I want you to open the left-hand drawer in my library table, and send me a certain paper you will find there, with names of books, &c. in my writing, in two columns, with crosses set against some of them.

. . . I hope you are all well and happy, that the pony still gets better, and that Edgar enjoys his swims. Ask him whether he remembers having the measles, and whether he is disappointed like Blanche[1] in his favourite *Punch*.

We had some strawberries to-day in the garden. The first this year.

Love to Curly Pate[2] and Lily[3] Catharina jocundissima and Florentilla dulcissima[4]. Also the kitten, Madlle. Thora[5], and Monsieur Panshère[6].

Your affectionate father.

At the end of five years spent at Lanrumney Hall he was again in search of a larger house, chiefly on account of the ever-increasing accumulation of his books. Writing to Mr. Webb in April, 1859, he asks, 'Do you know of a big house anywhere, and a little estate, to be sold? to wit, a house to hold six children and 3000 books (many of them folios), with pasture land enough to keep them in milk, butter, and mutton.'

CORRESPONDENCE, 1855–1859.

To the Rev. H. Thompson.

Lanrhymney, Cardiff, October 21, 1855.

Thanks for your letter and verses. Clevedon is visible to me most days across the Channel, looking something like

'The white streets of Tusculum.'

Had I set to work poetizing thereon, my theme would, I think,

---

[1] The reference is probably to some story in *Punch* which Edgar was fond of reading.

[2] His pet name for his son Edgar.

[3] Edgar's pet name for his sister Helen.

[4] Two younger daughters.

[5] A Newfoundland dog.

[6] A small stray dog adopted by the family and called Pincher.

have been Elton and Peace. Beati Pacifici. I have been diligently dispersing Sir Arthur's Tracts; I think some of them might be better, but they are the best things of the sort I have seen, and, I hope, may open some people's eyes to the infamous wickedness of the devastation we are carrying on against people who never injured us. All this for Louis Napoleon and the Pope! John Bull is making a fine recompense for his last frenzy [1]. Before Sir A. Elton put his name to the Tracts, F. Meyrick and I were thinking of writing to the anonymous author, suggesting co-operation; but I thought we could hardly do it, after he ceased to be anonymous. Do you think he would wish for any help? I want to put out something much simpler, explaining the whole matter to the meanest capacity.

I am not sure whether I told you that I am going to Edinburgh next month to deliver six lectures on the History of the Saracens, at the Philosophical Institution. These and my article on the Greek Kingdom for the *Edinburgh Review*, which is to appear in January [2], have pretty well occupied my time. At the same time you do err in recognizing me in the critical portion of the *Guardian*. As everything helps, I have been keeping up a constant fire of small philhellenic reviews.

To G. FINLAY, ESQ.

Lanrhymney, Cardiff, October 21, 1855.
MY DEAR SIR,

I am very much obliged for your last letter, as for its predecessor. I have finished my article on Greece for the *Edinburgh*, and I hope it will appear in the next number. I was obliged to cut recent matters somewhat shorter than I had intended; and, as I did not know whether there was, or was not, any chance of your forthcoming volume appearing in time, I alluded to it honourably beforehand, and shall probably get some opportunity of reviewing it retrospectively when it does come out. Your other books, I need not say, I have done my best to magnify, as I always do, whenever

---

[1] The outcry against the so-called 'Papal aggression'—the scheme of Pius IX for the division of England into twelve Roman Catholic dioceses.

[2] It did not actually appear till the April number.

I can get an opportunity or an excuse. Just now I am using them a good deal for some lectures on the History of the Saracens, which I have been asked to deliver this winter to the Philosophical Institution at Edinburgh. Your pamphlet—'The Hellenic people and the Greek kingdom'—I could not get, though I twice wrote to my bookseller about it. It is said to be quite out of print. So I only know it from some quotations in the *Westminster Review*.

Your last Revolution at Athens has come since I finished my article, so I must try and put in something about it in reviewing the proof. As far as I can judge, Kalerges must have made an extreme fool of himself[1], but it seems a pity to lose Maurokordatos for a miserable Court squabble. What sort of people are their successors? If Trikoupes does accept office, that I suppose will be some security for rationality. I want your little place simply to keep quiet while this loathsome and unrighteous war goes on, lest the Pope, or the Turk, or Louis Napoleon put you out altogether. As for Otho, I am really beginning to think whether he should not be regarded as Phocas or Michael the Drunkard, and some African or Slavonian be looked out for to smite him, and slay him, and reign in his stead. After the Parisian precedent really no one can object to any sort of coup.

My reading just now for these Saracenic lectures confirms me the more in the truth of your view, which I have been diligently preaching everywhere, about the falling off of the oriental provinces of Rome, because they were alienated in national and religious feeling from the rest of the Empire. Each province attacked by the Saracens, resists in proportion as it had been identified with the central government. Egypt openly joins the invaders, Syria seems only to be hindered

---

[1] Early in 1854 the Greeks had made an unjustifiable and unsuccessful invasion of Epirus and Thessaly, which were then Turkish provinces. In May, French and English troops were landed at the Peiraeus, and continued to occupy it to the close of the Crimean war, in order to enforce the neutrality of Greece. A new Ministry was formed, of which Maurokordatos was the President. In 1855 some breach of Court etiquette by General Kalerges, a member of the 'Occupation Cabinet,' as it was called, led to its dismissal. See Finlay, *Hist.* vii. 225-232.

from doing so by the presence of Heraclius and his army; Africa, orthodox but not Greek, resists for a very long period; the Greek provinces are not conquered at all. Of course we must take into consideration the internal disputes among the Saracens themselves; thus the war between Ali and Moawiyah stopped all conquest for a time; but when the Caliphate is again reunited, they can conquer Africa with difficulty, Spain with ease, but Constantinople they cannot conquer at all, nor do more than ravage Asia.

I have, as you may perceive, set myself up as a sort of preacher of the importance of the Byzantine Empire and of yourself as the historian of it. What I find on the subject is simply contempt arising from ignorance. People don't know what you are talking about. Or indeed some won't know. To allies of the Sultan it is inconvenient to know that Constantinople ever was Christian or civilized. They amuse me most about the Crimea. They have some notion about Mithridates, some notion about the Genoese, but not one man in a hundred thousand ever heard of the Republic of Cherson, for so many centuries the only free state in the world.

I suppose you may by this time have seen my review of you in the *North British.* I hope, as I say there, that your promised volume may tell us something about Sicily and south Italy. I am most curious to know how they ceased to be Greek. Overrun by Saracens, Normans, Germans, and Franks, they seem suddenly to become Italian without any reason.

I have a vague notion of getting to Greece next summer, but I do not know whether I shall be able to compass it. As yet I have never got beyond England, Wales, and the Channel Islands.

To Spyridon Trikoupes.

Lanrhymney, Cardiff, November 18, 1855.
My dear Sir,

Will you pardon me for two things? For reverting to my own tongue in writing to you; and for directing to you as an Englishman rather than a Frenchman. I want to ask and tell you two or three things which I really hardly know how to get into Greek. I am happy to say that my article, 'The Greek People and the Greek Kingdom,' is to be in the next *Edinburgh Review*, and I hope it may do some good. Of course you will remember two things, first, that I cannot write there quite so freely as when I write in my own name; second, that I do not hold your nation to be faultless any more than my own. But I have no doubt that you will be pleased in these days to get any good word at all in one of the first English periodicals; and by writing impartially I am more likely to get credit than by indiscriminate praise.

. . . I am leaving home to-morrow, ultimately for Edinburgh, where I have to lecture on the history of the Saracens, in which I contrive to introduce some side blows for you and against the Turks.

To G. Finlay, Esq.

Lanrhymney, Cardiff, December 26, 1855.

My dear Sir,

. . . I am glad you are pleased with my *North British* article; I believe it is the only at all elaborate review of your book which has appeared. Yet I really think the subject only wants introducing to be appreciated. I think I told you that I was going to Edinburgh to lecture upon the Saracens. The subject, of course, frequently coincided with yours, and gave me several opportunities of referring to you. In short, unless I greatly overrate my effectiveness, I inoculated my audience with strong Byzantine tendencies, and the name of Leo the Isaurian was always the sign for as much applause as your countrymen seem capable of. I found them most attentive and intelligent, but one thing I could not do,—make them laugh; not even when Nicephorus leads his army against the Cretan Saracens, and stigmatizes the latter as '*slow bellies.*' This fact I fished up fresh from Leo Diaconus. I do not think that either you or Gibbon mention this odd perversion of an old saying.

. . . I shall look out anxiously for your history of the Turkish and Venetian domination. I do wish you would give your attention to that most curious phenomenon of the extinction of Hellenism in the two Sicilies without any visible cause.

I mentioned this in my *North British* article. Sicily remains Greek through Arab and Norman invasions, and finally becomes —neither Arabian nor French (which would have been intelligible) but Italian. I cannot make it out at all.

To SPYRIDON TRIKOUPES.

Lanrhymney, Cardiff, March 5, 1856.

I am driven to write in English, because I am not clear that I can find Greek for all that I want to say. I am very much obliged for the *Spectateur de l' Orient* and for Professor Paparhegopoulos' Lectures. The former I did not mean to ask of you as a present; I meant to buy the set; but, as I see from the inscription that you intend it as a gift, I have only to offer you my best thanks, and to assure you of its finding an honourable place in my library. I should like to take it in regularly, if I knew how, if it still continues.

. . . The Tracts I sent you were contributions to a series published by Sir Arthur Elton, a gentleman in Somersetshire, who has been opposing the war all along. I shall be very much obliged if you can get mine at all known among the people most interested; as I am anxious your nation should know that it has one or two friends left in England. There is another printed, 'Turkish Reforms,' and another in the Press, 'Russia and her Conquests.' They have not yet sent me any copies of either; but I will send you some as soon as they appear.

You will see that in the Tracts, though even there I perhaps may not meet with exact agreement, I speak out more on many points than I could in the *Edinburgh*. In the latter I had to solve the problem of saying all that I could on behalf of Greece, without directly censuring the war. In the Tracts I can of course speak just as I please. I have put in a passage speaking strongly about the brigands, but adding that I believe the present Greek Ministry were setting vigorously to work to put them down. After all, excepting a few refinements which must have been learned from the Turks, I don't know that you do worse in Greece than we did in England, or at all events Scotland, 150 years back.

With my best remembrances to your son.

To the Same.

Lanrumney (Glanrhymney), Cardiff, April 15, 1856.

I have just received the *Edinburgh Review* containing my article on 'The Greek People and the Greek Kingdom.' I think it right to inform you that the present beginning and ending— from the beginning to 'present state of modern Greece,' p. 388, and again p. 420, 'but whilst these signs of progress,' &c. to the end, have been added by the editor; so I am neither entitled to praise nor blame, nor in any way responsible for any statement in them. I do not think, however, that they are inconsistent with the general tone of the article, though I should not have spoken so harshly of the events of 1854, nor do I expect so much from the boasted concessions of the Grand Turk. There are a few other editorial changes in the body of the article, but none, I think, of much consequence. Only the editor has made my spelling of Greek names inconsistent, I always use the Greek spelling; he has sometimes kept mine, and sometimes introduced the Italian way.

I trust that, on the whole, the article will prove to be, as it is certainly intended, of some service to the cause of Greece. And I would again thank most cordially both yourself and your son for the help which you have given me in its composition.

To the Same.

'Εν Λανρυμνίᾳ, τὴν 19 'Ιουνίου, 1856.

Φίλε Κύριε Τρικούπη,

Στέλλω σοι, ἅτε τῆς σῆς χάριτος μνημόσυνον, λόγους τοὺς περὶ Σαρακηνῶν ἐν 'Εδιμπύργῳ ἐκφωνήθεντας, ἐν οἷς πόλλ' ἄττα περὶ τῆς Βυζαντίνης ἀρχῆς καὶ ἔστιν ἃ περὶ τῆς νεωτέρας 'Ελλάδος εὑρήσεις.

Σοφώτερα ἴσως ἔπραξας ἢ ἐμοὶ χαριέστερα εἰς τὸν ἐν 'Οξωνίᾳ ἀγῶνα οὐκ ἐλθών· δεινὸν γὰρ ἦν μὴ οἱ νεώτεροι οἱ τὸν τῆς Τουρκίας πρεσβευτὴν κροτοῦντες τὸν τῆς 'Ελλάδος οὐκ ἴσῃ εὐμενείᾳ δέξαιντο· ἀλλ' ἑτέρῳ τινι χρόνῳ, ὅταν μεῖζον σωφρονῶμεν, τοιοῦτον ἱστοριογράφον τίμῃ τῇ πρεπούσῃ στεφανήσομεν.

Πολλὰς δέδεγμαι ἐφημερίδας, τὸν ἐν ἀνατολῇ θεατήν, 'Αθήνηθεν ἤκουσας. ἐν τῇ νεωτάτῃ οὐκ ἄνευ χαρᾶς ἑώρακα λόγον τινα τῶν ἐμῶν Φραγκιστὶ ἑρμηνευθέντα· ἔστιν ὅτε τῆς ἐμῆς γνώμης ἔσφαλται ὁ γράψας, οὐ μὴν ἀλλὰ τὰ πλεῖστα καλῶς κέκμηκε· πλὴν τὰ περὶ τοῦ Σουλτάνου Τερψιχόρῃ

† VOL. I.

230 . LIFE OF EDWARD A. FREEMAN. [1855-

θύοντος οὐχ ἡρμήνευκε. ἀκούω Γεώργιόν τινα Μάνον, τὸν λόγον τινα περὶ τῶν 'Ραγιάδων Φραγκιστὶ γράψαντα, τὸν ἐμὸν ἐν τῷ Edinburgh Review λόγον 'Ελληνιστὶ μεθηρμηνευκέναι, ἀλλ' οὐχ ἑώρακα τὸ βιβλίον.

Πῶς ποτε οἷόν τε ἐστὶν βίβλον 'Αθήναζε στέλλειν; θέλω γὰρ τοὺς περὶ τῶν Σαρακηνῶν λόγους Φινλαίῳ δίδοναι, ἀλλὰ πῶς πεμπτέον ἐστιν οὐκ οἶδα.   ὁ σὸς
                                                                    'Εδούαρδος Φρήμανος.
'Εξοχωτάτῳ πρεσβευτῇ Σπυρίδωνι Τρικούπῃ.

[*Translation of above.*]

Lanrumney, June 19, 1856.

DEAR MR. TRIKOUPES,

I send you as an acknowledgement of your kindness my lectures on the Saracens which were delivered in Edinburgh, in which you will find many things concerning the Byzantine government, and also some concerning modern Greece. You have probably acted with more wisdom, though less agreeably from my point of view, in not having come to the Festival at Oxford. For there was a terrible risk that the young men who applauded the Turkish ambassador might not have received the ambassador of Greece quite so graciously. But at some other time, when we are more sober-minded, we will crown so good an historian with the honour which befits him.

I have received many journals (the *Spectateur de l'Orient*) which have come from Athens. In the last number I have noticed, not without pleasure, a certain article of my own translated into French. The writer has now and then missed my meaning, yet for the most part he has done his work well. Only he has not translated the passages about the Sultan sacrificing to Terpsichore. I hear that one George Manos, who wrote a treatise in French on the Rayahs, has translated my article in the *Edinburgh Review* into Greek, but I have not seen the volume. Pray how is it possible to send a book to Athens? for I wish to give my lectures on the Saracens to Finlay, but do not know how to send them.

Thine,

EDWARD FREEMAN.

To his Excellency, the Minister Spyridon Trikoupes.

To THE SAME.

Lanrumney, Cardiff, August 12, 1856.

I am sure you must be quite tired of seeing my handwriting; but I hope it is generally about matters where I am likely to do some little good that I venture to trouble you with so many letters. I have now to ask you about an important matter, which I am constrained to deal with in English, as I doubt whether I can muster Greek enough for the purpose.

The editor of the *Edinburgh Review* has asked me to furnish another article on Greek matters, namely with regard to the position of the Orthodox Church. It was suggested by a letter of Mr. Manos, in which he called attention to the aggressions against your Communion now going on on the part of the emissaries of the Pope. The line I mean to take will be of course to deal rather with the political and social, than the strictly theological, aspect of the question, and especially to preach friendly union, without proselytism, between the Greek and English Churches, both representing the principle of independent national churches, as opposed to the foreign supremacy of the Latins. The fact that, both in Russia and in independent Greece, the Orthodox Church has been able to maintain full communion with a Patriarch whose authority it disclaims, will of course greatly help me.

Can you kindly furnish me with any facts or documents bearing upon the subject? especially any reforms or advances made in ecclesiastical matters in the kingdom as compared with Turkish Greece. I do not know much of your ecclesiastical arrangements, but I take it for granted that you have got rid of the simony which seems to be so prevalent in the latter. But you will know, much better than I can tell you, what facts will be useful to make out my case. I think you will allow the subject is likely to be a useful one.

. . . I see your third volume is published, which I hope to review somewhere or other. I wrote reviews lately of Finlay's last volume in the *Saturday Review*, and of Creasy's *Ottoman Turks* both there and in the *Guardian*. I hold that every little helps. I have just now got hold of *Ubicini's Letters*[1] by Lady

---

[1] *Letters on Turkey*, 2 vols., translated by Lady Easthope.

Easthope; I don't know who the woman is, but she is mighty amusing. One favourite dogma is that your nation has been better off under Turkish Sultans than under Byzantine Emperors. Balancing a thousand years and six hundred, I am fully willing to believe that *some* Sultans have been better than *some* Emperors; πῶς γὰρ οὔ; but the doctrine of course is that *any* Sultan was better than *any* Emperor; and the inference that a Mahometan government now is better than a Christian one! This is the way people argue.

To G. FINLAY, ESQ.

Lanrumney, September 1, 1856.

I have two letters of yours to answer, and that before I start, this very day, on my first continental tour, in which, however, I do not expect to get farther than the Pyrenees, and I hope to be back in the beginning of next month.

I am very sorry that you should think anything in my notice in the *Saturday Review* 'severe'—I spoke freely on one or two points, but I am sure the general tone of the article was meant to be one of strong sympathy and admiration. And I am sure *I* did not in the least doubt your philhellenism in the best sense : I only said that some expressions in your book might lead superficial readers to doubt it. But if anything that either I or anyone has said leads you really to write the history of the Revolution, I shall heartily rejoice.

I have taken to write a little in a penny paper called the *Star*, because it is the only one where I can abuse Turks (and oligarchs generally) *ad libitum*. I sent them a notice of the English translation of *Ubicini*, of which I will try and send you a copy. There are some misprints, as you will see.

I hope to review your last volume along with Trikoupes in the *North British*, in continuation of my former article about you. If you can give me any hints for my *Edinburgh* article on the Orthodox Church, I shall be very much obliged.

Some one at Hermopolis has been abusing my former *Edinburgh* article in a paper called Τηλέγραφος τῶν Κυκλάδων, which was sent me. I don't much care, as my facts rest on a consensus of Gordon and Trikoupes, which I suppose is likely to be right. It however reveals the fact of which I was uncertain, that some Greek translations of the *Edinburgh* article have appeared. I am very curious to see them. Is it asking too much to ask if you could get me one or two?

I am delighted that you think so well of my Saracens. Mine, you know, is a purely exoteric and Western view. I learned a little Hebrew years back, which enables me now and then to see the meaning of an Arabic name; that is all my oriental scholarship. I ought to have read Weil, but have not[1]. I had generally to get up the lectures rather quickly from my own library, away from Oxford, and a long German book takes me a long time to get through.

To the Rev. B. Webb.

Lanrumney, April 19, 1857.

There was your handwriting on a circular which arrived last night. Before I opened it I thought it was certainly going to contain a request for my long promised account of the restoration of Llandaff, which might have been again suggested to you by hearing of the re-opening on Thursday. There is nobody occupied in so many different ways as I am—standing for Cardiff and making radical speeches, preparing for my duties as Examiner at Oxford, writing in all sorts of places from the *Edinburgh* downwards, acting as churchwarden of St. Mellons, going hither and thither from St. Andrews to St. Bertrand de Comminges. Howbeit, whensoever I can steal a moment of leisure I will try and put something together for you, *ea lege atque omine*, that you at last break your amazing silence about my Tracery book[2].

Why should I write a history of Llandaff and also a history of the Saracens? The connecting link is to be found in the fact that Thomas *Omar*, joiner, set up the recently defunct Bishop's throne.

To G. Finlay, Esq.

Lanrumney, May 10, 1857.

. . . If I get upon general politics, there is a fear of my running on to a greater length than the post-office will send to

---

[1] *History of the Caliphs*, by Dr. Gustave Weil.

[2] Essay on 'Window Tracery,' which had not yet been reviewed in the *Ecclesiologist*, of which Mr. Webb was editor.

Athens for eleven-pence. I don't exactly know what I want, but certainly something different from what is now, beginning with the restoration of Bright, Cobden, &c., and the addition of my own self. From all I can learn, I believe I should have stood an excellent chance of coming in for Cardiff, had I only appeared sooner, and I shall certainly make another attempt, as opportunities turn up, either there or somewhere else. As it is, I have got a sort of popularity which I must keep up, though it may prove burthensome: and there is something novel and exciting in me, who have hitherto sat in my library and fought only with my pen, coming forth bodily before the ναυτικὸς ὄχλος[1] of a port which, when you first went to Greece, I conceive did not exist, but which now is very big, and gets bigger every day. I certainly want more straightforward dealings, and to clip the power of Premiers, who are really only despots on sufferance. I am not clear that, if we had war and peace brought more directly under the control of the House of Commons, our policy would be more bloodthirsty than it is. Possibly we might have as many wars, but I think they would be a little more respectable ones. This mere murder and brigandage out in Persia and China makes me half look back with envy to the Russian war, where the popular emotion, mistaken as it was, had something generous in it. The Persian war would certainly never have happened had Parliament been first consulted. As it is, the right or wrong of a war is never fully and fairly discussed; the people only hear of it when it is inevitable, perhaps when it is actually begun, and when the national honour is supposed to be involved. I don't want to fight anybody, because nobody has attacked us, but of the two, I had much rather fight Austria and Prussia on behalf of Wallachia and Neufchâtel, than fight Persia and China for absolutely nothing—for a Persian woman[2] or a Chinese pirate.

[1] 'Nautical crowd.'

[2] In 1855 the English Chargé d' Affaires in Persia appointed Meerza Hashem Khan to the post of British agent at Shiraz. This man was personally displeasing to the Persian Prime Minister, who threatened to arrest him, and when this was forbidden by the English representative he arrested Meerza Hashem's wife. Her release was demanded by the

To the Same.

The Schools, Oxford, June 19, 1857.

I am here hard at work at my office of ' Examinator Publicus in Jurisprudentiâ et Historiâ Modernâ,' which has revealed to me the existence of a mass of ignorance which I should not have conceived possible. I do not wonder at men supposing that the Turks were at Constantinople at the time of the First Crusade, or that 'the Saracens came out of Egypt and the *Turks out of Turkey*,' when I find some wholly ignorant of the old English cities, or supposing that all bills must originate in the Commons, and that, when they have passed both houses, the Queen may alter them. I commend those hints to the makers of the next paper-constitution on the Danube or elsewhere. N. B. Some men thought that the Crusaders in passing through Hungary and Roumania followed the course of the *Rhine*. I ought however to add that these are the pass-men, and I trust the class-men will do better. Still, such men grow into parsons, magistrates, and M.P.s—conceivably into Bishops and Cabinet Ministers. I can't think my Cardiff mob could do much worse. Don't we want the ballot to protect us against the brute force of *such* an oligarchy? I firmly believe that learning or intellectual power of any kind commands far more respect among the people than among the ' Nobility, Gentry, and Clergy.' Thus, instead of answering your politics, I give you my own. But I must now thank you both for your kind present of the new edition of *Greece under the Romans*, and also for your really setting to work on my Saracens.

. . . I have not yet gone through your new edition, and I greatly fear your numismatic labours will be lost upon me. I instinctively shrink (except when I have to receive them) from all mention of £ s. d., fr. dr., or the queer mark which denotes the American dollar. I trust people are beginning to appreciate your books—I am sure I have done all I could in my small way to make them—and that you will not find either the history or the soil of Greece so unproductive as hitherto.

English, but the Persian government would not give way, and in 1856 a little war was the result, in which the Persian forces were speedily defeated by General Outram.

To the Same.

Lanrumney, November 25, 1857.

. . . Can you tell me at all what is the truth about certain reported movements in Thessaly, which have excited my curiosity? The tale is, that a certain Pasha has been violating the amnesty passed in 1854—that was, I think, the year of the revolt, invasion, or whatever one is to call it—that the Christians are meditating an insurrection and the barbarians arming in all quarters. Latterly, though I have not forgotten south-eastern Europe, my thoughts have run rather in the direction of Wallachia than of Greece, as indeed you may have perhaps seen from the *Spectator*. I hope the Greeks are not too much bound up in themselves to see that the cause of all these nations is the same.

India is really very like Greece in these two things. First, it is impossible to find out the truth as to what has happened. Secondly, it is still more impossible to know what ought to be done. The Company does not do, and I am sure an Indian Government, going in and out with the Ministry, won't do. Πολλάκις μὲν ἤδη ἔγνων τὴν δημοκρατίαν ὡς ἀδύνατόν ἐστιν ἑτέρων ἄρχειν[1]. In short we have no business to go conquering India or anywhere else at all, and here is the punishment, τυραννίδα ἔχομεν τὴν ἀρχὴν ἣν λαβεῖν μὲν ἄδικον δοκεῖ εἶναι ἀφεῖναι δὲ ἐπικίνδυνον[2].

To the Same.

Lanrumney, January 25, 1858.

. . . I am quite surprised to hear that I have been stirring up anybody to make war upon anybody. I hold abstractedly that enslaved Greece has full right to revolt at any moment, and that liberated Greece has a full right to assist it in revolting. And I have often maintained this view in opposition to those wiseacres who lay down one rule for Magyars and Lombards, and another for Greeks and Bulgarians. But I don't think

[1] 'I have often perceived already how impossible it is for a democracy to rule over others.' Thucyd. iii. 37.
[2] 'We hold our rule as a tyranny which it seems to be unjust to have received and yet perilous to give up.' Thucyd. ii. 63.

I ever said that it was prudent to carry out that principle at
any particular moment. All experience shows that the tendency
of a newly liberated state is to extend itself, but, as things go,
it is much wiser in Greece to check that tendency, and rather
to dig and make roads. N.B. I have, with great difficulty,
and not without the intervention of the civil magistrates, procured the mending of a road close by here, so I sympathize
with you on that head and am prepared to canonize King
Archelaos as my patron hero. Was it not he who εὐθείας ὁδοὺς
ἔτεμεν [1].

. . . My article on the Orthodox Church will, I hope,
appear in the April *Edinburgh*. You will find a little about
your Othoman domination volume. I am going to do them
another on Sir F. Palgrave's Normandy and England. Are
you up in his writings? I don't remember that either of you
ever refers to the other ; I am not sure that you would appreciate
one another; but you always go together in my mind. I make
my historical system out of an union of you two. Between you,
you work out the fact that the Roman Empire did not die in 476,
but lived on as long as you please after. You do the East, which
has been forgotten, he the West, which has been misconceived.
But he does it only by hints and fragments, and in his present
book he has gone half wild in the form of his composition.
I should rather like to write the history of the Western Empire
myself; i.e. not so much the history of Germany or of Italy as
the history of the Imperial idea. Democrat as I am, I confess the
'Ρωμαίων βασιλεύς, the Romanorum Imperator semper Augustus,
impresses me with considerable awe—wherefore I have the
more loathing for these miserable pseudo-Caesares in Austria
and France.

. . . In my last Examination at Oxford, I was rejoiced to
find a man able to name three Eastern Emperors in succession—to wit Nikephoros Phokas, John Tzimiskes, and the
Βουλγαροκτόνος [2]. To be sure another could not name Constantine
Palaiologos, and another gave me Leo the Isaurian when he
was not wanted, which I looked on as a bad shot at my personal
favour.

[1] Thucyd. ii. 100.
[2] 'The slayer of the Bulgarians,' Basil II.

To the Same.

Lanrumney, March 21, 1858.

I am beginning to think that there is not, and never was, any such thing as truth in the world. At least I don't believe that any two people ever give exactly the same account of anything, even when they have seen it with their own eyes, except when they copy from one another. I believe that the very diversity is, in one sense, a proof of truth—truthfulness—in the narrators; but it increases the difficulty of finding out truth on the part of their readers or hearers. All this common-place is to prove that I shall not be in the least appalled, if I find you and Gordon and Trikoupes giving each a different account of many things in the Greek Revolution, and that it will not at all diminish my respect for any one of the three. It is just what I am used to—in the four Gospels, in the lives of St. Thomas of Canterbury (that purely western saint to whom, as Dean Milman says, no Greek ever prayed), of Alexander, of anybody you please. Observe the shifts to which divines put themselves to reconcile the manifest contradictions in the Gospels. A historian takes them with great calmness, and thinks them to be rather confirmations of the general truth of the narrative. Is not one reason why we deify Thucydides, because we have nobody to compare with him? Had we Philistos to compare him with, it might make a difference. It is only when I find evidently deliberate fiction, as in Q. Curtius, as in the Norman accounts of Harold, that I am seriously disturbed. As I don't suspect any of you three of this, I am not alarmed. I regard you as three witnesses, from three different points of view, and I expect a certain amount of contradiction. Gordon and Trikoupes follow such a different arrangement that it is hard to compare them in detail; but I have done it in some parts; e.g. in the Church-Cochrane-Fabvier-Karaïskakes campaign before Athens[1], and I found no such difference as to trouble me. The only very important case I remember is that Gordon makes Tombazes lay a deliberately treacherous scheme against the Turks in Crete, while Trikoupes makes the capitulation to be broken by the people after, as in several other cases.

[1] See Finlay, *History of Greece*, vi. p. 398 *sq.*

I pointed this out to T. and he quoted some authority or other which I forget. By the way, is 'plagiarism' quite the word? I don't look upon any of you as in the same light as I shall be if I sit down to the history of Charlemagne or anybody a long time ago, bound to give a reference for everything you say. As contemporary writers, and having all had more or less hand in the business, I regard you all as original authorities, just like Thucydides or Eginhard—yet it is clear that each of you must trust to hearsay for many things. I don't see any fault if Trikoupes copies Germanos' memoirs. How all mediaeval writers copy from each other.

It is just the same with the politics as with the history— I have no doubt all your corrections of facts are quite accurate, and Komondouros (whom I never heard of till I saw his manifesto) may perhaps be as great a rogue as Palmerston himself, who has so happily gone to the dogs. But I believe, all the same, that my *Star* article about it—the latter part of which did little more than repeat lessons learned of you— was calculated to do good here. People in England—you must see it in the *Spectator*—cannot be got to do Greece common justice. There is a tone of contempt always employed, and a refusal to make allowance for difficulties which you must allow to be thoroughly unfair. With your own writings for instance—you state the faults of the country strongly as a friend, but your words are taken up here and used by enemies. If you say about half of the truth, depend upon it people here will add the other half.

. . . I cannot help thinking, as Reeve of the *Edinburgh* suggested to me, that the condition of Greece now (bating mere talkativeness and consciousness) is not unlike that of Britain in Macaulay's times. Plenty of evils, peculation, klephtism, what not—but good stuff at the bottom. Trikoupes sent me an Αἰών, with a translation of my article, followed by an original one on the Financial system, which was, I believe, designed to carry out my, or rather your, argument. But it was so vilely printed, and in such queer Greek, that I gave it up before I had got to the end.

I admire your Pseudo Demetrios, such a man might have been made Czar in the seventeenth century.

I reviewed Trikoupes both in the *Star* and the *Saturday Review*, an odd conjunction. Also my article on the Eastern Church will be in the next *Edinburgh*. I am now on the tenter-hooks about the Modern History Professorship at Oxford, for which I am a candidate, but which I suppose I shall not get.

Why does constitutional government answer in Norway and not in Greece? Doubtless for one reason because the Danish despotism was, on the whole, a very good despotism, and acted, in many respects, as a schoolmaster to bring them to freedom. But is not royalty without a court a great help? The non-resident king has no means of corruption, while the constitution is constantly just so far threatened as to be in no real danger, but to keep people's affections constantly alive towards it. Also Norway had the good luck to be almost forgotten. But the contrast is certainly remarkable. I can't make out that the Norwegians have what we should call a *Ministry*. Both the king and the Storthing act. It is also curious that in Norway, the most democratic of all monarchic states, nobody asks for the ballot, and the election of members is indirect. The ballot I do not love for its own sake, but I see no other way in England of stopping the tyranny of landlords and employers. In Norway there are no such people, and the ballot is not wanted. Again, I fancy indirect election would not do here where there are marked political parties. In Norway there are none. All are of one party—Radical-Conservatives, so to speak—lovers of the existing democracy. The questions to be decided will be practical, financial, and such like : a man's personal ability will be of more account than it is here, and of this a select body of electors may be better able to judge.

Do you know anything of things in Bosnia and Herzegovina? Sir George Bowen wrote me a curious account of a visit to the Vladika, whom he affirms to be Lady Bowen's cousin.

I don't know Wallon's book, but I will look out for it. It is strange how people do not realize the existence of the Roman Empire at all—after when? perhaps 476. They always talk as if Charlemagne 'restored' something defunct. Turn to a mediaeval writer and the phrase always is that he transferred the Roman Empire from the Greeks to the Franks. It is curious in those chronicles which count by imperial reigns, to see Leo, Constantinus, Carolus, Hludovicus, following quite peaceably. You have set forth one side of this truth, Palgrave the other; I want to work you into harmony. I remember very well the article in the *North British*, by Senior I believe.

To THE REV. W. STUBBS.

Lanrumney, April 26, 1858.

I have licence to review your book[1] in what my Greek friends call ἡ ἐπιθεώρησις τοῦ σαββάτου[2], I have not yet heard from the Guardianic folk.

I must confess that I have never read W. Malmsb. de Pont[3]. His Kings[4] are enough to make me thoroughly despise him as a lying affected French scoundrel. I turned to the place about Ælfwold's death, and found it mixed up with a palpably Norman or monastic fable about Earl Godwine, which at once stamps it as mythical. Florence, my reverence for whom is measured by my dislike of Malmesbury, does not directly mention Ælfwold's death in 1058; but only by implication, if you believe the other man. There is Bishop 'Ailnotus' present at the consecration of Waltham by Kinsige, who I suppose must be the Ælfwoldus who signs the charter, though the mistake is an odd one. The charter DCCCI[5] is dated 1055, but it must be later (? 1065) by the signatures of earls as well as of bishops. Ælfwold is there plain enough. All this is as exciting to me as Greek accents to Linwood.

To G. FINLAY, ESQ.

Lanrumney, August 20, 1858.

I am very much obliged to you for your introduction of Professor Felton, though I had not the pleasure of seeing him. He sent me your letter with one of his own, as he was just starting for America. I am very glad to make his acquaintance, though only on paper, as I had been long wishing for

---

[1] The *Registrum Sacrum Anglicanum.*   [2] The *Saturday Review.*
[3] De Pontificibus.   [4] Gesta Regum.
[5] See Kemble's *Codex Diplomaticus*, vol. iv.

some correspondent in the United States, and I knew Professor Felton's name very well in his philhellenic capacity.

I have not had the kingdom of Greece so much in my head as other parts of the Eastern Empire and the Orthodox Church ; to wit, Montenegro, Wallachia, and Crete. Sir George Bowen who claims, through his wife, cousinhood with the Vladika, keeps me in news from the Black Mountain, but I should very much like to know the real state of affairs among the κακὰ θηρία, γαστέρες ἀργαί[1].

England is just now as dull as possible, wherefore I am going over for a tour in Ireland, where, as there has just been a bit of a στάσις[2] at Kilkenny, things may be rather more exciting.

I wonder whether I shall ever see Hellas with my own eyes. It is a thing I often dream of, but I don't know whether I shall ever really manage it—there is so much to see farther west.

To the Same.

Bickington, Newton Abbot, March 14, 1859.
I cannot think why you make apologies for your letters, which I am always delighted to receive, even though, as in the present case, I may be sometimes inclined to turn combative over them. Where I quite split with you on this Ionian business, is that you seem to take more than I should have expected the line of the *Times* and *Saturday Review* about ' subjects,' ' treason,' &c. Now surely you cannot call the citizens of a protected republic ' subjects,' nor their wish, wise or foolish, to get rid of the protectorate, ' treason.' That the Ionian Islands are not a direct British possession the *Times* and that school diligently keep out of sight. Now my one grand doctrine is the right of every nation to govern itself, or, if so be, to misgovern itself, without foreign interference. The protectorate was, one is bound to suppose, set up because the Ionian Republic was too weak to enter on the diplomatic arena for itself, but it is clear rascality to go and make it an excuse for assuming a sovereignty which is mere usurpation. And, surely, the institution of an independent Greek kingdom quite altered the case ; the two enfranchised portions of the Greek nation would

---

[1] ' Evil beasts, slow bellies,' see *Ep. to Titus*, i. 12.   [2] Insurrection.

naturally go together. I have no doubt that the Ionians are in
many things much better off than the Greeks of the kingdom,
but does not experience show that people prefer a bad government of their own to a good one of other people's. And I had
a vague hope that union might possibly open the eyes of the
continental Greeks to a thing or two. And I should stipulate
for an union preserving whatever advantages the Ionians have
at present. To me it seems that nothing but brute force can
hinder the union sooner or later. But then this nineteenth
century is pre-eminently the age of brute force. It seems to me
that in the wildest times of the Middle Ages a small state had
a better chance of holding its own than it has now, just because
of the modern abomination of standing armies.

I admired Gladstone throughout excessively ; there was
something heroic in going out on an errand which all the small
folk, crawlers, club-loungers, Saturday Reviewers, and all that
gang, were safe to make game of. And I admired his scheme
on the whole, i.e. to give the Islands the greatest degree of
freedom consistent with the protectorate, which, of course, in
his position, he was bound to assume. But, like you, I should
have doubts as to some of his details, his responsible ministry.
I have too great a dislike to our Cabinet system here to wish to
transplant it anywhere else ; and I don't see the wisdom of
prime ministers, &c., in the colonies. . . . So perhaps I can't
see the beauty of Premiers and the like.

. . . I am all agog about 'reform,' and I believe the nation to
be so too? but *Times* and Co. argue on this fashion—as long as
the people make their demands in a legal manner, they say
they are not in earnest; if they transgress the line, they say
they are unfit. What this unlucky ministry[1] may do, I suppose
no one can prophesy: I am hoping for a dissolution, to make
another dash at a seat for myself.

I hope you are getting on with your history of the War of
Independence. I want to see it very much. The only thing
I fear is that you may say things which enemies may turn
about to purposes which you do not mean, as they have often

---

[1] Lord Derby's. A new ministry with Lord Palmerston as Premier
came into office on June 18.

done already. I wish you could get rid of your *court.* If you must have a king, you should have got a hard-working, every-day king, open to break stones or shoot a Turk with his own hands.

To THE REV. W. STUBBS.

Lanrumney, May 14, 1859.

. . . There is an article of mine in the *National Review* on 'Mommsen,' and one in the *Edinburgh* (hard by Sir George[1] on 'Montenegro'), but Reeve has cut out all my theory about Rolf and Æthelstan, to my great horror. I therefore send you the proofs, which perhaps you will let me have again. I did the like to Thorpe, which evoked two letters which I enclose. I have also got two Record books[2] to do for the *Saturday Review,* and am taking the opportunity to abuse and magnify Shirley and Brewer.

I have not yet got my copies of Waltham. It strikes me that the East-Saxons are rather a slow race.

I have been reading Liutprand and Widukind and am now busy with Lambert of Herzfeld—also with Polybius, whom I have never before read straight through. I have got one or two things for you out of Lambert. Here is a portrait of a bishop, A.D. 1065. 'Successit ei [Arnolfo Wormaciae Ep⁰.] Adalbero, monachus ex monasterio Sti Galli, frater Ruodolfi ducis, uno pede omnino debilis, vir per omnia dignus spectaculo. Erat enim fortitudinis magnae, edacitatis nimiae, crassitudinis tantae, quae aspicientibus horrorem magis incuteret quam ad-mirationem ; nec ita centimanus gigas aut aliud antiquitatis mon-strum, si ab inferis emergeret, stupentis populi oculos in se atque ora converteret[3].'

---

[1] Sir George Bowen.

[2] In the series published under the direction of the Master of the Rolls.

[3] 'He, Arnolf Bishop of Worms, was succeeded by Adalbert, a monk from the monastery of St. Gall, brother of duke Rudolph, a complete cripple on one foot, a man in all respects worth seeing. For he was remarkable for great courage, excessive greediness, and such corpulence as struck the beholders with horror rather than admiration ; indeed, if a hundred-handed giant or any other monster of antiquity were to emerge from the lower regions, he would not in the same degree attract the gaze of the astonished people.'

Under 1066 I find : 'In festis paschalibus per xiv fere noctes continuas cometa apparebat. Quo in tempore atrox et lacrimabile nimis praelium factum est in partibus aquilonis; in quo rex Anglisaxonum tres reges cum infinito eorum exercitu usque ad internitionem delevit[1].'

Now the comet is an old friend; but is the battle Stamfordbridge or one that you and I never heard of? For S. was certainly not 'in festis paschalibus,' and who are the 'tres reges.' N.B.—Did last year's comet foretell L. N. B.'s pranks or what?

I trust you are not Austrian. I am severely neutral, wishing all conceivable bad luck to both sides alike. Yet there is this difference; France is a nation; one only wants to guillotine the tyrant and keep the nation within bounds; but for Austria it is just $\beta o \acute{\upsilon} \lambda o \mu a \iota \ \mu \acute{\eta} \ \epsilon \acute{\iota} \nu a \iota$ [2].

I suppose you got a paper containing one of my Wallingford speeches, and by exercising a little critical power over a corrupt text, you may have found out what I said. I did not expect to be elected, going mainly as an advertisement, so I was not disappointed, though I should certainly have liked a place in this next Parliament. All I know of your East-Saxon doings is that the chief weapon on both sides seemed to be to call the other side Puseyites. This is what I never can understand, as I (who bind myself to no dogmas, and think High Mass the finest thing in the world) see no reason why a man may not be a Puseyite as much as a Jew. If there has been all the screwing you say—which we can fully believe, as 'Liberal' landlords are no better than Derbyites, and of all things in the world a cut and dried, unprogressive, hereditary, aristocratic Whig is about the most loathsome—Why, I say, give them the BALLOT? Perhaps you don't.

I am still houseless, as well as boroughless, and am soon going to be governessless, which last, I think, involves the most

---

[1] 'During the Easter festival, for nearly fourteen nights in succession, a comet was visible. At which time a terrible and lamentable battle was fought in northern parts: wherein the King of the Anglo-Saxons destroyed three kings with their vast host so as utterly to annihilate them.'

[2] 'I wish it not to be.'

hopeless and fearful quest of the three. Do pray tell us of any houses anywhere, so that it be not in a land absolutely mortal with ague. I had rather stay at this end of the island if I could.

To the Same.

Lanrumney, November 17, 1859.

My dear Stubbs,

. . . I have been anxiously looking out hoping to hear of Isaac Gregory[1] being blest with twin boys, of whom the name of the elder should be called Esau Innocent, and the name of the younger Jacob Boniface. But lo, it is a lass; so I have written counselling him to call her REBEKAH MATILDA[2].

Otto Morena—who writes the worst Latin I have read, just, I take it, because he was an Italian and so did not *learn* it like the English and Germans—calls my redbearded predecessor[3] 'Dulcissimus Imperator quo dulcior nullus fuit a longis retro temporibus[4].'

Fred B. was a great man, but I should hardly have made him my type of the γλυκύθυμος ἀνήρ[5].

[1] The Rev. I. G. Smith.

[2] In allusion to the great Countess Matilda, the friend of Pope Gregory VII (Hildebrand).

[3] I. e. the Emperor Frederick I, surnamed Barbarossa ('red beard').

[4] 'Sweetest Emperor, than whom there was none more sweet from times long past.'

[5] 'Sweet-tempered man.'

CHAPTER V.

A.D. 1860-1866.

THE new home which Freeman was beginning to seek
in the spring of 1859 was not found before the following
year.   Those who have had any experience in house-
hunting know well how many houses which are advertised as 'beautiful,' 'commodious,' 'highly desirable,' or
'charming and enchanting residences' prove upon in-
spection to be ludicrously unlike these descriptions.
Freeman made an article upon the subject about this
time in the *Saturday Review*, a journal in which during
the next twenty-two years he gave expression week by
week to his thoughts and feelings on a vast variety of
subjects.   'The grammar of advertisements,' he said, 'is
perhaps more pitiful than that of any other kind of
human composition, unless it be that of addresses on
public occasions and of the answers returned to them.'
But sins of style were light matters.   The chief grievance
was that the veracity of an advertisement was about on

a level with the veracity of an epitaph. Some child or childlike person, who had looked at all the memorial tablets in a church, once asked where the bad people were buried. So one might ask where the undesirable houses were situated, and the estates which were not attractive.

It was too bad when a man was sent to view ' one of the most delightful estates in the western part of the kingdom ' to find a rather mean little house by the road-side. Or when one was told that a house was ' beautifully situated in its own grounds ' (and who would expect to find it situated in the grounds of any other house ?) it was provoking to be shown a house not situated in ' grounds ' at all, but only looking out on a ploughed field which happened to be in the same ownership.

After many disappointing visits of this kind, he saw Somerleaze for the first time in January 1860. In the following March the purchase was concluded, and he became owner of the place which was his principal home, and certainly the one which he most enjoyed, for the remainder of his life.

Somerleaze was a comfortable and fairly commodious house, without any architectural pretensions, distant about two miles from Wells, though comprised in the city parish of St. Cuthbert. In front of the house a small park, well studded with trees, slopes gently to the high road from Wells, and parallel to the road flows the infant stream of the Axe which has issued from the strange cave in the side of Mendip known as Wookey Hole. On the other side of the road and stream lies the little village of Wookey clustering round its church, while beyond rise the steep green slopes of the Mendip range. At the back of the house and

garden rises a steep hill, of moderate height, clothed with
a wood, such as in some parts of the country would be
called a 'hangar.' When he had not time for a ride
or a longer walk, a stroll in this wood in the intervals
of his work was Freeman's favourite recreation ; but
he loved to take his friends up through the wood to
the open top of the hill called Ben Knoll, whence the
view is full of beauty and interest. Facing north-west-
wards the eye ranges over the long green marshy valley
through which the Axe winds its way, to the Bristol
Channel faintly gleaming in the far distance. In early
times this tract was covered with water, and the round
humpy hills rising abruptly out of it, conspicuous
amongst which is Brent Knoll, called of old 'Mons
Ranarum' or the Hill of Frogs, were originally islands.
In the middle distance, the line of the valley is broken
by an elevated mass of ground which forms the Isle
of Wedmore, where the treaty between Alfred and the
Danes in 878 closed his long strife with the invader, and
left the English king not only master of all Wessex but
of all England south of Watling Street. On the right
rise the steep slopes of Mendip, concealing like a massy
wall the wondrous crags of Cheddar which are on the
further side. Turning to the left, the eye is caught by
the abrupt hill called Glastonbury Tor, or St. Michael's
Mount, overhanging the ruins of the great Abbey of
Glastonbury, the traditional burial place of the legendary
king Arthur, the real burial place of the great English
kings and heroes, Eadgar the peace-giver, Eadmund, the
doer of great deeds, and his noble descendant and namesake the mighty Ironside. Further westwards may be
traced the broken outline of the Quantock Hills, and in
clear weather even the massy height of Dunkerry, the

loftiest hill in Exmoor, may be discerned overlooking
Porlock, memorable as the spot where Harold landed
when he crossed from Ireland in 1052, to meet his father
Earl Godwine, and aid him in his return from exile.

Turning round in an easterly direction, the eye rests
upon the little city of Wells, calmly reposing in the
hollow of its surrounding hills. The full beauty of one
of the most lovely and loveable groups of buildings
in Christendom, the Bishop's Palace, the Cathedral and
its Chapter House, the Vicars' close and the stone
bridge connecting it with the Cathedral, cannot be
seen except from a nearer point of view ; but the three
towers of the Cathedral, and the still more stately
tower of St. Cuthbert rising solemnly out of the valley,
are clearly visible, especially if the dusky grey stone of
the buildings is lighted up with a golden glow by the
rays of the evening sun.

One special interest to Freeman in the situation of
Somerleaze, was that it lay on what became the border-
land of Welsh and English territory, after Ceawlin,
the West-Saxon king, had won the battle of Deorham
in 577, and conquered the tract which lay between
the Avon and the Axe. His advance had been checked
by the marshes which divided Mendip from Glastonbury. Wookey marked the farthest point which the
West-Saxon invader had reached. Somerleaze stood
on what continued to be Welsh ground until the
victories of Cenwealh about eighty years afterwards
advanced the English frontier from the Axe to the
Parret. Freeman was pleased at the discovery that
what had once been a national frontier was still a parochial boundary. Cenwealh's decisive battle was fought
in 658 according to the *Chronicle*, 'aet Peonnum,' i. e.

Pen, and Freeman sometimes indulged in the belief that
this Pen was no other than Pen or Ben Knoll immediately above his own abode.   At any rate, the
compound name, half Celtic half English, each word
signifying a head[1] or height, perpetuated the memory
of the struggle which had once been carried on in that
neighbourhood between the two races.   The special interest, indeed, of Somerset as a whole (the land of the
Somersetan) to Freeman, was that in no other part of
the country could the gradual growth of the West-
Saxon kingdom, which in time absorbed all England,
be so clearly traced.   The successive conquests of
Ceawlin, Cenwealh, Centwine, and Ine between 577 and
710, were marked stages in that process by which the
West-Saxon crept on winning the land from the Briton.
The history of Somerset thus furnished a clear illustration of the making of England, and the whole region
was rich in memories of kings and saints and heroes.
The following description of Somerleaze was written
by Freeman in 1882, when he was offering to let it to
a friend for a short time.

'I must tell you this is not a great and grand place, not so big
by a great deal as Dickinson's, of whom you speak, but it is
a good moderate-sized house, in which Dickinson often finds
himself very happy[2]. I am told by my antecessor's son, Alger-
non Bathurst, that nobody ever died here, which is something.

---

[1] Mongibello, the local name for Etna, is a parallel instance, being
made up of the Latin 'Mons,' mountain, and the Arabic 'gebel,' which
is identical in meaning. See *History of Sicily*, i. 56.

[2] F. H. Dickinson, Esq., of Kingweston, about twelve miles from
Somerleaze. Mr. Dickinson, who had been a Fellow of Trinity College,
Cambridge, was a man of great ability and learning, especially in Ecclesiastical history, and became one of Freeman's most intimate and highly
valued friends.

I don't know whether you shoot or do anything of that kind, you perhaps know that is not my line, but there is said to be *one* hare on my land. I have very little land in my own hands, and no cows, but my tenant's cows often form part of the general view, along with the trees and the hills.'

The greater part of May and June 1860, while his wife and family were getting into Somerleaze, was spent by Freeman in paying visits and rambling about chiefly in the Eastern and Midland counties, where of course he made many architectural sketches. The following letter was written to his daughter Margaret, when he was staying with Mr. Stubbs, in his country living of Navestock in Essex.

To HIS DAUGHTER MARGARET.

Navestock, May 5, 1860.

Thank you for your letter which came to me in Oxford. I daresay Mamma has told you about my going up Magdalen tower on Tuesday, and how well and bonny Harold looked, especially in his surplice—I don't mean that he wore it on the tower, as he is not a chorister of the college, but only in the school chapel. I was up so early, and did so much work on Tuesday, that I fancied it was two days, and so I have got wrong in the days of the week ever since, thinking Thursday was Friday, and yesterday Saturday. Waltham Abbey looks very well now; there is a very fine new ceiling, all painted with the signs of the zodiac; I saw at first what I thought was a *lobster*, and said, 'They have made the *crab* like a lobster,' but I looked again, and saw that there was a crab as well, and lo, my lobster was the *scorpion*. Yesterday I walked with Mr. Stubbs to several places, among them Greenstead, where the walls of the nave of the church are built of logs of wood. It is the place where the body of St. Edmund rested about 1014, and they are said to be the same logs which were built then, but they have been taken down and built up again. I went to sleep in the church, and just waking up, I took the eagle that there is to read the lessons from for Mr. Stubbs, and, when he really came

in, I asked him why the eagle did not catch the little birds
which were flying about the church ; so you see I was hardly
awake yet. Perhaps, if I make such mistakes, you will ask me
again whether I ever was plucked.

You must write to me again from Burnham and again from
Somerleaze, and tell me all about it. In the meanwhile Edgar
may write to me at Great Yarmouth.

You are taking something of a holiday, I suppose, but you
must not forget all about Publius, Hannibal, Massinissa, and the
rest of them.

Love to Edgar and Helen and Katharine and Florence.

By the end of June he had taken up his residence at
Somerleaze, but the workpeople engaged on the repairs
of the house could not be got rid of for some time, and
it was not till August that he was able to unpack and
arrange his books.

To the Rev. Henry Thompson.

Somerleaze, July 1, 1860.

Your letter reached me at Cannock in the course of the
very long ramble I took while my wife was taking possession
of this place—all round by Oxford, Wallingford, Waltham,
Navestock, Colchester, Yarmouth, Cromer, Peterborough,
Market Harborough, Cambridge, Houghton Conquest, Cannock,
Tedstone Delamere, Leominster, and Newport, in the course
of which I have seen a great many fine things. If you have
been at Brentwood you were a very little way from Navestock,
but I don't know whether we were both among the East-
Saxons at the same time. This post has brought me a capital
sermon from Stubbs about Jehu.

I am now at last settled as a Zummerzet freeholder, and
I am inclined to like my quarters very much. 'Tis certainly
a beautiful country, and my little property lies very compactly
and conveniently. But in the house itself we are in a state of
utter chaos. I never before so fully understood the meaning
of the words Tohu and Bohu [1]. An army of plasterers, masons,

---

[1] The Hebrew words in Gen. i. 1 signifying ' waste ' and ' void.'

and painters meet one at every step, and we go to bed with a practicable breach in the wall through which any number of klefts might march in at discretion.   When we are a little more in order I hope you will come and see us.

I staid two or three days with a friend of yours, I believe, H. J. Rose, at Houghton Conquest, a man of learning in paths altogether out of my beat, seeing he getteth up by cockcrow to read books in the Syriac tongue.

I don't think your bad character of the Italians is borne out by facts.   You say they are not fit for freedom.   Solvitur liberando[1].   Did any people ever go through the process so well?   I greatly respect the Dutch in the sixteenth century, and the Greeks in this; but I cannot say that either went through the trial, as the Italians have done now, with only one crime[2]?   Has a new-made constitution ever worked better than in Piedmont?   And pray what is your man at Vienna but an arrant impostor?   Who made him emperor or king or anything else?   You can't make him out to be anything but Duke of Austria, and that by a very doubtful title.   I don't know anything that makes me more angry than when people identify this wretched sham 'Kaiserthum' with my old Ottos and Fredericks.   N.B. I have this day unpacked Pertz's *Monumenta Germaniae Historica*, which I have bought for a great sum, but which I could hardly do without.   I certainly pant for the day when I can arrange all my books in their new library.   I have changed

certain windows from ⌂ to ⊞ which I think you will

approve, but *triplets* in the three chief rooms must still abide for a season.

To Rev. W. Stubbs.

Somerleaze, July 29, 1860.

We are now getting into a little more order inside, and outside everything (save the roads), is charming.   I have also found out why I am in Wells parish and not Wookey, I find from Guest's map that in 577 Ceawlin conquered up to

---

[1] 'The question is solved by setting them free.'
[2] The murder of Colonel Anviti, Oct. 5, 1859.

the boundary of my land and no further. *There* is a bit of English permanence ; the national boundary of 577 remaining the parochial one of 1860. By the way, this puts me in the Welsh part.

To THE REV. HENRY THOMPSON.

1860.

[*The first part of this letter is missing.*]

... I am very busy as usual with T[itus] Quinctius Flamininus, Divus Augustus Fridericus, and Lewis XI. Also writing in all possible Quarterlies—my last being the last Bentley—*Bentley's Quarterly Review*, not *Bentley's Miscellany*, I beg to put in.

I hope your invalids will soon be better ; I have not mounted a horse and scarcely stirred out of doors for the last week, owing to a sort of lumbago, dorsago, or some such thing, which would be mighty unpleasant if I wanted to dance, but which, as it does not reach to my head or my arms, in no way hinders reading or writing.

I find from William of Malmesbury that Brent Knoll was anciently known as *Mons Ranarum* [1]. Can you conceive such a scene as this?

ΔΕΝΙΣΩΝ. ΔΙΤΖΕΡ. ΒΟΥΛΗ.

ΔΕ. βρεκεκεκὲξ κοὰξ κοάξ.

ΔΙ. βρεκεκεκέξ, κοὰξ κοάξ.

ΔΕ. καταβρεκεκεκέξω σε.

ΔΙ. κατακοάξω σε.

ΔΕ. βρεκεκεκέξ.

ΔΙ. κοὰξ κοάξ.

ΒΟ. ἀλλ' ἐξόλοισθ' αὐτῷ κοάξ,
οὐδὲν γάρ ἐστ' ἀλλ' ἦ κοάξ.

I used to call it by the more respectful name of Mount St. Anthony, but I shall certainly stick to Frogsdoun, Mynydd Batrach, or whatever may be Welsh for the singer of the rhines.

---

[1] ' Hill of frogs.' The humorous imitation of the Frogs of Aristophanes which follows was suggested by a lawsuit on a question of doctrine which had been instituted by the Rev. J. Ditcher, the Vicar of South Brent, against Archdeacon Denison, the Vicar of East Brent.

The first ten years of his life at Somerleaze were the period in which Freeman's powers rose to their greatest height; a simple chronological outline of his work will best enable the reader to estimate the extent and variety of it. On Feb. 12, 1861 he began his *History of Federal Government*, of which the first and only volume was published on Feb. 5, 1863, but he was engaged upon a continuation of the work during the years 1864 and 1865. The volume of *Old English History for Children* published in 1869, was begun in February 1860, and on March 29, 1865 he began a *History of Greece* which he carried on at intervals throughout that year, then dropped it for a time and took it up again in January 1867. The continuation of the *History of Federal Government*, together with this *History of Greece* and the *Old English History for Children*, formed the staple of his literary work to the end of November 1865. On December 7, 1865, he started upon his *History of the Norman Conquest*, and by March 28, 1866 he had completed his fair copy of the second chapter. The first proofs of the work began to be received in August, and early in 1867 the first volume consisting of about 770 pages was published. He pushed on so rapidly with his manuscript that the first proofs of volume ii. were received on January 3, 1868. The first chapter of volume iii. was finished on April 1 of that year, the whole was completed by February 13, 1869, and the last proof was received on July 16 of the same year. In the latter part of that year he was engaged in preparing volume iv., and at the same time in revising volumes i. and ii. for a second edition, and making an index to them ; consequently the fourth volume did not appear before the middle of the year 1871. His diary under the date of November 24, 1869, contains the first notice of *Historical Geography*, a work upon which he was engaged at irregular intervals during the next twelve years, and which was published at last in 1881. It is a remarkable proof of the exuberance and versatility of his powers, that the period which saw the production of such great works as the *History of Federal Government*, the first three volumes of the *Norman Conquest*, and the *Old English History for Children*, was also the period in which he contributed the largest number of articles to the *Saturday Review*. For this journal he wrote from 1860 to 1869 (both years inclusive), 391 reviews, and 332 articles on miscellaneous subjects commonly called Middle Articles or ' Middles,' because they were placed between the articles on political matters at the beginning of the paper, and the reviews which were placed at the end[1]. The largest number of articles which he wrote for the *Saturday Review* in any one year was 96 in 1862, consisting of 52 Middles and 44 Reviews. Within the same period of ten years he also wrote 82 Reviews for the *Guardian* newspaper, and two articles for the *National Review*, one for the January number, 1860, on the new design for the Foreign Office, the other for the October

---

[1] List of articles for the *Saturday Review*, 1860-1869 :—

A.D.	Reviews.	Middles.
1860	20	6
1861	33	35
1862	44	52
1863	40	42
1864	40	37
1865	43	31
1866	38	23
1867	48	39
1868	39	24
1869	46	43
	391	332

Total of both kinds 723

number in that year on Herodotus. An article appeared
in the *Edinburgh Review* in January 1865 on Sir F.
Palgrave's *History of Normandy and England*, and four
articles in the *Fortnightly Review*, the first in October
1865 on the proposed revision of the Swiss Federal
Constitution, the second in January 1866 on the 'Grouping of Boroughs,' the third in April 1868 on Pearson's
Early and Middle Ages of England, and the fourth in
October 1869 on the 'Morality of Field Sports,' which
was the beginning of a long paper war on that subject.

The volume on Federal Government was only the
first instalment of a work in which he designed to trace
out the action of the federal principle as exemplified in
the ancient world by the Achaian League B.C. 281–146;
in mediaeval times by the Swiss Confederation, first
formed in 1291; in the intermediate period by the
United Provinces of the Netherlands, 1579–1795; and in
strictly modern times by the United States of America,
1778–1862. Although the book appeared during the
American War of Secession, it did not owe its origin in
any way to that event, being the fruit of more than ten
years' previous reading and thought. His first conception of it was due to the careful study that he had
made of the federal period of Greek history—a period
which seemed to him to be rich in political lessons and
to have been treated by English scholars with unmerited
neglect. His work being the history, not of any one
country, but of a system of government which had existed
in many countries, he made frequent use of the comparative method with respect to events and institutions.
'I have striven,' he says in his Preface, 'to make the
politics of Federal Greece more intelligible and more
interesting by showing their points of likeness and un-

likeness to the politics of modern England and America[1].'
But he maintains that in doing this he had not written
in the interests of any modern political party, or in the
interests of North or of South in the American quarrel.
He saw too much to be said for and against both sides
in that strife, to be capable of any strong partisanship
one way or the other. He held strong opinions on
many points both of home and of foreign politics, for
historical study more than anything else led the mind to
form a definite political creed ; but at the same time it
no less hindered the growth of narrow political partisanship. The historical student soon learned to sympathize
with individuals among all parties, but to decline to
throw in his lot unreservedly with any party[2]. In the
heat of controversy which was then at its height respecting the American War, it was difficult to make men take
a calm and dispassionate view of federal government as
a system. From the recent disruption in the United
States, some persons inferred an inherent weakness in
federal government as such, and because England had
suffered some wrong at the hands of one federal government, it was argued that all federal governments were
corrupt. In reality, however, these facts proved no more
against federalism in the abstract than the misgovern-
ment of particular kings, and the occasional disruption of

[1] The *History of Federal Government* was republished by Messrs.
Macmillan in 1893, and very ably edited by Mr. J. B. Bury, Fellow
of Trinity College, Dublin. The references in the present work are to
this edition.

[2] He held, however, that secession from the Union was as much
rebellion against existing law as the original revolt of the Colonies had
been against the English monarchy. The only question in either case
was whether special circumstances had arisen such as could alone justify
a breach of the ordinary law.

kingdoms, proved against monarchy in the abstract. No form of government was perfect, each had its special weaknesses and dangers, and the federal system did not enjoy any exceptional immunity [1].

The second chapter contains a very clear and masterly exposition of the characteristic advantages and disadvantages of large and small states, and of the federal system, which was a kind of compromise between the two. The principal advantages of the small state, of which the city commonwealths in ancient Greece afforded the most perfect examples, were that the political education of the individual citizen was carried to a higher pitch than was possible under any other system, and that patriotic devotion to the state was singularly fervent and intense. The chief disadvantages were, a want of permanency, the almost perpetual warfare in which neighbouring cities were involved owing to commercial jealousies and border disputes, the bitterness of political factions, and the cruelty with which war was conducted when the armies were composed of men who had a personal interest and stake in the quarrel.

In a large state, whether the government was that of a despotism, a constitutional monarchy, or a republic, the advantages were that peace was secured to a large space of country, containing, perhaps, hundreds of cities, which under the old Greek system would be continually harassing each other in war. In large states wars could not recur so often, and were not generally accompanied with so much cruelty and bitterness of feeling as in smaller commonwealths. On the other hand, under representative government, some form of which was necessary in large states, the political education of the ordinary

[1] *History of Federal Government*, pp. 71, 72.

citizen could not reach so high a level as in smaller
states. A large number of electors would always remain
ignorant and careless of public affairs to a degree which
was not possible in the case of an Athenian citizen, who
deliberated and voted in person upon every question of
importance which was brought before the Assembly.
And under an electoral system, if many were careless
and ignorant of public affairs, they were liable to be
either corrupted or deceived. Electoral ignorance, prejudice, and corruption were vices inherent in the representative system, and neither the ballot nor limitations
of franchise could thoroughly eradicate these evils. No
system had yet been found which would make the really
wise men and good citizens, who were scattered among all
classes and parties, the sole possessors of political power.
He sums up the result of this comparison in the following
eloquent passage :—

'On the whole there can be little doubt that the balance of
advantage lies in favour of the modern system of large states.
The small republic, indeed, developes its individual citizens to
a pitch which in the large kingdom is utterly impossible. But
it so developes them at the cost of bitter political strife within,
and almost constant warfare without. It may even be doubted
whether the highest form of the city commonwealth does not
require slavery as the condition of its most perfect development.
The days of glory of such a commonwealth are indeed glorious
beyond comparison, but it is a glory that is too brilliant to last,
and in proportion to the short splendour of its prime is too
often the unutterable wretchedness of its long old age. The
Republics of Greece seem to have been shown to the world for
a moment, like some model of glorified humanity from which
all may draw the highest of lessons, but which none can hope
to reproduce in its perfection. As the literature of Greece is
the groundwork of all later literature, as the art of Greece is
the groundwork of all later art, so in the great democracy of

Athens we recognize the parent state of law and justice and freedom, the wonder and the example of every later age. But it is
an example which we can no more reproduce, than we can call
back again the inspiration of the homeric singer, the more than
human skill of Pheidias, or the untaught and inborn wisdom of
Thucydides : they all belong to that glorious vision of the world's
youth which has passed away for ever. The subject of a great
modern state leads a life less exciting and less brilliant, but
a life no less useful than the citizen of an ancient commonwealth. But never could we have been as we are if those
ancient commonwealths had not gone before us. While human
nature remains what it has been for two thousand years, so
long will the eternal lessons of the great 'possession for all
time,' the lessons which Perikles has written with his life, and
Thucydides with his pen, the lessons expanded by the more
enlarged experience of Aristotle and Polybios, the lessons
which breathe a higher note of warning still as Demosthenes
lives the champion of freedom and dies its martyr, so long will
lessons such as these never cease to speak with the same truth
and the same freshness to countless generations [1].

He next turns to the consideration of federal government, as a third system intermediate between the two
extremes of great and small states, borrowing something
from each, and possessing many of the merits and of the
faults inherent in a compromise. Two requisites were
essential to a perfect form of federal government. The
several members of the union must be wholly independent
in the management of their internal affairs, but all must
be subject to a common power in those matters which
concerned the whole body collectively. A true federal
commonwealth consisted of many states in respect of
internal government, but formed a single state in relation
to other nations. It did not secure peace and equal
rights to its whole territory so perfectly as a modern
constitutional kingdom, nor did it develop the political

[1] Ib. pp. 67, 68.

life of the individual citizen so perfectly as an ancient city commonwealth; but it secured a far larger amount of general peace than the system of independent cities, and it gave its average citizens a higher political education than was attainable by the average subjects of extensive monarchies. It was a more delicate and artificial structure than either of the older forms of government; it was essentially the creation of circumstances, and was less tolerant than any other form of being transplanted to soils which circumstances had not fitted to receive it. Its warmest admirers, therefore, would hardly wish to propagate it throughout the world in general; no one could wish that Athens in the days of her glory should have stooped to a federal union with other Grecian cities. No one could wish to cut up our United Kingdom into a federation, to invest English counties with the rights of American States, or even to restore Scotland and Ireland to the quasi-federal position which they held before their respective unions. A federal union, to be of any value, must arise by the establishment of a closer tie between elements which were before distinct, not by the division of members which had hitherto been more closely united. The true end of federalism was to unite to a certain extent cities or states which were capable of that amount of union and no more. It was inappropriate where there was not sufficient community in origin, feeling, or interest to enable the several members to work together up to a certain point. It was equally inappropriate where community passed into identity. But in the intermediate condition, the condition of Peloponnesos struggling against Macedonia, of the Swiss League struggling against Austria, of the Netherlands contending with

Spain, and of the American colonies contending with England, it was the true solvent.

The Achaian League, the Swiss Bund, the United Provinces, and the United States, all had their origin in the purposes of mutual defence against a common enemy. The American Union had secured, for a long period of time, a greater amount of combined peace and freedom than was ever before enjoyed by so large a portion of the earth's surface. Yet it had been alleged that the recent disruption proved the inherent weakness of the federal tie. In a certain sense, indeed, it was a truism to say that the federal tie was a weak tie. It was by its nature weaker than the tie which united the geographical divisions of a perfectly consolidated State. But what federalism ought to be compared with was, not perfect union, but that complete separation which in most instances was the only alternative. The federal tie was weak, because it was artificial, depending for its permanence not on sentiment, but on reason and interest. But if the circumstances under which a federal union was formed remained unchanged, it might well be as permanent as any other form of government. It might be useful also as a transitional step, either to consolidation or to separation. Weakness of the federal tie only meant facility of secession. Separation between States federally united might become expedient and justifiable, and this being granted, a system which supplied the means of a peaceable divorce had its good side. He would not venture to pronounce whether the secession of the Southern States of America was right or wrong, though he thought a plausible case for secession might be made out on the grounds of expediency. In any case, American States might secede with safety, because they were not now threatened by any outside enemy. The members of the Swiss Confederation, on the other hand, notwithstanding diversity of race, language, and religion, could not separate because disruption would be fatal to freedom. The first State which seceded would inevitably be annexed, either by France on the one side, or by Austria on the other.

Some exposition of the main principles and leading characteristics of federal government, as understood by Freeman, seemed desirable in order to show that he did not entertain that blind admiration for the system which has sometimes been attributed to him. It also helps to explain the scorn and ridicule with which, as will be seen later on, he treated the idea of what has been called ' Imperial Federation,' and the distinction which he was careful to draw between Federation and Home Rule, so that while he advocated Home Rule for Ireland he was strongly opposed to the application of Federalism to the United Kingdom. On the other hand, his interest in tracing the history of the Achaian League was enhanced by the idea and the hope that what Federalism had done for ancient Greece, it might perhaps do again for modern Greece, or, if that were impracticable, might still do for some of the other nations in south-eastern Europe. At the conclusion of the ninth chapter of his history, after summing up the results of the Achaian League : how it gave for 140 years ' to a larger portion of Greece than any previous age had seen, a measure of freedom, unity, and general good government, which might well atone for the lack of the dazzling glory of the old Athenian Democracy,' he proceeds [1]—

---

[1] P. 554. This chapter was the last in the original edition. The two concluding chapters in the new edition have been added from MSS. found amongst Freeman's papers after his death.

'Never up to our own day has Federalism, the offspring of Greece, appeared again in its native land. Yet when we look at the map of Greece, and see each valley, and peninsula, and island marked out by the hand of nature for an independent being—when we think of the varied origin and condition of the present inhabitants of its several provinces—when we think of the local institutions, democratic here, aristocratic there, which preserved the life of the nation through ages of Turkish bondage —we may well ask whether ancient Achaia or modern Switzerland may not be the true model for regenerate Greece rather than a blind imitation of the stereotyped forms of European royalty. It may be that the favourable moment has passed for ever : it may be that it is now too late to dream of a Federal Republic in a land where thirty years of Bavarian corruption have swept away those relics of ancient freedom which the very Ottoman had spared.   However this may be now, there can be little doubt that a generation back the blood of Botzarês and the life of Kanarês would have been better given to found a free Hellenic Federation than to establish the throne of any stranger king.   And let us pass beyond the bounds of Greece herself, to look at that whole group of nations of which Greece is only one among many, although in some respects the foremost.   We may be sure that a day will come when the rod of the oppressor shall be broken.   We need no prophet to tell us that wrong and robbery shall not always be abiding, that all the arts of Western diplomatists cannot for ever maintain the Barbarian on the throne of the Caesars, and the Infidel in the most glorious of Christian temples.   A day will come when the Turkish horde shall be driven back to its native deserts, or die out, the victim of its own vices, upon the soil which it has too long defiled.   Then will Greek and Serb and Albanian and Rouman and Bulgarian enter upon the full and free possession of the land which is their own.   Already does Greece, free and extending her borders, Servia and Wallachia, held in only nominal vassalage, Montenegro, if crushed for a moment, yet unsubdued in heart, all point to the full accomplishment of the glorious dream.   And when the full day has dawned, are those lands to remain utterly separate and isolated, or are they, so many peoples, nations and languages, to be fettered down by some centralizing monarchy which would merely substitute a Christian for an infidel master. Here would be the grandest field that the world has ever seen for trying the great experiment of monarchic federalism. The nations of the Byzantine peninsula, differing in origin, language, and feeling, are united by common wrongs, by a common religion, and by the common reverence of ages for the Imperial City of the Basils and the Constantines. For nations in such a position the Federal tie, rather than more complete separation or more close connexion, seems the natural relation to each other. But the traditions of Servia and Bulgaria are not Republican : the mere size of the several provinces may seem, in the old world at least, to surpass the limits which nature has in all ages marked out for European Commonwealths. One set of circumstances points to federal union, another set of circumstances points to princely government. A monarchic federation on such a scale has never yet existed, but it is not in itself at all contradictory to the federal ideal. When the day of vengeance and of freedom shall have come, it will be for the people of those noble and injured lands—not for western mediators, or western protectors—to solve the mighty problem for themselves.'

The latest editor of the *History of Federal Government* rightly observes in his preface, that these remarks are as true to-day as they were in 1863. 'Bulgaria is now only nominally a vassal State. The Bulgarians have won their freedom, and have shown that they are perhaps more worthy to possess it than any other State in the Illyrian peninsula. But the " tinkering policy " of the Treaty of Berlin has not made it less true, and further tinkering by any such treaties in the future will not make it less true, that the only safeguard against Austrian and Russian aggression is a South Slavonic Federation, just as the only safeguard of Greece against absorption in the Macedonian Monarchy was found in the Federal tie[1].'

[1] P. ix.

Federalism is the topic which most frequently recurs in the following letters, generally in reference either to the war in America, or to affairs in Greece. There are also some allusions to events which had recently occurred in Italy. It may, therefore, assist the reader to be reminded that France and Sardinia had declared war against Austria in 1859, and that the Austrians had been defeated in the battles of Magenta and Solferino. By the treaty of Villafranca which brought the war to a close in July of that year, Austrian Lombardy was ceded to Sardinia. The duchies of Tuscany, Parma, and Modena, were also united to the kingdom of Sardinia, but Savoy and Nice were annexed to France. In 1860 Garibaldi set free Sicily and Naples, and in March, 1861, all Italy except Venetia and Rome was united under King Victor Emmanuel by declaration of the Italian Parliament. The American War of Secession began in April, 1861, and ended in April, 1865. In Greece, King Otho was expelled after a bloodless revolution in 1862. The choice of a new king was submitted to the Greek people, who elected our English Prince Alfred by an enormous majority. It was held, however, by the British Government, that England, France and Russia were bound by certain treaties and protocols not to permit any member of their reigning families to accept the crown of Greece. The British Government suggested the offer of the throne to the second son of Prince Christian of Sleswig-Holstein-Glucksburg[1], William George, a youth of seventeen, who was accordingly elected king of the Hellenes on March 30, 1863, with the title of George I.

[1] He had been appointed, though a second son, as heir to the kingdom of Denmark by a protocol signed at London, May 8, 1852, and he mounted the throne on the death of Frederick VII, November 15, 1863.

To G. FINLAY, ESQ.

Somerleaze, December 2, 1860.

I have not written to or heard from you for a long time. I suppose I have, for some time past, had less to do with Greek matters, old or new, than usual. Indeed just lately one has been tempted to forget English matters too: Garibaldi and Italy pretty well take up all our thoughts about such things.

I am delighted to see that your history of the *Greek Revolution* is actually in the press. I shall take and compare it diligently with Gordon and Trikoupes; the more contemporary narratives one has the better. I wish there were a Turkish version to match; that is, one by a regular orthodox old-fashioned Turk; I would not give a halfpenny for the Gallic twaddle of a Turk in tight trousers. Also the two volumes on the *Greek Revolution* form the natural finish of those which have gone before. It will be something indeed to have written the whole history of the nation, from its final conquest to its real or supposed regeneration. No other of our great historians takes in so long a series of years, and yet forms one whole and perfect subject.

. . . Do you know anything of the movement towards the Latin Church said to be going on in Bulgaria? It is not the first time the Bulgarians have played the same trick, and I am exceedingly sorry to hear of it. They surely have a perfect right to a Patriarch of their own tongue, and I don't see how it could damage the Grand Turk in any way to let them have one. (Is the common author of all mischief, L. N. Buonaparte, at the bottom of it?) The case is something like the Welsh Church here; not that I go at all with the cry that a Bishop in Wales must needs be a Welshman, but he certainly ought to be able to speak Welsh, as three out of the four now can. I can't see, however, how the Bulgarians will at all mend matters by going over to the Pope.

I should very much like to know what you think about Italian, Hungarian, and indeed European affairs generally. Here in England politics seem quite dead; at least such politics as I care about, for budgets and French treaties are things which I cannot at all understand. What is to become of

the old man at Rome, and the young man at Gaeta? Will
Victor Emmanuel be able to organize a really united Kingdom
of Italy? I wish him all good luck, but I should think it must
be hard. Anyhow, the more local independence the different
provinces have, the better ; what suits Piedmontese after twelve
years of constitution, and several centuries of a kind of national
life ; or again, Tuscans who have lived under despots indeed,
but not tyrants, can hardly suit the emancipated slaves at
Naples. 'Aπλῶς[1] I should have been for a Federation—not
Buonaparte's sham one, but a real Swiss or American one—but
I suppose between the Tyrant of Paris and the Tyrant of
Vienna it would not have answered, and I heartily accept the
Kingdom as a δεύτερος πλοῦς[2]. I am longing to see the Austrian
imposture fall to pieces. My hatred to it is exactly measured by
my love for the old German Kingdom whose memory it pro-
fanes. I should be much obliged for your thoughts on all
matters.

To THE SAME.

Somerleaze, January 8, 1861.

. . . I am very curious to see what will come this spring
in all parts of the world. There is something rather odd in the
sort of quarter's notice of a general revolution which has been
given all over Europe. In America they are more go-a-head,
and have actually begun. I am afraid people are rather
beginning to depreciate the American Constitution because it
has failed to keep Carolina, &c. I say rather that, looking over
the whole field of history, it is a very great matter to have
given such a great territory eighty years of combined peace and
freedom, such as I do not see how any other form of government could have done. So, if the whole Federation dropped
to pieces to-morrow, it would have done a great work. The
Achaian League lasted little longer as a substantive power :
happily America has had neither Macedonia nor Rome to
trouble it. But I think Achaian experience, in the case of
Sparta for instance, tells against any attempt to keep a seced-
ing state by force. Rather let the nigger-drivers go to the devil
their own way.

We are taught to believe here, that in the spring, when

[1] 'Absolutely,' i. e. in itself.   [2] ' Next best course.'

Garibaldi begins again and Hungary revolts, something is also to happen to the sacred person of King Otho. You do not say whether you expect it on the spot or not. As far as I understand Greek local politics (which is not at all), I should not be sorry. Only what are you to have instead? (I mean to come and see as soon as I can afford it, but I have impoverished myself for a year or two by buying and repairing this place, and moving thereto.) The 'Jupiter' amused me to-day by announcing the Bulgarian ecclesiastical movement in a telegram, as a piece of news, which I have seen discussed in various places, English and French, many weeks back. I have always tried to set forth, in my small way, that the Greeks ought not to assume any superiority over Bulgarians or anybody else, but just pull side by side against the common enemy. I am now and then haunted by a notion that Basil the Βουλγαροκτόνος[1] (though he is a bit of a hero of mine) was practically a mistake, and that Samuel ought to have reigned at Constantinople, as the Theodoric of the East. It would have been a fine εὐθανασία of the Empire to have been fairly conquered at its acme, instead of lingering on.

I am anxiously expecting your history of the War of Independence; you may be sure I shall blow its trumpet as loudly as I can. I hope you have worked out your views about the land-tax. That is, if I mistake not, a tithe in kind, which must be bad anyhow.

What I see of the Βρετ. 'Αστήρ[2]—though I can't say that I go through its politics very deeply—I like, as far as I can understand it. I wrote an article about it in the *Saturday Review* before Trikoupes gave me his opinion on it—but he says that he and the Greeks in London were satisfied with it. I take a sort of childish amusement in seeing English and French things expressed in Greek.

I hope you will come to England some day, and both make your way into Somersetshire, and let me meet you in Oxford. They ought to make you a D.C.L., but I can't promise that they

---

[1] 'The slayer of the Bulgarians.' The Emperor Basil II defeated Samuel, King of the Bulgarians, in 996, and subjugated the kingdom in 1019.

[2] Βρεττανικὸς 'Αστήρ, *The British Star*, a Greek newspaper so named.

would have sense enough. Though to be sure they did make Motley one last year.

To THE SAME.

Somerleaze, August 19, 1861.

I don't count myself a fair exchange for you, but here I am, such as I am, only I find the photographic art refuses to represent me with a beard of its natural colour. Some say I look fierce, and some sentimental; I am sure I don't know; it is hard to look anyhow when one has to screw up one's face into a state of artificial nothingness.

Do you think anything will come of this new Sultan, or is he simply a new broom, sweeping over-clean? It strikes me that a vigorous rule of any kind, whether for good or evil, must do good, if only by bringing the crisis about sooner. Anything must be better than a good-natured voluptuary, doing no particular harm himself, but allowing any quantity.

I am—at least I was a little time back, and hope soon to be again—hard at work at my *Federal Government.* I wish you had the League working still, meeting at Aigion, &c., and I should come out at once to look at it. Anyhow, coming to Greece is a thing which I certainly mean to do the very first time I can manage it.

I think I told you that the Camden Professorship of Ancient History had fallen vacant since you were good enough to give me a character for the other, and that my friends thought I had better not stand. It is very provoking; I should have liked it much the better of the two.

People think I can't know anything of what they are pleased to call 'ancient' because I am supposed to know something of what they are pleased to call 'modern.' You know, as well as any man, what utter tomfoolery this is.

To SPYRIDON TRIKOUPES.

Somerleaze, January 19, 1862.

I am very glad that you will let me attach your name to the first volume of my *Federal Government*[1]. I have always

[1] A dedicatory letter to Trikoupes is prefixed to the *History of Federal Government.*

imagined a certain analogy between you and Polybius, and he is naturally my great authority in that part of the book. So I think there is a special propriety in it.

I am very awkwardly placed between you and Finlay. I have learned so much from both of you, and have so much reason to respect and admire both of you, that I hardly know what to say between you. But I do not think either of you can object if I think better of both of you than either of you does of the other. Of course I cannot judge of the minute accuracy of either as to particular facts or particular people. But probably, at my distance of time and place, I can judge better than either of you of the general result of your two narratives as permanent pieces of history. I see many things in Finlay's book at which both your personal and your national feelings must be naturally, and I doubt not often justly, offended. But on me the general result of your book and his is essentially the same. I drew my notions of the Greek Revolution and the actors in it mainly from your book compared with Gordon's. You and Gordon write from different points of view, but I see no discrepancies of any importance in your two narratives, and not many in your estimates. Finlay writes from a third point of view, but his narrative does not differ in any important respect from your's or Gordon's. That is, there are only those differences which must exist in any different tellings of the same story ; differences which in no way lessen one's trust in either writer : differences which did they occur in two writers of past ages, no one would count to be of any moment. Nor is there really much difference in estimates of men and actions. To you, doubtless, the difference seems immense ; to me it seems very small. I formed my estimate of the actors in the Revolution from you and Gordon. On your joint showing I arranged them in three classes: first, pure and unmixed heroes, of whom Greece and human nature may be proud ;—Kanarês, Miaoules, Mark Botzarês, and several others. Second, utter rascals and traitors, Odysseus, Gogos, and so forth. Third, a much larger class than either, of *mixed* characters, men who did good service to Greece, being at the same time guilty of many faults and even crimes, but for whose faults and crimes I hold that much allowance is to be found in the circumstances in which they were placed.

Now I do not find that F's estimate of my first two classes differs at all from what I had drawn from you and Gordon. He admires the heroes just as much as you or I can do. It is in the third class that the difference comes out; he does not diminish the glory of the purely good, but he does certainly make out the mixed characters worse. This is the general tendency of his writings, whether he is speaking of present or past times, of Greeks, Englishmen, or anybody else. But I fully understand that to you it must constantly be most painful and irritating. To me it simply amounts to this: a man who has a tendency to severity of judgement, and to sarcastic vigour in his way of expressing himself, shows very little mercy to men, many of whom doubtless you know and esteem. But he shows just as little to living Englishmen and to men of past history. To the character of the Greek people as opposed to their leaders, you will surely allow that he does full justice.

I can easily see that he dislikes you, and finds fault with you whenever he can. At the same time he wishes to be fair to you : e. g. he allows you 'eloquence' and 'personal integrity,' and that you 'write in a spirit of fairness and equity.' . . . I fully understand that Finlay's history may most naturally seem to you a deliberate libel on your country : it does not seem so to me, and I do not think that Finlay means it as such.

In all this I am speaking of that part of F's history in which I have you and Gordon to check him by. On the latter part, which he has all to himself, I can give no opinion at all. It is evident that F's narrative is an *ex parte* statement : as such, I neither accept nor reject it. I have learned in my historical studies to trust no man implicitly in such matters : I would, therefore, neither approve nor condemn any man without, if possible, knowing what is to be said on the other side, or, failing that, without a more diligent and critical examination of the history itself than I have yet given to it. I will only venture to say, that when I see such men as Kanarès and Miaoules acting against one another, there must have been 'something to be said on both sides.'

I sincerely trust I may see you at Athens—I had rather see you at Mesolongi some day; but I do not in the least know when. I dream of a visit to Greece next year; I fear I cannot manage it this year for many reasons, among others, because I must go and see Switzerland before I write my second volume. Had the Achaian League gone on meeting at Aigion, I should have gone to see it long ago.

To Spyridon Trikoupes.

Somerleaze, October 31, 1862.

You may suppose that I am watching with intense interest the course of the new Greek Revolution. I know not what your own personal feelings at the expulsion of the late King may be. I rejoice at it, and I believe that every Englishman who wishes well to Greece rejoices also. You have got rid of a Government which nobody respected, and you have the opportunity of establishing one which may make the Greek name once more honoured.

You will not, I trust, think me presumptuous either in sending you the thoughts which occur to me on the matter, or in thinking that you may possibly deem them worthy of going beyond yourself. I do not see in what other way I can, just now, serve the cause so well. I therefore write in English, as I can express my thoughts more freely in my own language, and, if you should communicate them to anyone else, they will have more effect in your Greek than in mine.

I am very glad to see the friendly tone towards Greece which the *Times* has been taking up, both before and since the Revolution, and especially the important letter signed 'Digamma,' which is said to be written by Mr. Grote. The doctrine there expressed is the sound one ; let all other nations simply stand aloof, and let Greece, like Italy, decide its own fate. If Western diplomatists can be persuaded to leave Greece for once to herself, Greece will have an opportunity such as she has not had for thirty years past, for righting herself in the eyes of Europe.

The choice of a form of government, and the choice of the king or other ruler under the form of government that may be chosen, seem to me to be so wholly the affair of the Greek nation, and of no one else, that it would be simply impertinent for either individuals or governments of other nations to offer even advice upon the subject. Arguments can easily be brought for and against any plan, for a Republic and for a Monarchy, for a Federal and for a Consolidated State, for a native prince and for a foreigner. It is easy to see that something may be said for and against all of these: the question in each case is, on which side does the balance of advantage and disadvantage lie? But the practical answer to this question can, as it seems to me, be given by none but those whom the decision immediately concerns.

But, whatever may be the form of government which Greece adopts, Greece has such an opportunity as has never been before, and may never be again, for making it an honest and patriotic government, seeking the real good of the nation. The policy of Greece seems to me to be now to centre every thought upon practical internal improvements. Now is the time to do away with those practical evils which, cruelly as they have been exaggerated, neither Greeks, nor lovers of Greece, can pretend to be wholly imaginary. I know what the first impulse of a regenerate nation—or rather a regenerate fraction of a nation—must be; the first thought of every Greek will be to extend the area of the country, to extend the freedom which he himself enjoys to those of his brethren who are still in bondage. It may sound cold and heartless to say that such an impulse must be checked, but I believe that to check it for the present will be the best way to gain the desired object in the end. I am, as you well know, as anxious as any Greek can be to see the whole of Greece released from bondage, whether that bondage be English or Turkish. I trust to see a Greece which shall include at least Thessaly, Epeiros, Crete, and the Ionian Islands. But I am persuaded that the way to obtain this enlargement is to abstain from prematurely pressing it. If we in England should seize this opportunity of putting an end to our profitless and discreditable tenure of the Seven Islands, so much the better. But I think it will be wise in Greece not to demand them. The cry always is that Greece is ill-governed; therefore she is unfit to receive any addition of territory. I myself believe that one great cause of mis-government in Greece has been that she has been shut up within a narrow and unnatural frontier. But it might be hard

to make everybody take in a doctrine which, to conventional
politicians, would sound like a paradox. At any rate I am
sure that the true policy of Greece just now is not to clamour
for an immediate increase of territory, but to show herself
worthy of it. The stupid love of Turks is dying out in
England, but it is by no means dead. It is the part of Greece
now to give it its death-blow by showing that Greeks can
manage for themselves better than Turks, or even Englishmen, can manage for them. You have now an opportunity of
establishing a system of administration—whatever may be the
form of government chosen—which shall be the best practical
confutation of all the slanderers of Greece. Let it be seen that
the condition of liberated Greece is so incontestably superior
to that of enslaved Greece, as to take away from European
politicians all excuse for refusing you an increase of territory.
I do not doubt that its condition is already far superior, but
make it so indisputably superior that no calumniator can
venture to deny it for a moment. Let Europe see that the
detention of Crete and Thessaly by the tyrant of Stamboul
is a wrong even greater than the detention of Rome and
Venice by the tyrants of Paris and Vienna. Show, by material
improvements in independent Greece, the needlessness of
a British protectorate over Corfu and Kephallenia. The day
when Greece will obtain her rights must come sooner or later ;
I only fear that the happy moment may be delayed by some
premature outbreak of national feeling.

The choice of your form of government is, as I before said,
a matter wholly for yourselves. But I may perhaps not be
going too far in saying that the events of the last thirty years
must have taught Greece the vanity of copying the institutions
of other nations. You may possibly want a king ; I do not see
how you can want a court, or any of the gewgaws and trappings
of western royalty. Surely, if you must have a king, the
cheaper he is made the better.

But, under any form of government, now is the time to make
those improvements which are needed to give Greece her
proper place among nations. Now is the time to make roads,
now is the time to place free Greece at once above enslaved
Greece, by abolishing the land-tax in kind. And I do not

doubt that your long residence in England has shown you some points where—I do not say our institutions, but our principles, might be employed with advantage in reforms in Greece. I should be the last man to wish to see a slavish imitation of England, in Greece or anywhere else; I believe that our artificial constitutional system suits us, because it has grown up out of the circumstances of our history, but that it is dangerous rashly to transplant it ready made elsewhere. But I feel sure that you must have observed some things in England the remembrance of which may be useful to Greece in her present reconstruction. You must have seen the omnipotence of the Law, and contrasted it with the narrow sphere of action of the Government. You must have observed the utter absence of an official hierarchy, and the complete independence of local bodies. You must have seen that a Government official, as such, is of no account whatever, that he is subject to the ordinary laws and the ordinary magistrates, exactly like any other citizen. You must have remarked the freely elected Councils of our boroughs, in whose appointment the Government has no voice whatever. You must have remarked the Magistracy of our counties, not elective indeed, being appointed by the Queen's Commission, but having nothing whatever in common with the official classes of continental countries. I am here an unpaid Magistrate of this county; I have a share in the administration of justice and in the general business of the county, but I am in no sort an official; if I act amiss in any way, the Law can correct it, but I am not a member of a hierarchy, with anything to hope or to fear in the way of official advancement. My neighbours again in the neighbouring borough, manage their own affairs, and elect their Town Council without any reference whatever to the Government. Thus the whole local business of the country is done by councils, boards, magistrates; all independent, mostly elective, and none belonging to a professional class of officials; all subject to the Law, but subject to very little interference indeed from the Government. I have heard it said, and I am sure said truly, that the real difference between liberty and tyranny does not depend upon the form of the political Government, but on the subjection of all Government officials to the same laws and tribunals as other people. Now is the time, whatever may be the form of your general government, to restore, improve, and develope those free municipal institutions which the Turk spared and which the Bavarian destroyed. I do not of course mean that any particular English institutions can be transplanted whole into Greece; I only say that now is your golden opportunity to establish true local freedom and self-government, perfect subjection to the Law and complete independence of the mere Government. I am sure that these are sound principles in any age or country; the particular developments of them which may suit Greece at the present moment Greeks alone can determine.

I hope you will pardon the way in which a retired scholar like myself has ventured to enlarge upon these matters to a veteran statesman like you, who have helped to make history as well as to write it. My love for Greece and my ardent wishes for her welfare must be my excuse, and I ventured to think that the views of one who has done what he could—little as it has been—for Greece in darker days, might be worth setting forth now she has a hope of brighter times. And, if I can do anything in England, by writing or otherwise, you will, I am sure, rely on my doing it to the best of my power.

When I shall see Greece with my own eyes, I know not. I had dreamed of coming next year, but I do not know whether I can manage it, as I must go to Switzerland before I write the Swiss part of my *Federal Government.* My Greek volume—with your name attached to it—will I hope be out in a month or so. I could not help being pleased in seeing the country first and the capital last in the late movement, and in hearing the voice of freedom issue again from the land of both the Leagues.

To G. Finlay, Esq.

Somerleaze, November 2, 1862.

You can understand how intensely interested I am in what is now going on in Greece, and how delighted I should be to hear your opinion about it. I also hope that, as before

in the other στάσις[1]—this, I suppose, is allowed to be an ἐπανάστασις[2]—you will send something to the *Saturday Review*.
... Pray tell me all about what has happened and what is going to happen. I do trust the 'Great Powers' will, for once, have the sense to hold their tongues and mind their own business and leave other people to settle their own affairs. Do you go in for a king? I can't see the use of kings; that is, not of kings with courts and cabinets and civil lists and lords of the bedchamber and maids of honour and all such tomfoolery. A real ἄναξ ἀνδρῶν[3], if you can catch him, might be of great use. But why not have the League again? Without going that length, I do trust they will seize the opportunity to get rid of all centralization, bureaucracy, and such beastliness, and set up a good system of local administration. One thing delighted me; it is not a Parisian row, but a real national movement; the capital is the last to join, and my Achaians are the first to begin. The more you can tell me about it, the more obliged I shall be. If they would have put off the Revolution till the spring, and have sent me word in time, I really think I should have come to look at it.

I hope my *Federal Government*, vol. i, will be out in a month or so. I wind up with a few remarks on Modern Greece, to which I suppose I must now add something.

Do you know at all how things go on in Wallachia? And what do you think about Servia? I am intensely disgusted with Lord Russell's anti-Montenegrin despatch. It is really a great thing to see the *Times* coming round, not that the *Times* itself matters, but because it is a sign that public opinion is coming round too. I, who never bowed the knee to either the Turkish or the Napoleonic Baal, sit still and see the world go away from me and come back to me again.

The following letter from Mr. Finlay to Freeman serves to explain the two which follow it.

Athens, October 31, 1862.

I have not written to you lately because I despaired of living to see better times in Greece. I felt sulky and wished to

---

[1] 'Revolt.'   [2] 'Revolution.'   [3] 'King of men.'

feel selfish. But the Revolution and the manner in which the Greeks have behaved during it have put me into a better humour, and I feel again a return of philhellenism, though an αἰδόμαχος who can no longer be of much' use to the cause. . . .

I need not tell you my opinion, you know that I believe the vigour of the Greek nation can only be restored by a system of communal institutions that descend to the parish, and a system of finance that relieves the labour of agriculturists from all interference.

I leave the manufacture of political constitutions to others for I feel that I could without difficulty make two very different, and both equally good for Greece, and such as would pass muster in a dictionary of constitutions. I wish to see a Greece made by Greeks and not by protecting powers and foreign cabinets. The Greece that would suit congresses would not be a Greece with free institutions and an increasing population. I would fain address public opinion in England, but nobody reads what I write except my friends, and I have few left and they have no influence.

Now you may, in this crisis, do Greece good service. You have an inimitable style, and nobody knows both ancient and modern Greece so well. You alone are the man that can stave off both pedants and politicians. I beg you most fervently to turn your attention to the subject. Old men here are useless, and things must pass into the hands of younger men who have no traditions of Palmerstonian and Orlean intrigues. I think both the provisional government and the ministry are as well composed as could be expected. . . . The national assembly will have great authority, and if local interests are powerful, and phanariots[1] and the nominees of diplomatists are not intruded, I have hopes that much good will be effected.

One subject very naturally engages a good deal of attention. Who is to be the new sovereign? The Greeks very generally, and to my great astonishment, are eager to have an English

---

[1] Byzantine officials so named from the quarter of Constantinople in which they commonly resided. They were generally detested on account of their tyrannies and exactions.

prince, or a prince connected with England. It may be a passing fancy in which visions of annexation float. But there is
certainly also a reaction in favour of England as the freest and
best governed country in Europe. Not that Greeks overlook
its being the richest. The moment is not unfavourable for
reorganizing a better and even larger kingdom, without in-
juring the integrity of the Ottoman Empire, and with conditions
that would improve Ottoman finance. But I must indulge in
idle visions ἄρα? The best thing the Greeks could do would
be to elect Mr. Gladstone king. He has all the qualities
and some of the defects they want, which would make the
better king of Greece. Enthusiasm, eloquence, classic learning
enough to confound the professors, and powers of calculation
to confuse the merchants ; elevation of mind and rectitude of
principle, and, or I mistake, promptitude and energy in action.
I wonder why the three powers do not each choose a good
administrator, the best man that will accept, and draw lots for
the kingdom. The ancient Persians let a horse choose their
sovereign. Modern sovereigns generally select an ass for their
colleague, and tell us it is to keep royal blood pure, and ensure
paternity on thrones.

FROM F. H. DICKINSON, ESQ. TO E. A. FREEMAN, ESQ.

Kingweston, November 10, 1862.

I have sent on Finlay's curious and interesting letter to
Cox. I conceive the letter in 'Reviler[1]' is one of those he
mentions, and that the other will follow. It is very remarkable
certainly, the contrast you draw between the treatment of
Italian insurrections and those of Turkey. The fear of Russia
is defunct, but I suspect the real difficulty is that our statesmen
have got into a habit of protecting and bullying Turkey, and
by both processes, have acquired an amount of influence there
which they are not able to throw away. It will not do to have
an English prince on the throne of Greece ; we must not break
our word, even though it may have been given in trumpery
protocols. Besides, the continental powers will not believe
that we really care very little for the compliment. But there are
no protocols to prevent Gladstone being made king. That would

[1] I.e. *Saturday Review.*

be much the best thing as he has the personal qualities they want. He is sufficiently important to be placed above paltry jealousies, which would operate to prevent any native Greek being made king, or would pull him down if he were. The next best thing would be a son of King Leopold, though he would bring in the jealousy of the endless and aspiring Cobourg family, from which Gladstone would be free. I confess I like the system of new families being admitted to the royal rank, like the Buonapartes. I do not grudge the old kings and princes their perilous eminence individually, but I do feel a dislike of the (German?) feeling of caste attaching to them, and anything that pulls this down pleases me. In fact my antipathy to the royal marriage web connects itself with the elevation of Gladstone. Maybe, they may elect Prince Alfred to be king, W. E. G. as a pis-aller—if so, it may not be amiss to put him before the world as a candidate—I wish you could do so.

FROM E. A. FREEMAN, ESQ. TO G. FINLAY, ESQ.

Somerleaze, Wells. November 12, 1862.

Your notion of choosing Gladstone King of Greece, took me a little by surprise, but I have been thinking about it and conferring with a neighbour, a thoughtful man, who used often to write in the *Spectator* at the time that I did; I send you a copy of his letter. I really think there is a great deal in it ; cannot you put it forward at all, either directly, or indirectly ? Of course, you best know how. I do not see how I can say anything about it here, after distinctly declining to suggest anything, both in the *Daily News* and in my letter to Trikoupes. Also, I am afraid I am too republican to urge anybody's kingship with a really good heart. I see there is a party for the League. The more I look at the map of Greece, the more sure I am that it would have been the thing in 1830, but I fear it is too late now. Anyhow, I hope you won't go taking Austrians. I am urging Dickinson to advocate Gladstone's election himself. It would be a great thing to elect a private man, and so make another inroad into the vile royal caste with all their humbug and contempt for their betters.

Goldwin Smith seems to think I am too cautious, and that a dash should be made at Epeiros and Thessaly at once. He says that a patriotic war is just the thing to improve a people with whom a period of peace has been rather a period of - corruption. I think this is true ἀπλῶς[1] and I should say to the Greeks, Go-a-head, if only there were no such things as those filthy Great Powers. It will be a mercy if they let the Greeks alone to choose their own government. Doubtless they would at once crush any movement for the liberation of any Turkish province. That is why I said, Sit still and improve yourself.

I hear that my letter in the *Daily News* is supposed to be doing good.

To the Same.

Somerleaze, January 14, 1863.

. . . Dickinson remarks that your demarchs are chosen in a way very like our sheriffs, and yet the result is so different. I take it a demarch is more like a mayor than a sheriff, but the main difference is demarch being paid and sheriff unpaid. If the Mayor of Wells had a good salary, and had a prospect, by servility, of being Sheriff of Somerset with a better salary, I take it our mayors and sheriffs would soon be a very poor lot.

I have been serving my country all the morning on the Parochial Assessment Committee of this Union. That is real self-government in every sense, as it needs a little government of oneself to keep one's patience during the oratory of certain persons. I wish your Greeks would study our local institutions. We have some things to reform in detail, but the principles are good.

To Spyridon Trikoupes.

Somerleaze, February 18, 1863.

Many thanks for your speech, which has reached me both in Greek and English. I am getting very anxious about your affairs. The Greek nation has behaved nobly in bearing so long a state of suspense with so little disorder; but the con-dition seems most dangerous, and I long to see a settled government of any kind established. I hold that our Govern-ment has behaved very ill in not letting you have Alfred if

[1] 'In the abstract.'

you want him; at the same time, I confess that the national
wish for an inexperienced boy is something to me wholly
unintelligible. I care very little whether your chief magistrate
be called βασιλεύς, ἄρχων, στρατηγός, πρύτανις, or anything else:
all I do plead for is that he be a *man*, and not a *prince*. I cannot
understand the charm of Highnesses. If you cannot find
a Greek, or failing a pure Greek, an Albanian, Servian, or
Bulgarian, I should rejoice to see your choice fall on an
Englishman. But then surely it should be an *English man*
and not a nine-tenths *German lad.* Surely some man who
has had real experience in government, some statesman, or
Colonial Governor, ὁ περίφημος καὶ φιλέλλην Γλάδστων[1], or Lord
Stanley, or Sir George Grey of New Zealand (who I should
think, would be just the man to deal with any unruly elements
in the country), is what you really want, not Alfred of Saxe-
Coburg, or Leuchtenberg, or anything of the sort. It is the
most glorious opportunity for throwing aside all the wretched
caste-traditions of Royalties and Highnesses, and setting a real
ἄναξ ἀνδρῶν, a real ποιμὴν λαῶν, at the head of a nation. I find
most English friends of Greece quite agreeing with me.

The votes given, as usual, have some odd instances of what
the Americans call '*scattering*.' That Otho has *one* friend
is a parallel case to the strewing of flowers on the tomb of
Nero, but I am sorry to see that there are *two* Greeks who
wish to put their country into the jaws of the Tyrant of Paris.

. . . I heartily wish I could get to Greece this year, but
I don't see how I can manage it as I must go to Switzerland
as soon as I can leave home. If you would restore the League,
I would come at once, and put off the Swiss part of my book.
If you will have kings, I must go and work among them that
have none, and believe that I am carried back to Lydiadas and
Philopoimên[2].

To G. FINLAY, ESQ.

Geneva, April 26, 1863.

I got your letter a few days before I left England. You give
such a clear and full account of things that I heartily wish

---

[1] 'The renowned and Greek-loving Gladstone.'
[2] Two distinguished generals of the Achaian League, B.C. 233 and 208.

your letters were written to the *Saturday Review*, instead of to me, as they are worthy of a much wider circulation than the few friends to whom I can show them. What puzzles me is—and yet all that happens now, and all that has happened for a long time past, shows that your view is quite right—how a people with so much good in them as the Greeks send such poor specimens to the top. There is something like it in America, but there one sees the reason: politics are foolishly looked on as low, but this can hardly be the case in Greece. When you wrote, this King William business had not been finally settled; it disgusted me infinitely, more with the Great Powers than with the Greeks, and I fired off in the *Daily News*, which I suppose you have got before now. The Alfred move, silly as it was according to my principle, had still something native and generous about it, but this is merely ποιεῖν τὸ προσταττόμενον[1] and such a προσταττόμενον. 'Tis the Otho story over again, or rather worse. I suppose old Lewis of Bavaria had really done something for Greece. To be sure, that was a queer reason for making his son king, but still it is not quite so queer as to take this other unknown boy, because he is brother to an unknown girl, whom another unknown boy has gone and married. Truly it is comfortable to be here and breathe the air of a republic for a season. I really feel myself nearer to my Achaians here than you are. You are on the old soil, but among men who go and ask for a king, while I am here in a live confederation, and have some difficulty in persuading myself that I am not at Sikyôn or Megalopolis. It is such a relief, coming here out of the house of bondage, and seeing the outward and visible sign of freedom in the absence of those cut-throat rascals who swagger about everywhere in the tyrant's country, making one wonder how many patriots each murdered in 1851. At the same time, it makes one shudder to look at the mountains on both sides, and think that the thief has got both of them, and hems freedom in all round, except a bit of the lake.

Pray forgive this democratic ebullition; but I never was in a republic before, and I feel in a sort of paradise. I venerate every bill on the wall which has 'République' at the top,

---

[1] ' To do what is commanded.'

and even the words 'bon vin rouge, 90. c. le pot fédéral'
made me feel as if Philopoimên and I were hob-a-nobbing
at a 'pot fédéral' together, to commemorate the division of'
Megalopolis into small cantons. This city is one of the few
states in Europe which has not had a revolution for sixteen
years. Many people tell me that Fazy is a rascal; still they
seem to go on very well, without any such bother and tomfoolery as you see in Paris or even London. Surely princes
are a very costly luxury.

I hope you have got my first volume of *Federal Government;*
Charilaos Trikoupes promised to take both your copy and his
father's. Some of the papers have been snappish at it, but
on the whole it has fared pretty well, and I know that it is
approved by many of those for whose approbation I care most.
It must have been about the last thing which Sir Cornewall
Lewis was at work at; I had some correspondence with him
about it, of which you may perhaps have seen the result in
the shape of an article in *Notes and Queries* which was reprinted in the *Times*. What a loss his death is; just when one
could least afford to lose a real scholar and critic, when all this
Egyptian and Babylonish humbug is driving real history out
of people's minds. Some people don't like my pitching into
L. N. Buonaparte; others do: but I shall have to pitch into
him a great deal more in my second volume, where his evil-
doings to this land where I now am will come in, no longer as
illustration, but as an essential part of the story. I have come
to Switzerland to pick up materials of all sorts, and specially
to see a live *Bund* with my own eyes. On Sunday I trust
to see Δῆμος[1] face to face, in the form of the Landesgemeinde
of Uri, the true ἐκκλησία[2], which I suppose is simply the old
Gau-system of all Teutonic peoples, which has contrived
to survive in these out-of-the-way corners. My Swiss part
will, I fancy, be harder matter than the Greek, because the
story is so complicated, and the materials so infinite. (The
people here wrap up their parcels in odd leaves of their
constitution—fancy, if one could light on a lost bit of Polybios
by any such happy accident.) The main difference, I take it,
arises from the existence of the Holy Roman Empire. 'We

---

[1] 'The People.'   [2] 'Assembly.'

have no king but Caesar,' was as far as anybody in these parts
could get, at least till the sixteenth century; and so, granting
the nominal Caesar over all, counts and bishops and free
cities all grew up side by side, while in Greece the alternative
was simply republic or tyrant. Of course the internal question of oligarchy or democracy arises in both equally. I am
afraid from what I hear that the addition of a few French and
Savoyard parishes to this city in 1815 was not an addition of
strength. The French have brought some of their French
impudence with them—not that they are really French a bit,
but Burgundians, only France has such a wonderful knack
of corrupting everything she gets hold of, after her own
pattern—and the Savoyards, being Catholics, do not get on
well with the followers of Calvin. Small as the Canton is,
would not Philopoimèn in such a case have divided it? It
is an infinite pity that Bern did not keep her Savoyard conquests, south as well as north of the lake; then, everything
might have been straight, and one might have looked at Mont
Blanc—I wish it were Montebianco, or Weissberg, or Aspro-
bouni, or Snowdon or anything but a French name—without
the creeping feeling that the tyrant has got one paw upon it.

I have written a long rambling letter. I hope you will
excuse my enthusiasm. I really feel quite like a young lad
out here. I suppose I shall have to go back towards the end
of May, as I have got to examine again at Oxford; but I shall
come again either later this year or next; and I must get
a sight of the Hanse Towns before I put out vol. ii. Ah!
if Hellas had not turned back to this wretched vomit of
kings—and such kings—I should have come to you before
any of them.

To the Same.

Somerleaze, October 7, 1863.

I really fear that I have not written to you since your letter
of July 31, with the photographs of Kanarês and Hastings,
which I have put into my book, where I admit nobody but
private friends and the ἡμιθέων γένος ἀνδρῶν[1]; so I turned out
the Prince of Wales, whom one of my children stuck in. As

---

[1] 'Race of demigods,' Hom. *Il.* xii. 23.

Kanarês and Hastings are opposite to each other, that leaves a blank opposite Garibaldi, waiting for the next man who kills a tyrant or otherwise delivers any place. I reverence old Kanarês still, though I confess that he has gone down a good deal in my estimation since his king-hunting ramble to Denmark. It does seem to me a most ignominious ending of last year's struggle only to get another foreign boy. My Swiss journey quite knocked up what little notion of royalty I had left. I don't think that we in England are fit for the Swiss system, but that only proves that we are behind the Swiss. I am hard at work with both Swiss and other German matters for my second volume (I hope you have by this time found leisure to look at my first, and at its child, Warren's[1] *Coinages* also); it is horribly hard work, though intensely interesting—far harder than the Greek part, because one has to look to such an in- finite number of books, old and new, while I could get all my Achaian materials on my writing-table. It is especially so in the German part. The Bund is but a poor concern, and I don't think Francis Joseph will make it any better; still the phenomenon of a kingdom dissolving into a confederation of any kind is something which needs notice, from my point of view: the worst of it is that to get accurately at the special points which I want seems to involve almost as much work as if I were going to write a regular history of Germany, instead of one chapter about one aspect of it. But all my Swiss work is delightful, both in the land and out of it; your Greeks must take care and behave well, or I shall forget them for what seems to me to be the real living Greece.

. . . I am horribly afraid about Danish matters. I am Eider-Danish to the backbone, and should delight to see the Germans well whipped by the Scandinavians of all three nations; but then I fear Buonaparte will contrive to get a finger in the pie, perhaps help Denmark and go seize the Rhenish provinces as his pay. And it would be almost better to let Denmark pass under the yoke of those who are at least brother Teutons, than to let any more Teutons fall under Parisian bondage. My Swiss friends seem to be looking out in quietness and confidence for the fall of the Tyranny.

[1] Afterwards Lord de Tabley.

Nothing seems going on in England. The best thing a good citizen can do is to try to carry out the new Highway Act, to which I give as much time as I can spare from Federal Government. I think you will sympathize with this. We want King Archelaos, the cutter of straight roads, almost as much in some parts of England as you can in Greece—that is, if an impassible road be, as I am inclined to think it, an equal evil with no road at all.

I find I have twaddled on beyond French weight, so I send this *viâ Belgium*—if longer on the road, it will have the pleasure of passing through one free country.

To SPYRIDON TRIKOUPES.

Somerleaze, December 30, 1863.

I write at once to thank you for the new edition of your History, which reached me this morning. I wish it had come a little sooner, as I did not know that there was any new edition forthcoming. I have just written an article for the January number of the *National Review* headed 'Mediaeval and Modern Greece,' in which of course your history fills an important place, and of course if I had known that there was a new edition I should have said something about it. I trust you will be pleased with the article, if you see it.

. . . I hope matters are going on well in Greece. The accounts in the English papers are generally so vague that one can hardly make out anything. I wish your new king all manner of good luck, though I could wish you had chosen a more experienced ruler and, indeed, another form of government altogether. But you will see my notions better in my article. Part of it was written a long time ago, and it is curious how many passages I had to change, because of the happy change in general English feeling towards Greece.

With every good wish both for yourself and your country,

Believe me,

Very truly yours.

To G. FINLAY, ESQ.

Somerleaze, April 4, 1864.

There is one argument for a federal system in Greece, which with me outweighs all that can be brought against it. That is, if you had set up a league instead of a king, I should by this time have come to look at it, and should indeed have been bound to do so as part of my business. As you insist upon being consolidated, I find my prospects of getting into Greece more and more visionary, as I am now obliged to go about so much in other parts of the world. I hope to start for Switzerland again before the end of this week, and I want to get to the Hanse Towns, if possible, later in the year. Perhaps, however, I am better away, lest the Austrian thieves should slay me for an Eider-Dane, as I profess myself. My Swiss people, whom I love from the bottom of my heart and whom I wish your Greeks would somehow manage to copy, all go in for Denmark. They do not at all admire the fashion of big states making war on little ones for nothing; and, moreover, they think that it is quite possible to get on with two or three languages spoken in a country; I don't see what can come of this conference. I could understand a conference to settle the dispute between Denmark and *Germany*, where there is really much to be said on both sides, and where something between the two extreme views would probably be the right thing; but I don't understand a conference with Austria and Prussia, two revolted states which have trampled all federal authority under foot, and which, as to Denmark, are mere robbers and pirates, making war without a declaration of war; and who are withal to be allowed to go on robbing and murdering while the conference sits. All this puts me in a rage, and makes me anxious to fight, in a way that I never was before in my life.

You don't seem to be going on very prosperously in Greece. Your papers about the University raise my curiosity without gratifying it. Am I to infer that a body answering to the 'First Oxfordshire (University) Rifle Volunteers,' such is the idea suggested to me by an 'Academic Phalanx,' has been playing a part, as such, in Revolutions? I have also to thank you for another paper containing the beginning of a translation of my *National Review* article into Greek. I hope you don't disapprove of it, though you would see that I deal both with you and with others freely, according to my wont. I showed the article to Lord Strangford, who helped me to a fact or two and said it did very well, except that the *colouring* was not

his colouring. He has a certain love for Turks. Of course
Strangford, who has really been about everywhere and who
knows all tongues, is thoroughly fit to judge of any matter; but
it sometimes strikes me that the common run of diplomatists
are really less likely to come to right conclusions than we who
sit at home and think. Surely the mass of them see the facts
on one side only, and do not think at all.

You say that federalism has a natural tendency to civil war.
Doubtless this is true in a sense; that is to say, wars of the
peculiar character of the Sonderbund war in Switzerland or
the war now going on in America could arise only in a federal
state. But, supposing all the States or Cantons were completely independent, would there not have been very many
more wars between them? It strikes me that the utmost
you can say is that a federal system substitutes a smaller
number of civil wars for a greater number of foreign wars.
And, on the other hand, if America and Switzerland had
formed a consolidated state, whether monarchy or commonwealth, would not the disturbing causes in the two countries,
religion in the one case and slavery in the other, have caused
much worse civil wars, and brought on the civil war in America
much sooner? Fancy the attempt, which in a consolidated
government would surely have been made, to legalize or to
forbid slavery over the whole United States. Or compare the
religious wars of Switzerland with those of France. In consolidated France you have a whole series of horrible civil
wars, ending in the destruction of the weaker side. In federal
Switzerland you have a civil war once in a century, ending,
under the present constitution, in a real religious equality and
mutual toleration.

To the Same.

Somerleaze, August 28, 1864.

. . . Is there any hope for Germany, or for America, or
for anywhere? Even my Swiss, you see, have been making
disturbances at Geneva; but you may remark how much more
easily they seem to be put down there than they are at Belfast.
One thing seems to me plain, that this is emphatically an age
when might triumphs over right, and that a small state has less

chance of holding its own now than it ever had, except in the days of Roman dominion. Undoubtedly tyrants do not do quite so much mischief as of old ; they are to some extent restrained by public opinion, and to a much greater extent by knowing that mischief does not always pay. But when a wicked man determines to do mischief, he surely does it more effectually than in any past age. Witness the whole career of L. N. Buonaparte and these late doings against Denmark. I am delighted to find that the faith of one of the strongest Palmerstonians I know has given way under this last trial.

After the year 1860, a foreign tour became almost an annual event in Freeman's life ; but his tours were never made simply for recreation, but were always undertaken for some purpose connected with his studies in history and architecture. He had, in truth, no pleasure in travelling except as one means of carrying on those studies in which all his thoughts were absorbed. For these ends he would willingly undergo a great deal of fatigue and be contented with very rough quarters ; but for scenery, unconnected with any historical event, he cared very little, and to climb a hill or a mountain unless the ascent helped him to form a clearer idea of some battle-field or historic site, or of the general character of a country in which he happened to be interested, was to him utter weariness. To ascend a mountain simply for the sake of ascending it, seemed to him a sad waste of time ; and any climbing which involved risk of life was, in his judgement, culpable foolhardiness with which he had no sympathy at all. His tours, however, often involved an amount of physical and mental labour, such as few men would be capable of undergoing ; for after a long day of walking about and sketching, and taking notes of places or buildings from various points of view, he would sit up late into the night, writing descriptions of them, which were either introduced into the history which he had on hand, or appeared as articles in the *Saturday Review*. In regard to any place of historical importance about which he had to write, his rule was, first to read everything he could get hold of concerning it, then to visit the spot, then to read about it again, and write the first description of it, and then to revisit the spot, and correct the description with the scene before him. And, of course, in the case of many places of pre-eminent importance, such as the battle-field of Senlac, or the points connected with the Athenian siege of Syracuse, such processes were repeated again and again ; and he would secure, if possible, on such occasions, the aid of friends who were either specially acute in observation, like Mr. J. R. Green, or possessed of some special scientific knowledge, like Professor Dawkins. Although he did not begin to travel regularly upon the Continent till he was nearly forty years old, he had, as we have seen, been accustomed to ramble about England from a very early age, and this experience he considered to be a distinct advantage. He used to say that people would enter on foreign travel in a much more intelligent spirit if they had seen something of their own country first. The art of observation would have been learned among scenes which were comparatively familiar, before the attempt was made to practise it amid the excitements of strange languages and strange manners.

The countries in which he most loved to travel were those which contained the most distinct traces, either in their architectural remains, or in the situation of the towns, or the character of their institutions, of the days of Roman greatness and power ; or, on the other hand, those

in which freedom and unity had been won by valiant
efforts, whether in past ages as in Switzerland, or in more
modern times as in Greece and Italy.   He felt a natural
sympathy with the Scandinavian and Teutonic races, as
being kindred with the English, and took a profound
interest in tracing the growth of all Teutonic institutions.
Besides the close connexion between the histories of
Normandy and England, and his special interest in
Norman architecture, one reason why he enjoyed travelling in Normandy was the affinity of the inhabitants to
the English, especially in the regions of the Bessin and
Côtentin.   In an article in the *Saturday Review* upon
Normandy, written after his tour there in 1861, he remarks on the striking contrasts between Normandy and
France.   In Normandy, he says, men, women, horses,
cows, all are on a grander and better scale than in
France.   The stout, hearty, ruddy Norman farmer, presented a curious contrast to the puny, dirt-coloured
French soldier ; and it seemed a strange inversion of the
order of nature, that the palpably inferior animal should
bear rule over his manifest betters.   And the man who
had a Teutonic stomach, who liked to dine on roast beef
and breakfast on beef-steaks, would find Norman diet
nearer his ideal than the polite repasts of Paris.   To the
modern French he had a strong antipathy ; their rest-
less ambition and vaingloriousness, which had so often
been the cause of European disturbances, were especially
repugnant to him ; and as these evil qualities centred
in the Parisians, there was no capital in Europe which
he more heartily disliked, especially at this time when
France was ruled by a despot.   Writing to Mr. Stubbs
just after his return from Normandy, he says, ' we liked
the Normans much, the Picards somewhat less, Paris, of

course, is as beastly as ever.   Durand's shop is about the
best thing in it, as the churches are being spoiled.   How
different from Caen or Rouen!   Paris is just a collection
of shops and stuck-up people, with the Tyrant's house
in the middle.'

He could never breathe quite freely in a country
which was not under some form of popular government,
and even the smallest things, such as public notices,
which reminded him of despotic power, annoyed and
irritated him.   Switzerland was to him one of the most
delectable of all countries, not because of the beauty
of its scenery, or the freshness of its mountain air, but
because it was essentially a land of freedom, a land in
which some of the most primitive Teutonic customs were
preserved almost without change.   He visited Switzerland
in 1863 and 1864, and each time in the spring of the year,
in order that he might witness in some of the Cantons
the Landesgemeinde, or assembly of the people, in which
they frame their laws and choose their rulers.   The
antiquity and simplicity of the scene stirred in him
the deepest emotions.   'To stand,' he said, 'with the
clear heaven above, and the snowy mountains on either
side, and see the descendants of the men of Sempach and
Morgarten discharge the immemorial rights of Teutonic
freemen, is a sight which may well make us doubt
whether we are in the common world, or in some historical paradise of our own imagination.'   In the first
chapter of his book on the *Growth of the English
Constitution*, he has drawn a glowing and vivid picture
of the Landesgemeinde of Uri.   He describes the celebration of the early Mass in the church at Altdorf on
the morning of Sunday, May 1; the gathering in the
market-place; the procession to the place of meeting with

the little army of the Canton, whose weapons never can
be used save to drive back an invader ; the uplifted banner
of the bull's head of Uri, which led their forefathers to
victory on the fields of Sempach and Morgarten; the
horns whose blast struck terror into the heart of Charles
the Bold of Burgundy ; the mounted magistrates, and the
chief magistrate, the Landammann, with his sword by his
side ; the ranging of the assembly in the green meadow,
with its background of pine-wood and mountain; the
pause for silent prayer; the quiet and orderly speeches
by the people, ending with the re-election of their magistrates. His visits to Switzerland were undertaken also
with the view of observing the actual working of Swiss
federal institutions, in connexion with his *History of
Federal Government*, and it is certainly much to be
regretted that this chapter of the work was never
written[1]. He made great friends with some of the Swiss
politicians and men of letters, more especially M. Morlot
and M. Galiffe, with whom he kept up a correspondence
as long as they lived.

The two letters which follow describe the way in which
his time was spent in Switzerland.

To THE REV. W. STUBBS.

Einsiedeln, May 5, 1863.

I have been meaning to write to you for a long time, and
I think I cannot hit on a better place for the purpose than this.
I have seen two things this week which I fancy that mighty

---

[1] This regret has also been expressed by the most recent native
historian of Switzerland, Dierauer. ' Mann kann es nur lebhaft bedauern
dass der Englische Historiker nicht dazu gekommen ist in einer Fort-
setzung seines Werkes *die Geschichte der Schweizerischen Eidgenossen-
schaft*, den "angesehensten oder lehrreichsten" Teil seiner Aufgabe, zu
bearbeiten.'

few Englishmen have seen, the Landesgemeinde of Uri and the Abbey of Einsiedeln. My impressions of the former I will keep to form the materials of a middle; only I will add that you and I would most likely have both been pleased with an assembly, which is at once the most conservative and the most democratic in the world. The Abbey I wonder whether you have seen. I had some talk with a monk to-day who showed me the library, and told me that last year there came some learned men from Oxford, but he could not tell me their names. Was it haply you? 'Tis certainly wonderful to see a live Benedictine Abbey with real monks and a real Lord Abbot, howbeit the Illustrissimus and Reverendissimus Henricus IV is not here just now, having gone to St. Gallen for the hallowing of the new Bishop there last Sunday. They have cut up things so queerly in this land, that one knows not ecclesiastically where one is ; I find that there is no Bishop of Constanz, and there is one of St. Gallen. I have been delighted with everything that I have seen as yet; perhaps you will shake your head, and think I am getting lower and lower, for every moment that I stay in this republican and federal land, I am the more convinced of our folly at home in wasting our money on Alberts[1] and such like (the Landammann of Uri, a much more useful person than any prince, has 300 fr. per annum), and still more at the folly of the Greeks in asking for a king, setting up Omri the moment they have got rid of Tibni[2]. We shan't agree, I dare say, about these matters ; but I do want to convince you of one thing, the utter imposture of that man Francis Joseph. 'Tis my very respect for the Holy Roman Empire (whereof my Lord Abbot here was a prince), and all that belongs to it, which makes me loathe and spit at that most wretched of all humbugs. Why, the man has cut the rampagious lion of Habsburg—the Lorrainers' right to that might be doubtful— which I saw on Monday on a banner taken at Sempach, to set up the eagle of Caesar, to which he has no more right than you and I. I see eagles set up everywhere here ; πῶς γὰρ οὔ; I wonder whether summer-tourists and Rigi-climbers think they stand for F. J. V. or for L. N. B. They

---

[1] An allusion to the Albert Memorial.   [2] See I Kings xvi. 22.

had their election at Luzern on Sunday—ein liberale Sieg—
only the Habsburg polling-place sent up all conservatives.

. . . Is it right to sing vespers, &c. in a privy chapel
behind the high altar, so that the folk hear a voice, but see no
man? Also should not my Lord Abbot take the same stall as
a Dean, and not make him a throne in the middle of the choir,
finer even than that of the Dean of Bristol? At Luzern I think
I made out that there is, or was, a *mitred provost*. Is not that
rather funny?

To MISS HELEN FREEMAN.

Lausanne, April 16, 1864.

Thank Gretchen for her letter; but I think it is your turn
to have one now. I see my last letter was written at Neufchâtel
on Thursday, so I will tell you what I have been doing since.
One thing will sound like something which you may read
in a story-book. That same afternoon I was seized on by
a certain Baron, who said to me, ' Vous êtes mon prisonnier,'
and shut me up in his castle till next morning. Don't think,
however, that I was put in a dungeon among dead men's bones
and what not, as I slept in a comfortable bed, and had tea and
ham and breakfast. In short, the Baron is a very kind old
gentleman, De Büren by name, who lives in Vauxmarcus Castle
by the Lake of Neufchâtel, a real castle let me tell you, and not
a mere *château*. I was to call on him for him to show me his
castle, and to show me where the battle of Grandson was
fought. So we took a long walk that evening through most
beautiful places, not very unlike some of our own places, but
with the Jura just above us, and the great snowy Alps on the
other side of the lake. But I did not know that I was to stay there
all night till he said, ' vous êtes mon prisonnier.' The next day
he took me in his carriage as far as Grandson, where I saw the
castle and a very fine church, and went on by railway to
Chavornay, thence by omnibus to Orbe, a curious old town on
the top of a hill, looking on Jura one side and the Alps the
other, with a church with its tower at the east end, which
I never saw anywhere else. Then this morning I walked out
to Romainmotier to see the church, which is a very wonderful
one, and one of the oldest in Switzerland or anywhere else.

At Romainmotier, I was counting some money to give to
a boy, and I was reckoning in English, 'twenty, thirty,' &c., so
the lad chimed in, and counted straight up to an hundred in
something that might have been English. So I said, 'Com-
prenez-vous l'Anglais ou êtes-vous Allemand?' So he said he
was 'Allemand' and came from the Oberland in the Canton of
Bern. So we talked a little together in *Tütsch* (Deutsch) to the
amazement of the *Welsh* children who looked on. Do you
know why I call them Welsh? So you see the Deutsch boy
understood me when I was counting in English, because the
numbers are so nearly the same in the two languages. Then
I walked back to Orbe, dined, omnibus to Chavornay, rail to
Lausanne, where the Ritter seemed very glad to see me, and
gave me Margaret's letter. When I was at tea, Mr. Morlot
came in, and we have been talking all the rest of the evening.
I hope to be at the Landesgemeinde at Trogen in Appenzell
to-morrow week.

It is needless to say that in Switzerland, as everywhere
else, as much attention was given to architecture as to
past history and modern politics. The *Saturday Review*,
of course, contained the results of his thoughts and
observations on this, as on all other subjects; and on
June 13, 1864, a month after he returned from his second
visit to Switzerland, he read a paper on 'Certain
Romanesque buildings in Switzerland and the neighbouring countries' before the Royal Institute of British
Architects, of which he had been elected an honorary
member in the preceding year.

In the Autumn of 1865 he visited the chief towns of
North Germany, including Aachen, Dortmund, Pader-
burn, Hildesheim, Brunswick, Hamburg, Bremen, Lübeck, Wismar, Rostock, and Doberan. In the first part
of his tour he was accompanied by Mr. Stubbs, and
afterwards, for a time, by his Swiss friend, M. Morlot;
while at Hamburg he was a guest of Mr. Ward, the

father of Dr. A. W. Ward, the present Principal of Owens College, Manchester, and Pro-Vice-Chancellor of the Victoria University. To see the land which was the original home of our Teutonic forefathers, to tread the shores from which they set sail for the new home to which they gave their name, to look out upon the sea where the Vikings bridled the horses of the wave, were among the chief interests of this journey. And not second to them was the visit to the three old Hanse towns, more especially Lübeck. ' The first sight,' he writes, ' of that ancient head of the great merchant league, the mistress and civilizer of northern Europe, the chosen chief of eighty free republics, which once checked the advance of Denmark and gave kings to Sweden, is a moment in travel which stands by itself as unique.'

He delighted in drawing comparisons and contrasts between the Swiss confederation, made in defence of political freedom, and the Hanseatic league, made primarily for the protection of commerce. Lübeck was the Teutonic Carthage of the northern Mediterranean, as Berne was the Teutonic Rome ; and Berchthold of Zähringen was to Berne what Henry the Lion of Saxony was to Lübeck. A rough voyage home from Bremen, lasting three days, which to some persons would have been mainly occupied with the horrors of sea-sickness, were spent by him in much reading, and in meditation, especially when the shores of Thanet came in view, on the wonderful results of the voyage of the three Jutish keels which brought Hengist and his war-band to this island and determined the destiny of Britain.

His interest in travelling had been quickened, and in some respects enlarged, by the friendship which he had formed in 1862 with Mr. J. R. Green. Many years before that date, when Green was at Magdalen College School, Dr. Millard, who was then the head master, had pointed him out to his friend Freeman as a remarkably clever boy of great promise. Freeman saw him from time to time when he called on Dr. Millard, and was struck by his ability, but he had lost sight of him after he had left school, and had only heard that though he had entered the University, he had not taken any academical honours. In 1862, at the meeting of the Somersetshire Archaeological Society at Wellington, it was announced that the Rev. J. R. Green would read a paper on Dunstan. 'I had not the faintest notion,' said Freeman, 'who the Rev. J. R. Green might be, but I sat down ready to give his discourse, whoever he was, a fair hearing.' It was soon evident that the Rev. J. R. Green was somebody who had read and thought not a little.

'The discourse,' said Freeman, 'grew on the hearer. The knowledge, the thought, the power of putting things, were such as one rarely comes across. Who was this man, young and unknown, who was capable of such a work? I looked and thought, and it suddenly flashed across my mind, Why it is little Johnny Green that was at Magdalen School. When he had done, I went up and asked him whether he was not that same Johnny Green, and he said that he was.' . . . 'The paper on Dunstan,' continues Freeman, 'a noble defence of a noble and basely slandered man, I read over again not long ago. If I say that Green never surpassed it, I mean merely to show how early he reached the fulness of his powers. It was one youthful work out of several. He gave us in Somerset another essay, equally excellent, on the relations between Earl Harold and Bishop Gisa, again bringing truth to light out of a mass of old-standing confusion and calumny. These were critical papers in which all the authorities on a particular matter were thoroughly sifted and weighed.'

From that moment Freeman made it his business
to ' blow Johnny Green's trumpet,' as he expressed it,
on every opportunity, until, as the author of the *Short
History of the English People*, Green sprang at one bound
to an extraordinary height of popularity and fame. In
the opinion of Freeman, however, as of many other
scholars, that brilliant performance was far from being
the greatest or the most satisfactory of Green's historical
writings, and Freeman doubted whether there was anything in his later works quite equal to the efforts
of his younger days, when his name was wholly unknown. No one who reads Mr. Green's writings can
fail to be struck by his extraordinary power of seizing
and vividly describing the leading features, alike in the
geographical situation and in the history of towns,
and showing how they illustrate each other. And it
was in reference to this gift, that Freeman, whom Green
called one of his masters in the study of English history, admitted that he, in his turn, looked up to Green
as his teacher.

' I may truly say,' he writes, ' that it was from him that I first
learned to look on a town as a whole, with a kind of personal
history, instead of being simply the place where such and such
a church or castle was to be found. From him I learned that,
be it at Chester or be it at Rome, the city itself and its history
are something greater than any particular object in the city.'

Green was, as Freeman said, in everything ' municipal '
in his sympathies, but municipal according to the oldest
and freest forms of municipality. He would talk, as
only he could talk, of the growth of civic oligarchies,
and the way in which older rights of the people had
been swallowed up by them, so that Freeman used to
tell him, and he admitted the truth of the charge, that

though he did not greatly love a squire or a parson, he loved an alderman less than either. He was by birth a citizen of Oxford, and he certainly loved the city better than the University. Freeman used to say, that had Green been born at Abingdon, many pages of his history would have been written in a different spirit, because he would then have been a Wessex man ; but born as he was, north of the Thames, he was a loyal Mercian, and felt it to be a kind of point of honour to make the best case he could for any of his own earls. ' I was, in his eyes,' said Freeman, 'somewhat of an apostate, as a Mercian born, who had turned West-Saxon. It was no use to hint that Oxford was naturally West-Saxon ground, and became Mercian only through the encroachments of Offa. His allegiance was fixed, he held an hereditary brief for Ælfric and Eadric.' Mr. Green's topographical powers were far from being confined to the description of towns. He was no less skilled in catching the main features of a tract of country, and discerning how far they had helped to determine its military and political history. Here, again, he had a quicker eye than Freeman, and gave him valuable assistance by accompanying him to scenes of battle, as at Stamford Bridge and Senlac, Val-es-Dunes and Mortemer. They visited the latter places together in 1867, when Green made his first journey on the continent, and in the following year they travelled to Chartres and Le Mans, to Angers, Tours, Marmoutiers, Fontevrault, and Saumur, returning through Britanny and Normandy.

' In the first part of the journey,' said Freeman, ' Green was on his special ground, in the latter part, I was rather on mine ; but in either case it was a wonderful process, going through

such places, with such a man, each of us studying for our own
ends, ends which had so much in common. It was mutual
learning at every step, and I am sure that not a few passages
of my own history have gained not a little, from having been
designed, in some cases for having been actually written, in the
course of journeys, in Green's company, to the places of which
they speak.'

If Freeman introduced Green to Normandy and Anjou,
Green repaid the service in 1871, by introducing Freeman
to Italy.

' A first journey to Italy,' writes Freeman, 'is a wonderful
thing, and it is a great thing to have made it in the company of
such a man as Green. Yet it had not quite the freshness of
our Norman and Angevin journeys. Though in Italy we were
studying and learning, we were not, as we had been in Normandy, Maine, and Anjou, studying and learning for what had
been the main work of my life, and for what I had hoped would
be the main work of his. Still it was delightful to be with him,
it was delightful to listen, and learn from him. And none the
less so, because our tastes and objects were not exactly the
same. It is needless to say what were Green's primary objects
in Italy. Here was municipality on its grandest scale. Never
was he so thoroughly at home, as in the stately town-house of
an Italian city.'

Freeman thought that these visits to Italy also
quickened Green's interest in what are called the
classical periods of Greek and Latin history and literature, which he had formerly somewhat undervalued,
owing probably to the too exclusive exaltation of them
at Oxford. But Freeman thought also that this gain
was counterbalanced by some diminution of interest in
what was purely Teutonic and English. Green was by
nature and temperament southern, rather than Teutonic,
and he loved Italy with such passionate enthusiasm, that
although he worked to the last at English studies,

Freeman doubted whether, after crossing the Alps, he ever gave his heart and soul to them so unreservedly as he did in the days when he had talked about Dunstan at Wellington. What the two friends were to one another, will be most fully understood when the proposed volume of their correspondence appears. Certainly the day which first brought them together at the Somersetshire meeting, was a memorable event in the life of each. The elder of the two was unquestionably superior in range and variety of learning, and more exact and cautious in statement, and he enjoyed the advantage of a sounder training in Greek and Latin scholarship; but he readily admitted that he was surpassed by his friend in brilliancy of style, and power of vivid description. If Freeman had intellectual powers of the highest order, Green was endowed with some of the indescribable gifts of genius. He had also some of the caprices, the occasional carelessness and eccentricities, which so often accompany genius, and there were times, when these peculiarities manifested themselves in ways which were provoking to a man of Freeman's regular and methodical habits. But Freeman loved and admired him too warmly ever to be long or seriously vexed with him. He was accustomed to say that 'Johnny' or 'Johnnikin,' as he playfully and affectionately called him, was a wonderful creature, alike in himself and in his works, that he was not as other men, and was not to be judged by the same standard as other men, and that on the whole he could not wish him to be other than what he was.

The year 1862 was a remarkably fruitful one for Freeman in the formation of lasting friendships. In May of that year he first made the acquaintance of

Mr. Dawkins, who came to explore the hyena's den at
Wookey Hole; and it was through Mr. Dawkins, who
was an intimate college friend of Green, that the latter
was brought to the Archaeological meeting at Wellington.
In July of the same year, the annual meeting of the
Royal Archaeological Institute was held at Worcester,
and here a paper was read on Bishop Wulfstan, by
Dr. Hook, Dean of Chichester. The essay was characteristic of the writer, bespeaking a man who was full of
enthusiasm for goodness and nobleness, full of humour,
and possessed of that shrewd practical sense and insight
into character, which was partly an original gift, partly
derived from long and wide experience of his fellow men.
Freeman paid his first visit to the Deanery at Chichester
in the following year, and there was no one for whom he
came to entertain a deeper respect and affection than for
'old Hook' or 'dear old Hook,' as he commonly called
him. The Dean's sturdy independence, courage and
straightforwardness, the breadth and generosity of his
sympathies, the resolute industry with which in his
old age he toiled at his historical work, and steadily
raised the standard of it, all won Freeman's admiration.
Like himself, the Dean was thoroughly English,
thoroughly Teutonic; he was twenty-five years older
than Freeman, and while he looked up to Freeman as
a master of historical learning, and stood, like so many
others, in considerable awe of his criticisms—calling him
the 'Malleus hereticorum'—yet he did not scruple, in his
turn, to speak with fatherly kindness and plainness to
him concerning the occasional roughness of manner, and
fierceness of speech, by which Freeman often annoyed
others, and did injustice to the real kindness of his own
heart. Nor were these admonitions ever resented. 'He

was almost the only one of my friends,' said Freeman, in a letter written just after the Dean's death in 1875, 'who ever seriously reproved me for my faults, and I respected him accordingly.' And then, after speaking of some of the most attractive qualities in the Dean's character, he adds, 'dear, dear old man, you may easily believe that my eyes are not dry as I write these words.'

It was in the year after he had made the acquaintance of Mr. Dawkins, Mr. Green, and Dean Hook, that Mr. Bryce, to quote Freeman's words, 'astonished the world with the memorable prize essay, which grew into the more memorable volume, on the *Holy Roman Empire.*' He had, indeed, met Mr. Bryce in December, 1861, at the house of their common friend. Mr. Pinder, the Rector of Greys, near Henley-on-Thames, but their regular correspondence and intimate friendship dates from the appearance of the prize essay in 1863.

In some fragmentary notes of his own life, Freeman mentions that he had gradually formed two alternative wishes. One was for a seat in Parliament, the other was for an historical professorship at Oxford. He had already been disappointed in both these wishes, and he was destined to be disappointed again. He was an unsuccessful candidate for the Camden Professorship of Ancient History in 1861, and for the Chichele Professorship of Modern History in 1862. Thirty-five testimonials in his favour were forwarded to the electors to this latter Professorship. Amongst them was one from Dr. Thirlwall, Bishop of St. David's, who said, ' I have much pleasure in stating that I not only consider him eminently fitted for the office, but that I should not be able to name any living scholar who appears to me more highly qualified for it.'

He had already made two unsuccessful attempts to get
into Parliament. They were, however, of a very tenta-
tive kind, his only serious effort was made in 1868,
some notice of which must be reserved for the next
chapter.

He had a strong sense of his duty to the neighbourhood in which he lived as a resident landowner, and soon
after settling at Somerleaze, he qualified for a Justice of
the Peace. In that capacity he was one of the governors
of the County Lunatic Asylum, and he was an active
member of the Board of Guardians and of the Highway
Board. Nor was the insight which he thus gained into
practical affairs, without its value and influence upon his
work as an historian. Gibbon, speaking of his experience
as an officer in the Hampshire Militia, said, ' the discipline
and evolutions of a modern battalion gave me a clearer
notion of the phalanx and the Legion, and the captain
of the Hampshire Grenadiers (the reader may smile) has
not been useless to the historian of the Roman Empire.'
In like manner, Freeman maintained that his practical
acquaintance with various forms of local government,
gave him an advantage over the mere student in understanding the practical politics of past times. It was
one way in which he realized the truth of his favourite
dictum that history was past politics, and that politics
were present history. From lack of this practical experience of men and affairs he thought that the most
erudite of German historians sometimes failed to catch
the true character and complexion of political life in
remote times. Moreover, although the interruptions to
his literary work occasioned by magisterial duties were
sometimes vexatious to him, yet no doubt they acted as
a salutary diversion and relief to his mind, and often fur-

nished him with amusing studies of human character, which supplied materials for some of his most piquant and entertaining articles in the *Saturday Review*. In one of these he has sketched the peculiar and indeed unique position of an English Justice of the Peace [1].

'He is the most amazing person in the world except the High Sheriff. Both offices are utterly puzzling to the most intelligent foreigner, for there is nothing like them in any other part of the world. The English J. P. is a judge, a financier, an adminis-trator, a member of this or that Board or Committee, discharging ten or twenty functions, which in most countries are entrusted to distinct officers, or bodies of officers. And the greatest wonder is, that he performs all these duties without pay. He is indeed the most independent of men, having nothing to hope and nothing to fear. He is appointed by the Crown, but the Crown has no attractions with which to tempt him, and no penalties with which to alarm him. The men who find their way into the Commission for the Peace, form a kind of local aristocracy, not elected by the people nor responsible to the people, and yet, except in reference to the Game Laws, without any interests contrary to those of the people. The J. P. cannot spend the people's money, without spending his own also : what saves his pocket, save their's also.

In royal nominees or elected officials, on the other hand, he thought that there must always be a tendency to seek favour, either from the Government or from the people. The whole institution of the J. P. was utterly anomalous, it did not satisfy the monarchic, aristocratic, or democratic theory, it must be judged solely by its practical working, and on the whole it worked well, and might fairly be left alone until a better could be found.

[1] Vol. xviii, p. 804. Many other articles on questions of local govern-ment will be found in the *Saturday Review*, e. g. ' Highways and Turn-pikes,' vol. xv. 235 ; ' Highway Boards,' xvi. 518 ; ' Grand Juries,' xviii. 236 ; ' Cattle Plague Commission,' xxi. 750 ; ' Quarter Sessions,' xxii. 574 ; ' The last phase of the Turnpikes,' xxvi. 89.

Freeman always kept in touch with Oxford by attend-
ing the annual festival of his College on Trinity Monday,
as well as by constant correspondence with some of his
Oxford friends, and by frequent visits from them. And
in 1863 and 1864, his duties as an examiner in the
School of Modern History brought him up to Oxford
twice a year. He was a keen critic of the changes in the
University effected by the Act of 1854, and of the many
other changes which were from time to time projected ;
and he wrote various articles upon academical affairs
in the *Saturday Review*[1], in all of which he speaks in
the character of a conservative reformer. In the article
entitled ' Oxford, Past and Present,' written in October,
1862, he contrasts the Oxford of that day, with the
Oxford of his own recollections as a Scholar and Fellow
of Trinity. He observed that twenty years ago the
great High Church movement was in full swing, and its
birthplace naturally came in for the greatest share of its
results, both good and bad.

' That movement carried with it a very large proportion of
the intellect and vigour of the place. It carried a larger proportion than is commonly supposed, for many men who are
known to the world, or to the present generation of Oxford
men, as adherents of quite another school, followed the so-called
tractarian lead in their youth. There was no possible religious
movement which could have appealed in the same way to
young and ardent intellects. Puritanism is not and cannot be
the religion of scholars. The High Church movement, instead
of proscribing learning, fostered it. Its aesthetical and historical
side, its love of antiquity, its appeal to writings of other ages
and of other tongues, completely fell in with the spirit and
studies of the place. Here and there an enthusiast suffered

[1] ' Oxford, Past and Present,' vol. xiv. 466; 'Oxford Legislation,' xv.
300 ; 'The Hebdomadal Council,' xvi. 579 ; ' Oxford Class Lists,' xxii.
758 ; ' University Extension,' xxiii. 48, 108, 133.

a technical failure in the Schools, through over-attention to studies which did not pay there. But on the whole, the proper studies of the place, classical scholarship, ancient history, and moral philosophy, more than kept their ground alongside of the theological system. The attempts made to crush the leaders by authority, of course, only the more endeared them and their doctrines to their disciples. With the truth of particular dogmas, it is not our business to meddle; and quite irrespective of the truth of particular dogmas, the High Church movement like all other movements had its silly and extravagant side; but one professed object of a University, the union of religion and learning, was probably never so fully realized as during its prevalence.'

At the present time doubt was the fashion rather than belief. Doubt might seem to some more daring and impressive, but belief was certainly the more amiable condition, and it seemed to him that young men were more self-reliant and had less respect for age, authority, and tradition than they commonly had twenty years ago. Something, perhaps, had been gained in breadth of view and seeming knowledge of the world, but much also had been lost which was attractive in the earlier generation. Since the University Reform Bill, the process of statute-making and statute-tinkering had gone on at such a rate, that there was hardly time for any one to make up his mind whether a change was good or bad before it was succeeded by another change. None but residents could pretend to keep pace with the legislation, and consequently very few, save residents, voted at all. 'Congregation' consisted exclusively of residents, heavy dons at one end, and men without experience at the other; it included many unqualified persons, and excluded many who were well qualified. Residence within a mile and a half of Carfax was no guarantee for good judgement in

University affairs. Men whose opinion was most worth having were those who, having taken University honours, or filled University offices, had left the University for other walks of life, and thus had a twofold experience, not shared by those who had always resided, or who had never resided. The scholars, statesmen, lawyers, writers, who composed this class were the real glory of the University, and maintained its credit in the world; yet they were unrepresented in Congregation, and had no voice in University affairs except as members of Convocation, which was equally open to any one who had contrived, after endless plucks, to work his way up to the B.A. degree.

The frequent changes which were being made in the scheme of examinations he considered to be highly objectionable. The University ought not to be constantly making experiments upon the course of study. The multiplication of examinations and the division of subjects into separate schools tended, in his opinion, to narrow the range of study, to cramp the mind of the student by over specializing, to diminish the value and significance of academical honours, and to cool the love of learning for its own sake. And thus the University became less and less a centre for study and learning, and sank more and more into a mere educational machine, in which men who had got all they could for themselves found it a profitable trade to screw up others to the same point, instead of going on to build upon what was, after all, only a foundation. Meanwhile, the ablest works in philosophy and history proceeded from University men indeed, but not, as a rule, from those who were resident, but from the Cabinet Minister, the banker, or the country clergyman.

The subject of University extension began to be seriously discussed in 1865. In November of that year a meeting of graduates interested in the question was held in Oriel College, and committees were appointed to draw up various schemes. Freeman warmly advocated the principle of extension. The Universities in ancient days had been frequented by men of all ranks, and destined for all manner of callings. All went through the course of Arts, as it was called, to which other courses were added, suited to the special callings of Divinity, Medicine, and Law. The University, being now confined to comparatively rich men, was clearly not doing its duty. It could not, indeed, compel all men to come in, but it could at least throw open its gates that all might come in who chose. It was most desirable that professional men, like solicitors, bankers, surgeons, and physicians, should go through an academical course first. Men of that class who had not been to the University were often clever and well-informed, and yet lacked that nameless something which, though not always got *with* a University education, was yet hardly got without it. One of the committees recommended in their report that a college should be founded 'not exclusively, but especially for the education of persons needing assistance, and desirous of admission into the Christian ministry.' Freeman thought that though there were no theoretical objections to a clerical, medical, or legal college, there were great practical objections. The great social advantage of a University was its bringing together men of all ranks and all future callings; and of all class colleges he thought a clerical one the least desirable. Nothing had been a greater gain for the English clergy, and through them for the nation, than the fact that the future priest and the layman had hitherto gone through the same course of education at school and college side by side. A far wiser plan was that recommended by another committee, of adapting existing colleges and halls to University extension. But here a difficulty had been created by the recent University Reform Bill, which had taken what was intended for the poor and given it to the rich. College scholarships, designed for the support of students who were too poor to maintain themselves, had been turned into purely honorary distinctions, being awarded to mere proficiency, irrespective of circumstances. To give a man to whom money was no object £70 or £80 a year was so much *dead waste*. A sprig of laurel would serve the purpose of distinction just as well, and the money should go to those for whom it was intended—the most proficient amongst needy men. A rich man who wanted to exercise and display his cleverness might get six first-classes and all the University scholarships and prizes, without seizing on the college scholarships, which were intended for the poor.

A third committee, which included Mr. Goldwin Smith, Mr. Wayte, and Professor Mountague Bernard, recommended the system of unattached or non-collegiate students. They said ' there may not be the same need of an increased number of solicitors or medical men as there is of an increased number of clergy, but that there is need of better educated solicitors and better educated medical men is admitted on all hands, and most emphatically, as we believe, by the leading members of those professions.' 'This,' said Freeman, 'is the right sort of thing. This is eminently cheering to read after the somewhat dreary picture of a boundless inroad of curates on which the other sub-committee dwells with such delight.' Of course many objected to this proposal from apprehension of a difficulty in maintaining good moral discipline amongst men dispersed in lodgings ; but, as Freeman pointed out, what the opponents of lodgings had to prove was not that residence in a college was much better than residence in lodgings, but that residence in lodgings was so bad that it ought not to be tolerated at all. Otherwise the presumption was certainly in favour of a system which would restore to members of the University that freedom of choice which had been taken from them by a comparatively modern enactment [1].

A question which greatly agitated Oxford between the years 1860 and 1865 was the endowment of the Regius Professorship of Greek, to which Mr. Jowett had been appointed in 1855. This Chair was one of five Professorships founded by King Henry VIII, to each of which he had assigned an annual stipend of £40. In the case of three out of the five—the Chairs of Divinity, of Hebrew, and of Greek — the payment of these stipends was charged upon the Dean and Chapter of Christ Church. The endowments of the Professors of Divinity and of Hebrew had been augmented, the former by James I and the latter by Charles I, by annexing a canonry at Christ Church to each of the Chairs. The stipend of the Professorship of Greek, on the other hand, had not received any augmentation. The inequality, however, had not been severely felt before the appointment of

[1] Viz., A statute enforced by Dudley, Earl of Leicester, when he was Chancellor in the reign of Queen Elizabeth (though it was in existence before his time), which required that every student in the University should belong to, and reside within the walls of, some College or Hall. The restriction was removed in 1868, when a statute was passed for the admission of non-Collegiate students.

Mr. Jowett, because the Chair had frequently been occupied by men who held other offices which were well endowed ; and Mr. Jowett's immediate predecessor, Dr. Gaisford, appointed in 1811, had been Dean of Christ Church since 1831. After Mr. Jowett's appointment, proposals were made from time to time that the University should raise the stipend to at least £400 a year, which, allowing for the difference in the value of money, would be a fair equivalent to the original endowment of £40; but these proposals were constantly rejected, either in Convocation or by the Hebdomadal Council, through the influence of members who considered Mr. Jowett's theological opinions to be mischievous. In a letter to the *Daily News*, dated October 18, 1864, Freeman maintained that the Professor's stipend certainly ought to be augmented, only that the provision for it should be made, not by the University, but by the Dean and Chapter of Christ Church. He first stated the conditions of the controversy with his customary clearness and incisiveness.

' There is one party,' he said, ' who start from the position that Mr. Jowett has put forth certain theological views which they think objectionable, and who therefore argue that the University should in no case grant any further endowment to the Chair while he holds it. That the endowment is absurdly scanty, that Mr. Jowett has made a good and zealous Professor, that he has not, so far as I know, made his Professorship the means of insinuating his peculiar theological views, are facts, all of which go for nothing. He is guilty of theological error, and should therefore in no case receive anything from the University. There is another party, who start from the undoubted facts of the inadequate endowment of the Professorship and of Mr. Jowett's incontestable merits as Professor ; who either agree with his theological views, or think that theological controversies are alien to the question, and who therefore infer that the University should endow the Professorship in hot haste, without stopping to think whether there may not be other sources, from which the increased endowment may more justly be made to flow.

With Mr. Jowett's opponents I have no sympathy at all. Theologically I am neither an opponent nor a follower of Mr. Jowett. I must confess (I have no doubt that the fault is my own and not Mr. Jowett's), that such of Mr. Jowett's theological writings as I have read, I cannot understand; I can therefore neither approve nor disapprove, but I cannot see how his theological errors, if errors they be, can prove that his stipend ought not to be increased. If they prove anything at all, they prove something much more. If Mr. Jowett's opinions are so bad that he may not receive a decent reward for his services, he must be quite unfit to be a Professor at all, to be a Master of Arts in the University, to be a Fellow of Balliol College, to be a Priest in the Church of England. If he is allowed to be all these things, it is ridiculous to take issue on a mere question of income. . . .

But if I have no sympathy with Mr. Jowett's opponents, neither can I unreservedly throw in my lot with his supporters. I hold, as they do, that the stipend of the Professor is absurdly small, and that it ought to be increased, but I cannot leap to the conclusion that the University is necessarily bound at once to supply the deficiency. I am hindered from coming to this conclusion, because I see another body on whom it seems to me the duty imperatively lies. The body of which I speak is the Dean and Chapter of Christ Church. They are in enjoyment of the funds which the Founder alike of Chapter and Professorship intended to go to the maintenance of the Professor; and it is on them and not on the University that the moral obligation lies to provide an adequate endowment for the Professor. If they refuse to provide it, if Parliament, in case of their refusal to provide it, refuses to compel them to provide it, then rather than let the Professorship go unendowed, let the University come forward itself—but not before.'

Moreover, he found that ten years ago the Chapter itself had admitted its moral obligation to increase the

Professor's endowment. In a letter addressed by the Dean and Chapter of Christ Church to Lord Palmerston in 1854, they had proposed that unless the Crown should be pleased to make some other provision for the Chair, they should be empowered to set apart an estate of the value of between £300 and £400 a year, of which the lease was then running out, and that upon the next avoidance of the Greek Chair, the said estate should be made over to the new Professor and his successors. This voluntary and generous offer, however, was, for some reasons unexplained, not carried into effect. The last form of statute proposed on the matter was, in Freeman's opinion, bad from every point of view. It contained a proviso that the University, by voting the Professor's stipend, in no way committed itself to his theological views.

'I can conceive,' he said, 'no proviso more paltry and un-dignified. It is either the business of the University to judge of theological error or it is not. If it is not its duty so to judge, it should hold its tongue about the matter. If it is its duty so to judge, it *should* judge, and not guard itself against hypothetical judgements. It should not say, we should like to judge you, but we doubt whether we can, or in the unroyal words of Edward the Confessor, nocuissem si potuissem[1].'

In the following year the question was settled in the way which Freeman had advocated, and the Dean and Chapter of Christ Church raised the stipend of the Professorship to £500 a year.

[1] 'I would have hurt you if I could.'

GENERAL CORRESPONDENCE.

To the Rev. W. Stubbs.

Somerleaze, August 19, 1860.

. . . Pray don't 'destroy,' but only 'alter' your letter to Sylvanus Urban[1]. The latter part is just what I wanted, a calm backing by an *ab extra* scholar from the sure ground of facts. It is just the very thing, and I hope you will send it. I send you what I have written myself, which don't trouble yourself to send back. You will see that I have, ὥσπερ εἰκός, hit upon one or two of the same things as you have, but much the greater part you have all to yourself. You might add that people sometimes—I believe I did it myself in my younger days when talking about St. Cross—speak of Henry of Win-chester as Bishop De Blois, which is perhaps the greatest hash of all.

Not quite the same, but approaching to it, is the French fashion of calling princes, bishops, and abbots, M. de Bour-gogne, M. de Cambray, M. de Citeaux; wherefore I have seen somewhere in English *Cambray's Telemachus*.

N.B. Milman constantly calls Herbert of Bosham[2], *De Bosham*, as if it were a surname. That is just because Bosham is an obscure place. He would hardly say that *D'Oxford*[3] communi-cated with the schismatics, that *De London*[4] was killed in the Cathedral, or that *De Sarum*[5] ran away crying, 'A'Becket's almost dead.' If Morris' Italian Beckets were necessarily Thomas's kinsfolk, why not *Dr. London* in the sixteenth century, just as all Wickhams and Wykehams go claiming

---

[1] The assumed name of the Editor of the *Gentleman's Magazine*, in which there was much correspondence at this time about the architecture of Waltham Abbey.

[2] A friend and biographer of Archbishop Thomas Becket.

[3] John of Oxford, an adversary of Becket.

[4] Archbishop Becket, commonly called by contemporary writers Thomas of London.

[5] John of Salisbury.

Founder's kin at New College? May not Edward Oxford who fired at the Queen be a kinsman of John[1], Bishop of Norwich?
Yours ever,
Edward d'Harborne, alias Freeman.

To THE SAME.

Somerleaze, February 10, 1861.

. . . Don't utter such self-blasphemy as to talk of your letters being twaddle; I treasure them up as St. Edmund's barber did the bits of his beard.

I hope you are better again, nay, quite well. Won't you sit down and make something good on the whole subject of nomina, praenomina, and cognomina, from Titus Tatius to Field Flowers Goe. So many people write nonsense about it.

I have just—at last—begun my *Federal Government.*

To THE SAME.

Paris, May 5, 1861.

. . . A tour in Normandy does not teach one so much as one in Aquitaine, because everything, buildings, men, fields, horses, food, is so much more like England ; but for that same reason everything is in itself much better than in Aquitaine, bating the lack of Pyrenees. But this Paris I do from my heart abjure, detest and abhor, and it is only to please my wife that I stay an hour longer than is wanted to compare St. Germans in the Fields with the Norman churches and to look into some of the book shops on Quai Voltaire. Both Nôtre Dame and St. Eustache were shut up last night. N.B. The Normans are inferior to the Gascons in this, that they pew their churches and sometimes lock them—i. e. they approach our vices as well as our virtues.

To THE SAME.

Somerleaze, March 16, 1862.

. . . I hope to come to you either on the 27th or 28th, whether of the twain depends on certain dinners. Have you got Lanfranc's letters, and the ' Ingulf' and Continuation in Gale ?

---

[1] John of Oxford was made Bishop of Norwich.

If so, I might do a little work with you, if I can't finish it before I come. Meanwhile—

First. When did Abbot Thurstan of Glaston begin to reign?

Second. Did the Scotch Earls of Huntingdon ever marry any great granddaughters of Waltheof?

Third. Do you believe (I don't) that Earl Ælfgar had a daughter named Lucy?

You see I have taken a jump from Achaia to Holland, not Federal Holland, for a little bit.

Barlow wants to learn all that can be learned about John of Gaunt, specially in the matter of 'Katharine Swinford, a governess,' as she was once described in the schools.

To THE SAME.

Somerleaze, March 20, 1862.

What a man you are to know everything, Lucy and all[1]. We will talk about her and divers other Crowland matters on the evening of Friday the 28th. . . . I am always proud to be able to tell you anything back again. But add to your list of Irish Bishops in England[2], Nicolas, Bishop of Elphin, Suffragan to John [Chadworth], Bishop of Lincoln, who consecrated bells at Crowland in the days of Abbot John Lillington, therefore between 1452, first year of Bishop John, and 1469, last year of Abbot John.

To FRANCIS TURNER PALGRAVE, ESQ.[3]

July, 1862.

I meant to have brought back your book myself this evening, but, it being late, I asked a brother-in-law to leave it, who I hope did his errand faithfully.

I have been delighted with all that I have been able to read. I hope that you will publish this, and every word which your father left behind him, *as he left it,* neither adding, omitting, nor

[1] See preceding letter.

[2] In Appendix V. to his *Registrum Sacrum Anglicanum.*

[3] With reference to the proposed publication of two posthumous volumes of Sir Francis Palgrave's *History of Normandy and England.* The volumes appeared in 1864, and Freeman wrote a review of them in the *Edinburgh* for January, 1865.

altering, save plain slips of pen or press—one or two of these I ventured to mark in pencil. Let everything go out, as he left it, in its strength and in its weakness, as the memorial of a great, though eccentric mind, which no other hand could touch without marring. But in the volume you lent me, you get all the strength and hardly any of the weakness. Let it go forth, as it is, hiatus and all, mistakes (if there are any) and all. A few notes might probably be useful, and those no man could add so well as Stubbs.

To the Rev. W. Stubbs.

J. H. Parker's, Esq., December 2, 1863.

I write at once to tell you the result—*Shirley* is appointed[1]. I cannot say I am disappointed; I did not venture to hope for the success of the *best man* and it is a great thing to get a *good man*.

I spent yesterday afternoon in a *Parliamentum Tenebrosum*, Congregation and Convocation sitting at once; sitting on till it was pitch dark and all men growling and squeaking at each other through the gloom. It was the most ludicrous scene I ever heard, for I can't say that I saw it. My faith in residents is by no means increased.

To the Same.

Somerleaze, September 11, 1864.

Many thanks for all your answers, the which reached me at Burnham. Our little meeting there went off much better than anybody expected. Of course it was not like Wells last year, but as good as Burnham was likely to afford. We saw several churches, and climbed (clomb) up Brean Down and Mons Ranarum[2]. On the opposite sides of the latter we fraternized with Ditcher and Denison both—Ditcher is an old proser; G. A. D. had his arm in a sling, having fallen down on the railway. He says that men liken him to a bull; so I asked him whether he were the true *Bos primigenius*. Does not the occurrence of such a beast at the foot of Mons *ranarum* show

---

[1] To the Chair of Regius Professor of Ecclesiastical History at Oxford, for which Mr. Stubbs had been a candidate.

[2] Brent Knoll.

that the frog has at last accomplished what in Aesop's time it failed to do, and does not this confirm Darwin?

. . . What do you take to be the value of the Laws of William C., and Henry I? Palgrave quotes the latter without scruple, but Thorpe calls them the unauthorized compilation of an 'individual.' I should hardly have thought that 'individuals' were so old as 1101.

. . . I caught the *Dialogus de Scaccario* in Madox, and got a great deal out of it, though not that for which I was looking. Is it not odd that Henry I understood English and Greek?

I hope I shall meet you at Chichester, if nowhere else. I do love old Hook.

To W. F. HOOK, D.D., DEAN OF CHICHESTER.

Somerleaze, September 18, 1864.

I have three letters of your's before me, but I don't feel myself greatly to blame, because the last two have followed so closely on one another's heels. I confess to being a little amazed when I received the first copy of the Petworth book, with a letter from its author, talking about a certain article in the *Saturday Review* as mine, asking me to take some notice of him there, &c. &c. Of course this is strictly contrary to all literary etiquette, as nobody has a right to assume that I or anybody wrote any particular thing, and I should be only doing quite right if I pulled a donnish face like Tom Towers in *The Warden*. Of course I don't mean this to apply to you, or Stubbs, or Green, or half a hundred other people who have all a right to say exactly what you please. But I do think it applies to a man about whom I had to scratch my head a minute or two to remember who he was. So I really think it would be a kindness just to hint to him, not that I am offended with him (which I am not), but that a great many people would be if he wrote to them in the same way. Don't let him go writing any apologies to me, which would make things worse; only make him understand that the thing is irregular and should not be done. It is particularly awkward to have books sent in an irregular way by the author, as you don't know what answer to make to the author, nor do you know whether the editor may wish to have the book noticed at all, or whether he may not have given it to somebody else. Again, a merely local book is seldom worth noticing, unless it is either *very good* or *very bad,* or unless you have yourself some particular reason for talking about the place. So your good friend has put me in a bit of a quandary. But don't let him think that I am angry with him—I only exhort him for his good.

You, of course, have a right to assume what you please, and of course you are quite right in assuming that I wrote the article on Church Restoration and Destruction, and that I wrote it with special pleasure. Two or three lines where your name was mentioned were put in after it left my hands, as your letter and Scott's appeared in the *Times* in the meanwhile. Let it be understood of all men that I had not the faintest notion who 'Vigil' was, and that I judged him wholly out of his own mouth. Perhaps, however, I should confess a certain dislike to the whole class of Vigiles, Constant Readers, &c. (as doubtless some people would confess a certain dislike to the whole class of reviewers, middle-writers, &c.); that is, though I hold that leading articles, written in the name of the paper, should be anonymous, I hold that, when a man writes personally, not in the name of the paper, he should put his own name. I always do. The last thing I wrote without, was a little squib in the *Guardian* signed 'John of Salisbury,' when *Tite* and *Tait* made a speech about St. Paul's, calling it the *metropolitan* cathedral, so I quoted

'O Tite, tute Tati, tibi tanta, tyranne, tulisti[1],'

and asked whether the Bishop of London wished to revive the heresy of Gilbert Foliot and the Archflamens. But this I did as a work of charity, to mystify Dickinson and Stubbs.

. . . I wish more and more that I was dictator of Cathedral and Collegiate Churches. I should spare you and a few others, but I think that the punishments of the eleventh century and of the Levitical Law should be revived at Lincoln. An eye for an eye and a tooth for a tooth, whenever dean or canon mangles any old king or bishop. (N.B. There were once some new noses stuck on old bishops at Chichester, but that was before your time.)

. . . I have always looked upon A. P. Stanley as a man

[1] Ennius, *Ann.* 151.

capable of blunders, but I never caught him in any. The only thing I ever *read* of his was that about the Martyrdom, which is thoroughly good and accurate. I *heard* some of his lectures on the Eastern Church and divers sermons, which were mighty eloquent. I never went to sleep under Stanley; an honour reserved for him, Newman, and one or two more (I never slept under Stubbs except after dinner), of whom the Bishop of Oxford is *not* one.

. . . I am at work upon Palgrave, but I have got so much to say about William the Bastard, that I shall hardly have any room left to talk about Anselm or to cross swords with you. I am glad you are going through him again, as I am very fond of him. I look on him as the *raal article*, which Thomas tried, somewhat awkwardly, to reproduce. That is, both were perfectly sincere, but Thomas acted a part. He had a theory of what a saint ought to do and tried to do it, while Anselm was a saint naturally, without thinking about it. Depend upon it, the opposition of William Rufus to Anselm was simply the natural opposition of evil to good. As between Henry and Thomas, 'tis another thing; 'twas a controversy with much to be said on both sides. Remember my old case against ―― is that he can't understand either King or Primate. He is a fly sitting down to describe the manœuvres of two fighting elephants, because he has crawled over both their bodies and counted the number of bristles on each.

I trust to come to you in November, on my way to Oxford. Owing to the pestilent folly of dons, I never know exactly when I am wanted till just before the time. But I have committed myself to lecture at Bristol on November 14; so I shall be on the wing then, and shall be very glad to run on to Chichester about that time. I will leave my wife to answer for herself and Margaret, but let me anyhow thank Mrs. Hook for thinking of the lassie. Don't endow her with mythical virtues, but she is really very useful to me in my library, having helped me to verify all the references in *Federal Government*. If you can prove that our coming (or going) caused Mrs. Hook's recovery, I shall be very glad to believe it, and I shall send the fact to Oswald Cockayne of the Spoon and Sparrow to put into his next volume of *Saxon Leechdoms*.

To J. Bryce, Esq.

Somerleaze, Wells, October 2, 1864.

I don't know that it is your fault or anybody's fault that I have not been at Lübeck and Co. this autumn. I was half glad that I could not go, by reason both of time and money; yet if you or any one worth going with had been open to go, I should have essayed to go nathless. Go I must some time next year; there is hope of Stubbs to my comrade between Easter and Pentecost. But I yearn greatly either for you or your book—when am I to see either? Anyhow, woe be to any man who does not know his Burgundies, &c. next term. I have bidden Owen[1] announce by sound of trumpet that your essay is to be ygotten-up of all men. I also trust to say the same in the *Saturday Review*. I want to see you specially to discuss the plan of the Swiss part, as we may go on writing letters for ever, without either of us exactly understanding the other.

I was not at Bath, as there is hardly anything in the British Association that I care about: now and then a little ethnology, but then they care as much for an Ojibbeway as for a Greek or a Teuton. But I had a flying visit from a party of philosophers, and I have heard a good deal about it from Babington, who is here, but goes to-morrow with Owen.

I cannot keep pace with all that goes on. Denmark, Germany, Italy, America, and matters which concern us more directly at 'Gibenna[2], Burgundiae oppidum.' I have finished Palgrave for the *Edinburgh*, and am now writing Presidential Government for the *National Review*.

... I made an elaborate exposition of the law of Poundbreach last Monday. I suppose you soar above such small matters, but they are meat and drink to us Justice Shallows.

Come when you will between this and November 14, about which time I shall begin the journey which, by way of Bristol and Chichester, is to land me in the Schools—my last time, unless anybody gives me a *third* appointment. Jost Tschudi was thirty times Landammann of Glarus, which beats Philo-

---

[1] Mr. Sidney J. Owen, one of his fellow examiners this year in the School of Modern History.

[2] Geneva.

poimên [1], Aratos [2], Whittington, and Sir John Haberfield—the last named worthy being a Mayor of Bristol probably unknown to you. Phôkiôn [3], however, beats Tschudi.

To THE SAME.

Somerleaze, October 22, 1864.

I have read your Essay [4] with extreme delight, and I am writing a 'revilement' thereof agreeably. The only things I quarrel with are, an unsatisfactory style of reference, and here and there a Germanism (better anyhow than a Gallicism), in style. But you have done the whole subject nobly, and have brought out a vast deal that I should never have thought of.

. . . In my Quellen, the Act of Confederation of Rhein Bund is in Welsh. What authority have you for 'King of Italy' as a title of Odoacer? I know none. I find 'Germaniae Rex' in Hincmar's Annal. A. 866, Pertz. vol. i. p. 476. Do you find it again before Max? Was Ruprecht [5] ever crowned Imperator?

I trust you will manage to come here before November 9, when I start on my travels :—Clevedon, Bristol, Chichester, Oxford, &c. I want so much guidance. Why on earth do you go winter in Welsh places, ἐξόν [6] in Dutch?

To DEAN HOOK.

10 Welbeck Street, W., March 2, 1865.

. . . I think my notion of a cathedral is much the same as yours. A body of prebendaries, fifty, if you like, as there are at Wells, with a small endowment (enough to cover travelling expenses), no cathedral duty beyond preaching turns, votes in all matters above mere daily administration. These to be appointed by the bishop. A few laymen (e. g. Elton, Dickinson, and I at Wells) among them, with votes, but of course without income, would be a gain. These prebendaries *elect from among*

---

[1] Eight times elected General of the Achaian League between B.C. 208 and 183.

[2] Seventeen times General of the League, B.C. 245-213.

[3] Repeatedly General of the Athenians between B.C. 376 and 317.

[4] On 'The Holy Roman Empire.'

[5] Rupert of the Palatinate, A.D. 1400.

[6] 'When it is possible.'

themselves a smaller body of residentiaries, with much larger endowment, to do the duty of the cathedral (not excluding vicars for a choir), hold no other preferment, and keep the same residence that a rector does on his parish. The bishop, of course, to be much more than he is. I hold modern residentiaries to be an oligarchy, who have usurped alike at the cost of the monarchic and of the democratic element.

I have not got the Report of the Cathedral Commission, but I once read a good deal of it at Navestock.

To the Same.

Somerleaze, March 19, 1865.

We had such a laugh yesterday over ———'s criticism; it is so like a bookseller. Of course, I am a young man. Did not the 'Jupiter' (who must know) call me 'a fashionable young gentleman' less than four years ago? Nay, it is not ten years since I was called 'a handsome young man,' and I may add (in strict confidence) that it is less than three weeks since a lady conceived a—perfectly unrequited—passion for me, on the strength partly of my conversation (of which I gave her the least amount possible), partly of my personal charms.

But I am sorry that your son thought the tone of my first notice unfriendly. You have now got the second, and I think you will be more pleased with my going along with you about Shirley's *Zizania* [1], than displeased at what I say about the Prince Albert bit. Since then I have been doing Buonaparte's *Caesar*. I had feared he would have got Mommsen, or Merivale, or some one to correct his blunders; but no, there they all are.

If you ever see the *North British Review*, look at my article on Bryce's *Holy Roman Empire*.

I can quite sympathize with you under your lumbago, and I am sure I trust you have well got rid of it. I generally don't know about aches and pains; but this I do know, having had something of the sort (though doubtless much less sharp than

---

[1] *Fasciculi Zizaniorum*, literally 'little bundles of tares,' a collection of original memoranda concerning the doctrines of John Wycliff and other reformers, edited by the Rev. W. Shirley for the Master of the Rolls' Series of Chronicles.

your's), running about me for some time, becoming at different times lumbago, dorsago, humerago, and femorago [1].

To Spyridon Trikoupes.

Somerleaze, March 28, 1865.

I am much obliged to you and to Mr. Perbanoglous for the three notices of my book [2] in the Νέα Πανδώρα, which you have been good enough to send me. I have now been reviewed in three foreign languages, French, German, and Greek, the last being in one way the most pleasing, as the tongue of those with whom the book mainly deals. I owe many thanks to Mr. Perbanoglous for thus introducing me to his countrymen. I should certainly be well pleased to see myself in a Greek translation.

I have only written one chapter of the second volume, that which relates to Italy, but I am hard at work reading for the German and Swiss parts.

Do you think συμμαχία, which Mr. Perbanoglous uses, is a correct word to express the League? Συμμαχία to me means a mere alliance or confederacy, not a confederation. The Polybian words are ἔθνος, σύστημα, συμπολιτεία, expressing a much closer connexion.

I cannot well follow your various changes of ministry and the like ; but I do most earnestly hope to hear soon of a vigorous suppression of brigandage, and of something being done about the land-tax. I care very little what king doth reign or what minister, if only a few things of that sort could be done.

Mr. Victos, the editor of the 'Εθνικὸν ἡμερολόγιον, asks for my photograph and biography. He can easily have the former, but I am puzzled about writing my own life.

To the Rev. W. Stubbs.

Hamburg, September 9, 1865.

I was thinking of writing to you, when your letter followed me hither from Lübeck. I went on the day you left to Schwerin, where Morlot was. Big modern schloss, fair brick dom with

[1] 'Dorsago,' &c., back ache, shoulder ache, and thigh ache.
[2] *History of Federal Government.*

unfinished tower, all prince and bishop, no people. Then to Wismar and Rostock, two very interesting towns, the latter especially; I think, in this region, it comes distinctly next after Lübeck. You may be a Doctor there by sending in an Essay, which I suppose the barber may write for you, and paying a sum rather less than is needed to become a Justice of the Peace or a Prebendary of Wells. I went also to Doberan, where is a fine church full of pretty things and with the tombs of the early dukes. Thence I got a look at the Baltic at the Holy Dam [1], and a thorough wetting, not from the Baltic. At Wismar the *gassenbuben* [2] pelted me when I drew, but this is peculiar to Wismar. At Lübeck they are much better behaved, either because they are Dutch and not Wendish, or because they live in a Republic and not under a Grand Duke. I was on my second visit to Lübeck.

'Excepto quod non simul esses, cetera laetus.'

You would have been delighted with the library—all fine vaulted rooms of the Franciscans—and the Librarian, Professor Mantels. One night I went to tea, Swiss fashion, with Dr. Baumeister; the other two evenings I spent in correct Lübeck fashion in the wine cellar, with Peacock and the Archivar Wehrmann. Just now it is the only cool place in the town; was it ever so hot before? They tell me 'tis hotter in Sweden; so, by the law of contraries, I am wishing to be in Borneo. I saw nothing of their Magnificences, but I made acquaintance with one of their Wisdoms, Curtius by name, brother of Ernst and Georg C.

. . . The Wards here have been exceedingly kind and friendly: I dined there on Thursday and I am going again to-day. I had a visit yesterday from another Senator here, who is to take me somewhere, I know not exactly where, this afternoon. I go to Bremen in the night between Sunday and Monday; I mean to sail on Thursday, and I hope to be at home this day week.

. . . The canons of Lübeck whose tombs we saw were lay-men, mostly princes, but sometimes learned men got the place.

[1] Heiligendamm, a place on the sea-shore four miles from Doberan, so called from a great bank of shingle.

[2] Street boys.

It would just suit me. I don't think any prince has any authority at Lûbeck, but Hamburg was not clear of all claim of Holstein dukes till 1768. I saw a charter yesterday of one of the Christierns[1] talking of 'unser Stad Hamborch.' Of course this was not admitted, and there was disputing about it in the Reichstag. There were bishops of Hamburg, and a dom which was pulled down about 1805.

To G. FINLAY, ESQ.

Somerleaze, October 31, 1865.

I am utterly ignorant of all financial matters of any date or country.

. . . Am I right in understanding you to mean that the League coined good money, but that the Cantons coined bad? How would this agree with either interpretation of the famous piece in Polybios about their all using the same coinage? I hardly look on the League as having been so aristocratic as you seem to think it. I should not accept your description that it needed a revolution to displace the party in power. Surely it needed nothing but the annual vote of the Assembly, a vote in which the whole nation might take a part if it thought good. The party questions between Aratos and Lydiadas, and again between Philopoimên, Diophantos[2], and others, seem to be carried on in a strictly parliamentary way. It is only when the questions become geographical, when (as in America lately) the government has to deal with a revolted or disaffected state, that we get anything like violence, or again in the very late and corrupt time to which I do not go for precedents. No doubt there is this difference between Achaia and ourselves, that an obnoxious στρατηγός[3] and δημιουργοί[4] could not be got rid of by a vote at a moment's notice, but that a particular time of the year had to be waited for. But a condemned English ministry can generally contrive, if only by dissolving Parliament, to linger on for as long a time as it could ever be needful to endure an

---

[1] A common name of dukes of Sleswig-Holstein, and of kings of Denmark of the Oldenburg house.
[2] So in MS.; it must be a slip for Diophanes.
[3] General of the Achaian League.
[4] The ten Ministers who formed his Council.

obnoxious Achaian government. Either case differs from that
of America, where a President who has lost the confidence of
the nation may have to be borne with for three years or more.
An idea, however, has just struck me which I ought to have
worked out in my history. The prohibition of immediate re-
election of the President must have involved a more distinct
party organization in Achaia than there was at Athens. Perikles,
Nikias, and Phôkiôn, were elected generals over and over again,
sometimes by Assemblies which refused to carry out their policy.
The question must have become very much one of *personal*
confidence and esteem. But as Aratos or Philopoimên could
not be re-elected at once, they had to look out for someone else
of their party to be the candidate of that party in the alternate
year. You therefore get signs of a much closer organization,
caucuses, tickets, and the whole science of party electioneering.
I have no doubt that every year (unless while Aratos was
practically omnipotent) there was a distinct party struggle, but
that it came on constitutionally every year. And there must have
been more temptation to make it so, from the utter uncertainty
of whom the Assembly would consist. One year you have only
senators, another πάντας τοὺς ἀπὸ τριάκοντα ἐτῶν[1]. Each party was,
therefore, tempted to try its luck at that opportunity. But I
cannot call it an oligarchy ; I call it an aristocracy on sufferance.
The mass of the nation could always loyally step in when they
chose, and we know that sometimes they did step in. If at
any time they failed to step in when they ought to have done
so, the fault is their's, and it hardly makes the government an
oligarchy.

. . . Vischer's review pleased me very much. He had
evidently given the book that attentive study which an author
feels as the highest compliment that can be paid him. I wrote
him a long letter arguing some of the questions which he raised
about Boeotia being an *Einheitsstaat,* and the like. He touched
far more on those earlier matters than on Achaian times. He
then sent me a discourse of his on ' Ueber die Bildung von
Staaten und Bunden, oder Centralization und Föderation im
alten Griechenland.'

. . . I had indeed a very pleasant journey in North Germany,

----

[1] 'All who were above the age of thirty.'

of which, as you say, the records have been gradually appearing in the *Saturday Review*. I went chiefly to see the Hanse Towns, the three live ones, and as many of the dead ones as I could manage, and I did a good deal. Lübeck is a place with which I am specially charmed, and I have written it in the tablets of my heart next after Schweiz. The worst of all these federalizing journeys is that it seems as if I should never get into Greece.

I suppose the last letter in the *Times* is yours, and, if so, things must be looking up a little. What can Greece want with an army? Surely Switzerland is the model for a country in that sort of position; no army, but every man a soldier.

I have been figuring before a Queen for the first time in my life, to wit, Queen Emma of Hawaii, whose fame has probably not reached Athens, but who is the great lioness just now. I dare say it is very wrong, as she is a good woman and comes with a good object, but there is something grotesque about a Queen whose people are not even Aryans. However, I made a speech likening her to all the crowned saintesses in ecclesiastical history. I started with Helen, but I thought Pulcheria Augusta would not be understood, and I could not conscientiously hold up Theodôra[1] or Eirênê[2] as models for anybody. So I left your dominions, and got off among my own West-Saxons, Jutes, and so forth, where godly women abound.

To Dean Hook.

Somerleaze, December 23, 1865.

I have been meaning to write to you for a long time, but time slips away wonderfully when one is making *four* histories, besides Revilements and such trifles. First, there is *Federal Government*, vol. ii, for which I read a certain portion of High-Dutch daily, and write something ever and anon. Secondly, a *History of England*, for young folks, down to 1154 (where the *Chronicle* forsakes me), which I have been at, off and on, for a good many years, and which has crept down to 1016. I write it bit by bit for my own children. Thirdly, a *History of Greece*, which I undertook to do for the Delegates, and which also gets slowly on. Fourthly, but just now firstly,

---

[1] Wife of the Emperor Justinian.   [2] Wife of the Emperor Leo IX.

Goldwin Smith will most likely give up his Professorship next year, and I want to succeed him. It seems to be thought good that I should put out something more directly bearing on what they call Modern History than *Federal Government*, vol. i, so, as *Federal Government*, vol. ii, could not be done in time, and as no bookseller (at least neither Longman nor Macmillan) would take a volume of collected Essays at his own risk, I have actually sat down to make a distinct *History of the Norman Conquest*, which I can do easier than anybody else, as I have worked so much at the subject for twenty years past, that is, a great part of the story; there will be little more to do than to write down what is already in my head. Still, you see there is a good deal of work on hand, while gaols, lunatics, and meetings about cattle plague are supposed to keep me in play.

. . . Pray don't work so hard and make yourself ill again. We all trust you are well again ; but you must keep yourself so.

I shall be curious to see what you make of Cranmer—the Saint Thomas of Canterbury of sound Protestants. I confess that, if his conversion was real, it was singularly opportune. Was it not odd that up to Henry's death he should persecute every one who denied transubstantiation, and directly after, persecute everybody who believed it ? I cannot stand a reformer persecuting. I suspect I shall have to say some strong things about that when I get to Swiss matters.

To THE SAME.

Somerleaze, January 7, 1866.

I did not mean my two or three lines of Friday to be an answer to your most kind letter. I don't know how to tell you how much I value all your expressions (and still more the *signs*) of regard towards me, which you so constantly give me, not the least (which indeed I count the most valuable of any), when you criticize anything that I do, and point out the faults in it. When a man does not mind finding fault with me, then I believe him when he says any good of me.

. . . I believe I do stick to truth, as you are good enough to say, at any rate I always aim at it, as far as I can judge of myself, with a single eye. I can generally see good and bad on both sides, and I can constantly see good on opposite sides, so I never can be a partisan. It is only when one gets out of questions of opinion into the region of sheer wickedness, the land tenanted by Buonapartes and Palmerstons, that I get fairly in a rage. You say I am too impatient with fools. As you say it, I dare say I am. But I don't think I am impatient with them for being fools, which they can't help, but for writing books when they are fools, which they can help.

Of the Norman Conquest, I do hope I may make something which even that strangest of beings, the general reader, may deign to look at. I am reading again through Palgrave's *English Commonwealth*, which I had not read (as a whole) for some years. What a wonderfully suggestive book it is, though he certainly rides his hobby too hard. And then he could write in reasonable English, instead of the frantic style of many parts of the *England and Normandy*. Kemble, I deeply admire, and at the same time heartily dislike. I never saw either of them in the flesh. Guest is the man whom I do trust and look up to.

To G. Finlay, Esq.

Somerleaze, January 7, 1866.

Your changes of ministry—I suppose I must not call them your revolutions — are simply baffling. You must need a national Colenso simply to count them. I have long left off trying to do so, even with your help in 'Jupiter.' But they convince me more and more of what I have always said, that the ruin of Greece is the blind imitation of Western institutions. Our system of Cabinets and Parliaments answers here because it has grown up here, and it has been transplanted with fair success into two or three of the most advanced European kingdoms, but it does not do in the Colonies, and it clearly does not do in Greece. In a country like Greece is now, it can lead only to all sorts of jobbing and personal squabbles. It is much too elaborate and conventional. A στρατηγός safe for a year would be something permanent compared with these ministries of a day. But, republican as I am, I think that a real working prince would be better still. Read in our

chronicles how Eadgar, Godwine, Harold, William the Conqueror, and Henry the First, all put down the klephts[1] of their
day; how so doing was taken as an atonement for almost anything else, and how Robert of Normandy, William Rufus, and
Stephen omitted to do so, and what folk thought of them for the
omission. Really your case is something like ours 800 years
back. But then neither Harold nor William had to 'send for'
anybody to put together a Cabinet.

. . . I have no doubt that the Achaian League was aristocratic in your sense, nearly the same sense in which one might
call South Carolina aristocratic. But we do find a distinct influence of the people now and then, as in that violent Assembly
at Corinth, where Polybios complains that so many low people
attended. I learned first from you that the modern history of
Greece begins with Alexander. I am trying in my small
Greek History, to work out specially the growth of what I call 'the
artificial Greek nation' as distinguished from the pure Hellênes.
But I put the beginning of its formation much earlier, namely,
with the first beginnings of Greek colonization. It does not,
however, affect Hellas proper before the Macedonian times.

. . . I am thinking somewhat of the coming Reform Bill;
but more about the cattle-plague, seeing I have to help to
legislate upon the latter matter, and not about the former.
I wish some political philosopher would take up the subject
of Quarter Sessions. We are utterly unjustifiable in theory,
and utterly disorderly in practice, yet somehow I think we
practically get on fairly well. Bagehot (whose name you
perhaps know as a political philosopher) whispers that no
Parliament can get on without a Cabinet. But I don't think
the country would be better managed, if half the justices were
on a treasury bench and half in opposition.

I stick to my old scheme of contributory boroughs, fortified
as it is by the example of the Amphiktyonic Council.

To J. BRYCE, ESQ.

Somerleaze, February 28, 1866.

I am working at the Norman Conquest as nearly all my time as
the 'Reviler,' the cattle-plague, and the needs of eating, sleep-

[1] Robbers.

ing, and riding will let me. I think it will make two volumes —975-1066 and 1066-1154, with introductory and concluding portions. I dream of getting the one out by June, for manifest reasons, though October 14 would be the proper day[1].

Thanks for more papers. I wish I could find time to write something about it, as I am intensely interested in the matter.

I rejoice greatly in your appointment as Examiner. I conceive myself to have now nominated a whole board, Stubbs, Boase, Bryce, τρία ταῦτα, and I hope to come at Trinity Monday and see you all at work. As you are in a manner my ἔργα, στέργω ὥσπερ τέκνα[2]; only bear in mind your inferior condition[3] (the just penalty of heterodoxy), in that, if a man comes in wearing of a white coat, or even smoking of a weed, *you* cannot say 'Verte canem ex,' but must leave the power of the sword to your betters. On the other hand, how you will add to the aesthetics of the place, as you sit in blue and catskin. You remember about St. Wulfstan and 'cattus Dei'[4].

I am ashamed to say that, as I may not review your new edition, I have hardly looked at it. I did read Eginhard's bit about Scotorum Reges. I have been going through more charters, and I find a good many with 'Imperator,' and one with 'Induperator.' Conceive the curious learning of the clerk who hit upon that. I believe it has a meaning, but it does not get beyond the Latin charters. No *Casere*[5], only *Cyning*, in plain English.

Scotch writers seem to me to jumble three things, or rather they admit No. 2, and use it to get rid of 1 and 3.

1. *Commendation* of Scotland proper, north of Forth, to Eadward the Unconquered, 924.

---

[1] The day of the battle of Senlac.

[2] ' My works, I love you as if you were my children.'

[3] That of B.C.L.

[4] St. Wulfstan, Bishop of Worcester [A.D. 1062], being recommended to wear catskin instead of lambskin for warmth, replied, ' nunquam audivi cantari cattus Dei sed Agnus Dei, ideoque non catto sed agno volo calefieri.' Will. of Malmesbury, *Gesta Pont.* iv. § 141.

[5] Old English for Caesar. See on this whole subject *Norman Conquest*, i. Appendix B.

2. Grant of Cumberland in fief by Eadmund the Magnificent, 945.

3. Grant of Lothian, perhaps by Eadgar the Peaceful, perhaps later—I am trying to fix the date.

These two last differ in this. Strathclyde, hitherto independent, commended itself in 924. For some unknown cause Eadmund conquered it in 945 and granted it to Malcolm. The country had never been under direct English sovereignty, and was in Malcolm's hand strictly as a dependent principality. But Lothian was an integral part of England, as much as Somersetshire, and I conceive that the king of Scots, for Lothian, was simply an English alderman.

The vassalage of Scotland proper from 924 to 1327 seems to me one of the best authenticated facts in history, and I do not understand the feeling which makes its denial a matter of passion or a point of honour, instead of a matter of evidence. If a fact is a fact, why deny it? I am not quite clear whether Richard did homage for England or for Arles, but it is to me purely a matter of evidence, and I know beyond dispute that John did homage to the Paip. I can see with perfect equanimity my natural sovereign, the King of the Mercians, submitting himself to the King of the West-Saxons ; why should there be any different feeling about Scotland or Strathclyde?

I start from 924, because from that time there was a continuous vassalage. There are earlier instances of homage (one can't help using the feudal words, though it is before their day), from Scotland to Northumberland ; but it is clear that, in the evil days of Northumberland, that came to an end, and I find no instances of submission to any West-Saxon king before the general commendation to Eadward in 924. Therefore I do not insist on anything before 924.

But I do want to know whether there are any genuine Scottish, Pictish, Cumbrian, or Laudenian[1] (would that be the word?) authorities for my time. I have only Fordun's *Scotichronicon* in Gale, which tells me some things, but is nothing tip-top. Palgrave often quotes a *Chronicon Pictorum*, which I have not got. Stubbs says it is printed in a book called Johnstone's *Antiquitates Celto-Scandicae*, or some such name.

[1] I.e. Belonging to Lothian.

And he says that there are a lot of charters published by some of the Scotch publishing societies, which he looked through and found nothing to his purpose, but he thinks that I might perhaps find something to mine. Of course I want real contemporary documents. The chatter of the thirteenth century is equally valueless on either side. But if a real Scottish document of the tenth, eleventh, or twelfth century put any of the acts of homage in a different light from what I find in the English writers, such evidence I should carefully weigh. Are there such things?

The matter between Henry and Richard and William the Lion, as at present advised, I look upon thus. Henry exacted from William certain concessions beyond the usual homage, as the surrender of certain castles, and an oath from William's vassals, as well as from William himself. These extra submissions Richard gave back, but William was expressly to do what had been done of old, viz., the homage that Malcolm did to the purchaser of Abernethy[1].

I shall be glad to hear something from *North British* (if it will have me with such views) and from Pauli; gladder still to see you face to face.

To THE SAME.

Somerleaze, May 6, 1866.

. . . I have reason to believe that sound views on the subject of the Empire are spreading. There came some Christy's minstrels to Wells the other day, and in their bills, among their patrons they put 'The Duke and Duchess of Austria.' 'Tis pleasant to see the jackdaw plucked of his peacock's feathers, though to be sure I have stumbled on the wrong illustration, as the peacock's feather was the natural Austrian badge.

I have been scratching my head to find something for *North British*. Why not the Swiss Constitution and its History generally? Or a contrast between England, France, and Germany, how they started from the same point, and went different ways? Simon [2] I hold to belong in hotchpot (or is it

---

[1] See ' The relations between the Crowns of England and Scotland ' in *Historical Essays*, first series, and *Norman Conquest*, i. 116–130 with Appendix I, and iv. 517.

[2] Simon de Montfort.

coparcenary ?) to Blaauw [1] and Shirley [2]—moreover I have not yet come to him for any detailed work. I am still among Æthelred's Witenagemots. Or something about comparative mythology? Just now I can only offer subjects which are pretty well in my head. Perhaps the last, though by no means identical, comes too near to my *Fortnightly* article. Just think about it.

To the Same.

Somerleaze, May 8, 1866.

. . . What is there to see at St. David's? Everything: cathedral, palace, college, cromlechs, cyttiau [3], hills, rocks, sea, sea-calves, everything except trees, which seem not to be allowed.

I don't know any small book for you; there is a large one by your correspondents, Messrs. Jones and Freeman.

Gwent = Monmouth.

Morganwg = Glamorgan.

Dyfed = Pembroke.

Roma semel quantum bis dat Menevia tantum.

I have been to Rome $1\frac{1}{2}$ times; when you have been to Tŷ Dewi [4] you will equal me [5].

To the Rev. A. W. Jones.

Somerleaze, September 9, 1866.

Many thanks for the trouble which you have taken in the examination of coachmen; but we both shrink in a sort of reverential awe from a man who has driven four-in-hand for an Irish M.P. ! He is no doubt excellent in his own sphere, but

[1] W. H. Blaauw, Esq., F.S.A., an eminent archaeologist and historian, long resident in Sussex, who wrote the history of the Barons' War.

[2] The Rev. W. W. Shirley, Professor of Ecclesiastical History in Oxford, had edited some Royal and other Historical Letters illustrative of the reign of Henry III.

[3] Signifying in Welsh ' huts of the Gael,' the popular name, adopted by antiquaries, of the circular lines, sometimes surrounded by remains of walls, which are often found inside British camps.

[4] St. David's.

[5] Meaning that he had been thrice to St. David's.

that sphere is one wholly beyond mine. If by any chance
I should ever find myself master of Ford Abbey, I might think
of him when I had restored the refectory and dug up the church,
translating the croquet-ground elsewhere or nowhere.   Till
then I should as soon think of engaging the British Butler
himself, if he should chance to quarrel with our friend at
'Butler's House.' I am reminded of my old friend, Sir G. F.
Bowen, G.C.M.G. (who, like His Grace of York, was not always
so great a man as he is now; I have a third friend, of the
Roman Catholic faith, whom I design to be Pope, to take the
shine out of both of them), who, when I asked him to come
and see me, wrote back that he was staying with Sir John
Pakington, who drove him about in a drag with four horses.
So I made answer that I could not offer him a drag with four
horses, but that if it would make him any happier, I would put
on the children's pony—there was but one then—in front of my
two, so as to make an unicorn. Now my stud is larger, and
I could turn out the sort of thing on the other side.

I hope you understand that one of the foremost pair is an ass.

To G. FINLAY, ESQ.

Somerleaze, October 14, 1866.

. . . I am just now divided between writing the history of
Cnut and signing orders for the passing of cattle—writing
βουστροφηδόν [1], one might say. That is to say, I am hard at work,
at once writing and correcting proof for my *History of the
Norman Conquest*, which I have intercalated between Vols. i.

[1] Literally, 'turning about like oxen.' i. e. at the end of furrows in
ploughing, first one way then another.

and ii. of *Federal Government.* 'Tis the 800th year, and this October 14 is the day of the battle. I got up all the details on the spot two months back. These things give me just time to think about Crete and Frankfurt, and to curse Turks and Prussians—don't think I go in for Austria or Hanover or that sort of thing, but I should not mind keeping a tyrant or two going, if at no other price could I preserve a commonwealth.

I shall mourn if the Cretans are put down, as I fear they will be. The French papers talk disgustingly, and the more so because one knows it is for order, because the tyrant has a big bazaar which he does not wish to have disturbed, and the Cretans are to be sacrificed to this. At the same time I quite see your difficulty about the Cretan Mahometans. I suppose the days when the two creeds can sit down quietly together have not yet come. The real remedy would be a well-disposed Nebuchadnezzar—perhaps one or the other Rawlinson could lend one for the nonce, who should translate all the European Mahometans to Asia, and all the Asiatic Christians to Europe. One has heard of despots making changes almost as great. My philhellenism has borne up a long time, but I am really beginning to despair. The difficulty seems to be that, if the Greeks were really in the nineteenth century, or if they had never heard of the nineteenth century, in either case they might get on, but how can they in their half-and-half state? No doubt this applies more or less to all the Eastern Christians, but I suppose to the Greeks most of all. I fancy the less they know of Western things, and the less they are tempted to imitate them, the more likely they are to work out something satisfactory for themselves. Are not the Bulgarians, in this point of view, the most promising?

To W. B. DAWKINS, ESQ.

Somerleaze, Wells. November 18, 1866.

I have two letters of your's to answer, and a world of things to talk to you about. I will begin with the Esquimaux (I have seen them somewhere written Iskimos, which I recommend, as avoiding the look of Gal-Welsh about the other) down in Perigord. N. B. all about there is rather a Troglodytic country to this day, witness at St. Emilion, the church and many houses cut in the rock, Brantôme, &c. In some of them did the Girondins, even as Obadiah's prophets, seek shelter; but, if I remember rightly, they were worse off than Obadiah's prophets, and were dragged out again.

I am sending your paper to Cook[1] with some comments. He will most likely send you a proof, and then you can make any improvements. It strikes me that you have not quite caught the difference between a 'review' and a 'middle,' that there is rather too much of your author for a middle, and rather too little for a review. Also the beginning is rather too much like that of a longer essay; in these short articles you should get at once into the thick of your subject. Then, let me conjure you by Woden and all the gods (I won't invoke Jupiter, he being only a Rum-Welsh idol, not to be heeded of Dutchmen) don't talk of Saxons when you mean Englishmen, or of France when you mean Gaul. Now you will turn about and say that in the time of the Iskimos it was no more Gaul than it was France. To which I answer, yea verily, yet are Gaul and Britain, as the oldest names of those countries, their *geographical* names; you know when they became England and France, so I should not say England or France before that time; you do not know when they became Britain and Gaul, so I should call them Britain and Gaul at any time from the mammoths till now.

. . . About the plan of Senlac, you doubtless know how to make it and I don't. I want to show the hill itself, with the isthmus to show how it joins on to the mainland, the little hill and the two Malfosses. Size, to go into my octavo page, or haply, if need be, to fold. Then can you reckon anyhow the number of men that the hill would hold? This is important. Also what is its height? Many men have asked me, and I can only answer them by rough comparisons with our hills here, which are far higher.

To DEAN HOOK.

Upminster, Romford.   December 19, 1866.

There is really nothing I know of so good and kind as your letters. The more you blow me up the better, the more I feel

[1] Then Editor of the *Saturday Review*.

convinced that you really care for me. But don't mistake me.
I don't a bit despise or undervalue sermons where there is
really anything in them. E.g. I was at Rotherfield Greys last
Sunday, and *sat under* my friend Pinder (nephew of the
Precentor); now I did not sleep a wink during two sermons,
but listened attentively, because Pinder really had something
to say. But I cannot see how God can be honoured, or man
edified, by one getting up and talking sheer nonsense, eagles'
wings and so forth. If a man puts forth plain truths in words
of one syllable, that is another thing altogether. That I always
listen to; but how seldom one gets it. And I don't quite see
why you call me a 'free-thinker.' There are senses in which
I should not refuse the name; if it means one who has doubts
and difficulties, I do not refuse it; but if you mean that I am
committed to a non-believing school, I am not. The one thing
which I distinctly disbelieve and which I will have nothing
to say to is the damnatory clauses of the Athanasian Creed.
I will not declare that whole nations and churches in the East
and many very good people nearer home, shall *without doubt—*
there is no evading the words—perish everlastingly. And
I hold—and I see nothing in our formularies to hinder me from
holding—that a great part of the early Hebrew history, as
of all other early history, is simply legendary. I never read
any German books on those matters at all, but came to the
conclusion simply from the analogies supplied by my own
historical studies. And there are many points on which I seek
for further knowledge and enlightenment. But I am no un-
believer, and I hold very distinctly that a man should stay
where God has put him till he feels a distinct call to go somewhere else, which I do not feel. And, if you ask why I should
go to church, I answer to join, very imperfectly doubtless,
but very sincerely, in all that goes on there, bating the silly
talk of poetical curates. I am a long way from being perfect
either in faith, practice, or morals, but I don't feel myself
to be an utter reprobate in any of those ways. So whether
I allow myself to be a 'free-thinker' or no, depends on what
you mean by the word.

. . . The first volume of *Norman Conquest* is finished printing
but it is not yet settled whether it is to appear at once or not.

But I rather think it will. I wonder what people will say to it; I cannot help seeing that I have thrown life into some things into which nobody since the Chroniclers has thrown life. There is life enough in them. But that unbelieving Johnny Green won't believe that Harold's body was moved to Waltham, nor will he believe anything about Eadric. But he has begun *his* history, and has read out some parts to us about Charles of Flanders, the White Ship, &c. which will do very well. He is here with Dawkins, palaeontologist or man of bones, whose calling it is to connect geology with history. He has just written about Esquimaux in *Saturday Review*.

I venture to think I *should* make a good professor. People tell me that my enthusiasm for my subject kindles enthusiasm in others, and I can see that my writings have more effect when I read them out loud than when people merely read them to themselves. One thing is, that I always think how a piece of prose will sound, just as much as if it were verse. I fancy most people think not at all of rhythm in a prose writing. Also I think I have a knack of catching the intelligent youth. Indeed, some say I am forming a school which they call the Freemaningas.

. . . December 23. Have you attended to this decision of, I forget which court, about the non-residentiary canons of St. Paul's, pretty well smashing them utterly? How will that affect other old-foundation chapters? I don't like it at all. If chapters are to be of any use, or indeed to go on at all, they must be reformed after a more liberal pattern, viz. the old pattern. These modern changes seem to me to have simply kept the old abuses, and introduced some new ones; everywhere but at Llandaff, where they have really done some good. No doubt chapters and cathedrals generally have improved; but they have improved in spite of ignorant legislation, not because of it.

. . . We certainly want Godwine again to clear away all the strangers and teach the Court to talk English. But one can hardly say so openly. We do seem such a nation of flunkeys to fall down and worship whatever is called Prince. I am a republican in theory, but I should not go about preaching republicanism, because people don't seem fit for it. I don't

understand what people now-a-days call loyalty. I submit to
the Law in all things, and I therefore honour and obey the
Queen in the exercise of such powers as by Act of Parliament
she is invested with. And I understand almost boundless
personal devotion to a great man, which would not be lessened,
probably it would be heightened, if that great man happened
to be a king. But I don't understand this cringing to a lot
of trumpery boys and girls; this holding your breath as if you
were in the presence of Zeus and all his Gemót of gods, at
some —[1] thing called a Royal Highness is beyond me. I suppose
people will some day be ashamed of it. Or rather I fancy
people are ashamed of it, only each man is afraid of the other
and dare not speak out[2].

[1] Illegible owing to a rent in the paper.
[2] See more on this subject in his article on ' Loyalty' in the *Fortnightly
Review* for December, 1879.

CHAPTER VI.

UNSUCCESSFUL ATTEMPT TO GET INTO PARLIAMENT. A CONTRO-
VERSY ON FIELD SPORTS. CORRESPONDENCE.

A.D. 1867–1869.

A TEMPORARY interruption to Freeman's historical
labours was caused by the General Election of 1868,
when he made his first and last serious effort to obtain
a seat in Parliament, by coming forward as a candidate
for the Middle Division of the County of Somerset.
The resolutions which Mr. Gladstone had moved early in
that year for the disestablishment and partial disendowment of the Irish Church, had been carried by a large
majority in the House of Commons. Mr. Disraeli, the
Prime Minister, had immediately tendered his resignation, but afterwards agreed to make an appeal to the
constituencies, remodelled as they were and enlarged
by the Reform Bill, which he himself had introduced in
the previous year. The result of the General Election,
which took place in November, 1868, was a large majority
in favour of the Liberal party. Mr. Disraeli then
resigned, and Mr. Gladstone became Prime Minister.

The disestablishment of the Irish Church was a measure
which Freeman had long advocated on the ground of
simple justice ; so that he could declare himself a hearty

supporter of Mr. Gladstone in that question upon which the issue of the elections mainly turned. The request to become a candidate came to him quite spontaneously and suddenly. On October 19 he was presiding at a Liberal Meeting in Glastonbury, when information was received that a gentleman who had been invited, and who was expected, to stand in the Liberal interest, had sent in a final refusal. The name of another possible candidate was being considered, when the Mayor of Wells got up to say that he saw no need to go outside the room for a candidate, and thereupon proposed the nomination of the chairman himself. The proposal was received with acclamation, but Freeman, after expressing his great gratification at the proffered honour, replied that he could not afford to become a candidate, except on the condition that he was relieved from all electioneering expenses. To this condition the electors present cheerfully assented, and promises to the amount of £1,000 were received on the spot. In the address to the electors, which Freeman issued forthwith, he declared himself to be a Liberal by conviction.

'the thought and study of years have brought my opinions into conformity with those of the most enlightened statesmen of the day, among whom, as far as one man can rightly bind himself to follow the lead of another, I recognize Mr. Gladstone as my chief. To Mr. Gladstone's policy as regards the Irish Church, I give my hearty assent. I hold it contrary to every principle of religious freedom to maintain as a national establishment, a Church which is not only the Church of a small minority, but is also a badge of conquest, an unhappy reminder of evil days, of which it should be our object in all just policy to wipe away the memory. I may add, that as an attached and conscientious member of the Church of England, I cannot consent to stake the existence and the reputation of a religious establishment which I hold to be thoroughly righteous, on its connexion with another religious establishment whose circumstances are totally different, and which I hold to be thoroughly unrighteous.

While thankfully accepting many of the changes wrought by the late Reform Bill, that above all which has so largely increased the constituency of this Division, I feel that many of its provisions are imperfect, and others distinctly evil, and that one great duty of a reformed Parliament will be to reform the Reform Bill. I speak especially of the rate-paying clauses and the minority clauses. I further hold that as the example has been set of disfranchising several small boroughs, including the only one in our Division, the disfranchisement of several others must in consistency follow. While holding that open voting is in itself the better mode of conducting elections, yet in the existing circumstances of many constituencies I am prepared to support any proposal for vote by ballot.'

In conclusion he said :—

'I stand as a representative of purity of election. I hold that a candidate who believes he can be of use in the legislature of the country, and whose belief is confirmed by the unsolicited request of many electors, ought not to be debarred from coming forward because his means will not allow of a large expenditure. And as a landowner, a resident, and a magistrate of the county, and as having for some years taken an active interest in its local affairs, I feel myself as much identified with the welfare of the Division and as capable of representing its local interests in the great council of the nation, as men of greater estates.'

Soon after Freeman had consented to stand, another Liberal candidate came forward, in the person of Mr. Tagart, a wealthy London merchant, who had a country residence on the borders of Somerset. The two Conservative candidates were Major Paget and Mr. Neville Grenville. For the space of six weeks Freeman was engaged with his colleague in the usual toil of canvassing and speaking at public meetings up and

down the country, and of course very little literary work
was done beyond his weekly article or articles for the
Saturday Review. That journal and some other literary
papers commended Freeman's candidature as a recognition of the claims of pure learning and intellect to
a place in Parliament.

'If,' said the *Spectator*, 'Mid Somerset chooses Mr. Freeman,
it will be the one English constituency represented by its most
learned resident, and have for its member one of the few very
learned men admirably fitted to be a representative.'

'Mr. Freeman,' said the *Saturday Review*, 'presents the
exceptional case of a county candidate coming forward, not
on the strength of territorial influence, but distinctly as the
independent representative of public principle, and selected
by the Liberals on account of his intellectual eminence and
his high position in letters.'

Freeman had earned the gratitude of the Greeks
by the zeal and persistency with which he had long
advocated the independence of their nation, and the
following extract from *La Grèce*, an Athenian newspaper, shows how warmly his success was desired in that
country.

'The historian of Federal Government and of the Norman
Conquest was known and loved in Greece before his name had
acquired the fame which he so justly merited. The services
which Mr. Freeman has rendered to the cause of Hellenism and
the emancipation of the Christian East are invaluable. It is
owing to Mr. Freeman that the claims of the Christians in the
East have found a voice in the English Press, the *Edinburgh
Review*, the *Saturday Review*, the *North British Review* and the
daily newspapers, at a time when the interests and passions
of the English public would not suffer the sacred principle of
the integrity of the Ottoman Empire to be called in question.
Should Mr. Freeman obtain a seat in the British Parliament,
the little phalanx of the friends of Greece in the House of Com-

mons will have in him a powerful auxiliary, and the Greeks, the
Servians, the Roumanians, and Bulgarians will have one more
defender who will do justice to their cause and make a stand
against the London champions of Mahometan despotism.'

Mid Somerset was an old Tory stronghold, and the
invasion of the preserve by the Liberal candidates was
bitterly resented. Every effort was made to disparage
their claims. Some of the writers and speakers on the
Tory side sneered at Freeman as being only a small
landowner of insignificant position in the county, and
endeavoured to represent him as a mere writer in newspapers. Party feeling ran very high upon the Irish
Church question, and it was alleged or insinuated by
many that he who wished to disestablish that Church
was prepared, not only to disestablish the Church of
England, but even to demolish all the parish churches,
or to hand them over to the Roman Catholics. Freeman
was careful in all his speeches to refute these monstrous
statements, by informing his hearers that he had devoted
much of his time throughout his life to the study and
description of those splendid fabrics which the piety
of past ages had planted so thickly over the land,
and nowhere in greater beauty or more abundance than
in Somerset. He repeatedly insisted, also, on the
essential difference between the position of the Irish
Church, which had been thrust by a small and alien
minority upon an unwilling people, and the position of
the Church of England, deeply rooted, as he believed,
in the hearts of the people, and continually growing in
activity and influence. The election resulted in a clear
majority for the two Conservative candidates, who
obtained, each of them, more than 3,000 votes. The
Liberals, however, polled more than 2,000 each, which

was a larger number than they or their opponents had expected. In the market towns, indeed, and in some of the larger villages, there was a Liberal majority; but the Tory candidates were personally respected and popular, and the scale was turned by the rural voters in small places where the Tory interest was strongest.

Freeman threw himself heartily into all the stir and excitement of an electioneering campaign: he rejoiced in the opportunity of speaking his mind upon many topics in public, and he used frequently to refer to his 'going on stump,' as he called it, as one of the most enjoyable episodes in his life. He spoke with vigour and clearness, and although he sometimes introduced historical allusions which were beyond the understanding of his audience, he also made jokes, and dealt hard hits at his adversaries which were very intelligible and entertaining to his hearers. The only place in which neither he nor his fellow candidate could obtain a fair hearing was Wedmore, where a well-dressed and well-organized Tory mob burst into the place of meeting, drowned their speeches by yelling and hooting, and at last drove them off the platform by a plentiful discharge of rotten eggs and potatoes.

Freeman made fun of this exciting little incident in the following lines, supposed to be sung by the men of Wedmore on their way to the fray.

THE MARCH OF THE MEN OF WEDMORE.

Hark! the Wedmore men are coming; 'tis not fifing, 'tis not drumming,
It is our own sweet voices as we shout for ' Blue, Blue, Blue';
And the Yellow hearts are troubled, as they see our fists all doubled,
And our singlesticks all waving to the cry of ' Blue, Blue, Blue.'

The Yellow men may preach with their gabble and their
    speech,
But we know how to answer with a shout of ' Blue, Blue, Blue ';
The Yellow men may reason, but 'tis sadly out of season,
When our singlesticks can cut them short, with a shout of
    ' Blue, Blue, Blue.'

We mock their offered light ; we scorn to read and write ;
We only know our fathers always shouted ' Blue, Blue, Blue ' ;
And when men read and think, we see how low they sink,
For soon they leave off shouting with the shout of ' Blue,
    Blue, Blue.'

When they talk of right and law, we bid them hold their jaw ;
The only right and law for us is the shout of ' Blue, Blue,
    Blue ' ;
And we can give good knocks, enough to fell an ox,
To all who will not join us in the shout of ' Blue, Blue, Blue.'

We shout for Church and Queen ; true, we know not what
    they mean,
But the parson and the justice say that Church and Queen
    are ' Blue ' ;
And they say the Pope is Yellow, so we curse the dirty fellow,
And we'll shout for Beelzebub himself, if he'll shout for
    ' Blue, Blue, Blue.'

As for Gladstone and for Dizzy, what's the use of being busy?
We'll shout for either of the two that will shout for ' Blue,
    Blue, Blue ' ;
As for laws and bills and worry, we're in much too great
    a hurry ;
They're all the same to Wedmore men if they're only ' Blue,
    Blue, Blue.'

Then hey for Wedmore roughs, then hey for fisticuffs,
Drub hard on every Yellow back to the tune of ' Blue, Blue,
    Blue ' ;
Then hey for rotten eggs, broken heads, and broken legs,
All for Church and Constitution and the shout of ' Blue, Blue,
    Blue.'

No doubt it would have reflected great honour upon
the electors for Mid Somerset if they had disregarded
the traditional idea that the main qualifications for
a county member consist in the possession of a large
estate, and a certain familiarity with the ordinary
occupations and amusements of a country gentleman,
and had for once returned a representative distinguished
by first-rate ability and profound learning, as well as by
fearless integrity and a very high sense of duty. But it
is one of the greatest misfortunes of party government,
that a man who can be trusted to vote steadily, not to
say blindly, with his party, is more acceptable to constituencies and to leaders than one who, however much
attached to his party and to his leader, will always
reserve the right of speaking and voting strictly according to his reason, his knowledge, and his conscience.
Such a reservation of independence is distinctly adverse to
a man's success in Parliament. His speeches will often
be unpalatable to his own side, and any admiration
which they may excite in the opposite party is dis-
counted by the fact that he is not 'one of them' and
cannot be relied upon for lasting support.

There can be no doubt that if Freeman had entered
Parliament he would have made from time to time forcible,
interesting, and witty speeches, and he would have sometimes dealt telling blows to opponents which would have
gratified his party; but he was essentially, and before all
things, a critic, and neither his zeal for truth nor his
sense of duty would have permitted him to let a blunder-
ing statement, or fallacious argument, even if advanced
by one of his own party, pass uncorrected. Nor in
voting would he have hesitated to sever himself from his
own party in the case of any measure which in his

Aa 2

judgement was not based on thoroughly sound grounds
of reason, truth, and justice.   Such a deep and extensive
knowledge as he possessed of the history of various
forms and systems of government in all parts and ages
of the world, combined with special knowledge of the constitutional history of his own country, and of the origin
and growth of national institutions, might naturally
seem to be invaluable qualifications for a member of
a legislative body.   But practically they count for very
little in the House of Commons.   Arguments, illustrations, precedents, warnings derived from the teaching
of past history, may be respectfully received, or even
applauded, provided they do not clash with the exi-
gencies of party tactics and political expediency: otherwise they are utterly disregarded.   The House of
Commons is emphatically an assembly of partisans, not
of independent critics or impartial judges.   The influence,
therefore, of a man like Freeman in the House would
probably have been in no sort of proportion to his ability
and learning.   On questions of foreign policy, on which
he felt very strongly, his personal dislike for individuals
like Lord Beaconsfield and Lord Stanley (afterwards
Lord Derby), whom he could never forgive for having
forbidden English ships to rescue the fugitives from
Turkish oppression in Crete; his contempt also for the
ambiguous official language (the jargon as he called it)
of diplomatists, would have often betrayed him into
intemperate utterances, which would have injured the
cause he intended to befriend.   No doubt a great deal
of what he said would have been thoroughly true and
often unanswerable, and on that account all the more
irritating to opponents; but the vehemence of his
language would have somewhat weakened the weight of

his arguments and facts, by alienating the sympathy of his hearers. On the whole, therefore, none of Freeman's friends could regret that he was unsuccessful in obtaining a seat in Parliament. A man of his sturdy independence of character, irrepressible zeal for simple truth, and unvarnished plainness of speech, would be somewhat out of place in the House of Commons. Parliamentary duties would have seriously interfered with his literary work, and by his writings as an historian, an essayist, and a journalist, he spoke to a much larger audience, and exercised a far greater influence upon public opinion than he could ever have obtained as a member of the House of Commons. In his secret soul he was, I think, conscious of his unfitness, and although at times, when some critical question in which he took deep interest was before Parliament, he longed to have an opportunity of taking part in the debates, and although he had more than one attractive request to come forward as a candidate for election, he resolutely resisted the temptation. Meanwhile he returned with zest and contentment to his interrupted work on the history of the Norman Conquest, which he pushed forward at a great rate during the year 1869. In the course of that year the third volume, containing the account of the battle of Hastings, was completed and published, considerable progress was made with the preparation of the fourth volume, and the first and second volumes were revised for a second edition.

In October, 1869, an article by Freeman appeared in the *Fortnightly Review* entitled the 'Morality of Field Sports,' which provoked a long and lively controversy on the subject. There were probably not a few persons who marvelled how a man who held such heretical opinions concerning the immemorial and sacred privileges of country gentlemen should have dared to offer himself as the representative of a county constituency in Parliament. The main position which he maintained with great force and skill in this essay was, that any sport which involved the pain and death of the lower animals was morally unjustifiable. He began by citing from a police report the case of some boys who had recently been punished for setting on two dogs to worry a cat, and he asked in what respects such an act was more cruel, or more deserving of punishment, than setting on a pack of hounds to worry a fox. A bill for the suppression of bull-baiting introduced into Parliament in 1800, had been defeated by a majority of two. Windham opposed the bill in a long speech, mainly on the ground that no one who condemned bull-baiting could defend fox-hunting, or any other field sport. It would be the height of inconsistency and hypocrisy, he said, if the favourite sport of the lower classes was suppressed on the score of cruelty by men who indulged in the practice of other sports which were equally cruel. From the admitted right to torture the fox Windham inferred the right of torturing the bull. Nevertheless, bull-baiting had long been condemned and abolished, and from the now admitted wrong of torturing the bull Freeman inferred the wrong of torturing the fox. To prevent misunderstandings he stated at the outset that he was not a vegetarian or an opponent of capital punishment. He held that man and beast might be put to death when need demanded it, but that no pain should be inflicted which could be avoided. This principle was generally admitted in the case of man:

but in the case of the lower animals it was subjected to
many exceptions. Some sports, as bear-baiting, bull-
baiting, and cock-fighting, had been abolished, others had
been retained. To chase a calf or a donkey till it was
torn in pieces or sank from exhaustion would be scouted
as a cruel act, but to do the same thing to a stag was
a noble and royal sport. To worry a cat was a legal
crime: to worry a hare was a gallant diversion: and
men who would lift up their hands in horror at the torture
of a bull or a bear, deemed no praise too high for the
heroic sport which consisted in the torture of a fox. It
was instructive to trace the gradual revolution of feeling
with regard to various forms of sport. Gladiatorial combats were the favourite amusement of the Romans. In
our own country, in the fifteenth and sixteenth centuries,
rules for cock-shying in public schools were laid down .
by statute. When Queen Elizabeth listened to a sermon
two white bears were kept in readiness to be baited in
her presence as soon as the sermon was over. Now the
principle of all these sports was the same: the fox-hunt
was, of course, less revolting than the bull-fight or bear-
baiting, but in all three the pleasure of those who
indulged in the pastime involved the needless suffering
of some living creature.

He wished it to be distinctly understood at the outset
that he was not condemning *persons*, but *things*. Cruelty
was of course a sin, but of the degree of guilt in any one
who pursued cruel sports he declined to be the judge, for
it depended on the circumstances of a man's age, country,
education, and position. He granted that many high-
minded, cultivated, and generally humane men, indulged
in hunting and shooting, which were considered noble
and manly sports: but this fact was no proof that the

sports were in themselves justifiable. Windham was a high-minded, cultivated man, yet Windham countenanced sports from which the modern fox-hunter turns away in disgust. Titus and Trajan were high-minded, cultivated men, yet they patronized sports from which Windham would have turned away in disgust. Therefore he did not despair of a day coming when the English gentleman would look with the same disgust on some of the diversions of the present age, with which he already looked on the diversions of the days of Windham, and with which Windham looked on the diversions of the days of Titus.

He anticipated a great many of the arguments which would be brought forward in defence of sport.

It would be alleged on behalf of fox-hunting that it was a healthy, invigorating exercise. That was just one of the many disguises which marked the real cruelty of the sport. It was vain to say that the sport was followed merely for the sake of the exercise: for the essence of the sport consisted in its being the pursuit of a *living* animal.

Again, it was contended that hunting was justified on the ground of its social advantages, as promoting good fellowship amongst people of various classes, and that if hunting was abolished country gentlemen would find nothing to do, or that they would do something much worse.

It was also represented that a larger amount of animal suffering was inflicted in other ways, as by drovers, by butchers, and by cabmen.

All these arguments were produced and made the most of by Mr. Anthony Trollope, who came forward as the champion of sport, more especially of fox-hunting,

with a reply to Freeman in the *Fortnightly Review*, and
they were repeated over and over again by crowds of
other writers in various journals. Freeman, however, had
no difficulty in showing that not one of them touched the
heart of the question. He first combated Mr. Trollope's
arguments in two long letters addressed to the *Daily
Telegraph*. A few extracts from these letters are inserted
here, as some of them have an important bearing on the
subject, and others are amusing in themselves and
strongly characteristic of the writer.

'Mr. Trollope is so very, and so good-humouredly, anxious
to know something about my manner of life, that I must really
gratify him, so far as answering his questions goes. If he will
do me the honour of a visit at Somerleaze, I shall be glad to
enlighten him further on this mysterious subject. "Do I play
cards?" As a boy I learned to play Commerce and Beggar my
neighbour, but I cannot say that I give much time to these
now. "Do I read novels?" I have read many of Mr. Trollope's
novels with great delight. "Do I climb Alps?" When among
Alps I have found quite enough to study at their foot, without
going to their tops, but I do often climb Mendip, and I have once
climbed a Pyrénée. "Am I thoughtful about my cigar?" This
question I cannot answer categorically, as it involves the false
assumption that I own a cigar. "Am I good at croquet?" As
a layman, I do not presume. "Do I trundle the harmless
academic bowl?" I have in times past done such a thing, on
certain solemn feasts, but alas! the bowls in our college
garden have made way for croquet hoops. If Mr. Trollope
wishes to know the entertainment which I enjoy above all
others, it is one of which Mr. Trollope knows something as
well as I, but which neither of us can enjoy every day, viz.
an unsuccessful electioneering campaign. But supposing that
I indulged in any or all of these amusements, or in a great
many others which Mr. Trollope does not suggest for me,
whatever is to be said *against* any of them, there is this to
be said *for* all of them, that they do not involve cruelty to any
living creatures. Herein, according to my view, they differ

from Mr. Trollope's favourite amusement of hunting. Mr. Trollope thinks differently, let him speak for himself; "I have never followed any amusement of which the torture of an animal formed a part. As a boy, I never took a nest or worried a cat, and as a man I claim to be equally free from the sin of cruelty to animals, but I ride after fox-hounds very often, and am prepared to defend myself for so doing." Mr. Trollope does not say whether he hunts deer or hares. Perhaps he is like a writer in the last number of the *Spectator*, who thinks that fox-hunting makes the hunter a better man, while he denounces hare-hunting almost as strongly as I can. These are distinctions which I cannot admit, except as questions of degree. I said in my former article that to seek pleasure in the torment of a hare, probably needed a harder heart than to seek it in the torment of a fox. I will give Mr. Trollope this chance. There is a difference in degree among the three forms of hunting, and that difference is certainly in favour of the fox-hunter. But it is only a difference of degree. As a matter of principle the hunting, that is the torture, of stag, fox, hare, and cat, must all stand or fall together. Mr. Trollope then never worried a cat because it is cruel, he does hunt foxes because it is not cruel. Is then the fox not worried, or is it cruel to worry a cat, and not cruel to worry a fox? That the fox is worried, if there be any meaning in words, is manifest to all men. He is chased by dogs till his strength fails him, and then he is torn in pieces. In Mr. Trollope's own words, he is done to death by a pack of hounds, for the gratification of a hundred sportsmen. How does this differ from the worrying process which, as applied to a cat, Mr. Trollope condemns as cruel. Does the number make the difference? Is it cruel when street boys worry a cat only because the number of the boys is probably less than a hundred? smaller than the correct number of a pack of fox-hounds? In either case the beast is done to death by dogs, more or fewer, for the gratification of human creatures, more or fewer. Where is the distinction? What is the point of difference which makes the sport which Mr. Trollope eschews cruel, and the sport which he follows not cruel? I asked the question at the beginning of my *Fortnightly* article, I ask it still.

' But Mr. Trollope says that fox-hunting is not cruel because
the pleasure of the hunter is not derived from the pain of the
animal. He therefore rejects Windham's doctrine that fox-
hunting and bull-baiting must stand or fall together, because he
says in bull-baiting a pleasure is derived from the pain of the
animal. He goes on to draw out a contrast, in most respects
a perfectly fair contrast, between fox-hunting and bull-baiting;
but I drew the same contrast, doubtless not quite so forcibly,
in page 370 of my article. I maintained that bull-baiting and
fox-hunting were identical in principle, but I allowed that
the circumstances of the two sports were widely different.
I allowed that in a fox-chase the cruelty is masked and
disguised, while in a bull-bait it stands out in its native
ugliness. I said that both in bull-baiting and in fox-hunting
the pleasure is pleasure derived from the infliction of suffering; but I met Mr. Trollope's answer beforehand, by saying
that I did not doubt that in many fox-hunters the pleasure was
not directly drawn from the infliction of suffering, only, unlike
Mr. Trollope, I was charitable enough to extend this excuse, so
far as it is an excuse, to the bull-baiters also. I mean this.
I never fancied either Windham or Mr. Trollope rubbing his
hands and saying, How that must hurt the bull! or, How that
must hurt the fox! How I like to think he is being hurt!
I believe such a feeling to be perfectly possible, but I never
suspected Mr. Trollope of it, nor do I see any reason to suspect
Windham. Nevertheless, each alike took pleasure in a sport
of which the infliction of suffering is an essential part; he knew
that such suffering was being inflicted, and yet he found
pleasure in it. The cruelty therefore is there, in the fox-hunt
no less than in the bull-bait. But it is a great point with
Mr. Trollope that in the bull-bait people look on at the cruelty,
while in the fox-hunt, according to his description of it, they do
not. Mr. Trollope's morality, I must say, seems to me a little
like the prudence of the ostrich. The cruelty is done with
Mr. Trollope's knowledge and sanction and for his gratification,
for the fox is done to death " for the gratification of a hundred
sportsmen," of whom I presume Mr. Trollope is one. But so
long as Mr. Trollope turns away his head and does not look at
the cruelty, he holds that he has no share in it. This argument

would justify a good deal. It is only a few tyrants here and there who have always made a point of personally beholding the sufferings of their victims. We have heard of an illustrious person [1] who sat by a fire saying, " Tirez, tirez," while innocent men were being shot down in the streets. But no one ever thought that he was less guilty of their blood, because he did not himself see the shooting, or, like Charles IX, take a shot or two himself. Still, whatever the distinction may be worth, Mr. Trollope is fairly entitled to the advantage of it. Let us picture to ourselves Mr. Trollope in the hunting field. He has lately been described by an admirer as a conspicuous object in the first flight across country after the fox. But it is only in the first flight, or for some reasonable distance after it, that Mr. Trollope is thus conspicuous. At the last stage he is conspicuous only by his absence. He is never in at the death. As soon as there is any fear that the hounds will soon be running into the fox, Mr. Trollope draws his rein and turns aside, that his eyes may not be wounded by the ugly sight of the brief agony. He joins his less sensitive comrade, "only when there is no other ostensible evidence of the animal's destruction than a bit of fur hanging to the hound's mouth, or a bloody jaw." Mr. Trollope in short must draw the line somewhere, and he draws it "at a bloody jaw." Lord Sussex in *Kenilworth* goes a step further, and has no objection to hear "rib after rib crack." But that was only because such rib-cracking was "the bravest image of war which could be shown in peace." For the same cause he also enjoyed the sight of "blood and slaver" to which it seems that Mr. Trollope also does not object. In short, as Mr. Trollope says that the "horrid details" of a bull-bait did "harden the heart," so I must say that the "horrid details" of a fox-hunt, so graphically set forth by himself, have in some degree, no doubt in a far smaller degree, hardened Mr. Trollope's heart.'

In his second letter Freeman addresses himself mainly to the argument advanced by Mr. Trollope, that as many refined and educated men indulged in hunting

---

[1] Louis Napoleon Buonaparte in the Coup d'état, 1852.

and shooting, therefore these sports could not be such
very bad things. Freeman replied that of course this
was nothing to the purpose.

'If a thing can be shown to be wrong in itself, it makes no
difference whatever who does it. Still this kind of talk is just
the way to throw dust in people's eyes. Let us therefore
see what it all comes to. I am of course perfectly ready
to admit that a great many men whom I highly esteem do
hunt and shoot. And moreover though they do hunt and
shoot, they would, like Mr. Trollope, object to a bull-bait or
a show of gladiators as strongly as I do. That is to say, in
our age as in all ages, there are a great number of men who,
as they do not fall below the received standard of their
time, do not rise above it. They do what society allows and
approves, without going deep into the abstract right and wrong
of anything, and such men are not in any age to be harshly
condemned. In condemning modern fox-hunting I distinctly
refused in my original essay to condemn the modern fox-hunter.
I extend thus much of charity to the pursuits which I condemn,
but Mr. Trollope does not extend the same measure to the
pursuits which he condemns. Mr. Trollope says that the
spectators at a bull-bait were degraded. Now Mr. Trollope
has exactly as much and exactly as little right to say that
Windham was degraded by his bull-baits, as I have to say,
what I have not said, that Mr. Trollope is degraded by his fox-
hunting. I can hardly believe that "the statesmen, judges, and
senators of England" are as a rule men of keener intellect, of
more stainless honour, of more sensitive conscience, than the
"high-souled Windham." If the examples alleged by Mr.
Trollope prove anything in favour of fox-hunting, the example
of Windham proves just as much in favour of bull-baiting.
Like Mr. Trollope in the case of fox-hunting, he defended it on
principle, and on much the same grounds as those on which
Mr. Trollope defends fox-hunting. That the courtiers of
Queen Victoria hunt foxes, proves exactly as much as that the
courtiers of Queen Elizabeth baited bears, exactly as much as
that the courtiers of Titus and Trajan rejoiced in the combats
of gladiators and in the combats of lions and unarmed men.

That is to say, most men in all times act according to the standard of their own, the standard of Elizabeth being lower than the standard of Victoria, and the standard of Trajan being lower than the standard of Elizabeth; but this does not prove that the highest standard of the three is so high as it ought to be, or as at the same rate of improvement, it some day will be. In each age exactly the same defence might have been made for the favourite practice of that age, and in each age exactly the same defence was made. The same cry of "manly sport" was raised at all three periods. As far as example goes, there is as much to say for the manly sport of Trajan, as for the manly sport of Windham, and there is just as much to say for the manly sport of Windham as for the manly sport of Mr. Trollope[1]. . . Mr. Trollope's other subsidiary arguments are much of a piece with this notable argument from authority. He tells us, as all advocates of hunting tell us, that it has many incidental advantages, and he tells us that he hunts for the sake of these incidental advantages, and not for the sake of the mere worry of the fox. He says it, and I believe him. But again I had tried to meet this argument of incidental advantages in my first essay, page 379. Of course Mr. Trollope states the incidental advantages much better than I do, and he adds one that I should not have thought of, viz. the pleasures of conversation. This shows how tastes differ. I have heard of a lady being sent to the piano to promote conversation; but for a fox to be hunted down and torn in pieces to promote conversation is really beyond me. I should have thought that a cosy chat by the fireside, a quiet walk up a hillside, even a ride where no suffering animal was in front of the riders, was more likely to promote intellectual discourse, than the necessarily somewhat boisterous sights and sounds of a hunting field. Still I accept the fact, though I do not see what it proves. All this talk about incidental advantages is altogether off the point in a discussion

[1] When Freeman wrote his first article in the *Fortnightly* he was under the impression that Windham was accustomed to witness bull-baitings. He afterwards found that this was not the case, and that Windham was not even a fox-hunter. These facts, however, did not alter the position which Windham took up on the question, nor affect the force of the agument which Freeman based upon it.

on the morality of field sports. In a question of morality the
only point is whether it is right or wrong in itself, and if it be
wrong in itself, all the incidental advantages in the world
cannot make it right. This at least is my morality : that of
Mr. Trollope, who holds (page 625) that "the end justifies the
means" is doubtless different.'

As to another subsidiary argument, that more suffering
was inflicted on animals in other ways than by sport,
and by other persons than by sportsmen, it really came
to nothing better than the logical figure known as ' you're
another.' If sportsmen could prove cruelty against
other men, they proved them to be wrong, but they did
not prove themselves to be right. Somebody once said,
that when a man was charged with stealing a horse, it
would not improve his chance of acquittal if he could
prove that the judge had stolen two.

Since Freeman allowed that animals might be lawfully
killed, when there was any real need for their death,
Mr. Trollope asked a great many questions as to the
exact amount of need which justified putting an animal
to death. To this Freeman replied—

'I am not at all ashamed to say that in many cases it is not
easy to draw the line. There is exactly the same difficulty in
this case as there is in every other case, where virtue shades
off into vice. A man ought to be brave, but he ought not to be
foolhardy, he ought to be liberal, but he ought not to be
extravagant. Yet there are cases in which it would be hard to
say, whether a particular act was an act of bravery or an act
of foolhardiness, an act of liberality or an act of extravagance.
So in several of the cases put by Mr. Trollope, it would be
hard to say without knowing the exact circumstances of each
individual case, whether there was or was not real need to
justify the deaths of the animals. But none of the cases alleged
by Mr. Trollope at all touch the question of fox-hunting. He
puts the case of a lady's tippet, to provide which he says that

ten or twenty little animals are killed. I myself know nothing of the details of this matter, but I will take the fact on Mr. Trollope's authority. To kill an animal for clothing is quite as justifiable as to kill it for food. No sort of hunting stands less in need of apology than that described in the nursery rhyme :

> Baby, baby bunting,
> Daddy's gone a hunting,
> To fetch a little rabbit skin
> To wrap the little baby in.

This venerable poem seems to point to a primitive state of society, when there was no way of wrapping up the baby except by hunting a rabbit and fetching home its skin. But in such a state of things, no one can say that the hunting on which daddy went for that end was other than lawful and praise-worthy. Between this work of necessity and charity and the killing of ten or twenty little animals to make a lady's tippet, there is a wide gap—a field of debateable ground in which casuists may fairly dispute whether the undoubted necessity of the one form of hunting can be rightly extended to the other. But one thing is certain, that this question has nothing to do with the question of fox-hunting. Mr. Trollope does not say how the animals are killed, but he gives no reason to suppose that they suffer anything beyond simple death, or that the hunter derives any amusement from their deaths or sufferings. It is absolutely certain that the lady into whose tippet they are made does nothing of the kind. She stands in a very different position from the lady who looks on at the mortal agonies of a fox, and I suppose derives amusement from beholding them.'

There was one more argument which was so constantly put forward, that Freeman supposed it to be considered by the advocates of hunting as their specially strong and unanswerable point. This argument was, that the fox on the whole gained by being hunted. But for the practice of fox-hunting, the fox would long ago have been ex-terminated as well as the wolf. As it is, he is allowed to live and do as he pleases, his death without the prescribed circumstances of torture is held to be a crime worse than murder, only he enjoys all these advantages on condition of being tortured to death in the end.

'This argument,' said Freeman, ' I forestalled in my essay, pp. 369, 370, though doubtless I did not set it forth so graphically as the writer of bantering letters signed " Reynard," or " an old fox." The odd thing is, that this overwhelming argument on behalf of hunting seemed to me to be a strong incidental argument against it.'

It was monstrous, he said, that if a sheep was killed by a fox, the owner of the sheep must forego his natural right of killing the fox, and go to make his moan to the District Hunt Club.

' Mr. Trollope and his friends speak from the point of view of the fox, and tell us that he would willingly take his chance of being worried to death at last, on condition of enjoying the secure and merry life, which he alone of wild beasts is permitted to enjoy. When Mr. Trollope speaks on behalf of foxes, it reminds me of the days when American slaveholders were allowed an increased number of votes in the name of their slaves. Still it is possible that Mr. Trollope may know more of the inner mind of a fox than I do; I am certain that I know nothing. But we have really nothing to do with any balance of pain and pleasure, as weighed in the fox's mind. The fox is a noxious animal, which, like other noxious animals, we have a right to kill, but not a right to torture. He is, as far as we are concerned, a condemned criminal. He has the rights of a condemned criminal, and no others. These rights I take to be, that he may expect to be put out of the world speedily, and without mockery or needless pain. I can quite conceive that a man in the condemned cell might often be willing to take his chance of being hunted rather than be hanged at once. Still more willingly might two condemned criminals be ready to fight as gladiators, on condition that the survivor should be spared. A life would thus be spared, possibly in the one case, almost

certainly in the other, and the amusement of seeing the chase
or the fight might be given to those who like such things.
Still in either case, an act of justice would be changed into an
act of cruelty. So with the fox, the hunting code forbids him
to be killed when he ought to be killed, but thinks it noble and
manly to kill him after a brutal and lingering fashion. I have
not Mr. Trollope's gift of knowing the fox's thoughts, but as far
as I can guess at them, I should suspect them to be something
like the thoughts which Mr. Froude attributes to the Irish.
"Millions upon millions of Celts have been enabled to exist,
who, but for England, would never have been born, but those
millions, not wholly without justice, treasure up the bitter
memory of the wrongs of their ancestors." '

On a perusal of the whole controversy, no candid
person can, I think, fail to admit that Freeman remained
master of the field in argument. A victory in argument,
however, has but little immediate effect upon habits to
which large multitudes of people are inveterately attached. The love of sport is an instinct inherited from
the primitive ages, when hunting in some form was
a necessary and almost daily occupation, either for the
sake of procuring food, or of protecting life and property
from mischievous and savage beasts. The instinct is
not easily eradicated, and a practice which was a necessity
in barbarous times survives as a fashionable amusement
in civilized ages : and this amusement being the gratification of a natural instinct, and recommended by many
pleasant associations, is readily defended by many arguments which, however unsound, are sufficiently specious
to satisfy the reason and conscience of those who are
already strongly prejudiced in favour of it. On the
other hand, the principles which Freeman maintained
are not only sound in themselves, but are also in harmony
with that strong altruistic feeling which is one of the

most marked. and characteristic features of western
civilization; a feeling which has been the parent, especially
in recent times, of all kinds of benevolent and humane
institutions for relieving the sufferings, not only of
human beings, but also of the brute creation. And as
this feeling is continually gaining in strength, it does not
seem utterly improbable that in the course of time, such
forms of sport at least as stag-hunting, hare-hunting,
fox-hunting, and pigeon-shooting, will be condemned by
public opinion and cease to be practised.

And perhaps it is not beyond the bounds of possibility,
that in a still more distant future, the principle long ago
laid down by Wordsworth may be generally acknowledged and acted upon

> Never to blend our pleasure or our pride
> With sorrow of the meanest thing that feels[1].

Freeman, of course, received a great number of private
letters on the subject. Not a few of them, like many
of those which appeared in the public press, were abusive,
contemptuous, or derisive: but there were others in
which the writers owned that they had never thought
seriously on the subject before, and confessed that their
confidence in the morality of field sports was shaken, if
not shattered. Even some country gentlemen were
entirely converted to Freeman's view, and, although
admitting that they could not help deriving great
pleasure from hunting, doubted whether they could
henceforth conscientiously continue the practice.

The following is Freeman's reply to one who had
consulted him on this point.

----

[1] The two last lines in *Hartleap Well*, part ii.

To Captain Gillespey.

Somerleaze, January 14, 1870.
Dear Sir,

I feel much honoured by your letter, which is certainly the first case of my being applied to as a Ductor Dubitantium, or resolver of cases of conscience. If you have read my original article in the *Fortnightly Review*, out of which the controversy arose, you will remember that, while condemning hunting and all such amusements in the abstract, I distinctly refused to condemn this or that person who practises them. The wrongfulness of such pursuits seems to me to follow directly from certain principles which are commonly acknowledged among Christian and civilized men, but which many—perhaps most people—refuse, inconsistently as it seems to me, to apply to this particular case. Still, as it is only a matter of inference, and as the inference may not be so clear to every mind as it is to mine, I have no right to put the man who really and honestly thinks differently from me on a level with the man who breaks some distinct command either of the law of God or of the law of the land. As I believe the thing to be wrong, I believe there must be some amount of wrong, some perversion of the moral sense, in the man who fails to see that it is wrong, but further than this I have no right to say. But as soon as a man is convinced that the practice is wrong, or indeed so soon as he begins to doubt upon the subject, it is plainly his duty to give up the practice. Of the man who honestly feels no scruple, I decline to judge, but the man who does feel a scruple at once brings himself within the common rules of morality. If a man is in doubt whether it is his duty to leave the religious or political party in which he has been brought up, I hold that, while he is in the process of doubt, till his mind is thoroughly made up, he should stay where he is. It is his duty to take one side or the other, but he is uncertain which side it is his duty to take, and while the point is still uncertain, it is safer *for him* to stay where he finds himself. So with any other question, where it is a duty to act one way or the other, but where the path of duty is not clear. But the case of hunting—as at present practised—is different. It is no man's duty to hunt; the utmost that can be said for hunting is that it is an allowable amusement.

The man who hunts *may* be wrong in hunting; the man who abstains from hunting cannot be wrong in abstaining. Now it is a plain law of morals that we ought never to do a thing unless we are convinced that it is right. I hold, therefore, that the man who merely doubts on the subject ought to abstain from these pursuits. But if a man is positively convinced that these pursuits are wrong, his course is clearer still. It is his plain duty to abstain from them. Whatever the practice of them may be in the case of others, it becomes a plain sin in his case. This is clearly the stern rule of abstract morality 'Whatsoever is not of faith is sin.' At the same time it is not for me or for any man hastily to condemn those who may be led away, even against their better conviction, by habit or by strong temptation. No man is thoroughly consistent; no man is in every detail obedient to his conscience. The best man is he whose inconsistencies and disobediences are smallest. I do not take upon myself to judge you or any man, but as a question of right, nothing can be plainer to me than that it is *your* duty *in your frame of mind* to give up the practice of field sports altogether. May I take the liberty of adding how much I admire the honest and really manly spirit displayed in your letter? I have had many gratifying and encouraging letters since I began dealing with this controversy, but yours is the most gratifying and encouraging of all.

Of the three letters which follow, bearing upon this same subject, the first records the incident which seems to have first started the idea of writing the article in the *Fortnightly Review*. The last is a copy made by Freeman of a letter from Mr. John Stuart Mill. It is not stated to whom the original was addressed, but it reads as if it was written to the editor of the *Fortnightly*.

To F. H. DICKINSON, ESQ.

Somerleaze, May 3, 1869.

. . . About hunting hares, the Wells borough magistrates fined a boy for hunting a cat with dogs. The boy's father said it was hard that his son should be fined for hunting a cat, while gentlemen hunted hares. Now I don't see how you, or the Wells Harriers, or Sir Roger de Coverley, or the man whom Anselm rebuked, can answer that. I can't, but then I don't want to ; so some of you may try. I hold with Windham that he who disapproves of bull-baiting cannot defend fox-hunting, only I do not infer with Windham that it is right to torture bulls, but that it is wrong to torture foxes[1]. I know you think so in your heart, only you have a little bit of the *blue devil* hanging about you which makes you have coursings at Kenwarden.

I suppose I shall put my nose into Great Babylon[2] soon after Trinity Monday, and I will try and find you out.

To W. B. Dawkins, Esq.

November 1, 1869.

Many thanks for all your kindness in looking after Edgar, also for your hints about him, also for your lists of beasties, when they came in and went out. I have been a-judging of poachers this morning, and I wish, in the interests of morality and justice, that you could add Lepus cuniculus[3] (as well as Canis vulpes) to your extinct list. You may laugh; but I have converted one squire already, and I am getting much credit in divers quarters, from Mill downwards.

December 20, 1869.

I cannot too much congratulate you on such a paper as that of Mr. Freeman. I honour him for having broken ground against field sports, a thing I have been often tempted to do myself, but having so many unpopular causes already on my hands, thought it wiser not to provoke fresh hostility. He seems to have strongly coerced his habitually impetuous feelings and been studiously calm. It is a sign of the powerful effect he produces that the *Daily Telegraph* at once took up the cause with evident earnestness, though with timidity and reserve.

J. S. MILL.

[1] See above, p. 358.   [2] London.
[3] The rabbit.

GENERAL CORRESPONDENCE,

1867–1869.

To J. BRYCE, ESQ.

Somerleaze, February 3, 1867.

. . . Now about the evidence from history about democratic reform here. Of course, as you say, the Greek States afford no *exact* parallels, being, as you say, cities, often ruling cities, and what should not be forgotten, cities where everything depended on hereditary burghership, so that democracy did not necessarily imply the rule of a numerical majority. I don't count this as a merit, but the reverse; still it is a very important point of difference. Yet surely, with all this, you may still draw some very sound *general* inferences from the infinite superiority in life and vigour of every kind of the democratic states over the oligarchies and tyrannies. Then you have my Achaians, where the parallel, though still not exact, comes far nearer to it than that of Athens, as the Achaian Government must *practically* have come very near to a representative one—and that of Lykia nearer still. (N.B. I have written a book on this head, which might give people some hints, if they would condescend to read it.) They go on capitally *indoors*, and only failed before a power which they could not resist, and whose diplomacy was quite as dangerous as its arms.

As for Switzerland, of course the eternal democracies prove nothing; their virtue, I take it, is mainly in being eternal. But surely the modern constitutions, both of the Confederation and of the greater Cantons, prove a great deal. In some points Switzerland is a fairer comparison with England than America. as in other points America is a fairer comparison than Switzerland. Switzerland is, like England, an old country with a history, and, though its political history is not so unbroken as that of England, yet actual historical memories have perhaps greater influence. Again, in the establishment of democracy in the Confederation and in many of the Cantons, there were difficulties which we have not here. Here no class, no district, is actually the subject of any other class or district; a man has only to

acquire the requisite property, and his full political rights
cannot be denied him. But under the old League, the greater
part of the country had no political rights at all; cities ruled
over districts and over other cities, and the cities again were
often themselves ruled by hereditary oligarchies. And burghership and patricianship being hereditary, a man could not rise to
a higher political rank, except by special grant. (People are
misled by the words monarchy and republic; in truth we
are much nearer democracy than Switzerland—save in the
Urschweiz—was up to 1798 or even to 1830).

To sweep away all these hereditary distinctions was a much
stronger measure than any possible extension of the franchise
could be here. Yet it has answered completely, and the parts
of the country which were formerly subject do not in any way
lag behind, or show themselves less fitted for self-government
than their former masters. Then people are constantly saying
that in a democracy any stable government is impossible, that
Australian ministries change every week, and so forth. 'Jupiter'
said that no democracy ever did or could allow its executive to
remain in office a whole year. This sounded odd to me when
I read it just after being at the Landesgemeinde of Appenzell-
Out, when the late Landammann had fairly run away, as his
only way of escaping re-election. But it is odder still when one
thinks of these facts. The federal executive of Switzerland is
the Bundesrath, a council of seven. Every three years at the
beginning of each new diet, they come to an end, but are open
to re-election. This has gone on since 1848, giving six elections
since, at any of which the whole Bundesrath might have been
turned out of office. Instead of this (though of course several
changes have taken place through death and retirement), only
twice has a member of the Council who sought for re-election
failed to obtain it. At the election last year, one member
retired, two were opposed, but they were elected nevertheless.
Against the other four did not a dog move his tongue. Can
any monarchy show anything so stable? What ministry in
England or elsewhere has kept in for nineteen years? I am
not up enough in cantonal politics to say whether the cantonal
executives are equally stable. But the legislatures are, I believe,
invariably chosen by universal suffrage (unless when Jews have

been shut out and such like), and the general complaint seems to be that they are too conservative. In some Cantons the measures passed by the Legislature are submitted to a popular vote, a thing which I do not approve of, and I rejoice that the attempt to bring it into the federal constitution at the late *Bundesrevision* utterly failed[1]. It strikes me that the Swiss Federal Government is the most perfect specimen of parliamentary government anywhere. Reeve, Venables, and Co. would of course not understand this, as their only notion of parliamentary government is that which is much less parliamentary. But surely there is none where the Assembly exercises more direct power, and where the relations between legislative and executive are better.

To F. H. DICKINSON, ESQ.

Somerleaze, February 22, 1867.

. . . I don't think your arguments yesterday will do. An officer's orders to his soldiers, or a higher officer's orders to his subalterns, are like those of any other person in any sort of authority. The clergy are bound to obey their bishop, the police are bound to obey Goold, my children and servants are bound to obey me, the Scholars of Trinity are bound to obey Wayte, in all lawful commands coming within the measure of the superior's lawful authority—*but no further*. If Bishop, President, Chief Constable, orders them to do anything unlawful, say to put men to death by an illegal court, they must refuse, as the superior's command will not justify the illegal act. So a subaltern ordered to try and hang Gordon by ' court martial ' ought to have refused, and his superior officer's command is no justification[2].

The analogy of all the cases is exact. In the civil and ecclesiastical cases everybody would admit it, only in the military cases people's ideas get confused.

Firstly, because the soldiers have physical force on their side, and can murder people more easily than the others.

[1] It has since been accomplished.
[2] The reference is to the notorious case of Governor Eyre in the West Indies, who ordered a black man named Gordon to be hung, after a kind of mock ' court martial,' on very doubtful evidence.

Secondly, because they have on their side a silly public opinion, which falls in love with red coats and queer-shaped hats.

Cannot the Court of Queen's Bench restrain a military court transcending its jurisdiction, just as it can an ecclesiastical court? I suppose the difficulty would be that before the rule could be granted, the man would be murdered. Truly 'their feet are swift to shed blood ; destruction and unhappiness is in their ways,' and all other such like things as are written in the Law and the Prophets.

To J. BRYCE, ESQ.

Somerleaze, February 24, 1867.

. . . As for the rich, I conceive that save merchants at Basel and such like, Schweiz has hardly any people whom we should count rich. Aristocrats, or rather ex-aristocrats, abound, but they are mainly poor, having lost their two great sources of revenue, Condottieriship and Verres-ship. From all I can hear, they have no real grievances. Wherever, as at Zürich, they have frankly accepted the new state of things, and have gone in and taken their chance with other folk, they have got their share like other folk. At Bern for a long time they were sulky and held aloof from public affairs ; more fools they, as in many parts of the Canton they were distinctly popular, and would have been preferred to other candidates. Most of my friends are naturally democrats, but I saw some of the other sort at Chur, and specially at Welsh-Newcastle [1].

One man, James de Meuron, patrician, but who talked fairly and sensibly, told me that, just after the Revolution, there was an ugly rush of βάναυσοι καὶ ἀγοραῖοι [2] (vide Polybius or me), but that things had righted themselves, and that all sorts got into the Assembly, only too many lawyers, a fault not confined to Welsh-Newcastle. Then I stayed a night with the Baron de Büren, a charming old man, but who wanted the king of Prussia back again. The only intelligible grievance I could make out was that he had been compelled to sell some tithes. If he got a fair price, I don't see great harm. I should like to see all

[1] Neuchâtel in Switzerland.
[2] Artisans and market folk.

rights of one man over the land of another redeemed in the same way. On the other hand, he seemed to be in exactly the position of an English squire, people capping him and calling him 'M. le Baron.' He was, by election, President of the Communal Council, and his son was a member of the Legislature of the Canton. So I really did not see that his hardships were very great. He dwelleth in a real castle, Vauxmarcus to wit, whose name you will find among the doings of Charles the Bold.

The Federal Government seems to me as good a Government as can be, and I fancy people in general are well satisfied. What I don't like is the practice of carrying appeals to the Bundesrath, and thence to the Assembly, which ought to go to the Federal Court. 'Tis not business for the Government or the Parliament. Still I have read several of the causes, and they seem to be dealt with fairly and dispassionately, though, of course, I don't profess to judge points of Swiss law. In this and that Canton there are heaps of things to reform, mainly owing to the constitution of the *Gemeinden*, hereditary burghership not easily conferred, &c. So, if you live out of your own Canton (or even in your own Canton, but out of your own parish), you have a vote in Federal and Cantonal elections; but none in Communal as being μέτοικος[1].

I hope you will make something of all this. I have such a heap of histories, articles, letters round me that I have really no time to make it shorter.

To Dean Hook.

Somerleaze, April 7, 1867.

. . . I see a formula of making one Herbert, Dean of *Her Majesty's Cathedral Church* of Hereford. In what sense is it Her Majesty's church? I can think of none save that in which I am writing in Her Majesty's Library, viz. the Norman fiction of all land being held of the Crown. The freehold is most likely in the Dean and Chapter, the *cathedralitas*, if I may make a word, in the Bishop; the final cause, so to speak, in the whole folk of the diocese. What room then for Her Majesty?

---

[1] A resident alien, without civic rights.

And is not the form a new one? Did it not come in with
Ripon? It was certainly in a Ripon case that I first marked it.
Now 'Her Majesty's *Collegiate* Church of Ripon' being a royal
foundation, was sense when Ripon got a Bishop; did they not
substitute the word *Cathedral* and then extend the form to other
places?

The five letters which follow were written during
a tour in Normandy on which he was accompanied, first
by Mr. Sidney Owen, Student of Christ Church, Oxford,
and afterwards by Mr. J. R. Green, who joined him at
Caen on May 7.

To Dean Hook.

Coutances, April 25, 1867.

. . . Don't say I *accuse* you of being a controversialist, because
I do not look on it as accusation. I only state it as a fact,
which cannot fail to make a certain difference between your
way of looking at history, and my own, for instance. As
a controversialist, you have a constant temptation to see everything in the light of modern controversy, a temptation to which
I think you yielded in your lives of Lanfranc and Anselm, but
which you manfully resisted in the life of Thomas. Of course,
I have my temptations too of some other kind. If your correspondent be Rose, what he means by ignoring Christianity is
probably that I don't go in roaring for or against the Pope,
or the Culdees, or the early British Church founded by Saint
Paul, or something else which has nothing to do with my
subject.

April 26. I wrote this much at Coutances, and I go on at
Dol with somewhat better ink, though, to confess the truth, the
other was of my own spoiling, as I had put in *too much water*.
I don't know whether you know this country. This is the
place to which, if you like to believe it, the last Archbishop
of St. David's ran away, and left his pallium[1]. It has now

---

[1] The story is told by Giraldus Cambrensis of an Archbishop Sampson,
but it is very doubtful, and the Archiepiscopate of St. David's is altogether
mythical. See *Hist. of St. David's*, by Jones and Freeman, 263, 264.

ceased to be a bishop's see altogether, and the cathedral has
sunk into a parish church. This seems, however, not to make
the same difference here that it does in England. We were
at Bayeux on Easter Day; the services were magnificently
done—'rendered,' I suppose I should say—and Owen and
I believe that we were made Honorary Canons, seeing we
were caught up and set above other folk, not altogether in
the choir, but next door to it. I have now to run about by
myself a bit, but I trust that Johnny Green will meet me on
Thursday.

April 27. I am now at Dinan, as far as I mean to go in this
direction, because it is, as far as I know, the limit of Harold's
journey with William. I am journeying now, as I daresay
I have told you, to store my mind for the Norman part of my
second volume.

. . . You have found me out about the sixteenth century.
I fancy that, from endlessly belabouring Froude, I get credit for
knowing more of those times than I do. But one can belabour
Froude on a very small amount of knowledge, and you are
quite right when you say that I have 'never thrown the whole
force of my mind on that portion of history.' But I don't know
why I should be 'irate' and 'violent' when I read your history.
I confess to a certain inclination to the Popish side (the result,
perhaps, of being nourished by Sir Thomas Pope [1]), or rather
not [so much] to the Popish side pure and simple, as to Henry's
religion, Popery without a Pope; but I suppose it would not do,
and that it was necessary to be either bat or bird. I somehow
contrive to reconcile this with a very distinct horror of Henry's
wife-killing, abbey-smashing, &c. Of course, the monks wanted
greatly reducing in numbers and wealth; but that was no
reason for making Glastonbury into a factory, and hanging
Whiting.

It is very odd, in visiting monastic remains in France, to find
so much late work, as I did to-day in the Priory of Lehon near
here. Church and refectory beautiful thirteenth century work,
but cloister modern. It wants an effort to bear in mind that
there were real live Abbots down to 1789, though to be sure
I should not talk, who have seen Einsiedlen and St. Maurice.

[1] The founder of Trinity College, Oxford.

They seem to have had a great fancy for rebuilding all the domestic buildings at the beginning of the last century ; witness the buildings, not unlike the new part of Magdalen, attached to St. Ouen's and to St. Stephen's at Caen.

To the Same.

Undated fragment.

. . . Pray have mercy on Stephen Gardiner, for whom I have a lurking respect, perhaps because Sir Thomas Pope made the Bishop of Winchester our Visitor specially that we might be under his care. Johnny Green would plead for Bonner, in whose road he lives. (I want Johnny to set to on Henry Fitz-Empress, to be able to follow my Conquest straight off.) I find I have a reputation with some people for knowing the sixteenth century, of which I am profoundly ignorant. Of the tenth and eleventh centuries A. D., and the third and second B. C., I believe I do know something.

To W. B. Dawkins, Esq.

Dol, April 29, 1867.

I fell in with some of your folk this morning, to wit, Lubbock, Huxley, and one whom I think they called Hooker. They had been crom-stalking[1] here in the Lesser Britain, and I fell in with them at Dinan. They marvelled at my not going further, but I pleaded that, according to the tapestry, Dinan seemed to be the furthest point reached by William and Harold. N.B. I gathered from their talk that they knew me to be somebody, but I inferred that they knew nothing of *Norman Conquest*, vol. i. You had better amend that blindness. I was rather amused at Huxley asking me very simply whether I had read Thierry, and what I thought of it. I suppose this is much as if I should ask him whether he had read Buckland's *Reliquiae Diluvianae*, and what he thought of it. Howbeit they were all very jolly, and I ought to have known Lubbock, but it was he who recognized me, though he utterly puzzled me at first by asking whether I were a 'relation of Mr. Freeman.' Huxley took home a book and review for me to *Saturday Review*. Have

---

[1] Hunting for cromlechs.

you been doing anything more in that way? Our Johnnikin
seems getting on mightily. I trust he will join me at Cherbourg
on Thursday evening. I shall then have been a week by
myself, Owen having left me last Thursday. To return to our
philosophers, Huxley pronounced you to be 'heretical' in the
matter of Iskimos, whereon I could not judge either way.
But they told me also that you had become F.R.S., whereat
I rejoice, as I believe you wished so to be; as for me, I have
never craved to be a Fellow of anything since I ceased to be
Fellow of Trinity.

I have had a long pull to-day, getting up about four and
walking out to Mount Dol before breakfast, then coming hither
by diligences, not 'summâ diligentiâ,' as I have tried the ban-
quette, but like the coupé better. I suspect you would have
caught some geology to-day. From Bayeux to Coutances, and
again from Granville right into Britanny, the country is really
very like England, rich pasture-fields, with hedges, trees, &c., but
on the high ground like Coutances and Granville 'tis more like
other parts of France ('tis beastly to have to call Normandy
and Britanny France), no hedges, few trees, land rather dreary,
and oxen drawing, i. e. a horse in the shafts and an ox in front.
As a rule, horses draw in Normandy; south of Loire, oxen,
cows, all of them. There must be some reason for all this.
I fell thinking about stone, because Dol Cathedral is built of
granite, which makes a sensible difference in the architecture.
Why do Celts stay in stony places? On Mount Dol to-day
I could quite have believed I was in our own Bretland. There
is a tower crowned by a big image on the top, which at first
I took for some local bird, and lo! it proved to be Nôtre Dame
de l'Espérance!!

I hope you will be able to meet me at Senlac. I can't tell
exactly when we shall come over, least of all till Johnny has
met me, but I will write again when I can say anything more
certain.

. . . And I want you to come north to the Kingston-on-Hull
meeting, to work up Fulford and Stamford-bridge. I hope to
do Val-ès-Dunes and Mortemer now with Johnny. I am off
again decently early to-morrow to see Lessay Abbey, and so
make my way about to Carentan, where I shall be again on the

railway, and shall go on to Cherbourg for Johnny. I shall not
be quite comfortable till I have actually got him safe and sound.

To Miss Katharine Freeman.

Coutances, April 30, 1867.

'Tis your turn now for a letter, so I will tell you how hard
I have been at work just lately. I finished a letter to your
mother at Dinan on Sunday. I got up and drew churches
yesterday morning, and at breakfast in came three Englishmen,
none of whom I knew at all, but one of whom presently knew
me. He proved to be Sir John Lubbock, whom I think your
mother will remember once coming over with Mr. Dawkins.
With him were Professor Huxley, whose name some of you
will perhaps know, and another philosopher named Hooker.
I was pleased enough to meet them, though generally I don't
care to meet Englishmen when I am in foreign parts. When
they were gone I drew some more, then went back by my little
malle-poste to Dol, and walked out perhaps a mile and a-half
to see a big stone, a *dolmen*. How long it has been there
nobody can tell, long before *my time* anyhow. On the top
is now fixed a large crucifix, as if to triumph over the old
heathen stone. Then I drew a little more at the Cathedral,
where I had been at work on Friday, then dined or rather
supped—they call it 'un repas' in the bill, which will do for either
—wrote a letter and a-half, touched up a drawing *on the block*,
went to bed, got up before it was light and walked out about
two miles to Mount Dol, and back to 6.15 breakfast. Mount
Dol is a rocky hill, whence in fine weather is a very fine view,
as I do not doubt there would have been later in the day to-day,
but it was misty with a little rain in the morning. However,
'tis a fine rugged spot anyhow. Then after breakfast I got into
the diligence, and came right away to Granville (look at the
top). There I had to stay an hour and more, so I looked about
and drew, and then came on hither by another diligence.

. . . You will sympathize with me when there got in a priest
who would shut up all the windows during the hottest part
of the day. He said he had a bad tooth-ache, so I consented to
him out of pure Christian charity, and so got a head-ache,
which I believe was worse than his tooth-ache, as he managed

to chatter away merrily to a devout woman on the other side, while I got far too stupid from stuffiness to have talked to anybody. But I got plenty of air, sea-breeze, between Granville and Coutances.

To J. Bryce, Esq.

Hôtel Ste. Barbe, Caen, May 6, 1867.

. . . I have lost a good deal of time on this journey, mainly from Johnny Green not coming at the time appointed, which caused me to loiter about a good deal, both at Cherbourg and here. However, he (May 8) is come at last, and I took him to-day to Bayeux to see the installation of a new bishop, which is certainly a mighty fine sight.

. . . I am more and more convinced of the extreme folly of the people here in talking French. Why on earth did they forget their natural Danish, to say nothing of the still earlier Saxon? It seems so absolutely ridiculous to hear the Gal-Welsh jabber coming out of the fine Dutch carcases of so many of our Normans hereabout.

To Miss Florence Freeman.

Caen, May 10, 1867.

. . . On Wednesday we went, as I had intended, to Bayeux to the installation of the new bishop. It was a wonderful sight; such processions, not only of the clergy, but of almost everybody, the magistrates and lawyers, soldiers of various kinds— the sappers with axes on their shoulders, looking as if they had just come out of Harold Blaatand's ships, boys and girls of schools with their banners, gardeners, and what not. The Bishop walked in procession through the town from one of the other churches to the cathedral—a canopy being carried over his head. Then at the great door he stopped and took oaths, then entered the church and took his place on his throne in the choir. (Rouen, May 12.) Then all the clergy went up to him in the choir and, I suppose, sware oaths to him and became his men, but we were too far off to see that. Then we went to the library and saw the tapestry yet again, and I made my companion[1] swear oaths to me and become my man for the whole

[1] J. R. Green.

space of this journey. M. Puiseux and his wife were at Bayeux also, and I had a good deal of talk with him over the tapestry. Then in the evening we went back to Caen. Next day, Thursday, we went over the field of Val-ès-Dunes, where Duke William, with Henry, King of the French, to back him, won his great victory over his rebellious barons[1]. It is a rather dull kind of site, but I wanted to see what it was like. On Friday we went to Séez and saw the cathedral, and on to Alençon—there it was that they hung out skins and shouted 'peau,' when William besieged them; because his mother was a tanner's daughter[2]. Yesterday we left Caen altogether and came hither, stopping at Brionne (where there are remains of a Norman castle), and then on to Bec. The abbey stands in a lovely valley, with wooded hills on each side—not wild like Llanthony (your mother will remember), but rich. There is very little left of the church, but the detached tower is perfect. The abbey buildings, all very modern, are made into a place for cavalry. (N.B. I forgot to say that at Alençon I saw a bear led along the street.) We got here quite late last night; to-morrow (if it does not rain as it does now) we think of going to Château-Gaillard, Richard Lion-Heart's castle, and perhaps to Mantes, where William caught his death.

To J. Bryce, Esq.

Somerleaze, June 9, 1867.

Let me set before you my geography and chronology for some time to come, as far as I know it. My mode of life may be called, *Norman Conquest*, tempered by Trinity Monday and Quarter Sessions.

1st. On Friday next, my wife, Margaret, and I, are coming up to Oxford to tarry with *the President*. So we shall anyhow meet on Trinity Monday, and I trust you will have viva voce going on, as Margaret is anxious to contemplate you in your blue hood.

2nd. On or about Friday, the 21st, we go on to London for divers causes. This makes Roundell and Co.'s coming on the 23rd a blow, whereon I am writing to him. On the 24th I have to

---

[1] See *Norman Conquest*, ii. 256-267
[2] Ib. ii. 291-298.

preach ; on the 29th to dine, as I trust you will also ; also on
some unfixed day to go to Lunacy Commissioners about a new
chapel for our asylum.

3rd. July 1 I must go back, not exactly home, but to Taunton
to Sessions, to strive lest the Sumorsaetas be made to imitate

'Uno contentam carcere Romam[1],'

(vide *History of the Norman Conquest*, pp. 49, 50[2], which arose
wholly out of Quarter Sessions debates). Thence I want to run
to Porlock, to look at the site of Harold's landing in 1052—then
home.

4th. I take the advantage of the two archaeological meetings
at Hull and Hereford to work up Harold's Northumbrian and
Welsh campaigns. I shall leave home towards the end of July
and come back about the middle of August.

5th. It is quite possible that I may have to go into Normandy
(and Maine) again before the year is out, at any rate before
vol. ii. is finished.

Now you will see that for me geographically it would be very
convenient to go and see my Kent and Sussex places between
June 24 and 29, as I shall be in London, nearer to them than
I am likely to be for some time. On the other hand, it would
suit the composition of the book better to get rid of Wales,
Normandy, and Northumberland, before I touch Kent and
Sussex, as coming later. But I value more than either to get
you, Green, and Dawkins, or as many of you three as may be,
to come with me. And it is not irreverent to you other two to
say that Dawkins is *pro hâc vice*, the most valuable, as he can
put me up to divers things about ground, which I don't understand myself, and specially about the coast-line at Pevensey,
which I am given to understand has changed a good deal since
my time. So I am inclined to go whenever it may best suit
a majority of you three. Green said he would see you and talk
about it. I should like, if I could find such an animal, to talk to
an intelligent soldier on the hill itself. I had some thoughts of
asking General Lefroy, if I chance to come across him. Though
a soldier, he has brains.

[1] 'Rome content with one prison.' There was a proposal to have
only one gaol for Somerset.
[2] Vol. i.

To W. B. Dawkins, Esq.

Somerleaze, July 7, 1867.

Do you know anything about the changes of the coast at Porlock? How is it likely to have stood in 1052? They told us there that the sea had come in a good deal within memory, and they get up the wood of the ' submarine forest,' marked in the ordnance map. Was that forest land in 1052? On the other hand, the coast looks much as if the sea had some time come in further, but that may have been before the time of Harold or of the flint folk either. Pray tell me as soon as you can, as I want to make a flourish about Harold's landing [1].

To the Same.

Somerleaze, July 14, 1867.

Pray don't write to me 'all you know' about 'alluvia, &c., &c.,' which would be simply overwhelming, but do tell me, in your

character of geologist to *Norman Conquest*, enough to enable me to draw a picture of Porlock as it stood in 1052. *Where* did Harold land? By the present weir or pier? Or could he then get up to the present town? There are fairly old houses—

[1] See *Norman Conquest*, ii. 314–316.

sixteenth century, perhaps—close to the present pier, so that spot has been land for a good while.

Your postscript suggests to me the most amazing picture. ' Harold sailed over those trees, and I found mammoth remains under them.'

The bones I was most eager to find were those of the thirty thegns[1], but I missed them.

To THE SAME.

Barnburgh (perhaps Brunanburh), July 25, 1867.

I am here in Northumberland, on my way to Stamford-bridge, Kingston-on-Hull, &c., &c., tarrying with Dimock. Johnny Green is coming to Hull—I wish you were also—you will doubtless be at Bristol and come and see us before or after.

I gather then that Harold may have sailed up to the present town (or village) of Porlock, but that it would not be safe to say so, but that he certainly landed within the two horns of the bay. I came yesterday by a train from Bristol to Derby, which I take it went slower than his march to Tadcaster, though I doubt his keeping up with the train by which I flew from Derby to Chesterfield. I have written all the Northumbrian campaign, subject to what new light I may get on the spot, and I am going to spout it at Hull.

To DEAN HOOK.

Somerleaze, September 3, 1867.

I believe it is I who have been an undutiful dog in not having written to you all this time. It is not from lack of thinking of you, as I missed you mightily at Hull[2], as well as Willis, Stubbs, Guest, and divers other good people who did not appear. The absence of you and Stubbs I specially smoked at (the Welsh-talkers would say *fumed*, but I stick to my natural English, which I find used about the time of the blessed Reformation),

---

[1] Harold's landing at Porlock was opposed by the people of that district, under the leadership of thirty thegns, who were slain in the fight with Harold and his followers. *Norman Conquest*, ii. 316.

[2] At the meeting of the Royal Archaeological Society there.

seeing I trusted you would both feel a call to revisit your old haunts north of Humber. Stubbs, indeed, though he would not come to Hull, was minded to go to the parts of Ripon. I hope he will come here soon. I wrote my mind about the Hull meeting in the *Saturday Review*, so I won't trouble you with it again. From Hull I went to Lincoln, to pay a long promised visit to Praecentor (you taught me the spelling) Venables, who, when I had got there, presently turned me out to make way for his wife's sister. Wives' sisters are a mystery to me, why people make such a fuss about marrying or not marrying them. I can't see why a man should not, if he is fool enough, but I can't fancy any man wanting to do it.

At Lincoln I saw somewhat of the minster, but none of the two early churches down below, which more immediately concern me. I met the Bishop and the new Dean of Chester, who is very jolly. I also went out to pay my respects to Earl Leofric's handiwork at Stow, but they have been a-restoring of it, so I found it less easy to make out than I had hoped. From Lincoln I went right across to Worcester, then plunged into the hills (such a comfort to see hills, after Holderness and even Lindesey), and paid a short visit to my old friend, Isaac Gregory Smith (sometime 'dilectissimus scholaris meus' at Trinity), at Tedstone Delamere, where he has rebuilt a church so small that the choir barely holds him, and has put out a book on faith and philosophy. Thence to Hereford, to the Cambrian meeting, whereof I also spoke in the *Saturday Review*. It was the week before the fiddling. I call it a beastly desecration, not because of the music, but because of taking money, hired singers, and general tomfoolery, in a word, turning a church into a playhouse. All the talk about the excellence of music does not meet my objections, and it is more ridiculous still when — goes and preaches about the 'antiquity' of a custom which began in some dark time in the last century. From Hereford I came home, *slept* a week, for I really did little else, then went to the meeting of our own local society at Bristol, paid visits at the mediaeval houses, Congresbury Vicarage and Clevedon Court, and then came home to stay quiet, I hope, for a good bit.

Both at Hull and at Hereford I read out such parts of my

second volume as were appropriate to the places, to wit, Stamford-bridge at Hull and Harold's Welsh wars at Hereford. But I don't think that anybody but Lord Talbot and Johnny Green knew that there was such a thing as the *History of the Norman Conquest* a-making. A Hereford paper said that ' Mr. Freeman read extracts from a work which he is *compiling*' —what a word! The result of this is that I have several parts written in advance, forming in truth a large part of the reigns of Eadward and Harold. But what I am now regularly at work on is the early reign of William in Normandy. It has its interests, and the more so as I have seen most of the places which I have to talk about, but my heart does not go forth towards it as it does towards our own people and our own subjects. At Stamford-bridge, as you may guess, I was quite at home.

. . . Last week I have been working at the early life of Lanfranc, and have therefore been comparing your life of him with the authorities. It is a very great puzzle why he left Pavia for Normandy. Your notion about his wife and son you of course propose only as a guess, which can neither be proved nor disproved. But if Paul had been a legitimate son, born of an avowed marriage before ordination, would he have been spoken of darkly as 'nepos, vel, ut quidam autumant, filius '? Again, I don't think the use of the word 'exsilium' at all implies that Lanfranc was driven from Pavia by political disturbances.

To F. H. Dickinson, Esq.

Somerleaze, October 25, 1867.

I rather like your notion of holding the county elections in some place not a town. It would make it more of a real Scir-gemót. The two or three county elections I have seen elsewhere seemed to me rather a humbug, men professing to talk to the δῆμος [1] of the shire, while they were really talking to the ὄχλος [2] of Northampton or Dursley. For the boundaries of the divisions, I confess to a lingering weakness for the frontiers of Ceawlin and Cenwalh, which seem to represent north (surely it should be north, and not east) pretty fairly. They might take

---

[1] People.   [2] Mob.

Mendip—only what point of Mendip?—instead of Axe. I fancy that a swamp was then the greater barrier, as a hill is now. My only quarrel with Ceawlin is that he makes us here Welshmen.

If I had had a horse and had not had things to do in Wells, I think I should have gone to Axbridge to the Scirgemót for choosing a Crowner. I have never seen the ceremony, which I take to be as old as the great founder of Crowners[1], and therefore a thing one ought to see.

. . . Would it not be much better if justices' clerks were paid by salaries? I am sure there is dodging about fees here which I don't understand. I see there is a permissive power. Why not act upon it? Of course I don't mean to let all the world summon all the rest of the world for nothing, but treat the fees like *Lovell's*[2]. N.B. I delivered myself the other day of this doctrine, that everybody was underpaid, save Lovell and the Prince of Wales. Do you agree? I mean, of course, of people who should be paid at all—there are many whom I should send away altogether, like Heads of Houses, Clerks of the Closet, and courtiers generally.

To Dean Hook.

Kingston-upon-Hull, December 4, 1867.

I sent a very scrubby answer to your last long letter, which, however, I have been treasuring up ever since, and which I have carried off specially to answer more decently while I am in these northern parts of the world. I have come here by request, to make a talk to the good folk here in honour of their founder, King Edward of famous memory. I could not well refuse to come, as they were very civil to me in the summer, and they certainly gave me a very good hearing last night. I think I must have had fully ten hearers for every one I get at Bristol—a large theatre all but full, and that though divers were kept away by the weather—all the municipal swells present, who at Bristol certainly never care to come near one.

---

[1] He probably means Henry II, but see Stubbs, *Constit. History*, i. 505, 506.

[2] Clerk of the Peace for Somerset.

Am I to infer that the mixed race of Hwiccas and Sumorsaetas has less go in it (to be sure *Field Flowers Goe*—called by his more intimate friends 'All Flesh is Grass'—is one of the local clergy here) than the Danes up here? Mercian by birth and West-Saxon by choice, I don't like the notion. I go on from hence to Bishopthorpe—to the Archdeacon, not the Archbishop. I have to preach at Eoforwic [1] on Stamford-bridge (December 5). I have to have another look at S. B. to-morrow, and on Saturday go to Eoforwic viâ Scarborough, to see where Harold Hardrada threw down the burning timbers.

Till I came away hither, I have been chiefly quietly at home, working away at *Norman Conquest.* I was a few days at Butleigh, where I met Hope, and I went to Bristol to lecture ; otherwise I have been almost wholly engaged with Harold— Godwine's sunu I mean, not Eadwardes sunu. I have persuaded the Delegates to let me expand my book to five volumes instead of three, which will enable me to do justice to the great central portion of my subject, which would otherwise have been quite hopeless. I have thus done vol. ii. which contains the reign of Eadward, and it is gone to the Press.

And now let me congratulate you heartily on the finishing (Bishopthorpe Vicarage, December 8) of your great work at Chichester [2]. It would never have done for me to come to it in the flesh, just occupied as I was with writing ; but I (December 11) did not forget you and I have heard about it from more people than one, i. e. Venables (Praecentor) and Sir S. Glynne. I shall come and see it and you (if you are in the way) at the proper time for finally getting up the South-Saxon and Kentish parts ; but I must go to Le Mans first. All things now are ruled by the book. My coming here has given me a sight of Scarborough, and another sight of Stamford-bridge, and to-morrow I hope to get to Tadcaster, another of my sites.

I made my York preachment to-night, that is, I read out

[1] York.
[2] The restoration of the central tower and spire of the Cathedral Church which had fallen in 1861. They were rebuilt at a cost of £60,000.

my account of Harold Hardrada's invasion, ending with
Stamford-bridge. It went off well, as far as I could judge; not
so many hearers as at Hull, for the room will not hold so
many, but it was well filled. But none of the clerical swells
were there, save my host Jones. Kaine, whom I met last
night, was a-dining somewhere. I wonder whether my
Northumbrian audience was scandalized at my saying that
York did not hold out like London and Exeter; but I would
not leave out anything to flatter them. Roman walls ought to
have held out more than four days.

Oxford, December 14. I will really make an effort, and try
and finish this nomad letter; but I think you will allow that
this style of writing at least shows that I have you pretty constantly in my thoughts. I think Jones and I have been talking
more about deans and canons than anything else. Thomson
and his babies are of course veiled in a sort of mysterious
primatial awe; to my mediaeval notions an Archbishop's baby
is a somewhat grotesque object, specially when the nursery
supplants the roof of a thirteenth century chapel.

. . . I have been reading over again your last letter, which,
to my undying shame, bears date September 24. I know
I have scribbled something to you since, but nothing that
(December 15) was good for anything. I like, and I think
I take in, your distinction of writing up to a thing and writing
down to it; only you see it lays a terrible burthen on me when
I have to review your Reformation volumes, which I suppose
I shall have to do as well as the rest. I have not seen your
last volumes yet, and I do not know whether they are out;
maybe I shall find them when I get home. You say you
began your work in 1821, two years before I was born—that
makes me feel young—generally now I am reminded in all
manner of ways how old I am, which otherwise I am apt to
forget. I feel very much what you say about being criticized
by people who really do not understand one's work. I have
had nothing to complain of in the tone of the notices of me
now (except perhaps *Spectator*), but nearly all have been so
thoroughly weak. I suppose they are what Macmillan calls
'commercially valuable'; otherwise, as far as my own personal
feeling goes, it is less nauseous to be abused by fools than to

be praised by them. I also am particularly amused at the kind of commotion which seems to be caused by my writing Eadward and Ælfred—how would they have me write Eadric and Ælfhelm?—they all speak exactly as if I had been the first person who ever did so, which lets one into the fact that people think themselves fit to review such a book as mine who have not read Kemble or Lappenberg. I hope you will not have to talk of me in this way. You speak of my avowing my articles; I can't well help it, as I am always found out, except that now that Johnny Green writes much in the 'Reviler,' I fancy that many of his things are pretty generally fathered upon me. You say you don't refute or criticize any who have written before—I can't help doing it sometimes. 'Tis best done in an appendix; I am, in correcting vol. ii., throwing large parts of the notes and somewhat of the text into that form.

How people do talk. I don't see that I am, as examiner, lenient or fierce, or anything but simply just. I don't believe the coaches know what sort of questions I should set; but I know very well the sort of tips the coaches give the men, and what blunders they put them (December 18) up to. When a string of men, one after the other, all tell you that Thomas of London went to the Pope at Avignon, you know that the blunder is not their own, but that they have been put up to it by some blind leader of the blind. As for plucking, if I slew my thousands, Bryce has slain his tens of thousands—thirty a day and fourteen plucked—see the doings of Boase, Burrows, and their colleague, one Ramsay.

. . . I can't tell a bit what you mean by my being so narrow-minded as not to tolerate those who throw their intellectual power into a different line from mine. Ask Dawkins, my palaeontologist, whether it be so. I don't know what you mean about 'Musical Science'—is music a science?—as I am not aware that I ever said anything about it. But about meta-physicians I have somewhat to say, quite irrespective of the Mansel job. That has nothing to do with the merits of metaphysical study.

. . . I allow that I don't worship the metaphysical people. And why? Because I suspect them of being humbugs. I know quite well that Phillips and Brodie and Rolleston and Henry

Smith know a heap of facts which I don't, and I respect them agreeably. I only ask that, as I know a heap of facts which they don't, they should respect me back again. But I am not at all convinced that Mansel and that lot know anything that I don't. They seem to me to simply bamboozle one with hard words. If Dawkins tells me that the bones of the ichthyosaurus are found only in this or that stratum, the idea that it gives me is, through my ignorance of the subject, a very vague one ; but it gives me some idea ; the words clearly have a meaning; but when a man says that 'marriage is love founded on right and developed into rightfulness,' or that 'children are the objective expression of their parents' existence,' I am not clear that the words have any meaning at all. They seem to me to be pure gibberish, which would be just as much to the purpose if you read it backwards. I can understand that hydrogen and oxygen are something, though I don't know what, but I am not clear that the objective and the absolute and the ill-conditioned are anything at all.

To F. H. DICKINSON, ESQ.

Somerleaze, April 10, 1868.

This is too bad. I know you love pitching into a Government office, and here is a fine opportunity. When a letter of mine, without the word Somerset, goes to Wells of the East Angles, I hold my peace, but when it goes to Tunbridge Wells (why not Sadlers Wells ?), I kick up a row, or even create a rumpus. But I did not expect it would ever happen to a letter posted within the bounds of the Sumorsaetas. It proves, I will not say the 'mira simplicitas et innocentia,' but rather the 'stoliditas et desidia[1]'—I quote *Ann. Wint.*[2] and Saxo—of the folk of 'such out-of-the-way places as Taunton and Wellington' —I quote Rogers.

Don't tell Sinkins, but it came into my head that one of my arguments for eating horse-flesh would in a slave-holding country equally defend eating men's flesh. Such a practice would clearly tend to the kind treatment of weak and aged

[1] Stupidity and sloth.
[2] *Annales de Wintonia.* 'Rex Edwardus erat mirae simplicitatis et innocentiae.'

slaves. If Sinkins pressed this, I should say 'How wicked
then is slavery, which needs cannibalism to temper it.'

To MISS FREEMAN.

Paris, May 9, 1868 [1].

MY DEAR GRETCHEN,

I wrote to your mother from Rouen; I suppose she got
my letter this afternoon with the ' Reviler.' We got here yesterday morning—it seems longer ago—by the quick train, and took
up our quarters at Hôtel Voltaire on the Quai. We have bought
a few books, not very many, chiefly a D'Achery, which will
enable me to release that belonging to the College. Johnny
Green is mightily pleased with this idle place, but I will say
that I left him upstairs reading a new book of Angevin Chronicles that he bought. I showed him Nôtre Dame and St. Germain
des Près, and one or two other things; also to-day we went all
over the Louvre, which I had never seen before. We were to
have gone to Chartres to-day, but we had so much to see that
we are driven to a 'sobbath-braich,' and shall go to-morrow
morning. However, like Henry IV going to Sicily, we hope
to get there in time for vespers. I took Johnny to a *café
chantant*, which was much to his taste; also he greatly delights
in the *Diner Européen*, especially when the band plays below.
I liked better the dinner at Rouen, when they did give us a bit
of real beef; remember, first, Rolf got into Rouen and stayed
there, while Hasting could not get into Paris; secondly, that the
English—was not Duke John dead?—kept Rouen after they had
lost Paris, T. R. H. vi. I think that a vast number of houses
have sprung up all along the *Elysian Fields*; it seems much
more part of the town than it used to be. We saw a mighty
grand carriage with outriders and what not, and Johnny swore
he saw the Tyrant and Mother B [2]. in it, but I could not distinguish—or rather I did not look. Since then Johnny has been
a little disgusted, and more ready to come away.

[1] The six letters which follow were written during a tour in
Normandy, Maine and Anjou, with Mr. J. R. Green.
[2] Buonaparte.

To Miss Edith Thompson.

Dinan, May 19, 1868.

My dear Edith,

The Delegates have increased the number of copies of my second volume which I am allowed for myself; so I have asked Macmillan to forward one to you, which I hope you will receive in a few days, if you have not received it already. I am sure nobody deserves it more, as a little offering for all the help which you gave me when you were with us, and a little memorial of the many pleasant (to me at least) talks which we have had about matters connected with it. I only hope you will come and *earn* the third volume in the like sort. N.B. Isaac Gregory[1], in the *Christian Remembrancer*, rebukes me for saying 'in the like sort,' but I mean to say it, maugre Isaac Gregory. If the book and I were together, I would write something in the fly-leaf, but that must wait till we three—viz. you and I and the book—meet again.

I am wandering about with Johnny Green, going over the steps of divers of our Normans, Angevins, and others, from Tib the Tricker[2] at Chartres, to Conan[3] at this Dinan. Our course has been Rouen (*per accidens*), Paris (just to show Johnny what it was like and to pick up some books), Chartres, then Le Mans, where real work began, as I hope you will some day see more largely expressed in the *Saturday Review*. My part is done : whether Johnnikin will do his is, of course, uncertain. 'Tis a glorious city, and belongs to both of us. Then to Tours, which I had seen before, to which was now added a walk to Marmoutiers. From Tours to Chinon, Candes, Fontevrault. At Chinon died Henry II, at Candes St. Martin—you may draw out a contrast, if you like, yet are there points of likeness, as Martin gave half his cloak to the beggar, and Henry founded

[1] Rev. Isaac Gregory Smith, an old college friend, see above, p. 45, now Vicar of Great Malvern.
[2] Theobald, first Count of Blois and Chartres, a crafty, unscrupulous politician.
[3] Count of Rennes and first Duke of Brittany. (See *England under the Angevin Kings*, by Miss K. Norgate, i. pp. 121, 122, 137-139, 146-148.)

divers hospitals for poor and sick folk, including a noble one at Angers. At Fontevrault we saw, not indeed Martin, but Henry, as also Richard, the statues which foolish people wanted to move[1].

Chinon Castle stands grandly atop, with the town below, looking down on the Indre (a river which always sounds to me like a Hindoo god). Distinguish between a town grown round a castle, and a city like Le Mans or Chartres, which has grown out of a primitive hill-fort, and where the oldest part is always the highest.

'Tis a rich and fine country, all that part of Touraine south of Loire—but Anjou is dull enough : but the city of Angers has plenty to show—the castle, unluckily, is all later than the time when the French broke in, but there is much of old times in the churches and in the Bishop's Palace—a grand hall over a substructure, now made into a chapel—well turned into Romanesque, as you get a Romanesque Glastonbury kitchen at Fontevrault. I have left out Saumur, between Fontevrault and Angers, full of Huguenot memories.

To Miss Freeman.

Caen, May 27, 1868.

My dear Gretchen,

Your letter looks now rather old, dated May 9 ; you know it waited some days at Le Mans before I got it at Angers. But you have doubtless heard all about me since from your mother and sisters, to whom I think I have written very diligently. I wrote last on Sunday. That day we dined with Le Gost and Puiseux in an arbour—I should like to call it a harbour, which is the real word—in Le Gost's garden, which reminded me of Edgar's story of Sir James Bathurst. We were merry enough ; I don't know any one whose French I can follow so well as Puiseux's. In the evening Johnny Green started for Paris and Stepney—his way, as he thought it—owing me 10 fr. 50 c., which I suppose he won't pay me, so I now have not a soul to chatter to in mine own tongue. I purposely did not go anywhere on Monday, as I wanted to write some things for the *Saturday*

---

[1] To Westminster Abbey.

Review, as also I have taken to write the bits of my history which touch on a place, at that place, or soon after I have been there, so I shall come back loaded with scraps of vol. iii. So I merely wrote and toddled about, and went to both the abbeys and had a good muse in St. Stephen's, and talked to Le Gost and Bouet, who was to start for Paris the next morning to meet Parker *père* on his way back from Rome. But yesterday I went by rail to Bayeux, and there took a trap and went about to some of the seaside churches, specially Ryes, where William found Hubert standing,

'Entre le mostier et sa mote[1].'

The church is there, and part of it may be as old as that time, but there seem to be no traces of the castle. I was a little disappointed in my round, for, though every church had some part or other very good, Ryes was the only one which I could call a fine whole. I have made better rounds in this country.
. . . To-day I go with Le Gost to Varaville, and to-morrow with him and Puiseux and Le Comte to Val-ès-Dunes, and go forth on Friday, I know not exactly whither. But write to *Poste Restante, Dieppe*, where I mean to be sooner or later for the sake of Arques.

To MRS. FREEMAN.

Caen, May 29, 1868.

. . . In my letter to Margaret I think I told her of my going to Bayeux and making a circuit among the churches. Wednesday I went with Le Gost and his wife in a trap to Varaville and mouth of the Dives, whence William first meant to set out. Varaville is where he whopped the French. It was great fun on Sunday in the castle to hear Puiseux talking to the Commandant about Varaville as 'une bataille entre les Normands et les Français,' at which the man of war seemed utterly

---

[1] In 1047 there was a formidable revolt amongst the vassals of William, Duke of Normandy. A plot was made to seize him at Valognes. He received timely warning and escaped, riding for his life all night. At dawn he drew near the castle of Ryes, the home of Hubert, a faithful vassal, whom he found standing 'between the church and the mound' of his castle. Roman de Rou, l. 8846. *Norman Conquest*, ii. 246.

puzzled. Le Gost is a very pleasant companion. Yesterday we set out early—that is, Puiseux, Le Gost, Le Gost fils, and I— for Cintheaux, where dwells Le Comte, the priest whose little book I reviewed, with which he is intensely delighted. He is a dear old man, and knows a good lot, and is busy putting his church, a good Norman one, to rights, which his predecessor had done all he could to spoil. His admiration for me seems boundless, but I find it hard to persuade him and others that I am not professor at Oxford. He lives in a much better house than I expected, and he fed us well twice. He has two little pupils, and I am sure must from some source have much more than his pay of 1200 fr. yearly. There joined us one St. Maclon, at once baron, doctor, pontifical zouave, and philosopher, who nearly slew me by prating without end at the top of his voice. I understand some people's French so much better than other's. Puiseux I can understand every word ; he gave a capital lecture to the two boys on the battlefield, Val-ès-Dunes. After dinner we walked to Quilly, a church with the earliest tower I have seen in Normandy.

. . . I am a good deal struck by the ignorance of English geography of people here ; they seem to have no idea where an English place is, while one would be ashamed not to know the same sort of place in France. Puiseux understands an English book quite well, so does Le Gost, but they can't speak it a bit, nor pronounce it when they read ; quite different from the Nether-Dutchmen, where my difficulty was to get a chance of airing my Dutch. Here I confess I am getting a-weary of Welsh talking ; so that, seeing Le Comte's dog, who had a Pomeranian look, I made it an excuse to speak to the beast in Dutch—perhaps Gretchen will say that I ought rather to have tried Wendish.

To Miss Freeman.

Fécamp, May 31, 1868.

My dear Gretchen,

It is very pleasant to look out by moonlight from one's window on þam haligan mynstre aet Feskamp, as I am doing now. But you will ask what brings me here to-day, and wherefore I am not a-keeping of my Pentecost at Rouen, as I said

VOL. I.   D d

I should. Of a truth I have been driven out of the city by no less an arm than that of the Tyrant himself. *Je m'explique.* Don't fancy that I have got into any political row; 'tis only as followeth. On Friday I went from Caen to Evreux, and looked over the place a bit, where I was with your Mother seven years back. Well, yesterday morning—it seems so long ago—and now it is longer, as it is now June 1,—I have been to bed and got up since the other page: well—on Saturday morning, *avant hier*, I was at Evreux, whence I went to Mantes (you know about Mantes), where I looked about me, and drew most part of the day. In the evening in my innocence I took a ticket for Rouen. The train was late and full, but I thought that might be only because of Whitsuntide. But when I got to Rouen, the station was all over big N.'s and E.'s, which I thought must mean some mischief. I gradually found out that the Tyrant and mother B. were coming bodily the next morning to open some tomfoolery or other. 'Twas too late to go on by that train, so I tried to get a bed at my usual place in Rouen, Hôtel de France, and at one or two others. 'Twas hopeless; the city was chuck full, and seemingly raving mad. It had seen Rolf and William and Henry V, and had driven away Otto[1] from before its walls, so why such a row about this chap? So I studied my Indicateur, and found I could start for this Fécamp at 3.40. So I supped and coffeed myself, and walked about Rouen by lamplight, starlight, and early dawn. It was by no means an uninteresting process, getting the big churches in quite new lights. Amongst other things I walked up to St. Gervase, and mused awhile—you know wherefore[2]. The train was awfully late starting, but at last we got off. I took a first-class ticket that I might sleep, but in the carriage were two brutes of men who smoked, and two brutes of women who shut up windows. Yet I managed to sleep till

---

[1] Otto the Great, King of the East Franks (afterwards Emperor), in alliance with Lewis, King of the West Franks, and Conrad, King of Burgundy, was repulsed in an attack upon Rouen, the capital of the Duchy of Normandy, A.D. 944.

[2] William the Conqueror, after receiving his death wound at Mantes, was carried to Rouen and died in the priory of St. Gervase. *Norman Conquest*, iv. 704.

I got to Beuzeville junction, where one changes for Fécamp. There too was a brute who smoked, but I could have lots of air. So we got to Fécamp about an hour after our time, and about 7 a.m. Sunday *I went to bed* and slept till 11. So I missed High Mass of Pentecost, but I came in for an afternoon worship which lasted nearly three hours, vespers, compline, two sermons, and some hymn-singing, all at a pull. I got on pretty well by help of my book and of a woman who sang her Latin very clearly. One of the preachers praught about Achilleus and Priam, to prove the efficacy of prayer, so I suppose Homer is studied at Fécamp; the other set forth that the month of Mary was over, which is a good job anyhow. The church here is magnificent—a long nave more Englishwise than French, and all fairly kept, save the monks themselves made a beastly west front, and in 1802 they pulled down the *jubé* or roodloft. In the evening I walked over the hills—the view of the abbey and over the sea is splendid, and I caught rather a good church, half ruined and partly set up again. Fécamp is now a sort of watering place, but I am now in the old town, a good way from the sea, close by the abbey.

I fear I shall lose Jumièges, (I have seen it before, as your mother knows), but I hope to manage Lillebonne to-morrow, and to get to Dieppe (for Arques) to-morrow night, or Wednesday, as may happen.

To THE SAME.

Dieppe, June 3, 1868.

MY DEAR GRETCHEN,

I walked out to Arques to-day. The castle is horribly spoiled, all the ashlar picked away, but one can make it all out, especially as I bought a capital history this morning. Such fosses —but the popular mind seems to dwell more on Henry of Navarre[1] than on either William[2], and they have actually gone and carved him—no, inaugurated him, 'inauguré' is the word— over one of the old gates. I was guided part of the way by

---

[1] Henry IV, with a band of 4,000 Protestants, defeated the army of the League, 30,000 strong, in 1589.

[2] William the Conqueror and his uncle, Count William, the builder of the Castle. *Norman Conquest*, iii. 121.

a good old soul, who seemed to think that Arques had once belonged to England, but had been conquered from it by Henry. I tried to make him understand about 'le grand duc Guillaume,' and how there was a time when 'l'Angleterre et la Normandie n'avaient qu'un seul souverain.' But he seemed to stick much more to the second period man. N.B. Do they confound him with Henry who helped W. of Arques? My man had been in England and spake much of 'fabrique de papier,' and 'chapellerie,' but said he spake 'patois.' So I told him it was not 'mauvais Français,' but 'bon Normand,' which he seemed rather to like, but I could understand very little of it.

I bought some chocolate this evening.

10.40. Start for Eu, 6.15 a.m. and a letter to Bryce to finish, so good night.

To Dean Hook.

Kilcolman Lodge, Oxford, June 8, 1868.

I carried about a letter, or more truly, two letters, of your's, through a large part of Normandy and the neighbouring countries, in the hopes of finding an opportunity for writing you a long story thence. The opportunity, however, never came. I am now staying a few days with Stubbs, to keep to-day's feast, and also to do some work in Bodleian for vol. iii. . . . (June 12) I have been working somewhat in the Bodleian, and among other things at coronations. I looked to the point which you speak of about Cranmer smuggling Edward VI into the kingdom without any election. I find the word 'elect,' which occurs very distinctly in the office used for Henry VIII, is left out, but the assent of the people is asked in much the same form. My Margaret said a rather sharp thing about it, namely that as Parliament had allowed Henry to name his successor, election was not needed in that particular case. It is very curious to trace how the notion of the elective kingship gradually died out, and then to think of the impudent ignorance of Blackstone, saying that the English Crown had never been asserted to be elective, except at the trial of Charles I.

. . . I won't look at the letters which I carried about through Normandy, because I do not doubt that they would start half-a-dozen subjects which would set me a-going, and I should not finish this in time to post it before I leave Oxford. Of vol. iii. I have written (besides the battles in advance) the first chapter, on the Election and Coronation, with the Appendices thereto. I now go home to write the days of William from 1051 to 1066. Then I must make my journey into Sussex and Kent, in the course of which I trust to find you at home at Chichester, but you see that I can't as yet say exactly when it will be.

The young folk who rule this place are, as usual, tinkering and statute-making till nobody but themselves can tell what anything in Oxford now means. I really think that the Great Unpaid are a touch more sensible. If I vote with Dickinson on point A, he does not call me names if I vote against him on point B.

To W. B. DAWKINS, ESQ.

Kilcolman Lodge, Oxford, June 8, (Trinity Monday) 1868.

I can't come and see you this time, as I must get home as soon as I have done a little Bodleian work which I have to do here. But you must certainly come to us before the year is out. Can't you come, as of old, for our Williton Meeting? Williton of itself is nought, but it takes in many nice things, as Dunster, Porlock, Dunkery, and Cleve Abbey. At any rate you must come to us. I don't know exactly when I shall make my Kentish and South-Saxon journey—whenever I get to that stage of my writing which calls for it—I will give you full notice, as I must have you 'in epitumo Senlac,'[1] and, if you can construe ' epitumo,' so much the better.

June 10. I am tarrying here with our Professor[2], partly for Trinity Monday, which is now past, partly for work in Bodleian. I have not yet been home. I landed and got here on Saturday. I saw a good deal after Johnnikin left me, as—besides excursions from Caen—*Evreux*, Mantes, Fécamp, *Lillebonne*, *Dieppe*, Arques, Eu, *St. Valery*—(I mark the places where I had been aforetime). Fécamp is delightful in every way, but I maintain that

---

[1] Ordericus Vitalis 659 B. See *Norman Conquest*, iii. 758.
[2] Rev. W. Stubbs, then recently made Professor of Modern History.

altogether Le Mans has been the roof and crown of my journey
this year. I came from Boulogne by the boat which goes
straight (or crooked) to London Bridge, thus following in the
track of Godwine [1].

To the Rev. W. Stubbs.

Somerleaze, June 14, 1868.

Both friends and enemies seem to make your house an
ἀποδυτήριον [2] or λωποδυτήριον [3]; is there not such a word as λωποδύτης? Professed thieves carry off Wayte's coat and hat, then
I take first your waistcoat—vestment κατ' ἐξοχήν—and then
Owen's coat, and lastly Owen takes your coat. But I think
my sin against Owen was very venial. If a man will leave
his coat about in the room where another is packing, he must
expect it to be crammed in along with the other coats. But
I should like to have seen him when he came down in his
shirt-sleeves to seek a coat from you. . . .

I slept most part of yesterday and part of to-day. To-morrow
I hope to begin some work.

To J. Bryce, Esq.

Somerleaze, July 9, 1868.

My hand is quite tired with writing about Richard and Adela,
so I will dictate this letter.

First about Normandy. You say, round Caen, Bayeux,
Avranches; but Avranches is quite away from the other two
places, and I don't see how you can get there without going by
St. Lo and Coutances, places well worth seeing. At Coutances,
besides the cathedral (where do not forget to go up the tower),
mark the imitation of the lantern in the two smaller churches,
and make out, if you can, the thing like an aqueduct, a little
way out of the town. At Avranches there are no buildings that
matter, but the finest view in Normandy from the point where
the cathedral once stood, taking in a lot of Brétland as well, and
St. Michael-in-peril-of-the-sea. If you are tempted to go on to

[1] See *Norman Conquest*, ii. 390.
[2] A room for undressing.
[3] A thieves' dressing-room. The writer has coined the word from
λωποδύτης, a clothes stealer.

Dol, a place which is a special pet of mine, besides the cathedral and the old houses, walk out to Le Mont Dol for a view, and also on the other side of the town to a gigantic standing-stone, which they call chaindelac or some such name, for I have never seen it written. The last syllable I take to be the Welsh λίθος and lapis.

On the other side of Avranches, if possible, get to Mortain, *Moretolium*, undoubtedly the most picturesque spot in Normandy, with rocks, waterfalls, and what not, and where there should be the castle of William the Warling, only they have pulled it down to build a Sous-Préfecture[1]. There is also a good church, and there is said to be a still finer view from a higher point, which we did not reach.

Find out also if you can, why a certain castle not far from Avranches, which I did not see, built by William to keep out the Brets, and called Castrum Sancti Jacobi, is always now called St. James, and not St. Jacques.

But, to come back to Caen and Bayeux, I need not tell you to go see the cathedral and the tapestry at one place, and the two abbeys at the other. But also see the castle with the exchequer in it. It will want an order from the commandant, but he is a douce man, only he was sore puzzled when Puiseux said that Varaville was a victory of the Normans over the French. But, to see anything in Caen or thereabouts, make the acquaintance of my worthy friend Le Gost-Clerisse, bookseller in the Rue Ecuyère, on the way to St. Stephen's. Tell him you are a friend of mine and the historian of the *Holy Roman Empire*, and he will go endless kilometres with peas in his shoes to help you.

About Ireland, of course Cashel is *the* great thing of all, but Kilkenny and Limerick are not to be despised, neither yet are Athlone and Killaloe. I could not make out what they meant by Spanish houses at Galway. I did not see the battle-field of Aghrim, which I am sorry for, as the account in Macaulay reads mightily like Senlac. North of Dublin, don't forget Drogheda, and, of course, not the Boyne, and in quite another way New-grange, the grandfather of Croms[2]. If your friend

[1] See *Norman Conquest*, iii. 151.
[2] Cromlechs.

cares about buildings, it is very curious to distinguish the natural Irish buildings (not the work of the Cuthites) from the buildings under English influence; it is not always merely a difference of date. Among the latter, the most interesting to me are the Friars' churches, very numerous and characteristic.

To F. H. DICKINSON, ESQ.

Somerleaze, July 11, 1868.

Your doings at Sessions are not exactly a case of wretches hanging that jurymen may dine. 'Tis a case of thieves escaping that chairmen may catch the bus. Let me set forth that, according to my books, this is to walk in the way of Robert and William the Red, not in that of Godwine, Harold, William the Great, and Henry the Lion of Justice, all of whom, however different in other matters, are painted as very stout and terrible towards evildoers.

. . . And now I have to 'consult the oracle.' My wife laughed at the phrase. (But don't flatter yourself you are the only one. Delphi stood not alone, but Dodona, Abai, Branchidai, half-a-dozen others, had something to say. So if I consult you, I also often consult Stubbs, Elton, Wayte, Bryce, Pinder, Strangford, Warren, and certain others in their several lines.) But you will remember about the pollution of the Axe some time back. It has been going on again, more or less, for a long time, and was frightfully bad a few weeks back; everybody was complaining, and many of the poor could get no water at all. So I wrote a memorial, which Margaret copied, to the Board of Guardians, asking them, as Local Board of Health, either to act themselves or to suggest some other way of acting. This was signed in a trice by seventy-seven people, farmers, millers, labourers, all sorts—(my hand is tired, so I will dictate)—and I laid it before the Board. Meanwhile, —— at the Lower Mill, who was the chief sinner—Hodgkinson was hardly complained of at all—got scent of it and came up to me. You know I can do better either in writing or in making a speech than in talking to one person. —— began rather by whining, and then, as I thought, waxed insolent, telling me that I said things which I could not confirm, &c., &c., so, that

I might not get in a bigger rage, I told him to go away, and walked off myself. Then at the Board I soon found that my usual friends would be my enemies, and vice versa, as all the Wells people were hand in glove with the paper-makers, while the farmers had a natural feeling for their half-poisoned kine. Well, they made a committee to go and inspect the mills—me, Welsh, Bumpstead, Garrod, Lawrence the postmaster (a very good fellow generally), and the two Wookey guardians. I begged to be let off, as I knew nothing about mills and had had a shindy with ——, but they would have it so. So we went, all save Bumpstead, who was a great loss. Of course I could learn nothing from looking at the mills, and Welsh and Garrod were determined to stick by their friend, and I could not even get them to come and look at the stream near us, and hear what the people had to say. Meanwhile —— followed and stuck to us and kept on talking, not letting me have a moment to speak to the rest of the committee; at last I got in a rage and said, 'We can't listen to this man any longer.' The words were contemptuous doubtless, but I should have used them to a duke, if the duke had been bothering and hindering business in the same way; but Mr. Paper-maker fired up—'*A man!* I'm not a man; I'm as much a gentleman as you are; I don't care for magistrates; I hold my head as high as you do; my education is as good as yours' (which I did venture to doubt anyhow), and much more which I could tell you by word of mouth; and at last ended by something like threatening my life, saying that if I lived near him, and his people heard what I said, my life would not be safe. Carrying this out, I got the enclosed letter this morning. Now give me your advice. Of course I shall go on pressing the matter at the Board of Guardians, as it is simply standing up for the rights of the poor, or, rather, of the whole neighbourhood, against one selfish fellow who has shamefully broken his promise. But shall I take any notice, either there or at the magistrates' meeting on Monday, of ——'s threat or his man's letter. I had rather leave it alone, but I am not clear it will be right to do so, as it savours of a breach of the peace. I will tell you more face to face at the Asylum on Thursday. All this is a great bother; I had much rather stay at home with William and Harold, and the rest of them, but if one has duties, I think one should perform them, though the youngsters who are set to help me seem not to think so, so no more.

To THE REV. W. STUBBS.

Somerleaze, July 22, 1868.

I have awakened to a heap of things, among others to my utter ignorance of Spanish history, and to my utter lack of means of learning anything, having only a Gal-Welsh crib of Mariana[1]. Can you help me at all? I am very busy with William's daughters, and I want to know something of the Spanish king—Alfonso, or whoever he was—who did not marry one of them. Any views on the subject of William's daughters will be thankfully received, but anything about the Spanish match more particularly. Will. Pict.[2] says two Spanish kings' brothers squabbled about her. Some place the non-marrying in 1068—on what authority? What was her name—Agatha or anything else? Do the Spaniards say ought about it? Art de verifier[3] quotes Ferraras as calling her Aqueda. But I see from Potthast that Ferraras (I believe I have spelt it wrong) is a modern chap. Are there any original accounts? Do find out and tell me, as a blank space yawneth.

July 24.—I see his name is Ferreras, and there is a copy of him in a French crib in Barthe's and Lowell's Catalogue, but he is too dear to buy, and hardly worth buying just for this one girl. I have no doubt that you either know all about it or can find out in five minutes. So pray tell me. Then there is something about William's daughter Matilda in Mabillon, *Ann. Ord. Ben.* vol. v. Appendix lxxxiii, which is again in the same catalogue, but too dear for me. Then I want to know a good deal about William's marriage; I have got a reference to Mansi, xix. 867, for the fact that Normandy was absolved from the interdict in 1059, but the dispensation was not granted till 1063. I have my doubts about these dates, and I went to Kingweston, not on purpose for this, but for several other

---

[1] Author of *Historia General de España.*
[2] William of Poitiers.
[3] ' L'Art de verifier les dates.'

things; Dickinson, who generally has the books which I have not, and vice versa, has a Mansi, but it has only six volumes, so I could not refer to the nineteenth, nor could I find anything about it elsewhere. Then Thorpe quotes Saga Játvarthos Helga, p. 12, ed. Copenh. 1852, for that queer story about William whopping Matilda, which I think is a piece of comparative mythology, as you will see in Appendix to vol. iii[1]. But still I should like to know something about the Saga. Is it likely to be in Dasent's collection, and when is that likely to be out? Could you get me the extract from the *Tours Chronicle*, Bouquet, xi. 348, which gives the date of the marriage in 1053, and also the details of the whopping? 'By a piece of stupid, ignorant carelessness,' to speak after the manner of Dimock, I forgot to look it up when I was last in Bodleian, as I had fully meant to do. Also Mrs. Green, i. 3, refers to *Chron. Flandriae*, i. 552, in a series published by the Belgian Government, giving the date as 1047, which I think cannot be, but I should like to know what is said.

. . . Dear old Hook talks of asking you and me and Johnnikin, and divers others to be named by me, to meet at Chichester and go on pilgrimage to Senlac. He can't come himself. Of course I must have Bryce and Dawkins, and I have a dream of trying to get General Lefroy to meet me there. A really rational soldier, as he seems to be, would explain several things. A mere routine dog would be better away.

To Miss Edith Thompson.

Somerleaze, September 20, 1868.

I have been thinking of writing to you ever since I came back from Normandy, and I have had a letter of yours on my *hand* (not *hands*) all the time—but it is so hard to find a spare moment. I am at last stirred up by your last letter to Margaret to stand forth and show that I am a raal man of flesh and blood, and not merely a thing that writes books. For why, you ask Gretchen a heap of questions and tell her a heap of things touching me in this last character, as you might ask about Florence—of Worcester I mean, not my daughter—and then

---

[1] p. 662.

at the end, when you scatter greetings and blessings broadcast among mine household, you have not the least scrap of a blessing for me personally.

All from the top of this page has been written on September 28, in the solar[1] of the manor-house at Fifield—more truly Fifehead—in Berkshire, the house of Godric the sheriff, who died on Senlac, as more largely is expressed in my third volume as is to be[2]. 'Tis a curious place, a fourteenth century house—for when I call it the house of Godric I only mean that it is most likely on his site—which James Parker has done up. It belongs to St. John's College, and J. P. has got a lease at a rent of, I think, £5, on condition of doing it up. As it really is a house, James has done it much more successfully than his father at Wells, though 'tis rather wonderful to sit here, with the massive beams of the wooden roof over one's head. I am come to be godfather to their seventh child, who is to be baptized to-morrow by the name of Edward Godric. . . .

September 29.—So you recommend me as light reading. Did I ever tell you how Sir George Lewis—whose memory I greatly worship—when standing for Peterborough (when the Peterburghers, just set free, chose Whalley over his head) asked Dr. Paley, in whose house he was staying, for a 'light book' to read on Sunday. Dr. Paley showed him such books as he had, and Lewis chose, neither a sermon nor a novel, but Alison's *History of Europe*.

Eadward Godric was baptized this morning. I was specially bidden to give him his *ea*, when I had to 'name this child.' So I spake out manfully ' Yadward Godric,' but the parson said ' Edward.' But when it came to register the babe, James Parker yet again bare testimony that it was ' Eadward '—on which the parson wanted to write it Gal-Welsh fashion ' Edouard,' on which we both bare testimony, and he was written ' Eadward Godric.' So, O Eadgyth, your rights are asserted.

---

[1] A room at the end of the hall in a mediaeval house, generally behind the dais, with a small opening through which the occupant could see and hear all that went on in the hall.

[2] *Norman Conquest*, iii. 428.

They do queer things here. Last night the parson hallowed
the choristers' cassocks. I did not hear till after, or I should
have gone to see it. Also to-day he came into church with one
manner of stole, put on another at the beginning of the baptismal
service, and a third when he came actually to baptize the bairn.
This is queer, is it not? I wonder he did not carry the goose
in procession, with some pots or cups of apple-sauce.

Mark that my godchild, born here, is a natural-born West-
Saxon—Parker's other children having been born on the wrong
side of the Thames. What would Johnny say, if he heard me
say that? or you either, who go in for not only north of Thames,
but north of Humber?

They had the choir boys to supper this evening, and after
supper they were asked to sing songs. I was really sorry to
find they had not a single local song, only cockney slang. I did
not expect a hymn in praise of Godric or of Ælfred, but they
might have had some ditty about the miller of Fifield or the
brewer of Abingdon (which brewer left two daughters, whom
Short used to call Swypena and Swyposa), not about ' Not for
Joseph,' which I objected to as a local, sectarian, Jerusalemite
psalm, dishonouring to the tribes of Ephraim, Benjamin, and
Manasses. I am not sure that there are not here materials for
a ' middle [1].'

To W. B. Dawkins, Esq.

October 8, 1868.

I don't know whether I told you that that dear good old
Dean of Chichester had made a delightful scheme of asking
me, and divers men to be chosen by me—of whom I had of
course set you down as one—to meet at his house before going
on to Senlac. But all this has broken down through a sudden
illness of Mrs. Hook's. I must, however, go on my South-Saxon
and Kentish campaign all the same, and I must have you to
help me 'in epitumo Senlac'; and if I can get Bryce and any
other like-minded so much the better. So far from being
obliged to go in October, I am pretty well fixed here till the end

---

[1] Articles in the *Saturday Review* which are placed between the
political articles at the beginning, and the reviews at the end of the
paper, are commonly called ' middles.'

of this month; so it will just do if you will come here on your way to Torquay, in the neighbourhood of which some erring folk, confounding Harold Hardrada and William III, do place Stamford-bridge. We can then settle the exact time and have a sit in the summer-house, *quaere* winter-house, about other things.

To the Same.

Portsmouth, December 23, 1868.

I went to Hastings yesterday from Dover, walked out to Battle, and back by train; to-day I looked about Hastings, came to Pevensey, walked about endlessly, and came on here. I trust to get home to-morrow.

Out of all this I have a heap of questions to ask you.

First, if you please, if you don't mind, write me a little note of the two roads, north and east, commanded by the English position at Senlac. You know I am dull about such things.

Second, I did not manage Romney. Was William's Romney Old or New? Can you give me any hints about the place? (The sea seemingly went back between William and Leland[1].) This leads to the Marshy book which I left with you.

Third, Is there any evidence for the site of William's camp at Hastings? I see the present castle is between the old town and the new. Perhaps the army covered all the hills. Where did William want Harold to fight? I see very little 'planities' about Hastings—most perhaps where the new town now stands.

Fourth, The march from Hastings to Senlac would, I suppose, follow mainly the line of the present road, allowing for the spreading of the army on both sides?

Fifth, The landing at Pevensey means, I suppose, all along Pevensey Bay? What was its state then? Was all that strange wilderness of shingle there? Did the sea ever come up to the walls of Anderida?

I found it a weary pull from Hastings to Battle. Truly King Harold knew what he was about. What a pity you did not come; but really Johnny's military eye is most valuable. I told

[1] Between the times of William the Conqueror and Leland, A.D. 1066–1536.

him that he ought to have been a soldier, adding that I did not
see what military function he could have discharged, save only
that of a drummer.

At Anderida to-day I wellnigh forgot William, and thought
mainly of Ælla and Cissa, and that jolly smiting of Brets, leaving
not one remaining[1].

To Miss Edith Thompson.

Bishopthorpe, January 5, 1869.

There is a fate of some sort which in matters of letter-writing
binds together you and the Dean of Chichester. I am always
hearing from you two at the same time, and writing to you two
at the same time, and that often long letters written page about
—or more strictly two pages about—to each of you. So again,
when I was sorting letters before I set out, a thick letter of
your's and a thick letter of his forced themselves upon the eye
by abiding in their covers. (N.B. The dear old Dean's address
was not nearly so legible as your's.) So I carry out the principle still farther, and as I take a big sheet for him, I have also
taken a big sheet for you; but, as it is now 2.7 a.m., I certainly
do not mean to fill it before I go to bed.

First of all, let me very much thank you and your mother—
or was it your father? if so, I hope to thank him bodily before
I leave Hull—for all the trouble which you (Hull, January 6)
have taken about the Brunanburh matter. I now know that it
was your mother, as I saw your father to-day and yesterday—
yesterday at my preachment, and I learned from him that you
were gone to Bournemouth. How you do gad about. Hardly
back from Deornarice when you are off to the Dornsaetas—and
for a ball, too—*Vanitas vanitatum.* So I sent off a paper thither
this morning, with a report of my second talk better than re-
porters commonly do make. I go to Bishopthorpe on Saturday,
and preach again at York on Monday.

Now to return, about Brunanburh[2]. If I had thought it likely

---

[1] See the *Anglo-Saxon Chronicle* under year A.D. 491. 'A story,' says
Gibbon, vi. 372 (Milman's edition), 'more dreadful in its simplicity than
all the vague and tedious lamentations of the British Jeremiah,' meaning
Gildas.

[2] A great victory was won by Æthelstan and his brother Eadmund in

to be the right place, or if, not thinking it likely to be the right place, I had had anybody to go with me, I should have gone over to-day or to-morrow to see it. As I have nobody to go with, neither you nor Margaret nor Bryce nor Johnny, and as I see no reason to think it is the place, I stay and read Froude, prepare my lecture, and write letters, besides pottering by the banks of the rivers Ool and Oomber[1]. I am really sorry you and your mother had so much trouble about what is so transparently nothing. But it is rather amusing. ' It is agreed on all hands that Anlaf[2] sailed up the Humber.' Harold Hardrada did certainly, but why Anlaf? Οὐ γὰρ ἦν οὕτω φρενοβλαβὴς ὁ Ἄνλαφος[3] as to sail up the Humber, when it was so much easier to sail up the Dee, unless he liked sailing round Cape Wrath or the Land's End for the fun of the thing. Then on what hands is it agreed? I can find nothing like it either in the Chronicles or in William of Malmesbury. (I greatly admire your way of putting it, that to him 'a book is a book.') Howes hill is a good case of μυθοποιία[4]. Howe is simply hill; a local (perhaps not local) word, which I should have thought might still have been understood. Howe hill is just like Ben knoll, Bar Gate, and such other cases of repetition. Then comes Howes Hill; then King Howes Hill; then your W—— turns Howe into Howel, though the reason or motive for carrying Howel to Brunanburh I cannot even guess at. The thing was well summed up by dear old Dimock. ' He has proved that his place is some battle-field, and, if Brunanburh had been the only battle ever fought in Britain, he would have proved it to be Brunanburh.' We both thought that the leathern belts savoured much of the days of what President Wayte used to call 'The Troubles.' You know that Brunanburh is placed at all manner of points from

937 over a combined army of Danes, Scots, and Welsh from Strathclyde, at Brunanburh; but the site of Brunanburh has never been identified. See *Norman Conquest*, i. 60. The letter is a criticism on some book or paper by a Mr. Surtees, who thought he had discovered the site.

[1] Local pronunciation of Hull and Humber.
[2] Leader of the Ostmen, from Ireland, who took part with the Danes in the fight at Brunanburh.
[3] 'For Anlaf was not so crazy.'
[4] Myth-making.

Lincoln to Edinburgh ; I have no theory about it, but I incline to the west coast rather than the east.

Talking of local words, I said, 'The keels of Hengest and Horsa led the way.' For some inscrutable reason the reporter changed *keels* into *followers*! Now I should have thought that here in Deornarice all would have known their own tongue. Did I not see keels at Tatha, yea, and at Riccale ? Did I not speak with the keelers to find out what manner of ships either the Ouse or Hwarf could stand ? The reporter eke left out a flourishing contrast between Le Mans and Anderida. 3.11 a.m. Friday morning. So good night, and dream as pleasant a dream as I did in my chair, viz. an undergraduate having spoken of ' Mods.,' I dreamed that I was floating in the air (like Gladstone's Lords) and despising examinations.

January 7. I heard your father torture a witness to-day in the Court of Record, holden before £10,000 a-year[1]. I am convinced that there is some virtue in a periwig. I am sure that I could not, and I greatly doubt whether Sir W. Miles could, remind a witness that he was ' on his solemn oath ' in the thrilling tones in which Warren did.

To G. FINLAY, ESQ.

Somerleaze, February 8, 1869.

. . . I wish that, when you were in Switzerland, you could have come on to your native island. My chances of getting to Greece seem to get ever fainter and fainter. My present work has almost naturalized me at Caen and Bayeux, but I have by no means forgotten Switzerland. You will see that my Swiss work has told in several passages of the *Norman Conquest.* I am more and more convinced of the absolute identity of all the old Teutonic constitutions (aye, and the oldest Greek constitutions, too), and I believe I can (February 10) describe either an Homeric ἀγορή[2] or an English mickle-gemot all the better for having seen a Landesgemeinde. But I am half inclined to have a fight with you for talking of the Norman Conquest as having made Englishmen slaves. I suppose my sympathies are about

---

[1] The late Samuel Warren, Esq., Q.C., D.C.L., Master in Lunacy, Recorder of Hull, author of *Ten Thousand a Year.*

[2] 'Assembly.'

† VOL. I.　　　　　　E e

as purely English as any man's; but I cannot help seeing that the Norman Conquest in a most strange and indirect way worked for good in the end, and still more that the popular conception greatly exaggerates the amount of immediate change and suffering. I write, in fact, to substitute a real state of the case for Thierry's pretty picture. I don't know whether I ever told you that I am also making—or supposed to be making— a *History of Greece* for the Oxford Delegates. I am writing it on a plan of my own, founded mainly on ideas which I have learnt from you; but as yet I have only got as far as the Homeric catalogue. I want to make it, as far as may be, a history of the Greek nation; both the Greek nation proper—the Ethnological Hellenes—and what I call the artificial Greek nation; that is to say, the various peoples who have embraced the Greek speech and Greek feeling from the beginnings of Greek colonization down to the last of your Albanian neighbours who has succeeded in Hellenizing himself. It seems to me that it is all one long story, and that during all those ages one process has been going on—that of the Greek nation gradually losing itself, or, to say the least, getting hid among the mass of its proselytes, who became Greek by adoption. I think that something of the same sort went on in the case of the Romans, though you know better than I, that all the people who gradually came to call themselves Romani, or 'Ρωμαῖοι, were far from becoming Romans in the sense in which the artificial Greeks became Greeks. I am not clear that something of the same sort is not going on with the English nation also. I think this is not a bad way, and I think it is an original way of looking at Grecian history. The Delegates say I am to cut it short after Greece became a Roman Province, to which I answered by asking them to tell me when that was, as all I knew about it was that it was not in B. C. 146. They also want me to write the Greek names Latin fashion, to which I answered that as I meant to come down to quite modern times, I wished to know in what year of what Emperor I was to leave off writing Αἴακος—Aeacus, and take to spelling it Eaco. It seems to me that the only way by which you can maintain consistency is to *spell* letter by letter, and leave people to *pronounce* how they choose.

To Miss Edith Thompson.

Birch Villa, June 10, 1869.

I have not yet recovered from my amazement at receiving all the things which I had so carelessly left behind in a way which I can't account for, and at which I can only say that 'it is merveille.' I won't flatter you by saying that I think you had any hand in it, as I feel sure that it was all the νοῦς πρακτικός[1] of your mother. I thanked her once, please to thank her again. And let me thank her, and you, and your father, very much for the pleasant time which I spent in your house—specially for what I had much looked forward to, making the acquaintance of your grandfather[2]. What a noble old man he is! I shall put his note which he sent me on Sunday in my drawer of things to be kept. I thought it was not worth while bothering him with anything of mine.

But pleasant as it was being with you at Blackheath, it is pleasanter still having you with us at Somerleaze. I will explain myself philosophically. The duty of a guest is to obey, a duty which I always strive to fulfil diligently, even to the enduring of shut windows. (N.B. You will crow over me, as I have somehow or other picked up a cold.) Now, though it is oftentimes pleasant to obey, as I found it from May 31 to June 7, yet to command is always pleasanter still. So I hope that it will not be long before you again 'seek me to lord' in my own house. And I hope that your father, and mother, and Nellikin to boot, will manage to appear there also.

I have written to Parker to send you some books which I thought would be profitable for you, as also one for the little lass, which I hope have reached you by this time, and which I hope you will both accept from me. I won't make fine speeches, as you know the interest I take in all your real work, but I think you rather want system. And remember what we were talking about dates and geography. I quite understand your difficulty—in the latter matter at least—from my own experience. I am specially particular about it for one reason, because I remember my own difficulties. Remember, you can't

[1] Practical mind.
[2] General Perronet Thompson.

E e 2

do anything without effort. That sounds like a platitude, but it is what most people do not take in. It is nothing to work, as long as it is pleasant—the fine thing is to do what is unpleasant, and have the pleasure of victory. . . .

To the Same.

Somerleaze, July 8, 1869.

Edithula gnavissima et benignissima[1]!

There is a title which surely quite beats Eddeva pulcra or dives, and which shows withal that, if I can't make you a diminutive in English, I can make a very pretty one in Latin. (Might you not in High-Dutch make something like *Gittchen*, like Gretchen and Trüdchen?) But I am sure you deserve all the superlatives that I can make and more also, for the great trouble which you have been good enough to take for me about the inscription. Thanks many, many. 'Tis just the thing, and I can print it nearly as it stands.

I had a great cruise in Domesday last night and yesterday, searching for one Ælfgyth who taught Godric's daughter to embroider in gold. I caught her at last, and on the road I fell in with three people whom I will take as texts to hold forth to you.

First, 'Eddeva puella, homo S. Archiepiscopi[2].' This sounds as if she were a modest and retiring young person, but I have not that reverence either for Titus Tatius at Lambeth or for the ἄναξ ἀνδρῶν at Bishopthorpe, to recommend you to take her as your model.

Second, 'Eddid quaedam libera femina[3].' Neither do I recommend her, as savouring too much of Lydia Becker.

Third, 'Eddid, quae potuit ire quo voluit[4].' This, rightly interpreted, is exactly the right thing. For may we not hope that the 'velle' will, when you have reached the old borough Acemannesceaster ('which in other words men Bath name'[5])

[1] 'Little Edith, most diligent and most kind.'
[2] 'Eddeva, a maiden, vassal (literally 'man') of S(tigand) the Archbishop.'
[3] 'Eddid, a certain free woman.'
[4] 'Eddid, who could go where she would.' A common phrase in Domesday to signify one who was not dependent on any feudal lord.
[5] A favourite quotation of the writer, from the *Chronicle* under the year 973.

bring you on hither to finish the rest of the visit which was so sadly cut short in February? Prythee do so; it will be a sin against St. Andrew of Wells (who as elder brother and elder see claims precedence over Peter of Bath) to come so near, and then tarry in the place 'ad portas inferi' to which the Tours doctor[1] moved our bishoprick. Prythee come, and bring also your mother and the Nellikin, that she may say how near I come to hàving the real Bayeux Tapestry.

To the Same.

Somerleaze, July 14, 1869.

What an undutiful 'homo' or 'puella,' or whatever you are to be called, you are! I sent you what I thought was a most charming little parable, the moral of which was that you should not go so near as Bath without coming on hither. (Do I not see weekly advertised everywhere a book on *The Baths and Wells of Europe*, showing how the two do go naturally together in all parts of the world, and not only in the bishoprick of the Sumorsaetas?) But of that parable and the request which it wound up with, and that touching not yourself only, but also your mother, and the Schwesterlein, you take no heed whatever. Now I don't like to be despised, at least not by you, so you must send me to make up some specially precious balm, warranted not to break heads, like that in the Psalms, but—what shall I say? I want to say something poetical—bind up hearts or the like. The idea of balm I have got out of your own letter, where you go off into raptures about the air in the Isle Wiht, which you say is

'Balmy, and soft, and soothing to the mind.'

Excuse my apparent familiarity, but this line sounds to me exactly as if it came out of a sermon by the Rev. A. C. P., and described the atmosphere into which the eagle wished to soar, when he was hindered by one feather being plucked from his wing. Why on earth your mind should want soothing (which implies a ruffling thereof going before) I don't in the least

---

[1] John of Tours, a physician, the first Bishop of Somerset after the Norman Conquest, A.D. 1088, moved the See from Wells to Bath. See *Cathedral Church of Wells*, by E. A. Freeman, pp. 35, 36.

understand; but I don't see that our air here need be less balmy and soothing than that of Iktis—for Iktis your isle undoubtedly is, though the unlearned and unbelieving West-Wealas and such like, move it to Scilly. . . .

Do you remember the frightfully revolutionary talk (grievous to my conservative mind) which your father and Bryce held the day Bryce dined with you—how they wanted to abolish magistrates, grand-juries, everything that is lovely and of good report, and set up instead convenient berths for lawyers at the cost of the British tax-payer? Perhaps, however, as such talk could not be good for the youthful mind (that's why I tell it you now), they waited till you had gone out of the room. Well, at Manchester I saw the first step thereunto in the new courts, which certainly make a fine thing on the whole; they have put the grand jury room a stadium or more from the court instead of opening into a gallery. This is clearly with the object of wearying grand jurors by journeys to and fro, till the poor things, respectable old gentlemen very often, are worn out and cease to be. . . .

St. Swithun, 10.26 p.m.—I thought you must either have heard me speak of A. W. Ward or have read my review of his lectures on the Thirty Years War. He is Professor of History at Manchester, and knows more of German history and literature than any one I know. His father is (unless Bismark has quenched him) Minister, Consul, and what not, to all the small dukes and free cities on the North Sea and the Baltic, and he was very civil to me when I was at Hamburg. But some years back he went to the Pope, an odd thing for an elderly diplomatist to do. George Stephens is English Professor at the city which we corruptly call *Copenhagen*, but whose real name is Kiobenhavn, which in English is pretty well expressed by Chipping or Cheapingham. But ask your uncle, who has been there, and may have seen him in the flesh. I don't see the use of writing distinguis*ht*, but I would fain write *tung* if I dared. . . .

TO THE SAME.

Somerleaze, August 8, 1869.

It is a pleasant thought that I may hope to see you here next week. Last year you gave us a full month, a reign of Menahem (see O. T.[1]), all in a ring-fence; this year you are cut up into bits, like the county of Cromarty; but take care that the aggregate is not less. . . .

To me Salisbury[2] is too uniform, too perfect; add something or knock down something and it would be better. But why? (August 9) because of the barbarous pulling down of the bell-tower on the usual silly notion of opening a view, whereas I have no doubt that the bell-tower gave that very effect of varied grouping which is now wanted. At the same time they did all the other evil things that were done, opening the lady chapel to the choir, putting the tombs in two rows in the nave, and other such wicked deeds of James Wyatt. The west front is a wretched sham; as great a sham as Wells, and without its dignity. I wonder at your admiring the *town* of Salisbury, which, when you once get out of the close, always seems to me singularly uninteresting. One tidy church and, I think, one wooden house. You speak of buns at the station; there is also a place in the town where you can eat mutton-chops and read the *Family Herald.* Romsey is a very old favourite spot of mine, and out of it came one of your many namesakes; viz. she who became 'Mold the good Queen[3].' We are going to see this week several places of which I am very fond, as Llandaff, brother to Glaston.; Ewenny, brother to Dunster; and Llantwit Major, which is like nothing else in the whole world. More about this and many other things when we meet.

I don't think I told you—and it has now almost passed out of memory—how on June 20 I went to church, expecting to hear something about Her Majesty that now reigneth, and heard instead, to my great delight, a most savoury and fruitful discourse of Samuel Ealdorman—or shall I rather say Landammann?—of the Hebrews, setting forth the many evils of

---

[1] Old Testament. It was not Menahem, however, but his predecessor Shallum, who 'reigned a full month in Samaria.' See 2 Kings xv. 13.

[2] The Cathedral Church.

[3] Matilda or Eadgyth, daughter of Malcolm, King of Scotland, and his wife Margaret, became the queen of Henry I. She was brought up in the Abbey of Romsey, where her aunt Christina was a nun. See *Reign of William Rufus*, ii. 31 and 599.

kingship[1]. I don't look on knowledge of the Old Testament as one of your strongest points; so I won't give you the reference, as it will be good practice for you to find it out, as well as Menahem.

To THE SAME.

Somerleaze, September 7, 1869.

I have hardly a moment my own, as we are just starting for Axbridge. But I must write a line to tell you my sympathy for you in your sorrow—most likely the first deep sorrow that you have ever felt. You have lost one whom I know you deeply and deservedly loved, and whose loss will leave a gap which can be filled only by time. But the separation must have come before very long, and we cannot but rejoice in the painless and peaceful end of a useful and noble life. You know, I had learned to reverence your grandfather before I saw him, and that I was charmed with the little that I did see. I am glad indeed that I had the opportunity of seeing him. I know I am writing common-places, but I believe that at such times common-places are not unacceptable, and that mourners are well pleased to hear that they are in the minds of their friends, as you assuredly are in mine to-day. And I have a loss of my own, utterly different in degree from yours, but which will come home strongly to me to-day. I have to make the ἐπιτύμ-βιον αἶνον ἐπ' ἀνδρὶ θείῳ[2] for my dear old friend Warre.

Other matters I hope in a day or two.

Pray give my best condolences to your father and mother, and take all the sympathy and good wishes that you can ask

from Your sincere friend.

To THE SAME.

September 12, 1869.

.   .   .   .

September 13.—I told my wife and Margaret about your article, as I was sure they would find it out, and indeed they had guessed it already; they saw there was something in

---

[1] Probably June 20 coincided with the 4th Sunday after Trinity, when the first lesson for the morning is 1 Sam. xii.

[2] 'Epitaph in praise of a divinely good man.' Aeschyl. *Agam.* 1553.

which you and ——— were concerned! δειναὶ γὰρ αἱ γυναῖκες εὑρίσκειν τέχνας [1]. There is no keeping anything from any of you. But I have asked them to let it go no further.

And now I am well pleased to have done you this little service, and I thank you much for your pretty parable of the ' beneficent fairy,' only to have been called a ' kindly elf' would have gone more straightway to my Dutchmanship. Remember that *Ælfred* is the greatest of all names, and the *rede* of that *elf* will be *ready* for you on all matters whenever you ask for it. Indeed, I must give you a bit without being asked. . . . Don't let the reading and reviewing of ' Mudie history' (that is a very good name—did you make it, or where did you find it ?) become your main work. You have certainly read a wonderful lot, and you continue to remember a wonderful deal of it, but I can't get rid of a notion that you are a bit desultory and do things by fits and starts. I should like to be certain that you were working steadily and thoroughly at something or other; it is for yourself to choose at what. And don't forget your Greek and your Dutch.

I shall be delighted—at least, I hope I shall be delighted—to hear your mind upon vol. iii. Johnny, you see, was in a better humour this time, save the bit at the end—I never talked of ' the Great Dunstan,' and ' the Great William '; I mean to represent ' Willelmus Magnus.' I have seen no other notice as yet.

I have written to Cox to say that both Harolds are clearly solar myths [2]. Each kills a dragon—Hardrada bodily; our Harold mystically, to wit the Red Dragon of the Cymry. Then Queen Elizabeth and Eadygth Swanneshals supply the necessary forsaken one returned to or returning at the last moment. Then the *Ea* in Eadgyth is clearly the Io in 'Ιόλη, &c., and I am not clear that Elizabeth=Isabel='Ιέζεβελ does not contain the same element. So consider yourself, O Eadgyth, for the future as a violet cloud, and, if you have any special Elizabeth, consider her the same.

Duke and *Duc*, &c. I always write English after the manner

---

[1] ' For women are terribly clever in discovering plans.'

[2] A playful allusion to the *Mythology of the Aryan Nations*, by the Rev. Sir G. W. Cox.

of Macaulay. I should no more say 'the Duke d'Orleans' or 'the Duc d'Orleans,' than 'the King de France' or 'the Roi de France.' We never say 'the Herzog von Friedland,' nor does a Welshman ever say 'le Prince of Wales.' But your question is to the purpose. With a country or city, Burgundy, Orleans, &c., the case is clear; but how when the estate and the surname are the same? Macaulay introduces his man as 'the Count of Avaux,' and goes on talking of 'Avaux.' I presume that La Trémoille is a place. If so, one might fairly say 'Duke of La Trémoille.' No more to-night.

September 14 (anniversary of Godwine's return).—Index is done, that is one comfort, and I must work as hard as I can to do the greatest number of 'revilements[1]' that may be by Friday. On that evening Gretchen and I have fixed to cross from Southampton to Havre. We were to have gone last night, but this Index has hindered us; I hope I may get the proof before then, and also that by that time I may know what you mean to do. I think we shall spend Sunday either at Fécamp or at Rouen, and if any lucky fate (elf?) should bring you to that quarter it would be delightful. Fécamp is a charm-ing place, any way. I suppose that we shall go on in a day or two to Amiens; if you are at Boulogne, you might drop down upon us there and help us to worship St. Philumena in her own city. Think on these things.

I have seen no paper with anything about your grandfather save the *Star* that you sent me. I am very sorry the *Daily News*, generally my favourite paper, has done amiss. Dear Edith, you must now be getting better to realize and be reconciled to your great loss. I am sure I am glad if I have given the least comfort to you or to any one belonging to you. You have been much in my thoughts both about that and about other matters. . . .

---

[1] Articles for the *Saturday Review*. *Saturday Reviler* was a nick-name originally given to the paper by some person or persons who had smarted under its criticism, and it came to be adopted by writers on the staff.

The three letters which follow were written during a tour in the north of France with his eldest daughter and her friend Miss Macarthur [1].

To Miss Edith Thompson.

Laôn, September 25, 1869.

I need not put my finger in my eye like the mythical baby, nor yet bring out a plate full of onions, like Octavius Morgan, as I was really very sorry that we could not meet you at Rouen or anywhere. I should have greatly enjoyed leading you about some of these old Norman and French cities, and I heartily trust we may manage to do it some other year. Your letter to Margaret found us at Rouen, where my duty was mainly to lionize her, as it was at Amiens also. After that we plunged into lands as unknown to me as to her; first, St. Quentin, a place which I fancy is very little known, and of which I knew nothing beyond the fact of the battle [2]. You have got up all the disreputable kings of the sixteenth century, so you doubtless know all about it. I don't feel myself bound to know second-period battles, save that I must do something at Jarnac [3] and Coutras [4], as I am carrying about the Duke of Aumale's book to review. There is a superb church there, which nobody seems to know anything about, and an Hôtel de Ville, which looks so kindly and Hanseatic that I felt inclined to call it the *Rathhaus.* Thence this morning to Noyon ; some hours there to see the cathedral, and hither in the evening. I should like to have stayed longer at Noyon, both to see the church again and to walk up a very tempting hill which overlooks the town. Here in the city of the Karlings there is no talk of hills overlooking the town, as Laudunum verily is a city set on an hill which cannot be hid. We have as yet only gone round the church by moonlight, but it is glorious indeed with its many towers. But my thoughts have run back to Hluthwig and Gerberga, and all

[1] Authoress of the *History of Scotland* and *Historical Course for Schools*.
[2] In 1557, when Gaspard de Coligni, Admiral of France, was defeated by the Spaniards.
[3] Where the Huguenots were defeated in 1569 by the Duke of Anjou.
[4] Where Henry IV, King of Navarre, defeated the forces of the League under the Duke of Joyeuse in 1587.

that I writ about Laôn in my first volume[1]. I wish I had seen it first. Indeed, I am not quite clear as to the rightfulness of bringing the Capetian Duke's book here among the ghosts of Karlings. I do remember the Count of Paris talking of ' my family' doing this and that in the tenth century. And all that 'my family' did just then was to do despite to their lords up here. The tower, Hluthwig and Gerberga's tower, is gone—not very long ago, according to guide-books. We shall see more of the place to-morrow.

We see the French papers by fits and starts. I have seen nothing about a certain personage abdicating, but I am amazed at the boldness of language in the papers and the freedom with which (September 27) every possible measure and every possible chance is discussed. The walls are still covered with election bills, many of which are very comforting to read, and remind me of my own. The old insolent formula, 'Candidat du Gouvernement,' seems to have disappeared, and I read no more such pieces of impudence as I read last year at Eu from the Senator-Prefect of the Lower Seine. Also, the windows are full of both royal and republican photographs. The change seems marked in everything.

Margaret and I went to bed last night in the belief that we should have to appear this morning at the Laôn Petty Sessions, or whatever answers thereto in these parts. Don't think that we were summoned as criminals, but we fully expected to be summoned as witnesses. There was a mad woman at dinner yesterday, who went on holding forth and preaching in a strange way in bad French and worse English. I fear she was some kind of Dutchwoman, but, as I am not sure, we will hope she was a Russian. Well, at last she took to abusing and assaulting the *garçons*, on which they brought in a *gend'arme*, who took her to prison, and solemnly took down all our names and ages all round the table (including *Marguerite à vingt ans*, the title of a godly book which I see in the windows), that we might bear witness. Howbeit, when she was in prison came two Commissioners of Police (like the magistrates of Philippi in the Acts of the Apostles) and let her go, so she started for Paris (Hôtel du Louvre), as, I suppose, the common sink where

---

[1] *Norman Conquest*, i. ch. iv.

anything may be sent. She praught a sermon to a little girl at the table till the poor child wept and ran away. One stave I remember, because the cadence is just like some of the hymns which some of you sing.

> 'Quand vous êtes sur le lit de mort,
> Pensez à moi.'

'Twas much more solemn, I assure you, than the tune of Rory O'More, which—so Margaret tells me—was played yesterday at high mass in Laôn cathedral.

This Laôn is, in point of position, the finest place I ever saw. In everything but the lack of a river it beats Le Mans itself (of course, towns with lakes and mountains in view, Geneva, Lausanne, Bern, are different again). But I won't write a long story about it, because I shall certainly write a middle thereon. . . . To-morrow we hope to get to see Coucy-le-château, i. e. if Margaret can come, as she is gone to bed with *mal à la tête*, and, what to me is very grievous to look upon, she can eat nothing. She is writing a journal, but I call it hard that you asked to see hers and not mine, as I look on mine as a model of annalistic simplicity (and Cicero says, 'annalibus nihil jucundius,' or words to that effect) worthy of Flodoard himself, whose memory I shall duly honour when I get to Reims. I must now, while my last bit of candle serves me, add one more day to it; so good night.

September 28.—We have been to Coucy to-day, and a wonderful place it is; bear it in mind, if you ever come into these parts. It is said to be the grandest castle anywhere, though I was just a bit disappointed at not finding a square donjon like Falaise and Rochester. The situation, too, is magnificent, as is that of this city. If there were only a good inn *and a Ghost*[1]— I think you must know my Caen friend by that name—I should like to stay ever so long; but I can't say much for our quarters at La Hure, and we must get on to Reims to-morrow. Margaret has eaten somewhat to-day, but she has still got headaches.

Tell me about vol. iii., how it strikes both yourself and other people. I have seen no notices save Johnny in *Sat. Rev.*, but I hear it is going off well, and I had a most pleasant letter from

---

[1] M. le Gost-Clerisse; see above, p. 399.

R. W. Church (besides others) about it. I feel that I am really beginning at last to hit people's tastes, and it is not an unpleasant feeling, when I know that I have not done it by any unworthy means. The little book will, I suppose, be out soon—perhaps it is out by this time.

You asked about Rouen streets. The city has been what Pinder calls Hausmannized. Crowds of old houses, and, I cannot help thinking, a church or two also, have made way for a long street called after Madame B., stretching from the Quay almost up to the West Station. I dare say it is fine in its way, but it is very beastly to my taste. . . .

I have got to work for *Harwood*[1] even here. I have sent off a thing on the Wallace Monument, and have begun another on this Laudunum itself. Also, I am getting somewhat slowly through the Duke of Aumale's book. Really, next to the Patriarch David, Henry the Great appears in it as the first of recorded scamps. The book is good and solid, but sometimes a little heavy. I was rather glad to see the author's picture in a window here.

I am sure that here in France they talk a different sort of Welsh from my people in Normandy ; I can understand the Normans far better.

I am sure you would enjoy this place. The town and its suburbs cover a sort of amphitheatre of hills, and are almost wholly at the top, not coming down the sides like Le Mans and Angers. The views, both of the town and from the town, are glorious. The cathedral, with seven towers begun and five finished, stranger perhaps than beautifuller, but vast and varied ; the other big church, St. Martin, with two towers at the other end; the walls of St. Vincent occupy the other end of the curve, and the slopes all rich with vineyards—it is a fine sight. But the old castle, with the tower which professed to be *the* tower[2], has made way for an ugly citadel. You must allow that all modern warlike works are ugly, save the martello towers, which somebody told me were of no use.

---

[1] The second Editor of the *Saturday Review*.

[2] I. e. the tower of ' Louis-from-beyond-sea,' one of the last of the Carolingian kings who reigned in Laôn. See *Norman Conquest*, i. ch. iv.

To W. B. DAWKINS, ESQ.

Paris, October 4, 1869.

I don't know how to thank you and your wife enough for your kindness to Edgar[1], as set forth in a letter, part of which my wife copied and sent me.

. . . October 5.—Margaret and I have come pretty nearly to the end of our journey, as we hope to cross to-morrow night. We have been a delightful round, and all, after Rouen and Amiens, as new to me as to her. If you want a city in a noble position, go to Laôn, but Rheims beats it in churches, and one thing there specially brought you to my memory. Our inn was exactly opposite the west front of the cathedral, which we sat and contemplated whenever we had nothing else to do. Besides its higher beauties, never was a place so rich in gurgoyles; one is an ox's head in lead, looking so natural that at first I thought it was a real skull. There must have been palaeontologists or anatomists of some kind in the thirteenth century.

Also, do you know anything of the legend of a lord of Coucy killing a lion, which is carved about at Coucy? Perhaps he did it when out on a crusade; if he did it at Coucy, why that, as well as the lion-hunt of which we saw the picture at Axbridge, is a fact for you in the history of the retreat of the lion from Europe. Otherwise I have seen no strange beasts, save a rum beetle or two. I have not been far southard enough for special lizards and grasshoppers.

We are, so to speak, on the Surrey side of the river, on Quai Voltaire, looking out on the Seine, with the Louvre, Tuileries, &c., beyond it, which I humbly conceive to be a finer view than the Louvre, Tuileries, &c., without the Seine, which you get from the more fashionable hotels. Margaret is delighted with her short sojourn here; to me it is just idleness, a day or two of which is very well now and then; in the other places I am studying just as much as at home, though in a different way.

[1] His second son, who was at this time at Owens College, Manchester.

To Miss Edith Thompson.

Paris, October 6, 1869.

You will not, I hope, think it disrespectful in me that I tore off the stamp of your letter to give it, along with that of another letter, to a crowd of boys who meet you on the steps of the Poste Restante asking for the English stamps. What think you of that?

Off with its stamp—so much for Paris and the whole land of the Gal-Welsh. I am now again at my own desk in my own library (Friday, October 8) a little tired, but not worse, having had a charming passage, which landed us so early at Southampton that we were able to run out to Winchester and to stop at Salisbury, to hear matins in the one cathedral and evensong in the other, and yet get home last night. I felt a little like Henry of Navarre, breakfasting at Milan and dining at Naples, and perhaps reaching Sicily in time for vespers [1]. (N. B. The paragraph before this last is one which, if you sent it to *Saturday Review*, I should certainly call on you to cut into two or three.) I wrote to you from Laôn. Hence we went to Rheims, and sat ourselves down in excellent quarters just opposite Notre Dame, so that we could enjoy the sight of the west front whenever we were not specially doing anything else. Rheims Cathedral is certainly one of the most perfect things anywhere, it is at once so good and so uniform, and with such glorious glass; but the great towers lack their spires, and the smaller towers have not been carried up. Still, the most interesting thing for me in Rheims was not the metropolitan church, but the great abbey of St. Remigius, *þæt micele mynster æt Rémys*, of which see somewhat in my history, vol. ii. pp. 112, 459 [2]. The nave and transepts of

---

[1] See the note in Gibbon to his account of the massacre of the French in Sicily in 1282, known as the *Sicilian Vespers*, vol. xi. p. 331 (Milman's edition). 'The French were long taught to remember this bloody lesson.' 'If I am provoked,' said Henry IV, 'I will breakfast at Milan and dine at Naples.' 'Your Majesty' (replied the Spanish Ambassador) 'may perhaps arrive in Sicily in time for vespers.'

[2] Pp. 111 and 456 in second edition.

Heremar's[1] church are there, though with much change, and it was something to think that one was in the church which Leo IX hallowed, and that the pillars which I saw Gyrth[2] had seen. But more of this in a middle. Notre Dame is eminently the *high* church, and St. Remy the *broad* church, and there is a third, St. James, which may be called the *low*. But whatever you say of *lowness*, breadth has a certain dignity, as St. Remigius showeth beyond all doubt.

Rheims does not stand like Laôn, but besides other things it is, to the carnally minded, a much more attractive city than Laôn, seeing food and lodging are much better, and cheaper withal. We had the good luck to be there for St. Remigius' day and his ceremonies. The archbishop (not a cardinal this time) said pontifical high mass—mighty fine ; and Gretchen had a talk with the organist—but I craved greatly to learn the fate of a dog who profanely ran into the choir, and who I thought might perhaps come to the same end as the famous jackdaw. Dogs in the choir suggest the question whether the English ambassadors in 1049 took with them each man his *pig* to assist at the hallowing. (You remember about Thrapp and the pigs, don't you?[3]) Moreover, all folk crowded round the shrine of St. Remigius (a gift of your man, Francis the First), and there were brought unto them from the shrine handkerchiefs and aprons ; so I trust that the evil spirits, if they had any, departed from them[4]. It certainly seems to me that, whether through the blessing of St. Remigius or other-wise—I think the baptizer of Hlothwig might be *trusted*—the evil spirit of all[5] is likely to depart afore long. It makes one's

---

[1] Abbot of St. Remigius, at whose request the newly-built church was hallowed by Pope Leo IX in 1049.

[2] Earl of the East Angles, a brother of Harold (afterwards king), and of Tostig, with whom he went on a pilgrimage to Rome in 1061. On their return they halted at Rheims.

[3] An allusion to a book in which it was stated that 'the Anglo-Saxon nobles' had so little sense of reverence that they brought their dogs, hawks and PIGS into church. The writer had got hold of a law or injunction of Eadgar's, that pigs were not to be allowed to get into churchyards.

[4] Acts xix. 12.

[5] I. e as represented by Louis Napoleon Buonaparte.

hair stand on end to see how every man speaketh and writeth as he listeth, where before all was dumb. Why, the very *garçon* at [Hôtel] Voltaire spake openly unto me of his own free will, while other while I have never ventured to utter a word save to one I trusted, and that only either in a privy chamber or on a lonely road. As Aeschylus saith :

Οὐδ' ἔτι γλῶσσα βροτοῖσιν
ἐν φυλακαῖς· λέλυται γὰρ
λαὸς ἐλεύθερα βάζειν
ὡς λέλυται ζυγὸς ἀλκᾶς [1].

To THE SAME.

Somerleaze, November 7, 1869.

Herewith I send the proof of your note about Harold Hardrada. The law in such cases is that all extracts are to be compared on the proof sheet with the original, and Margaret and I always find something to correct in our own extracts. I suspect you are a more careful copyist than either of us; still, it would make assurance doubly sure to have it thus verified, and the more so as it is in a tongue which neither of us very well understands. But, as this involves a journey to the British Museum, I do not like to ask you to take so much trouble without at least giving you an alternative. So if you can't go at once, or if you don't feel inclined to go at all, just drop the enclosed letter into the post—if you go yourself, burn it and keep the half sheet to yourself—and send the proof to the same address. Here I make two comments. On the one hand, I feel sure that, if you undertake to do it, you, *Eddeva homo mea*, will do it, while I don't feel so sure of *Johannunculus homunculus meus*. On the other hand, if he won't do it, or does it ill, I can kick him, while, by the present rules of society I can't kick you. I say the present rules, because if you and Lydia and the rest establish your rights as *liberae feminae*, including the right to kick us, you must in common fairness expect to be kicked back again. . . .

[1] Aeschyl. *Persae* 591-594. His memory was a little at fault in the last line, which is ὡς ἐλύθη ζυγὸν ἀλκᾶς. It is curious that he should have put the rare form ζυγός instead of ζυγόν.

I am not sure whether you ever saw old General Coles, who died the other day. He was a good old soul (like his namesake, the founder of Colchester and father of St. Helen), but could never be persuaded to put a question from the chair with which he did not agree. He was the superior officer, and acted accordingly. On the other hand, when not in the chair, he always voted with the chairman, as being *his* superior officer. He had waged war in India, Spain, and divers places: Spain I count for a good work, as helping to put down a tyrant.

END OF VOL. I.